A CHUGHTAI QUARTET

ISMAT CHUGHTAI is the author of several collections of short stories, four novellas, three novels, a collection of reminiscences and essays, *My Friend, My Enemy*, and a memoir, *Kaghazi hai Perahan* (The Paper-thin Garment). With her husband, Shahid Latif, a film director, she produced and co-directed six films, and produced a further six independently.

TAHIRA NAQVI is a translator, writer, and Urdu language lecturer in the Department of Middle Eastern and Islamic Studies at New York University. She has translated the works of Sa'dat Hasan Manto, Munshi Premchand, Khadija Mastoor and Ismat Chughtai into English.

ALSO AVAILABLE

The Crooked Line: a novel
Vintage Chughtai: a selection of her best stories
A Very Strange Man: a novel
Masooma: a novel

A CHUGHTAI QUARTET

The Heart Breaks Free
The Wild One
Obsession
Wild Pigeons

ISMAT CHUGHTAI

Translated from the Urdu by Tahira Naqvi

women UNLIMITED
an associate of
kali for women

A Chughtai Quartet
was first published in English in India in 2014

by
Women Unlimited
(an associate of Kali for Women)
7/10 First Floor, Sarvapriya Vihar
New Delhi 110016
www.womenunlimited.net

ISBN: 978-81-88965-87-8

Cover design: Neelima Rao

Typeset at Women Unlimited, New Delhi 110016
Printed at Raj Press, R-3, Inderpuri, New Delhi 110012

Contents

Prefatory Note

It is quite by accident that we have four novellas in this collection, spanning Ismat's literary career from its early stages to the last years of her writing life. *Dil ki Duniya* (*The Heart Breaks Free*) written in 1918; *Ziddi* (The Wild One) in 1939; *Saudai* (Obsession) in 1966, and *Jungli Kabutar* (Wild Pigeons) in 1971. As such, the works offer valuable insights into the ways Ismat develops her characteristic themes revolving around the lives of women. Even a cursory reading reveals that her writing style sustains its exceptional form and technique, its vivid imagery and richness of language, even though, in terms of thematic configurations, she steps out of an insular domestic space into a more expansive universe comprising the home and the world.

For now, I will focus on another aspect of Chughtai's work that offers food for thought in these four novellas: their protagonists, like many others in other Chughtai stories, despairing in love, faced with tragedy when they try to cross social boundaries, seek and find agency in the exercise of an obdurate will that cannot be bent; they cannot therefore be regarded as tragic figures.

At first, struggling against society's harsh mores, suffering its blows, these women appear to be hapless victims. However, even as they pass through fire they do not let it consume them. They achieve what we may not regard as "triumphs" in the usual sense, but which do translate into a victory of sorts; tragedy pursues them, but in the end they swim against the tide. They make their own choices which, however drastic and tragic, afford them a special kind of supremacy. In other words, Chughtai berates the social ills that inflict tragic consequences on the women, but she does not allow the reader to pity them or feel they are a lost cause. How does she do this? Not by discounting or diminishing their suffering, but by highlighting festering mores and the maladies that infect society in such a manner, that the relationship between victim and oppressor remains clear in its dimensions and implications.

In *The Heart Breaks Free* Chughtai draws on her childhood memories of life in Bahraich to write what, in my opinion, is one of her very best stories. Here, society is made up of the women in the narrator's household, aunts, mothers, mothers-in-law, housekeepers. Chughtai has repeatedly brought to our attention the cruel treatment that women dole out to each other. Together, the women of the household—steeped in old-fashioned custom and intransigent tradition that impel them to engage in practices that border on the inhuman and inflexible—proceed to ruin the life of Bua, a free spirit who "had created a free world of her own where she ruled". All seems to be lost, but in a clever twist Chughtai stirs up the dying embers. A strange and unexpected exchange takes place, a masterful turn of events in terms of plot development that culminates in a tour de force. Qudsia Apa, docile and weakened by attacks of hysteria as an abandoned wife, suddenly gains ownership of her life even as Bua loses control over hers.

Published in 1938, *Ziddi* seems to be a traditional love story complete with a love triangle, but on closer examination we see that the plot has been complicated by Chughtai's critique of class differences. She revisits this trope repeatedly in screenplays (*Sheesha, Buzdil*), short stories ("Kallu", "The Third Hand"), and novellas (*Saudai, Badan ki Khushbu*). Her critique is located in the relationship between master and servant; the playful, dashing, fun-loving Puran and the timorous and beautiful servant girl, Asha, fall in love with each other. Set against the backdrop of a feudal family, their affair, an unexpected recurrence of an earlier relationship in the same family, makes for tragic consequences for Asha, as well as for her lover and master, Puran. The lovers flail, wilting into shadows of their real selves as society demands unflinching submission; in the end Asha, the stubborn one, unwilling to give up, succeeds in outwitting the demons society has set upon her trail and finds a way to be with her beloved.

Chughtai's connection with the film world in Bombay, both as a writer for the films her husband Shahid Latif directed, and as an independent filmmaker after his death, is often overshadowed by her literary achievements. As a matter of fact, the films bear an important relationship to her writing. Her stories, with the potential inherent in their detailed narrative structure as well as the imagery that enriches her writing style, can almost be read as screenplays. She received credit for writing *Garam Hawa*, the award-winning film on India's Partition, which is actually drawn from two or three of her stories, most notably "*Chauthi ka Jora*" (The Wedding Shroud) and "*Jarein*" (Roots). A novella, *Saudai* became the famous film, *Buzdil;* noted Urdu poet, Kaifi Azmi, began his career as a lyricist with this film. And in1948, ten years after the publication of *Ziddi,* Ismat and her husband turned *Ziddi* into a film that launched the careers of Dev Anand and Kamini Kaushal, and introduced Kishore Kumar as a playback singer with his song, "*Marne ki dua'ain kyun mangun.*" Lata's "*Chanda re jaa re jaa re/Piya se sandesa mora kah'yo ja*" is memorable, as are the other songs. The music was by Khemchand Prakash and the film was a hit. Never impervious to box office expectations, either Ismat or Shahid, or both, decided to change the ending although the rest of the film remained faithful to the novella. The altered ending detracts from the effect Asha's actions have in the novella — she is diminished somehow, although the exquisite songs and Kamini Kaushal and Dev Anand's youthful and exuberant romance on screen let one forget the novella's dark ending.

With *Saudai*, the process was inverted. In 1951 Shahid and Ismat made *Buzdil (The Coward)*, and in 1966 Ismat turned her screenplay into a novella. Ismat's style is always rich in imagery and description, but *Saudai* actually reads like a screenplay. Here, too, she continues with the trope of master-and-servant romance. In this story about two brothers in love with the same orphaned girl, Chandni, played by Nimmi, Kishore Sahu provides a masterful performance as the two-faced older brother, Suraj, who presents his sober, serious, god-like demeanour to the world, but is tormented by his inner demons that eventually destroy him; they shake the foundations of the very world he has promised to protect. Chandar, the younger brother, playful, charming and romantic, was played by a very young Premnath. Chandni, discovered as a little girl on a pile of dead leaves in the garden, becomes the foil for all the other characters in the story who evolve, develop or unravel in relationship to her. She was Ismat's favourite female protagonist, a woman who defies convention and, despite her lowly position in the social scale, commands everyone's attention.

Jungli Kabutar was published in 1971. Chughtai already had a substantial and impressive body of work to her credit and was now probing new themes, in this case infidelity. Reading the novella I could not help but see a resemblance between her plot and a real-life situation involving a well-known film personality. Chughtai's treatment, however, is distinctive, an exploration of feelings and emotions that wrack both the person who betrays and the one who is betrayed. Once again, ignoring all conventional reactions, Chughtai created a female character who thinks too much, whose cerebral responses become a vehicle for tragedy; she is as "stubborn" as Asha, and her will cannot be bent. Her triumph comes at great cost, and makes the ending complex and problematic.

Not content with writing for films and with directing and producing, Chughtai tried her hand at acting as well, and what a natural she proved to be! Not everyone knows that she has played an important and interesting role in Shyam Benegal's classic film, *Junoon,* with Shashi Kapoor, Shabana Azmi, Jennifer Kendall and Naseeruddin Shah. Chughtai plays a Muslim noblewoman from Rampur, married to an Englishman, and now an ageing grandmother to Ruth, the young woman for whom Javed, the dashing young Pathan played by Kapoor, nurses a consuming passion (*junoon*). Dressed in a crisp white gharara, dupatta covering her head, her glasses set firmly on her nose, her intonation very much that of an Urdu-speaking person from U.P., she sits at the table of this British family and asks the cook to make sure he prepares "sewayyan and sheer khurma for Eid tomorrow".

Chughtai is never a comfortable read. She jolts the reader out of any sense of complacency, creates havoc and practically bullies the reader into digging deep into the many meanings concealed in her powerful idiom, her tapestry of images and her rich symbols and metaphors. But she never disappoints.

TAHIRA NAQVI

The Heart Breaks Free

(*Dil ki Duniya*)

WHAT a strange and mysterious moment it is when you suddenly open your eyes and can't tell whether the sun is setting or just rising, which way your feet are or where your head is, and you don't know where you slept and what this place is where you've awakened! It becomes imperative then, to determine where your head and feet are, and you have this feeling that if you don't find out immediately you'll be lost forever.

When we were children our first reaction to this was tears, but then a flash came down from some unknown source and right away we were able to place ourselves, to determine where everything was. All at once fountains of mirth burst forth, and to provide further proof of our existence we ran after the chickens or began grappling with one another like dogs. At that point Amma would order us to make ourselves scarce and this we happily did. Making a run for the garden we proceeded to pluck off half-opened buds from the bushes and gathered them in our laps.

Thus we occupied ourselves until it got dark. Then Ali Bakhsh would slip in a bunch of lanterns from behind the curtain on the front door. The wicks were raised and lighted and the lanterns dispatched to every corner of the house so that the walls and doors which had been engulfed in darkness were visible again.

The watchman climbed a ladder and lighted the boxed lamp on the front door. Frightened, the bushes hastily retreated into the darkness and the buds we had collected in our laps began to flower. At that time, and for no apparent reason, we were assailed by feelings of dread. A stealthy chameleon, its cheeks ballooning as it manufactured poison it its mouth, turned red like an ember and then scampered up the tamarind tree. And we felt as if our feet were melting like wax.

This was when that mysterious voice floated and vibrated as it travelled across the water:

"Kanhayya, your flute has become my enemy ..."

We ran without a moment wasted, dashed through the curtain on the front door, threw the flowers down on our grandmother's prayer mat and took refuge under her dupatta.

"Dadima, please read ayat-ul kursi quickly and blow on us!"

Only when we felt Dadima's "Ahmed Hussain, Dildar Hussain," soaked in tobacco and betel juice blow on our faces did we breathe sighs of relief.

"Kanhayya ... yo ... u ... r... flooote ... has become my ... enemy..." The sound weakened and then disappeared altogether, leaving behind only the rustling of the wind.

Our father had recently been transferred to Bahraich. Situated across from our spacious, two-storied bungalow was the shrine of Sayyed Salar Masud Ghazi. Adjacent to the house was a garden where we spent the major part of our waking lives. At the end of a long line of modest-sized quarters was a white mosque and rows of har-singhar, jasmine, chameli and mogra trees that extended as far as the eye could see. Not too far from the mosque was a Muslim cemetery and on the banks of the river, some distance away from the mosque, beyond the melon plantation, was a crematorium. We dreaded these two spots the most. The mysterious voice appeared to come from this direction and anything coming from there struck fear in our hearts.

Whenever we stepped out of line, or if we made a row, we were frightened into docility by references to that voice. "She's a demon, she'll eat you up alive, she's a ghoul, if she lays hands on you she'll cast a spell on you. Don't you know what they say? A wedding party once drowned in the Ghagra stream but the bride didn't die, she turned into a demon and floats about in the stream to this day."

There was another factor associated with this voice. No sooner was it heard than Aunt Qudsia suffered a paroxysm; her jaw locked, she'd begin to foam at the mouth and the house turned into an abode of anguish.

"O Mighty Qadir, bring us Qudsia's husband," Nani Bi (our maternal grandmother) chanted, swaying. But Mighty Qadir seemed to have clogged his ears with oil; he paid no heed to anyone's pleas. Perhaps he was ruminating on the matter of returning Aunt Qudsia's husband to her.

She had been married for nearly ten years. Her father packed her husband off to England soon after the wedding–that was one of the conditions of the marriage. In keeping with custom, he returned from there with an English wife, a mem. Now he had a clinic in Mainpuri. This is why Aunt Qudsia endlessly chanted verses from the Quran, spent long hours in worship and prayer, and when all of this proved fruitless, suffered from attacks in which her jaw locked and foam gathered at her mouth. Unfortunate woman, what else could she do? She penned several letters beginning, "My master, may you live long." She wrote: "Give me a spot in a corner of your house as a maid of the memSahib, I'll serve you both, I'll eat your left-overs, wear your cast-offs, and if I utter one word of dissatisfaction, you may punish me as one punishes a thief. You are the master, I your slave, what better fate can I ask for than dying at your feet," etc., etc.; but the master apparently thought it foolish to bother with a reply.

Usually Aunt Qudsia was introduced to people like this: "This is Qudsia, her husband has taken in a white woman." People were quite impressed. At that moment Aunt Qudsia, too, would forget her misfortune and experience a certain degree of pride. Her rival was the daughter of the rulers, who knows, maybe she was even distantly related to the King! Not everyone can take in a white woman. In a way her husband had honoured her by bringing a white woman to be her rival; he could have taken in a washer-woman or a sweeperess.

Aunt Qudsia was married at the age of fifteen. Six months after the wedding her husband left for England. For two years a fervid romance flourished. Her face lowered, she was seen either writing to her husband or reading one of his letters. Gradually the letters cooled off. She continued her frenzied writing but replies there were none! Then all kinds of bad news started trickling in. After the First World War white women diminished in value and whoever went abroad returned with a catch from the free-flowing Ganga. But Aunt Qudsia's husband turned out to be rather strange. There were other men as well who were bringing home white women, but once every six or seven months they also showed their faces to their Hindustani wives. Her husband, on the other hand, maintained absolute silence and made no effort to find out how she was doing.

And that's why Aunt Qudsia became hysterical during Urs (the celebrations at the shrine), that's why whenever there was a wedding in the neighbourhood her jaw locked, or when, in the darkness of night, someone sang a song of separation, she frothed at the mouth. The mysterious voice affected her the most, so much so that she paced restlessly, cracked her knuckles, nervously twisted the corners of her dupatta, and suffered an attack of hysterics.

*

We were picking off buds. Our laps were full, but we lingered to see the lighting of the boxed lamp on the front door. Suddenly the voice floated up right behind us. Our hair stood on end. We turned in surprise. She was sitting on a fallen fig tree trunk that had come down during a storm and now lay among crumbling gravestones in the cemetery behind the mosque. Her face wore a sad look. She paused in her singing. Our feet weighed heavily like sacks stuffed with straw.

"Let go of my dupatta," she murmured petulantly, as if addressing someone behind her.

Terrified, we ran wildly from there. No one was holding her dupatta, there was no one there.

She stood up hastily, and tugging at a corner of her dupatta ran away laughing, as though she were being pursued playfully. Soon she had disappeared into the trees.

Fear gripped us, our feet seemed to drag us down.

"We'll meet in Meerut." Her voice echoed in the distance and we ducked around the curtain and into the house.

"*You, beloved, so dark, and I so fair/ We shall gaze at each other in the mirror.*"

Her voice vibrated again like a top and we felt as if there were beadwork-needless running down our backs.

"*You, beloved, so stout, and I so thin/ On scales we shall both be weighed.*"

What a coincidence! Aunt Qudsia's husband was both stout and dark, but there was not a ghost of a chance of meeting him in Meerut. What could she do except have an attack of hysteria?

Nani Biwi was busy with something else. Dadima, who was still murmuring over her prayer beads, blew on us, but our fear did not abate. Uff! How many grandmothers there were, and aunts, both maternal and paternal, but what good were they? There was no vigour in their blowing.

"Stay away from her, child," the attendant at the shrine said one Thursday when we arrived there with our usual offering of flowers. "She's very dangerous."

"Why?"

"She brings bad luck, she ate up her parents and her husband."

"She ate them?" We thought she had sprinkled salt and pepper on them and really eaten them.

"If she catches you alone she'll pull out your heart and eat it," he frightened us further.

"Is she a demon?"

"Of course."

"May God help us!" Chacha Mian, who had come with us, interjected. "What nonsense is this. No, dear children, she's just insane." He glared threateningly at the attendant.

"Insane?" We didn't like Chacha Mian's explanation. All the romance was gone. She's just insane? And not insane in an amusing way, either, she doesn't smell or rip her clothes, nor does she throw stones at anyone. Instead, whenever you chance to run into her you find her singing.

"*Beloved, I'll be a flower in your lap/ A flower in your lap, beloved.*"

What a melodious voice. That's why Aunt Qudsia became so agitated when she heard her sing.

"Amma dear, please send for her, we'll hear her sing."

"No, child, I'm not going to send for that mad wretch. She's from a good family and look how she wanders all over the place without restraint, her parda forgotten. She's possessed, you know; everyone drowned in the Ghagra stream, but she remained afloat for three days as if there was something holding her up."

"But the unhappy creature sings well." Aunt Qudsia nursed an obsession for songs. When Uncle Shabir sang devotional songs, streams and rivulets flowed from her eyes.

"*O Rasul-e-Arabi? To you I offer my life,*" he sang and Aunt Qudsia, her dupatta held to her nose, sobbed as she swayed to the rhythm of his song. Everyone sat at attention, waiting for the paroxysm that invariably overtook her when Uncle Shabir sang. Her hands would rotate, her eyes roll up in their sockets, and foam bubble at her mouth. Nani Biwi and Dadima would run towards her, blow holy incantations on her while Uncle Shabir, seated on the wooden divan, tried to conceal the shaking of his hands. Until Aunt Qudsia calmed down, he would pace up and down outside the front door.

Uncle Shabir was related to Aunt Qudsia by marriage, he was a brother-in-law. The only child of poor parents, he was a timid, uninteresting and ineffectual man, and it was indeed lucky he was an only child or we might have had to contend with several uninteresting and ineffectual uncles instead of one. He was very thin and nearly three feet taller than Aunt Qudsia. Humped over like a camel, he was in the habit of taking long strides when he walked.

"Shabir Bhai, please sing something," Aunt Qudsia would entreat in a melancholy voice, "please, it will calm my nerves."

"What can I sing, I have a scratchy throat today." He always presented the same excuse. Then he cleared his throat, blinked his eyes a few times, flared his nostrils, pressed both hands together between his knees, and:

"O east wind, if you travel to Tayyabba/Promise that you will embrace the curtains of the sanctuary."

He sang in a clear, unsullied voice. You felt sorry for him. The east wind had also clogged its ears with oil it seemed; it didn't hear him nor did it travel to Tayyabba at his behest.

It was common knowledge that Uncle Shabir was in love with Aunt Qudsia. But what a sluggish, timid love it was. Other young men and women in the family also loved, and what a sprightly and energetic love it was! Amorous embraces in secret or a tussle during a game of pachisi, grabbing hold of each other in dark corners! Grandmothers, uncles and various aunts cursed and remonstrated endlessly but the laughter and giggling continued unchecked.

Uncle Shabir, on the other hand, never sat close to her, never allowed even his little finger to touch her; she was forbidden fruit which belonged to another, to a man who had put her somewhere and forgotten about her. She had recently turned twenty-five and already there were silver strands gleaming in her hair. Everyone hoped she would age quickly so that the matter would end once and for all.

"No, I'm not going near that mad wretch," the old smelly crone, Pathani Bua, retorted when Aunt Qudsia solicited her help. "That husband-eater threatens you with a stone every time you go near her."

"What's amazing is that the ruffians out there don't harass her. If it had been some other girl she'd be in shreds by now. The wretch, she roams around in the woods all night dressed up in her finery. Isn't she scared?" Chachi Bi asked.

"Why, what's she got to be scared of?" Pathani Bua said, "no one dares to look at her with a crooked eye."

"Why? Is she a lioness, will she tear you to pieces? She's always alone, isn't she?"

"No, she's not alone, her husband is with her."

"What husband?"

"Bale Mian..."

"What nonsense! Don't be a fool, woman."

"This isn't nonsense, I swear she's the beloved of her husband, she's a true faithful of our Ghazi Mian."

Pathani Bua proceeded to explain in greater detail. She was Ghazi Mian's beloved, and this despite the fact that Ghazi Mian was martyred four hundred years ago. Love is not fettered by the chains of time.

There was an Urs at Ghazi Mian's shrine every year. Qawwali singers and others came from far and wide. People of every religion and caste, old and young, children, women and men, all made the pilgrimage to the shrine. Offered vows and received answers to their prayers.

Every Thursday the dancing girls from the town and its neighbouring districts arrived with their offerings. They sang thumris, dadras and ghazals in honour of Ghazi Mian. When a dancing girl was about to surrender her virginity she would first sing and dance at Mian's shrine. A fair was held during the flame-ridden heat of May and June, and the faithful came months ahead of time and set up camp. Such enormous crowds gathered during the actual days of the fair that you couldn't find an empty spot anywhere. Stretched in front of the main entrance to the shrine was an over-sized shamiana on which the arriving pilgrims threw garlands, sweetmeats and money.

Flags were transported here from neighbouring towns and districts. There were sixty-foot high bamboo poles with clusters of black or white hair attached to the top, while below them hung streamers made from rupee notes. Anyone whose wish was granted offered the standard at the shrine. Dancing and leaping to the beat of kettle-drums, the men arrived at the entrance of the shrine and formed a circle; a muscular man built like a wrestler, balancing the standard, stationed himself in the middle of the circle; in order to keep the banner steady, to prevent it from tipping, four other men held on to ropes extending from the spire of the standard. Then, lifting up the standard, the man danced and executed tricks with it. Sometimes he'd place the base of the standard on his forehead and wriggle his body, at other times he'd catch it between his teeth and sway. Finally, when everyone began sweating, or maybe when the group ran out of time (there were other groups with standards waiting their turn), the weary flag was furled around the pole like a sail tied to its mast, hitched on shoulders and carried into the shrine through the tall entrance-way. And then another flag dance began. At the end of the fair days all the flags were auctioned off.

Our mother bought flags every year for use as floor cloths –these were the best examples of tambour-work. Embroidered on the rough cotton fabric were colourful designs in the shape of elephants and horses. Here you could see whole armies on the march with their spears hoisted, there a caravan of camels; in another corner were flocks of sheep and goats, herds of cows, along with groups of men and women exchanging secrets. We would roll around on the divans all day long, observing the scenes belows us, never tiring of what we saw.

Besides the flags, those whose prayers had been heard also offered, in accordance with what they had promised, gold and silver figurines, tables, chairs, beds, and pots and pans. All this was followed by Ghazi Mian's wedding ceremonies. A kettle-drum was placed at the entrance. Early in the morning the playing of the drum commenced to one's annoyance and continued late into the night. All day, one group after another came and surrounded the drum players, and sometimes one or two men broke into sad songs about lost love. As soon as one group had exhausted itself another took its place. Women possessed by evil spirits came to Mian's door to be rid of them; they loosened their hair and shook their heads rhythmically from side to side, and when the person chanting holy verses blew smoke over them, they screamed and fainted. But it wasn't long before they regained consciousness and started swaying again. If the spirit were a stubborn creature it would not budge for days; red and green clubs were used to punish it and only then, after a terrible struggle, did it depart. Happy and contented, the women who had been healed then made offering at the shrine and went their way.

On the fifth of the month came the ceremony of the fan, on the seventh the sandalwood ceremony and on the ninth, the henna ceremony. At night on that day, Ghazi Mian's kurta, on which the Quran was etched in its entirety, was brought out for viewing. Frenzied crowds engulfed it. On the eleventh day, the ceremony marking the readying of the marriage procession took place.

A long time ago, Radha Bai, alias Zehra Bibi, a child widow from a family in Raduli, lost her heart to Mian. Ghazi Mian appeared to her in a dream and accepted her love. She made her home in his shrine. She was known to wash the tomb with her tears and sweep the floor of the shrine with her hair every day. Her father was an oil merchant. He forcibly dragged her away from Ghazi Mian, but Radha refused to give in. All girls with the name 'Radha' are stubborn; boldly and fearlessly they announce their love, suffer every dishonour and stigma happily, and put life and soul on the line. And the dice rolls in their favour. Unfavourable winds are compelled to give in when confronted with the ardour of their love, people begin to worship them, sing songs about them, and finally worship them as goddesses.

Ghazi Mian's Radha also had to walk on coals. She too had to drag herself through thorns. Her mother beat her senseless, her father whipped her with moistened rope and tied her to a peg in the cowshed. And the whole village spat at her. In the middle of the night when poor Radha, starving and thirsty, weary from her wounds and splattered with cow-dung, was taking her last breath, Ghazi Mian came to her. He washed her wounds with his tears, clasped her to his sacred chest, and dipping his forefinger into his heart's blood, he made the bridal mark in the parting of her hair.

When the demented Meera fell in love with her Girdhar Gopal the world let vipers loose on her life and gave her a cup of poison to drink and then–Krishan Murari's flute came to life and the viper turned into a garland of flowers, the cup of poison brimmed over with the elixir of life.

The next morning the inhabitants of Raduli awoke to the sound of temple bells and the azan echoing from the minaret of the mosque. Immersed in the fragrance of sandalwood, dressed in majestic clothes, Radha lay on a bed of flowers in everlasting sleep. There was not a single scratch on her, her body glowed like burnished gold, her hair shone with sindhur.

People in Raduli were thunderstruck. A meeting of the village elders was called. It was decided that the girl now belonged in another's house, there was no reason for her to stay in her parent's home. So she was delivered to her groom's dwelling.

The Hindus called her Radha, the Muslims referred to her as Zehra Bibi. Her plain, unpretentious grave sat at the foot of Mian's tomb. At one end of her grave grew a tamarind tree whose bark was known to exude the fragrance of sandalwood when burnt.

Since Radha's death, the Raduliwallahs had been bringing an offering of Mian's barat to the shrine every year. Children were put to bed early so they could be aroused around three o'clock at night to witness the arrival of the wedding procession. As soon as the familiar sound of trumpets was heard everyone was awakened. Quickly splashing some water on our faces, we all ran up to the roof to see the wedding procession enter the village.

It's been so many years, but to this day my eyes are blinded with the memory of that barat. A white steed in front, heavily laden with silver and gold ornaments, covered with flowers, the silvery strands of the sehra kissing the hooves.

"Look, there's Bale Mian!" We thought we could really see him seated on the horse.

Behind the horse was a palanquin with fine red muslin curtains, and inside it was the Quran with a candle burning alongside it.

"The bride, the bride!" We were spellbound. The trembling flame of the candle behind the red muslin curtains appeared to take the form of a shy, reticent bride. Following the bride were the wedding guests carrying tiny umbrellas. These were decorated with small stars between embroidered bands, and beaded silver and gold tassels hung from their edges. Twirling these umbrellas like reels, swaying, dancing, the members of the wedding procession filled the streets. It was a dazzling sight. For days afterwards little umbrellas continued to dance in my vision.

Sometimes, when you see something very beautiful you feel a lump in your throat. Aunt Qudsia always had a lump in her throat and all she needed was an excuse to start weeping. Resting her head on the window sill, she shed voluminous tears; seeing a wedding procession always cut her to the quick. But everyone was saddened by this barat. Was it a barat or a funeral? Life's doors are shut on a young, frail girl, she wants to create a world of dreams and open a small window in it. But the stupid people around her don't allow it because she threatens their beliefs. And what happens? She shatters all their beliefs and turns away from them.

Now Uncle Shabir was neither Krishan Murari nor Ghazi Mian. He was an incomplete, hollow man. He could not turn the snarling vipers in Aunt Qudsia's life into garlands with his flute, nor could he change the cowdung that enveloped her soul into sandalwood by sheer dint of his faith. His total assets were his two trembling hands which he could use well to stifle turbulent emotions. And Aunt Qudsia, at the age of twenty-six, was fading away like a forgotten remark. She didn't even have enough courage to be like Bua and lose her sanity. At least then people would fear her. As things stood now, her Ghazi Mian was ridiculed and pitied. There are those who are more alive in death than the living.

Bua was probably just a few years older than Aunt Qudsia. From the time she is young, a woman's heart is filled with a thousand fears, so that when she reaches puberty she thinks of herself as a fragile, unbaked clay pitcher that must encounter stones at every step. Because she had lost her mind, Bua's fears had vanished, especially her fear of losing her honour. She was no longer a hollow clay pitcher, she was solid rock. In a manly fashion she went where she pleased, regardless of whether it was night or day. Somehow she had managed to make people fear her. Nobody really knew how, but one or two miracles came about and people began to believe. Once a ruffian, finding her alone, tried to grab her. Ghazi Mian slapped his face with such fury that it caved in. At another time an unfortunate fellow tried to force himself on her, and it is believed that the hand which he fastened upon her wrist decomposed and fell off.

Our uncle, Chacha Mian, was an apostate. He used to say, "Every year thousands of lepers throng to the shrine with hopes of being healed. Decomposition of limbs and their subsequent falling off is not a miracle, it's a disease. And it's not unusual for an alcoholic to suffer from an attack of facial paralysis."

But we were afraid of doubting Bua. What would you do if your whole face fell in and collapsed? She had the temperament of an ogress. However, ever since we had discovered that she was not a ghoul or a spirit and was only a little mad, we ceased to be terrified of her.

One day we found her standing under the oak tree, wiping mud from her slipper. I gave her Aunt Qudsia's message.

"I'm not coming," she said rudely. "I'll come when I feel like it." Muttering, she walked away towards the path across the small bridge.

Finally, after a long time, she felt like it and there she was suddenly. Without standing on ceremony, without saying a word to anyone, she went directly to the water pitchers, poured some water in a brass cup for herself and sprinkled some on the chameli buds she had tied in a corner of her dupatta. Then she drew the dupatta over her head, placed her hands on her hips like a nautchi and started smiling. Amma had always warned us that girls from good families don't stand with their hands on their hips, only nautchis do that. While you're growing up there's a time when your hands become a nuisance, you don't know what to do with them. So, driven by the fear that I might become a nautchi if I weren't careful, I would sometimes place both hands over my head.

"What is this, you wretch, why are you slapping your head?" vexed, Amma would scold me.

"Where should I keep my hands then?" I would wearily ask.

"In the fire!" She'd get more irritated. "Get out of here." And I would quickly slip away.

Suddenly Bua laughed. Then she came and sat down on the divan and proceeded to adjust the folds on her tight pajama. Her clothes were clean and spotless. A starched pink dupatta was draped neatly across her shoulders while the bunch of chameli buds tied in a corner swung next to her cheek.

Unable to withstand her stare, Aunt Qudsia lowered her eyes and pretended to busy herself by adjusting her dupatta over her shoulders.

"My eyes are red from weeping…"

She seemed to be teasing Aunt Qudsia.

"Smoking, chewing paan, my beloved/ My cruel beloved didn't come today/My eyes are red from weeping…"

Aunt Qudsia was holding her tears in the palm of her hand; she began sprinkling them. But before she could bring on an attack of hysteria, Bua leapt up and was gone out of the back door in seconds.

Her voice glided in the distance: *"My eyes are red from weeping…"*

Everyone was impressed. Bua had knowledge of hidden things, she knew how to handle Aunt Qudsia.

"She must have heard it from somebody," Chacha Mian said. He was an apostate, you see. But no one paid any attention to his remark. After this episode Bua became a frequent visitor to our house. She'd come, sit down, and if she felt uneasy, she'd just get up and leave.

"Come, stay," Aunt Qudsia cajoled pleadingly.

"No, no I can't…he'll be waiting for me…"

And I'd imagine Ghazi Mian actually standing under the shade of the kadamb tree, waiting for her.

"She's lost her wits, the unfortunate creature, and she's from such a good family, too."

"You know, she doesn't look mad to me."

"Why, you'll think she's mad only after she picks up stones to throw at you? Doesn't she have that low-caste woman in her house, and what does she know of the value of money? Anyone can come in and steal all she's got and she'll never know."

"Don't say anything about her, please, I'm not sure it's safe."

"Why, I'm not saying she's a bad person, am I?"

Once Maulvi Sahib, the village cleric, said to Bua, "You had better get married, girl. What's the good of roaming around like this?"

Enraged, Bua pounced on him: "Why don't *you* get your mother married to some ruffian walking on the streets!"

"A woman is not safe without a man by her side," Maulvi Sahib explained.

Bua exploded: "I have a man by my side, your father's father…if he hears you talk like this he'll set your beard on fire."

Who could chide Ghazi Mian's cherished beloved without incurring his wrath? While returning from the well with a bucket of water, Maulvi Sahib's son was bitten by a snake. Maulvi Sahib's wife fell at Bua's feet, rubbed her nose on her shoes and it was only then that the boy's life was spared.

"It must be a water snake, they're not the poisonous type," Chacha Mian remarked. But who will listen to talk that mocks belief? Fear of Bua grew in people's hearts. She wasn't just anybody, she was Ghazi Mian's most treasured beloved, Ghazi Mian, who made it possible for a barren woman to conceive, who healed a leper, who turned beggars into kings and kings into beggars in seconds. Was it any wonder that he cared so much about his favourite girl?

Since she hadn't produced even a mouse as yet, Aunt Qudsia was sure the mem was barren. Nani Biwi's fasting and prayers had surely put a lock on her fertility. Allah could change everything in no time. Nani Biwi had also made a vow at Mian's shrine that when, with Allah's grace, Qudsia's luck changed and she became pregnant, she woud make an offering of a silver figurine.

For three years Nani Biwi's silver cradle had been placed at Mian's feet with the entreaty, "Ghazi Mian, please fill this cradle." And along with that continued the pleas to Qawi Qadir to bring Qudsia's husband back to her. But all the vows, prayers and fasting came to nought. The cradle was filled up, but it was the mem who became the instrument. The day she heard the news that her rival had given birth to a daughter, Aunt Qudsia was weighed down, as if a marble tomb had been erected over her soft, newly-dug grave. On the day of reckoning the angels of death, Munkar and Nakir, would be slow to breathe life into her.

Bua, who had been absent for many days, suddenly appeared. Nani Biwi was busy scolding the nain who had arrived with sweets to offer felicitations on the occasion of the baby's birth. Tossing the ladoos into the gutter, Nani Biwi threatened to shave off the nain's hair; the woman clasped her lahnga about her legs and bolted from there.

On hearing of the arrival of the baby girl, Bua began twittering.

"Listen girl, your soutan's lap has been blessed, aren't you going to distribute sweets?" Then she took down the drum and embarked on silly songs about childbirth.

"*With bells on his ankles/ The little tot will play* cham, cham, cham..."

There was no little tot, what cursed cham, cham was there going to be? This uncalled for singing angered Nani Biwi. She railed and ranted at Bua who dropped the drum, left the house and trudged off to sit behind the mosque. She was gone for many days. This was not unusual. Not caring whether it was night or day, she started off on foot, wandering from one village to another. Somewhere along the way, standing on the edge of a well to catch her breath, if she heard a new song, she'd include it in her repertoire of lyrics. Then she moved on. Often she travelled without food for days. The crazed have great strength. We had never seen her sleeping. She wasn't bothered by either snakes or scorpions or wild animals. In the village on the other side of the stream a lion was spotted, but it stayed out of her path. We had heard rumours that the lion offered her salutations by placing its head on the ground before her.

Bua told her stories of Ghazi Mian's playfulness with such aplomb that it became difficult to doubt her word. When you live next to a shrine everything seems to make sense. Mian was very stubborn and mischievous. He teased her, always tugging at her dupatta or clutching her bangles.

"Now listen, how did he fall in love with you?" Aunt Qudsia asked.

"His heart led him to me," Bua replied, smiling proudly.

"That's what I'm asking, how did his heart lead him to you?" Aunt Qudsia was always anxious to find out how one could win someone's heart. Although she had sacrificed her body, soul and everything she possessed, she had not succeeded in winning anyone's heart.

"I don't know, why don't you ask him yourself, he's standing in front of me, smiling." She pointed to the wall with her finger and all of us followed it fearfully. Our eyes could see nothing, but for her the world around was filled with blinding light.

"How did you meet him?"

"I was on my way to the well, to draw water, he stood in my path blocking my way."

"And then?" We all moved closer to her.

"I tried to run, he clasped my wrist."

"And then?" We edged closer still.

"My father was very amgry." She was in a world of her own already. "He said, we won't give him our daughter, he's a boatman's son."

"A boatman's son?"

Bua explained that Mian had taken the form of a boatman's son in order to beg for her hand; he fell at her father's feet and pleaded. But her father got angry and rejected him, and arranged her marriage to someone else. A terrible storm arose while the wedding party was attempting to cross the Ghagra stream in the middle of the night. It was Mian, transformed as the boatman and oaring their boat, who had summoned the storm. He ignored everyone else and made an attempt to save her from drowning, but the others tried to interfere. Enraged, he tipped the boat and let everyone drown. Surrounded by flowers, Bua floated for three days on the surface of the water in her bridal clothes.

"And then?" We had moved practically into her lap by now.

"And then nothing!" Exhausted, she pushed us away and left the house to wander in the cemetery in a daze, lost, singing love songs.

Bua was a virgin. No man had touched her. After the barat drowned she managed somehow to get to the banks of the stream. For days she strayed in the woods. When her parents heard she was alive they came after her to take her home, but by then Bua had retreated into a world of dreams. She refused to shatter her bridal bangles; she was a bride, and Bale Mian was her bridegroom. No one had the courage to tangle with Bale Mian.

"He's calling me," she'd suddenly say and wander off into the woods, singing songs of love. Considering her desire to be Bale Mian's, no one dared stop her. Gradually, as time passed, certain miracles came to be associated with her and people seemed to be more and more intimidated by her. Then they began to worship her. If someone needed to ask a favour of Mian, she was the one who was pampered first. Wherever she went she was treated with deference, and to have the opportunity of doing something for her was regarded as a stroke of good fortune. When a prayer was answered, a pink dupatta, fragrant oil and attar, bangles and flowers were offered at Ghazi Mian's shrine for her, along with the offering that had been promised for Ghazi Mian. How much did she eat? She could stay without food for days. People filled large decorated trays with food and brought them to her house and she distributed the food among beggars. She had been living alone since the death of her parents. A low-caste woman took care of the house. The village washer-woman, who was careless with everyone else's clothes and frequently lost or misplaced laundry, washed Bua's clothes with the utmost care, giving them the best crispness and lustre. Bua owned some land, but never bothered to make any profit from its tilling. Perhaps that was why people had begun to view her as Ghazi Mian's cherished beloved, there were hundreds who were ready to surrender their lives to her. Therefore, although she was a weak woman, she was not handicapped or helpless; she claimed all the rights of a man. She moved about alone, as she fancied, declared her love in a loud voice, sang boisterously, made bold comments without reserve, swore unabashedly, sat in the company of men while a qawwali was going on and generously threw money to the singers.

During the annual fair at Ghazi Mian's shrine, thousands of ruffians and scoundrels trooped in along with the lakhs of pilgrims and worshippers; every other day you heard about kidnappings and rapes. Upper class women considered it dangerous to come out even in enclosed palanquins or guarded carriages. And Bua, all the while, sailed about without a care among the crowds, her dupatta floating behind her.

"My word, Bua, the world is a dangerous place, don't go to the fair," Amma warned her. "Aren't you afraid to wander around all by yourself?"

"But I don't wander by myself. I'm not alone, he's with me." In other words, her *he.*

There was no one among us who could contradict her. What could you say? And if we said something she didn't like we'd be in trouble; who knows what miracle might follow.

"She's a degenerate, the wretch!" In the beginning Chacha Mian didn't like her at all. "And she's not mad, either. She's just making a fool of all of us."

That very night Chacha Mian suffered an attack of liver pain that left him gasping for breath. He kept insisting that he'd had a liver ailment for many years, but who was going to pay any attention to what he said? "He's an ignorant man," Amma admitted to Bua in an attempt to win her over. She secretly begged her to speak to Ghazi Mian on their behalf.

The pain would have subsided on its own, but Amma was sure he had been cured because of Bua's intervention. And she warned Chacha Mian that if he ever said another unfavourable word concerning Bua again, she would beat her head with her hands. What did he have to lose? He had no children and no God, while she, by God's grace, was a mother and could not afford to antagonise anyone. As for Abba, she had already sworn that if he said anything hostile with regard to Bua he would surely see her dead. Abba had often maintained that this business of believing in spiritual leaders and their followers was a sinful undertaking. But Amma's family was dearer to her than concerns about the next life.

When our friendship with Bua grew it seemed as if we'd come to terms with God; because of Bua we felt as if we too had some connection with Ghazi Mian. Sometimes, when she was in a good mood, she spent the night at our house and all of us quarrelled for the opportunity to sleep with her on the same bed. She exuded a wonderful fragrance of soft-smelling, freshly-dug earth. When, after several days of absence, her voice floating in song reached our ears, we became frantic with excitement and ran to fetch her. Like ants we clung to her, dragging her home. The very same voice which used to strike fear in our hearts now fell on our ears with the magic of an ancient melody.

As soon as she stepped into the house, everything brightened and came to life, the drum beat vibrated:

"*Ho, my raja, bring me some medicine from Dilli/ So I can be cured.*" She sang the new songs and new tunes she had picked up.

"*The rains are here/My brother, will you not put up the swing?*"

Dark clouds swirled, raindrops fell, young hearts stirred with emotions, flames smouldered in Aunt Qudsia's eyes. Who was going to put up a swing? Aunt Qudsia became dizzy and nauseous when she saw anyone swinging. But Bua brought a length of rope from somewhere, we made a swing, and with a down pillow for a seat we swung high and low. Bua sang long, high notes and Aunt Qudsia, from her place on the divan, joined in:

"*My heart yearns, the clouds pour/ My friend, how will I endure these days of spring...*"

Sitting at a distance Uncle Shabir stared at the floor like a criminal, as though he had a hand in making the clouds pour and the heart yearn, as if Aunt Qudsia's spring had soured because of him. Qudsia belonged to someone else, she was forbidden fruit. Secretly he consulted maulvis, talked to lawyers, but we're talking of the time when the Khul's Bill hadn't been passed. At first no one thought of divorce because of the fear of bringing dishonour to the family. Then, after some of the rebels in the family succeeded in bringing Nani Biwi around to the idea, Aunt Qudsia's husband stubbornly refused to give in.

Rejecting our world, Bua had created a free world of her own where she ruled. She had sealed all doors but after all she was a woman; a chink remained somewhere. We became very fond of her and sometimes affectionately made obstinate demands; when she got ready to leave we trailed her tearfully, forcing her to turn back.

"Bua, these silly children are crazy about you, why don't you take them with you," Amma would say, and Bua would cancel her trip.

If she hadn't been slightly demented, Bua was fit to be weighed in gold. She had started helping out with chores in the house. Cleaning was her particular obsession. Accompanied by an army of kids she went about tidying up and threw out basketfuls of rubbish. If only she could come back with us to our hometown after Abba's retirement.

"Can't she be cured?" Amma asked Hakim Sahib who used to be called in to treat Aunt Qudsia. He came to our house once or twice every week.

"Of course she can, Begum Sahib. There is no ailment in this world for which medicine doesn't have a cure. Start giving her a laxative and God willing, her mind will return to its normal state."

Hakim Sahib had only one medicine for every ailment: laburnum purgative. When Aunt Qudsia felt unwell, it was this vey laxative that was administered to her. Not only did you feel that your life was slipping away but your body also seemed to be threatened by the effects of these laxatives. She had no recourse but to be cured, and for days afterwards she was afraid to blink for fear that it might be mistaken for an oncoming attack. Chacha Mian, too, had been given these laxatives for the pain in his liver. After the first dose he threatened to kill Hakim Sahib.

"The heat from the body travels to the brain. Purging the stomach helps get rid of all noxious matter." Hakim Sahib proceeded to throw light on the advantages of purgative therapy and everyone was convinced. Bua, however, ignored his advice.

"Come now, what's this silly hakim going to do for me." Irritated by all this talk, Bua made off. No one could discuss her illness for any length of time.

It was while a treatment for Bua was being sought that something tragic occurred, which clearly confirmed her unbalanced state of mind. One of our cousins, the third among her siblings, was rather homely and the family faced constant hurdles in finding her a suitable match. After much hard work an aunt from Saharanpur finally got something going. The boy's mother arrived to talk things over. The house was cleaned so thoroughly to impress her that we began to feel like guests in our own home. Displayed all around us were items which we had never been allowed near for fear that we might break or tarnish them.

Bua had not made an appearance for many days. After a frantic search lasting three or four days, we gave up on her. A lengthy menu was being prepared for the mother-in-law, the samdhan. Suddenly, chameli buds dangling from a corner of her dupatta, a new song on her lips, Bua arrived in her usual way. First, she was taken aback by the manner in which the house had been cleaned and decorated. Then she spotted the guest and lost control altogether. Going up to the woman, Bua flicked her eyelashes and knit her brows as if searching for a microscopic tic. The samdhan was not invisible. True, she was short, but her lack of height was amply made up for by her massive bulk.

Amma was perturbed by Bua's behaviour and made an attempt to distract her with some silly chatter. But, pushing aside Amma's restraining hand, Bua asked the samdhan-to-be:

"I say, sister, what kind of grain do you eat?"

The samdhan's face came alive with a variety of emotions. The diamond nose-pin vibrated in the smooth, black nose and it seemed as if she was about to explode with a loud bang.

"Bua dear, will you take this ice-water to the men's quarters?" Amma pulled her away from their guest. "Number Three has received a proposal, why don't you go and see the groom and tell us what he's like–he's outside." Amma managed to get her to leave.

"She's mad, the wretch," Amma apologised.

But the samdhan would not be appeased.

Bua left the room and returned within seconds. Dumping the tray with the ice-water on the divan, she beat her forehead with her hand.

"O my mother! Is that a groom or a tobacco leaf and a dwarf to boot!" She placed her right hand over her left, fingers extended, thumb to thumb to show them what she meant.

Bua continued: "I tell you, they don't make a proper pair. The groom is no good, you'll only ruin the girl's life. I say samdhan, go and find someone who's a fairy like yourself for your son, and leave our girl alone."

The samdhan didn't explode, but she did leave Number Three alone.

Vexed, Bua kept swearing; Amma could not calm her down. Taking the drum down from the peg she began a song on a high note:

"*A dark lover I won't take, sister, a dark lover…*

When my groom sits beside me on the nuptial bed, I'll kick him so he falls, sister…

A dark lover… I won't take…"

Poor Number Three was fated to live with hurdles. The whole household reprimanded Bua for her actions, but thrusting the drum to one side, she continued to mutter: "Is she unwanted baggage, hunh?"

She was gone for many weeks this time. We thought she wasn't coming back. The house was lonely without her and Aunt Qudsia's attacks recurred with greater frequency. Her temperament also soured. In the past she had complied with everything Nani Biwi said.

"Qudsia, child, drink some milk."

"Yes, Bi Amma."

"Child, lie down, give your back a rest, you've been stretched like a rod all day."

"Girl, how long are you going to remain in bed, get up now."

In other words it was always "Get up," "Eat this, drink that." Like a disease, Aunt Qudsia was affixed to Nani Biwi who constantly expressed her grief at her daughter's fate and continuously scrutinised her. What else was there for her to do, anyway? And Aunt Qudsia answered with, "Yes, Bi Amma," to everything.

Suddenly, no one knows why, Aunt Qudsia began to get irritated with Nani Biwi. The two would quarrel with each other, sometimes Aunt Qudsia would cry and sometimes Nani Biwi. And Dadima invariably jumped in. One by one all the aunts in the house would also be embroiled in the battle and before long two separate parties emerged. It all started with one thing and ended somewhere else altogether.

Members from our mother's side of the family formed one group while those from our father's side formed another. Attacks directed at seven generations of each party commenced. And later, their faces swollen, all the women stiffly avoided each other for days.

Every skirmish originated from Aunt Qudsia's camp. The bitterness in her temperament grew with each passing day; she seemed to derive pleasure from hurting those around her. Her behaviour towards Uncle Shabir also became chilly.

"*Why, when I called for you, did you take so long?*," he began with one of Aunt Qudsia's favourite pieces. She turned her back to him. The poor fellow squirmed uncomfortably.

"You should go, it's getting dark and it's the rainy season," she said dryly, feeling sorry for him. Grateful that she was thinking of him at least, he got up and left.

And then one day we went mad with joy. We found her. It was spring, the woods were blazing with palash blossoms, our eyes seemed to be brimming over with the red of the flowers. She was standing next to an amber-laden tree, dusting sand from her slippers. Her pink dupatta glowed from the fiery reflection of the flowers, spring blossoms danced in her eyes as if she had just come from a visit with her beloved or was on her way to meet him.

"Wait, wait a minute, I'm coming." We dragged her. Suddenly she paused, cast a glance behind her and said in a pleading tone, "I'll be back soon."

We were nonplussed. To whom was she making a promise of return? There was no one there. She took a few steps, then stopped. Angrily she said, "Don't put on an act with me, I'm warning you!" Then she made as if to walk on. Once again, as if she had heard some objectionable remark, she knit her brow and scolded: "All right, you can go, I won't come back...I'll see what you'll do...you don't trust me... I don't care..." She was fighting the air and our legs seemed to be melting. If we hadn't loved her so much we would have made off from there a long time ago.

Bua's arrival caused a stir in our house. It was a strange coincidence that whenever she came, a parcel containing fruit or sweetmeats arrived or we received some good news. Her appearance livened everyone's hearts; if a fight was in progress, it ceased, or maybe in the ensuing commotion people forgot what they had been fighting about. Shrugging off her despondency, Aunt Qusdia also got up and took note of what was going on.

"I'm not coming ," Bua scolded the air in front of her. Everyone became fearful.

"What's the matter?" Amma asked.

"Such grief. He's pestering me, he doesn't trust me, he says I have another lover, I have eyes for someone else!" She screamed as she complained about Bale Mian. "Who does he think I am...a hussy?"

"Ahhh...you crazy girl," Amma said sadly and sighed again.

"He's burnt to a cinder with jealousy, he says I'm fickle!"

Her imaginary lover was an odd composite indeed; a little bit of James Bond, a little of Krishan Murari, you might say. James Bond is a hero for every age, whether he appears as a hero from *Dastan-e-Amir Hamza* or as Hatim Tai. And her beloved was also a reflection of Krishan Murari because people generally sang song about Krishan. As a matter of fact, Bale Mian's antics reminded you of him: tugging at her dupatta, twisting her wrists so that her bangles broke, and when moved to anger, resorting to slapping or upturning a boat.

He exhibited all the traits of a suave young man. No matter what anyone might say, Bua's Bale Mian was undoubtedly more colourful and vibrant than Aunt Qudsia's Uncle Shabir. We believed everything Bua told us. Why was it so surprising that she could see Bale Mian? Didn't we observe elephants and stallions in the clouds, and Raja Inder's court in all its glory in the peeling plaster of the crumbling, saline-ridden walls? We didn't think she was deranged. If there were a few deranged people like her in every household, life would certainly be more tolerable.

"I say Bua, won't you come here for a minute," Amma cajoled; she had something to say to her that was important. Perhaps because Bua was angry with Mian, she didn't bolt when Amma brought up the question of Hakim Sahib's treatment. It seemed that she was listening intently.

"Ahhh…what treatment…my suffering at his hands will take my life…he grumbles at every step, then he tyrannises me…"

Taking the drum from its hook she gazed at it ruefully.

"Little mouse, why do you gather all this treasure/Soon all will be taken away…"

When the drum failed to perk her up she began quarrelling with Bale Mian:

"Beloved, your tantrums I won't tolerate anymore…
I tell you, if you climb a horse, I'll climb an elephant…
Beloved, your tantrums…"

She wore her beloved out. If he climbed the roof, she climbed a mountain, if he followed her to the mountain, she darted into the infernal regions under the earth; in other words, she made him huff and puff.

"Look, here he is, touching my feet, begging forgiveness."

The insane are like kings in their own realm. What confidence Bua had in herself. The king of kings bowed at her feet, one smile from her and he was no longer himself. If you can find someone who cares for you like this why should you not discard the life of reason and good sense?

When birds who are caged gaze at the flight of those soaring freely in the skies, they are bound to dash their heads against the wooden bars of their cages. And, unable to find escape, they conspire with their captors. Isn't it true that domesticated fowls or birds with clipped wings are used by hunters to ensnare their own kind?

The good women enclosed in the four walls of their homes, tightly bound by the constraints of society, also could not tolerate Bua's freedom. She was a woman, but she enjoyed the rights of men and everyone resented that. Bua didn't refuse to take the laxative, but she also didn't protest strongly.

Amma said that the wretch's yes or no was all the same; after all, the treatment was for her own good.

All night long amaltas pods, amla, har, bahir and other items from the same disgusting family continued to be emptied into a large, unpolished copper pot. After her morning prayers Nani Biwi raised the heat under the pot again. Bua had been detained under some pretext.

The first dose had to be taken on an empty stomach, first thing in the morning. We also awoke. The whole house was putrid with the smell of amaltas. The sight of the large tin bowl filled with a mixture that looked like rotting cow-dung, made my stomach turn.

Bua tried to shake her off, but Amma pressed on with pledges on her own life. Nani Biwi pleaded on Mian's behalf. They brought her to the edge of the water drain and told her to squat.

"Hold your nose with your dupatta," Dadi Amma suggested.

The entire family had gathered as if a fighting match between rams was about to commence. Bua pressed her nose with her dupatta and with Tai Amma's help she balanced the large bowl with one hand.

"Don't make her drink this... Amma bi... O God, Apa bi, leave the poor wretch alone." Suddenly Aunt Qudsia was pleading with everybody. "Please, you're so nice, Tai Amma..."

She had suffered the tortures of this laxative.

"My word, girl, are you out of your mind!"

"Alakh! Alakh!" We made gagging noises as we sat close by with our noses pressed between our fingers.

"No, Apa bi...please, don't make her drink this. I've had it, may God help us!"

"Because you've had it you're still in one piece. You might have been picking at straws by now if you hadn't."

With great ceremony Bua took one sip from the cup and "phurr!" she spat it all out on Tai Amma's breast. Throwing the bowl into the drain, she made a beeline for the tap and gargled until she was spent.

"May he die, that bastard hakim, it's his mother's crushed liver in this drink."

Each time she washed out her mouth she delivered a solid invective intended for Hakim Sahib. "May his mother's grave be filled with worms!"

"You foolish girl, you've dumped such valuable medicine into the gutter. If you didn't want it you should have said so in the beginning, we could have saved it for Qudsia."

Aunt Qudsia winced.

"I didn't throw it, he pushed it out of my hand." Placing the blame on Bale Mian, Bua calmly began chewing cardamom seeds.

"But he was not talking to you," Tai Amma said irately.

"Oh, he is such a vagabond! Who can fight him? Last night he wouldn't leave me alone, he clasped my feet, begged forgiveness and cried."

May God forgive us!

Bua rose nonchalantly and got ready to leave. "Why, where are you off to?"

"I have to go, he's getting angry with me again. *Beloved, I'll be a chameli in your lap…*" She was one with her beloved once more.

A travelling theatre was in town, we were all longing to go. Bua went without a ticket every day and picked up new songs of burning love.

Aunt Qudsia's behaviour was changing. Instead of reading Rashid-ul-Kheri's *The Morning of Sorrow* and *The Night of Life* and sobbing, she now surreptitiously read *The Poems of Love's Poison,* and at night she paced the courtyard.

"Sir, the wretch will absolutely not take the laxative," Amma complained to Hakim Sahib.

"No matter. By Allah's grace, I have other drugs, she will never guess she is taking anything. Here, give her these three tablets rolled in paan or some sweets. Continue this treatment once every three days and, God willing, she will be completely cured."

"Here, Bua, have a paan." As soon as Bua appeared Amma would open her paandan.

"No dear, no, my breath will smell." Bua dodged Amma adroitly.

But if women don't have anything better to do than meddle, how long can you escape from them? Perhaps she had a quarrel with Bale Mian or maybe his attention strayed, but somehow the first dose finally went down Bua's throat. And everyone waited for the results. Nothing happened. Except that Bua placed a rope cot under the neem tree and went to sleep, something we had never seen her do before.

Everyone was convinced that Bale Mian had played a trick by impeding the progress of the tablet, or possibly it hadn't been administered first thing in the morning and that was why no results were in evidence. Suddenly Bua awoke with a start. For the first time we saw a strange expression of undefined fear on her face. She undoubtedly had knowledge of the unknown. She got up and left angrily.

"I say, to hell with this wretched treatment! What if she leaves a curse or two behind, where will we be? One shouldn't tangle with the pious." Amma made her decision.

"It is truly amazing, the tablet had no effect on her," impressed, Nani Biwi proclaimed.

But in the evening surprise fell upon us like a mud slide. Bua's sweepress came running to our house with the message that Bua had been suffering from dysentery all morning and now she was also vomiting. Bewildered, Amma sent off a servant to Hakim Sahib.

"It's the heat flowing out," Hakim Sahib remarked, and handed the servant a potion which reduced the flow of the heat, but caused Bua's temperature to rise at an alarming rate.

Amma sent for her several days in a row, but she refused to come. She hardly ate much earlier and now her sweepress came and fetched some watery rice and khichri and sago pudding, but Bua didn't touch a thing. All she did was drink large quantities of water.

When she came after several weeks, we felt as if she was distanced from us, as if we had remained children while she had matured. When we tried to put our arms around her neck she tottered and sat down.

"Come now, what silliness is this." She spoke in a brusque tone, as though we had never draped our arms around her neck like a garland before this. Her clothes were rumpled, her hair dry and bedraggled. She had always been thin, now, after the illness, she was worse. When we requested her to play the drum she hedged. Amma placed a tray of pea-pods before her. She started shelling them.

Nani Biwi and Amma exchanged meaningful glances above her head. They both expressed relief; if the remaining two tablets could also be administered, no signs of the illness would remain.

"I say, Bua, Mian isn't upset with you, is he?" Amma probed.

"Am I the one to fight?" This meant that a dispute was in progress. "I don't know what he thinks of himself, that son of a lat sahib!" She seemed perturbed. There was, without a doubt, a falling-out between them.

Bua's sweepress had gone to a neighbouring village to perform an abortion. Her usual trade was rolling twine, but occasionally, as a side business, she helped the needy. Amma persuaded Bua to spend the night at our house.

Amma was ready to swear on the Quran that she had not given Bua the second dose, but Dadi Amma insisted that she and Nani Biwi had been conspiring; the second dose had been given and had acted like an acid bomb. Bua collapsed from a wave of diarrhoea that seemed to have no end. That night things became so bad that Abba also got wind of what was going on. The doctor was sent for, he prescribed medication, but Bua suffered helplessly from loose motions all night long.

Abba thundered that the Hakim Sahib ought to be whipped, he was a fool, and that if he prescribed any medicine for anyone again he would be handcuffed.

Dadi Amma had been kept out of all this good work. It was Nani Biwi's special case and she wanted to man her position herself.

"I say, girls, what is going on?" Dadi Amma, who was quite deaf, would occasionally repeat this question.

"Nothing, sister dear...mind your own business!" Nani Biwi uttered the first part of the sentence loudly and the second almost inaudibly.

"Nobody tells me anything," Dadi Amma muttered. The two were always at odds with each other. They were samdhans, but were also sisters-in-law by marriage. However, the real reason for their dissent lay in the fact of their beliefs. Nani Biwi belonged to the Sunni sect while Dadi Amma was a Shia. Their cantonments were set up in the different verandas. Amma came and sat in Nani Biwi's veranda early in the morning. Amma was the nucleus around whom our household revolved; it is obvious that her veranda assumed greater importance. After offering salutations to Dadi Amma, Amma came and sat down. The door to Aunt Qudsia's room also opened on this veranda, Aunt Qudsia, who was the family's most urgent social issue. Her comings and goings caused the place to bustle. Uncle Shabir too sat there. And as for the children, they will be where all the activity is. Dadi Amma was jealous: because the children's paternal side of the family was Shia, they should be raised as Shia as well. However, Nani Biwi had all the power; at every step she praised the tenets of the Sunni sect.

We were backed by Amma. When we didn't heed Dadi Amma's injunctions, Amma reprimanded us with a smile and we were emboldened. But if we ignored Nani Biwi's orders, we had to listen to threats of bones being shattered.

Both sides attempted to show us the straight road leading to heaven. Dadi Amma taught us one kalima, while Nani Biwi taught us the other. Confused, we jumbled them up, something that had an effect on us similar to that of Hakim Sahib's tablets, we felt as if we had taken a mental purgative. The keys to heaven got all mixed up and both sides showered us with damnation.

Nani Biwi held milad in answer to Dadi Amma's majalis; we got fine-grained sweets in earthen cups and immediately became Sunnis. But when the coverings were removed from the chandeliers in Dadi Amma's veranda and the taboot was brought out, we became hers completely; when nobas were recited in tremulous voices we donned black shirts and beat our chests with vigour. Nani Biwi pummelled us and tempted us with colourful sweets, but it was wise to be a member of Dadi Amma's party during the holy month of Muharram. For us the doors to heaven opened on the side where goods were most plentiful.

"Girl, are you Sunni or Shia?" Dadi Amma would frequently ask.

"Shia," I would reply promptly.

"Are you Shia or Sunni?" Nani Biwi usually queried before handing out sweets. Thank God the two verandas were at some distance from each other and both grandmothers were somewhat hard of hearing.

The question of Bua's treatment took a rather unpleasant turn. Dadi Amma filled Abba's ears with gossip, he scolded Amma, Amma cried heartily.

Abba's retirement was approaching. Prosperity makes you large-hearted and you feel great affection for your relatives. But with the onset of hard times, the fountains of love also dry up. All his life Abba had spent money indiscriminately. Now, with only a few years left before retirement, he wanted to make up for all that careless spending.

Everyone stiffened when a crow cawed. Here comes another guests. The crow cawed at our house every day; when our relatives from our father's side poured in, our mother's relatives, not wishing to be left behind, arrived as well. If paternal aunts showed up with their spouses and children, then maternal aunts also made an appearance with their entire families in tow.

The guests fell into two camps. Two tables were set up and spies were sent out to make sure that the opposing camp was not receiving preferential treatment. Usually Nani Biwi's party had the upper hand since Amma was in her camp.

Abba had no time for party politics. In addition, he was the one who made the money and Amma the one who spent it. The situation was very similar to what it's like in America these days; everyone, regardless of which party each person belonged to, pampered her. Abba, on the other hand, was neutral. He treated both parties in the same way.

However, Chacha Mian, my father's younger brother, was the one who was always looking for an opportunity to make trouble between the two parties.

Amma entertained her in-laws well, but in a way that reeked openly of disaffection. If there was a shortage of food she would announce the fact in a loud voice: "Send it over there, we'll eat with chutney and pickle."

But Chacha Mian was a sly one; he ate with Amma's party, partaking of whatever special dish it was that had proven unplentiful, and then went over to Dadi Amma's camp and said, "The liver and kidneys cooked today were excellent."

There were no liver and kidneys cooked that day.

Dadi Amma grumbled: "My word, I've had a hankering for so many days; no one bothered to send us any, they wolfed it all down themselves!"

And the following day when Abba came from court and went to greet her, she immediately complained about the liver and kidneys. Abba said to Amma, "I say, why didn't you send some liver and kidneys over there?"

"My word! When did we have liver and kidneys?" Amma would stand up in a huff.

"I swear, I saw it with my own eyes, Bakreedan took over a bowlful," Dadi Amma declared, relying on Chacha Mian's word. Oaths would be taken, faiths dragged in, and finally Chacha Mian would be called. He would say innocently, "What liver and kidneys? I've said so many times we shouldn't eat watermelon with rice, now I have a pain in my kidneys and once the pain starts..." Chacha Mian tried to change the subject.

"Did you eat liver and kidneys over there or not?" Dadi Amma persisted.

"When? I didn't get any. This is not fair, such rich foods being cooked and eaten by others."

No one really knew what was going on. Witnesses were brought forth, then someone who was feeling heavy-hearted burst into tears, in answer to which another person broke down; old wounds were rubbed anew.

"All I did was ask for a tiny morsel and she was downright evasive..."

"Such a blow it was, the fingers left a mark on the poor wretch's face..."

"I say, sister, it's quite another matter when it comes to your own kin..."

"Yes, indeed, and we're just enemies..."

When all of them were exhausted, Chacha Mian stepped in.

"What's all this bickering? You sound like butchers and common people...what kind of decency is this...fighting over morsels like dogs."

Hearing him scold, everyone, exhausted and worn out by now, felt contrite and went off to bed. Members of the paternal side of the family were glad that Nani Biwi's party had been severely reproached on account of Bua.

Bua was very sick. The time for the third dose never came; she was no good to herself after the second. If Qais had been administered all three doses prescribed by Hakim Sahib he would never have become Majnun, the crazed lover. He would have lost the vigour needed to roam the desert and the energy to cry out 'Laila! Laila!' the poor fellow would have forgotten all about love's sprightliness.

The fever subsided, but for several days afterwards Bua was so weak she could barely talk. Because the second dose had produced immediate results, she was still at our house.

All day long she sat silently in a corner, her eyes shut. Her reason had made a comeback; she seemed quite sensible now.

Bua's sweepress had not yet returned. Amma pampered Bua no end and personally prepared soup for her. But Bua, her face drawn, would not budge. After much coaxing she would take a few sips but immediately throw up; either that, or she had to set up her cot next to the toilet. Her digestive system was permanently damaged; heat seemed to flow out without the aid of medicine.

Where has Bua gone, I wondered sometimes. That jaunty, proud Bua who ran about with the children shaking the branches of the jambolana tree for jamuns, our mad Bua who stole melons and cucumbers from the fields! Why did Allah give her back her reason? She had even forgotten to laugh.

And singing?

After the second dose her throat became hoarse.

O God, she'll never again put up a swing on the neem tree and sing songs about the rainy season.

Amma had appointed herself Bua's guardian. She arranged to have her house rented and Bua began to live with us. When the sweepress returned, she came to Bua distraught. Bua's health was relatively better at this time. She was peeling potatoes for potato bharta. Because winter had begun, she spent most of her time in the kitchen.

There was a time when, during the coldest winter months, Bua went around with just a light shawl draped over her shoulders at night. But that was when she had been filled with warmth.

Amma scolded the sweepress and sent her off. Bua continued to sit quietly with her head lowered. As soon as the rent from the house started coming in, Amma put it all together and ordered a pair of gold bracelets for Bua. When the bracelets, decorated with carved lion heads, arrived, Bua turned them over a few times in her hands, then handed them to Amma.

"Keep them."

"I say, girl, put them on," Nani Biwi insisted.

"My word, no, what's the occasion for wearing bracelets?"

she replied tartly. Bua had also developed the ability to tell the difference between what was proper and what was not.

"Do you see her? Who can say the poor girl was once mad. How mature she is now." Nani Biwi called her dullness, maturity.

Bua didn't mention Bale Mian either. If one of us asked, "Bua, how is Mian?" she pretended he had been nothing to her, as if he were a stranger. We teased her further.

"Don't chew my brains!" she'd snap at us and Amma would censure us and shoo us away.

"I say, don't remind her, the wretch, she'll lose her mind again." Nani Biwi also scolded, but she too teased Bua sometimes.

"I say, it seems your Ghazi Mian has forgotten you altogether."

Bua sat still as if she were deaf.

But one day she showed some of her old spirit.

If she watched her diet carefully she was able to keep everything down. By now she had taken over most of the housework and had graduated from light jobs to frying garlic in ghee and pouring it over the dal. Every day she kneaded five seers of dough and before long she was also cooking rotis.

"He's unfaithful," Bua said archly. Then she became emotional. She had been drying her hair after a bath. She looked a little like the Bua of old. Suddenly she broke into songs in a lifeless voice:

"*Ho, raja ji, my rival has long tresses/Don't get caught, raja ji...*"

The old passion was gone from her voice. Bale Mian had been unfaithful to her or was about to be. Seeing her own dry hair she was suddenly threatened by her rival's long tresses.

"*Ho, raja ji...my rival has pink cheeks...*"

Bua's once wheatish complexion had become muddy and

lustreless. All of a sudden she was stooping like an old woman. When she got to her feet she braced herself by putting both hands on her knees. The old vitality and sprightliness had disappeared; after forsaking Bale Mian's love, she was dispossessed and vacant, a ruin.

*

Childhood never mourns any loss for long. We moved on, leaving her behind as she lagged. Aunt Qudsia was no longer the same either. Instead of constantly complaining about the noise we made, she now called us to her and resolved our disputes, tutored us, scrubbed our dry, chapped hands and feet and massaged them with Vaseline. It wasn't long ago that she had wandered listless and morose, her hair uncombed for many days, her clothes filthy because she would forget to change. Why would a woman adorn herself if the person whose gaze matters the most turns away from her? However, in consideration of her married state she continued wearing two glass bangles on each wrist. People recounted tales of her patience and loyalty with awe and wonder.

A soft, delicate change had begun to appear in her. Instead of staying in bed for hours she started walking regularly. Her complexion blossomed, perhaps because she used a turmeric paste prepared from a fine selection of herbs. In the past when Nani Biwi combed her hair, big clumps would fall out. Now her hair was silky and shiny, probably because it was washed with shika kai, nagar motha and other fragrant roots that are generally used by brides. Or maybe we now liked everything about her because she no longer considered us a curse from God, but thought of us instead as mischievious children.

In the past she carelessly dipped her dupattas in any odd shade of purple or yellow dye (in deference to her wedded state), and threw them out to dry on the line. Now, ever since she had sent for the bale of muslin # 26 from Agra, the dupattas were dyed in soft, sober colours. First the clothes were tailored to match the season, and then matching gold or silver lace was stitched on to the dupattas. For Muharram the colour was green, and for spring they were dyed in five-toned, wavy stripes. We happily transported bucketfuls of water to her, flung her gold-embroidered dupatta up and down, this way and that in the sun to dry, and dumped heaps of half-opened buds next to her pillow.

We looped her earrings with clusters of buds, wrapped the earrings in moist cloth and left them by the water containers. In the evening she bathed, donned a soft-hued, crisp gharara along with an embroidered muslin shirt, with which she wore a gathered dupatta, put on the earrings laden with flowers, and smilingly gazed into the empty air before her as if she too had a Ghazi Mian standing there, teasing her.

The responsible women in the household were a little concerned about the changes they saw in Aunt Qudsia. The attacks of hysteria she had suffered from were understandable; every unfortunate woman who is rejected by her husband occupies herself thus. But dressing up and wearing flowers does not become a woman whose earthly God has turned away from her. She must thank God for whatever meagre clothing she can obtain, cover herself with it, and eat whatever little comes her way. What would people say if they got a glimpse of her fanciful behaviour?

Surely she would be spat at.

All this adornment, these rosettes, they enflame wicked thoughts, the devil gets encouragement from them.

"I say, Qudsia, you don't look well, should I send for Hakim Sahib?" Nani Biwi, fearful of her daughter's well-being, suggested.

"No, Amma Bi, I'm feeling fine." Aunt Qudsia guiltily evaded her mother's gaze.

"My word, sleeping late again! Why, you've missed your morning prayers, girl!"

"I've said the make-up prayers, Amma."

"God knows what rubbish you read all night. Is it any wonder you can't get up in time for morning prayers?"

Every other day Aunt Qudsia received a fresh batch of novels in the mail. Not once did she show them to anyone. As soon as a fresh shipment arrived, she immediately hid it under her pillow.

These days when Aunt Qudsia wore earrings or bangles, Nani Biwi reacted with indignation: "What's the occasion for these earrings?" she'd ask.

"No occasion, I just felt like wearing them," Aunt Qudsia would reply, tossing her head, making the earrings swing.

"My, oh my, what feeling is this?" Nani Biwi grumbled.

There was a time when Nani Biwi had mourned, expressing sorrow at the sight of Aunt Qudsia's unadorned wrists, lamenting that she couldn't wear earrings. "Ahhh, what hopes went into all this jewellery...the poor girl wasn't destined to use any of it. I say, Qudsia, put on a thing or two at Eid or Baqr-Eid at least."

"Who shall I wear it for, Amma?" Aunt Qudsia would respond with a deep sigh.

But all that was in the past. And now? No, the signs were not at all good; reading those wretched, cheap books all night long, pacing the veranda and sighing, looking up at the sky and smiling to oneself...no, these are not the ways of girls who sacrifice their lives for the family. Why were buds sprouting from this old, dried-out trunk?

No longer did Nani Biwi pray with the same zeal for Aunt Qudsia's husband's return. The groom didn't show his face, but Uncle Shabir, on the other hand, came regularly. He seemed to be getting taller with each passing day; he gave the impression that, like a juggler, he had stilts attached to his legs.

Assuming an air of indifference, he would come and sit down at some distance. Aunt Qudsia nonchalantly played with her dupatta which kept slipping from her shoulders, and the gold buttons, in the meantime, became heavier and sank deeper into her chest. Those two didn't need to use their eyes to gaze at each other.

Soon she'd prompt one of us to ask Uncle Shabir to sing "*Sarkar Madine-walle.*" We preferred "*The eyes spoke/ plunging a dagger into the heart.*" However, in order to make Aunt Qudsia happy we would pester Uncle Shabir to sing the *na'at.*

"Let him sit on the stool here," she would say encouragingly, and we brought him over to the stool.

He would start singing and if, impelled by boredom, we tried to slip away, Aunt Qudsia caught hold of us and, whispering promises of carrot halva and laddus in our ears, made us stay. It was as if she were guilty and could not be left alone with him. Our presence gave them an opportunity to say God knows what to each other; we never understood much. Often, Aunt Qudsia suddenly broke into a laugh for no apparent reason and continued laughing. We too joined in; children don't always have to know why they're laughing. Auntie's complexion glowed and the flower-laden earrings swayed and kissed her cheeks. With everyone laughing, Uncle Shabir's eyes also brimmed with light and his wooden mouth came to life.

"You're laughing for no reason, you silly girl!" he'd say ever so softly. But Auntie heard him.

"So, do you want me to weep all my life?"

"No, Qudsia! I…I want…"he fumbled.

"Whom do you want?" Aunt Qudsia interjected, twisting his words to suit her meaning.

"Qudsia…" Mumble, murmur…whatever he said was unintelligible to us.

We stared at them like idiots.

Mumble, murmur...Aunt Qudsia was saying something. We didn't know what they were saying to each other. But we were aware that a delightfully sweet conversation was in progress. The expressions on their faces filled us with joy; children often understand unspoken words, feel them. We giggled loudly and they used our laughter as a screen behind which to hide.

"Liar! Swear on my life!"

"But how can I swear on *my* life?" he would reply so softly that stone-deaf Nani Biwi could not hear a thing. Dadi Amma's encampment was some distance away.

The two parties were embroiled in battle these days. Dadi Amma sent over some sweetmeats.

"It must be impure."

Nani Biwi maintained that Shias spat into food before handing it out to others or else mixed excrement with it. She threw the grainy, sugar-sweet laddus to the ducks in front of everyone, leaving Dadi Amma fuming with anger. But when Nani Biwi sent her some loquat that had arrived from Saharanpur, Dadi Amma immediately handed the fruit over to her sweepress.

"Be sure to wash them," she said loudly to her, hoping to rile Nani Biwi.

Anyway, Aunt Qudsia would say something and the atmosphere would become taut. She insisted on forcing Uncle Shabir to look into her eyes. However, he avoided her, pinning his gaze instead on the bricks on the floor with an intensity that made one think that, if he looked away, the bricks would jump up and run from there.

When it was evening Uncle Shabir left, but lights continued to glimmer in Aunt Qudsia's eyes, and the smile that played on her lips was reminiscent of the cocky one that hovered on Bua's lips when she saw Bale Mian. That was if she and Bale Mian hadn't quarrelled. But now Bua's eyes had an empty look, like dried-out, smoking oil wicks. A staleness hung about her. Some time had passed since her treatment, but Hakim Sahib's tablets seemed to have become permanently glued to her stomach lining; she would get the runs frequently and was always burping.

There was a time when Bua had the appetite of a bird, but now she heaped her plate high with maize bhat and arhar dal and constantly complained of heartburn. She also spent the better part of the day asleep; leaning against a wall, her mouth open, she could be found sleeping quietly most of the time. In her state of madness she didn't seem to need sleep, now she dozed all day. She had also become quite shrewd. Every day she visited her tenants and bickered with them.

"The bastards aren't paying rent on time, they're out to rob me."

As soon as Bua regained her sanity, she saw that the world was full of thieves and brigands. Her vision cleared and brightened, as if someone had applied a magical kohl to her eyes. The roof was leaking, but who can you get to repair it? All the workers are thieves, they'll clean you out.

After the bracelets came a matching gold necklet with the same lion's-head, and this too was immediately placed in Amma's steel safe. Still she wasn't satisfied; every once in a while she'd ask about her jewellery.

"You're sure the lock's working?"

If a robbery took place in the neighbourhood, Bua felt the world was coming to an end. Right away she would have Amma open the safe and check its contents. No longer was she our dear, sweet Bua; she seemed to us now like all other stupid women.

All old associations slowly slipped from our minds. We were irritated by the sight of Bua grinding spices. Clamouring to sleep with her now seemed like a foolish thing to do. Instead of the fragrant odour of freshly-dug earth, her body now gave off an offensive smell of garlic, onions and stale food.

Meanwhile, Aunt Qudsia blossomed some more.

Nani Biwi tried every trick in the book, but Aunt Qudsia did not take the laxative and openly solicited Uncle Shabir's help in reading Mir's poetry. Evening came. No sooner had Aunt Qudsia turned her face to the left with the salaam at the end of the *asr* prayers than Uncle Shabir appeared magically at the front door like the storybook giant. He would explain and she would understand; their eyes remained lowered, their faces wearing masks of strangeness. Their eyes met just once or twice and, for no apparent reason, our hearts raced like colourful kites entwining cords in the sky.

If we, the children, could guess what was going on, surely Nani Biwi, who was exceedingly clever, was not fooled. Dadi Amma, meanwhile, didn't spare her meaningfully judgemental smiles.

'I say, woman, if something untoward happens, the head of the household will have to face dishonour,"

Dadi Amma proceeded to explain the intricacies of philosophy to smelly old Pathani Bua while the woman pressed her feet. She raised the subject as if they were discussing everyday politics. God help her, she wasn't pointing to anything specific, but it wouldn't be her fault if suspicion was raised by what she was saying.

Nani Biwi heard all this and fumed.

"Please, break off some tamarind pods, won't you? We'll make some chutney." Aunt Qudsia was playing with the buttons on her shirt front.

Uncle Shabir had just arrived.

"What shall I break them off with? Is there a stick or a pole around here?"

"My word! You're no less than a pole yourself, why don't you just reach up and break some?"

For a split second a rod of brightness flashed in Uncle Shabir's eyes. He appeared alive, and if no one had been around he would certainly have done what Manjhuji's fiancé did when he found himself alone with her...

After Uncle Shabir left, Nani Biwi reprimanded Aunt Qudsia for her flighty behaviour.

"Why, have I committed adultery?" snarled Aunt Qudsia.

"Tsk, tsk, you wretch! What will people say? Agreed that Shabir is a decent man, he's not an outsider, he's your brother-in-law, but the world is an unjust place. It doesn't take long for a mole-hill to become a mountain."

"What do I care about the world? For ten years that man–may he die–has been making me weep and no one says one word of reproach to him."

It's true, girls should not read such peculiar books. There's all kinds of rubbish in them.

"Child, he's a man, no one can harm him. A woman's person is like a mirror, once there's a crack in it you'll forever see a crooked image of yourself."

"Hunh!" Unable to pursue the argument further, Aunt Qudsia turned her attention to the box of bangles. *"My Girdhar Gopal/ There is no other..."* she began humming as she selected bangles to match the colour of her shirt.

"The vine has spread, what can anyone do now...My Girdhar..."

"My word, child! How many times have I told you not to sing these dreadful, profane songs? And you neglected the afternoon prayers, too. I tried to wake you up, but you were too lazy. Of course, when you stay up so late at night you're sure to sleep late in the morning, like a bat."

Aunt Qudsia rose to her feet so abruptly her dupatta fell to the floor and the tiny bells on her buttons jingled. Picking up the lota she went to wash for prayers. Nani Biwi was not the only one who was upset; all good women were disturbed by the sight of girls striding about brazenly. Decent girls walked respectfully, taking small steps. Aunt Qudsia's newfound agility had shaken Nani Biwi to the core.

"I say girl, what kind of a gait is this, like a singing girl's, the front and back all sticking out?"

*

Trying to talk to Aunt Qudsia was like hitting oneself with a shoe. Nani Biwi conspired with Amma.

"This wretch Shabir just won't leave us alone. I've told him off so many times, but I think he's not budging because of encouragement from Qudsia. I'm very worried."

"I say, Amma, you're just imagining things. Now you're suspicious of poor Shabir. Because of him the unhappy girl gets to laugh and relax a little. She must have a reason to continue living, don't you think?"

If Amma was in a good mood Nani Biwi became more agitated.

"To hell with such living! What is she planning anyway? And seeing your sister's false tears, you're melting too?"

"I ask you, why would such a thing be so terrible?" Amma said after a pause.

"What do you mean?"

"Machu was saying, he had consulted with a lawyer friend of his, he was saying..."

Uncle Machu's real name was Mustaqeem and his nickname was Machu. Mustaqeem means straight; but Uncle Machu didn't have a straight bone in his body. He was crooked beyond measure.

"May the contemptible wretch's mouth burn! What is he but a good-for-nothing raised on the crumbs of prostitutes!" Nani Biwi went so far as to dig up his grave. He, in the meantime, alive and well, was receiving a hair massage from Aunt Qudsia.

"All right, please..." Amma fumbled for words.

"How dare you! Do you want your sister to have a second husband?"

"Get out of here!" Finding me listening intently to this conversation, Amma smacked me.

Unaware of what going on, Aunt Qudsia, at that moment, was blushing in response to something Uncle Machu had asked. Just when her glowing, white cheeks seemed to disappear into the folds of her pink dupatta, the curtain moved and Uncle Shabir erupted into the room.

The air around us seemed to hold its breath. Gathering the front folds of her wide-legged pajama, Amma tucked them in at the waist and, ready to serve her lord and master, left the room. The bell on Abba's cycle could be heard from a distance. On his return from the club he usually went straight upstairs to his room, calmly keeping to himself on the second storey, very much like the leader of a caravan. Her keys jangling, Amma strode off to wait upon her husband and Nani Biwi took charge of the fort.

Uncle Machu generally slipped away as soon as he heard the sound of the bell. He was terrified of his serious, sober older brother and made every effort to stay out of his way in order to avoid being questioned on one matter or another. Considering the sort of thing he was involved in, it was certainly prudent for everyone to refrain from questioning him.

Placing the bundle of books on the bed, Uncle Shabir mumbled something, Aunt Qudsia inaudibly mumbled a reply, and off he went to pay his respects to Dadi Amma.

Nani Biwi was on guard for him like a cat waiting to pounce on a mouse. As soon as he emerged from the veranda, she grabbed him.

Aunt Qudsia, feeling a little bashful, walked off to the kitchen to prepare a tray for Abba. Food was being dished out and, presuming that Nani Biwi was sharing some pleasant secrets with Uncle Shabir, she started humming.

The drum had been refurbished. Aunt Qudsia sat down on the divan, picked it up and proceeded to tighten its rings. Leaning wearily against a wall, periodically spitting on the floor to one side, was Bua; perhaps she wanted to spit out the taste of amaltas from her mouth. These days she would start spitting wherever she was sitting.

"Bua dear, please play the beat you heard at the theatre, show me how the man struck the drum with his palm."

Bua cast a glance at the drum as if asking, "What is this thing?" and then, turning, spat on the floor.

"Oh, Bua! For Bale Mian's sake," Aunt Qudsia implored, pushing the drum towards her. She reached for Bua's hand, pulled her, then hastily let go. "Bua! You have fever!"

When she touched Bua's forehead she discovered it was burning.

Nani Biwi had been complaining for many days that Bua had stunk up her veranda. "I can't breathe," she said, "tell her to go back to her own house, the tenants have gone, we'll send her two meals a day."

She egged on Amma who had lost interest in Bua by this time. Whatever they had all done for her had been done for her own good. Abba had been warning us about tightening our belts. This constant waiting upon guests was taking its toll; we had guests every day, elaborate dishes were prepared, clothes were made for them depending on whether it was summer or winter, and in the end the guests, barely escaping indigestion, grabbed their gifts and left, vacating their beds for a new set of visitors.

Bua's future had been satisfactorily taken care of. It was no one's fault that she wasn't well. Why, didn't she eat everything and anything that came her way? Her sweepress had been gone a long time. The woman did visit once, pressed Bua's feet, crying all the while at her condition, but she was scolded and driven away again. She made her home under a peepal tree and eked out a living by begging.

But now they had no choice.

Manjhu was coming to attend Urs along with her-in-laws. Her mother-in-law wanted to pray and make an offering at the shrine for a grandchild. So Bua returned to her house. However, her precious sweepress became a constant presence on the veranda again. Three times a day, tea and food were set in a tray and sent out. If Bua was feeling well, she'd come herself and stay for several days in a row. Since Nani Biwi had had her veranda whitewashed, she had become extremely cautious; Bua hesitated to be about in such a clean and tidy place. There was a time when Bua's clothes were whiter and cleaner than those donned by the lady of the house and when she visited she sat with the other women. Now when she appeared, a small wooden stool or a bamboo chair was quickly pushed towards her. She either sat on the stool or if one wasn't around, she'd seat herself in the doorway, just like the sweepress, washerwoman, or any other low-caste person.

Sometimes, when she didn't have the energy to make it back to her house, Bua slept in the cowshed, a part of her cot inside the shed, the rest sticking out. The foul smell from Bua's body was lost in the stench of cow-dung and chicken droppings.

*

Uncle Shabir disappeared after his talk with Nani Biwi. Aunt Qudsia paced about restlessly and it seemed that she had vowed not to sleep; all night long she tossed and turned. Nani Biwi was beside herself with anxiety.

About this time Sanjhli's fate once again showed signs of changing. Her prospective in-laws had come and were being appropriately entertained.

"I say, is she the one whose husband brought in a mem?" the prospective sister-in-law inquired in a sorrowful tone.

Instead of trembling with pride, for the first time in her life Aunt Qudsia laughed crudely at this remark. "Yes, sister, my rival is a mem, but I hear yours is an oil-manufacturer's daughter."

This was true, but it was something that had been covered up like cat's shit. The sister-in-law burst into tears.

When the guests left it was discovered that the young man in question had a squint in one eye. But everyone was sure it was Aunt Qudsia who had created a hurdle for Sanjhli this time. When Hakim Sahib was consulted on the matter of Aunt Qudsia's condition, he presented the same diagnosis as before: an excess of melancholic matter in the body. As for treatment, it was that same wretched amaltas prescription, the only cure for heat in the blood!

Nani Biwi ignored Aunt Qudsia's protests and, setting up a brick stove in her veranda, she prepared the elixir with her own hands.

"Child, say 'Allah is all, Allah will help' and toss it down." Nani Biwi handed her the copper bowl and patted her back.

Aunt Qudsia calmly flung the bowl exactly where Bua had thrown it that day, in the gutter.

"A curse upon you! What are you doing!" Nani Biwi screamed, but Auntie walked away, calmly took the drum off the hook and began humming a song she had learned recently from the sweepress.

Furious, Nani Biwi tried to snatch the drum from Auntie, who pushed her away with such force she nearly lost her balance and fell.

"If I'm a burden for you why don't you bury me alive, why do you want me to die like a dog? I will not drink this poison, I will never drink it!"

That was the day Aunt Qudsia discovered how Nani Biwi had instructed Uncle Shabir, in very polite tones, to stop coming to the house.

"You consider her your sister, dear boy, but people are very narrow-minded..." she explained to him and Uncle Shabir understood.

"Are you out of your mind, wretch!"

"Why shouldn't I be out of my mind? I'm human, I'm not a stone. You hurled me into hell when I was fifteen, the colour of my wedding henna hadn't yet faded when he crossed the seven seas to a faraway place, and there he was stung by a white snake. But tell me, is this all my fault? Did I dally with anyone, did I give a thought to another man?"

"You were destined for a tragic fate! Who can interfere with God's will?"

"What sin have I committed that I should be punished while that scoundrel continues to lead a happy life?"

"You miserable creature, aren't you ashamed to call your husband a scoundrel...he's your earthly God."

"A curse upon his face, the worst villain that ever lived!" Aunt Qudsia advanced threateningly.

"You wretched girl! Have you no pride in your wedded state? He hasn't done anything wrong, the Shariah allows a man to have four wives. You are not the only one in this world, there are thousands who suffer like you, but they endure hardship gracefully. A man is unfaithful by nature."

Finding that she was losing ground, Aunt Qudsia began to curse herself.

"O Allah! Please take me from this world! Mighty ruler, make my body dirt so I can at least be rid of this hell, or else take his life so I can be rid of the vile creature."

"You witch! Who is this you're cursing?" Nani Biwi shuddered. A husband is, after all, a husband.

"Baqar Hussain, your beloved son-in-law, the bastard, the son-of-a-bitch!" Aunt Qudsia was sliping away. "May he burn in hell! May worms gnaw at him in the grave!" Spreading out her dupatta, she swayed as she cursed.

"So, will you go after a second husband?"

"Yes, I will...I will..." No, this wasn't Aunt Qudsia, this was an ogress.

"Then go and sell yourself in the bazaar!"

"I will do that, I dare anyone to stop me."

Aunt Qudsia had no intention of selling herself, but anger led them from one thing to another. Nani Biwi remembered Nana Mian and cried bitterly. Ever since Uncle Shabir had stopped coming to the house, mother and daughter engaged in altercations of this nature nearly every day. Finally Aunt Qudsia's in-laws received news of what was going on. Her father-in-law expressed alarm.

"Amma has spoiled her thoroughly. If this continues any longer the girl will no doubt bring dishonour to the family. It's better that we send for her, she'll come to her senses when she's here."

Nani Biwi agreed to send her. She could no longer bend her to her will. "Yes, this is how it should be," she decided, "it's between them and their daughter-in-law. How much longer can I wrack my brains, anyway?"

But as soon as she heard that her in-laws had sent for her, Aunt Qudsia became enraged.

"Why doesn't he rebuke his son, the hypocrite! May his beard go up in flames, may his face burn!"

"You wretch, he's your uncle!" Nani Biwi screamed.

"To hell with such an uncle! Couldn't say one word of reproach to his own son. I say, they're very happy, there's a mem in the house, they butter her up, sit down at a table to eat dinner with forks and knives. After all, they're living on the crumbs their son throws them, they have to wag their tails in the mem's presence. She's going to make God bless them in the next life no doubt, they're sure to follow even her shadow into heaven."

"You won't stop this nonsense, wretch? Oh God, save this miserable creature from dishonour. May your tongue burn!" Nani Biwi picked up a shoe and crushed Aunt Qudsia's lips with it.

That was when Aunt Qudsia became like a woman possessed by a ghoul from the cremation grounds. She gnashed her teeth and, grasping both of Nani Biwi's twiggy wrists, she twisted them.

For a split second Nani Biwi peered into her raging eyes. Her heart convulsed. She could not see her dearer-then-life

Qudsia Bano there; instead she saw a wounded lioness, a female cobra whose hood had been crushed, and she felt her own life was being squeezed by that steely grasp. The old woman doubled over in fear. Everyone ran towards them with cries of "Hai! hai!" Nani Biwi was trembling from head to foot like a doe surrounded by hunting dogs.

"Oh God, Qudsia, what have you done? You raised your hand to Amma!"

Feeling completely helpless, Aunt Qudsia struck her hands against the stone slab laying on the terrace, smashing her bangles to pieces.

"I say, people, what is going on?" Dadi Amma, who was deaf, asked impatiently in a stifled voice. "Girls, will someone turn up the wick on the lamp. What is happening?" She was surrounded by lanterns, but who could dispel the darkness in her eyes?

The whole house was in an uproar; all the servants crowded near the front door, the women lifted their pajama folds and ran, the children began to whimper, the hens cackled.

"If anyone comes near me, I swear upon the Quran, I'll split her head open!" Aunt Qudsia lifted the stone slab above her head. All the women valued their lives; they continued to rant and rave, but no one dared take one step in her direction. Aunt Qudsia started crushing the broken pieces of glass. Before she could bring her hand to her mouth, Uncle Shabir calmly placed his hand on her shoulder.

For ten years no man had touched her. Her hands fell limply to her sides. She turned and looked into Shabir Hassan's eyes. This was the moment when she would have even returned from heaven. Closing her eyes, she swooned and fell upon his chest.

Shabir Hassan's worthless hands hesitated for a split second. Then, in front of everyone, he clasped her to his breast with a force that made his ribs crack. The whole family was silenced as if a snake had been spotted. We forgot our play and gaped with our mouths hanging open. The air around us was stilled. Nani Biwi collapsed like a weak roof.

"What is going on, why this sudden silence?" Dadi Amma felt under her pillow for the *sajdah-gah*. "Is everyone getting ready for prayer, is that why no one says a word?"

Shabir Hasan gathered Qudsia Bano's slender body in both arms. It seemed as though he would never let her go, that he would carry her off somewhere. We were all holding our breath. Steeling himself, he gently put her down on the bed and, calmly stationing himself some distance from her, proceeded to stare at the floor as if to say, 'Well, here lies Qudsia Bano, she's unconscious, this is a good opportunity, come quietly and quickly strangle her, but don't kill her slowly, agonisingly.'

*

Hakim Sahib checked her pulse and immediately came to the conclusion that the heat had travelled to her head, causing her brain to become numb. No one has any say in what Allah has fated, he added.

"The hakim speaks nonsense," smelly Pathani Bua remarked as she dusted her lehnga, "it looks like something else to me."

"Yes, I suspect that the sprit that had bewitched that wretch, Bua, has abandoned her and taken over the poor girl instead. Don't you see, sister, as Bua's condition improved poor Qudsia Bano's ways deteriorated." Aunt Baqar did her best to convince Nani Biwi. "What a terrible thing it was to see–the girl would wear white clothes, attar and aromatic oils and wander in the garden at all times of the day."

Aunt Qudsia's status began to improve. She was no longer alone. A sprit, demon, jinn, or some saint was with her. My poor Amma was taken in right away. Amma was a simple soul, anything she didn't understand she feared as a matter of caution.

Saint, demon, sprit or jinn, whatever it might be, she was reluctant to lock horns with any one of them. This was why she regularly sent a donation to the temple for Vishnu and, every now and then, made arrangements to provide fodder for a five-legged cow and milk for snakes.

"Daughter, this is blasphemous," Nani Biwi used to warn her, "offerings and niaz is one thing, but don't ruin your chances of going to heaven by getting involved with these good-for-nothing rituals."

But Amma was more concerned about her husband's life and the well-being of her children than she was about life after death. Now, who was to say that you could do anything if the gods and goddesses got upset? Right next to the cemetery were the cremation grounds and the children wandered around all day like bulls let loose. One day they went into a temple and showed disrespect to Bhagvan. Mahantji came to the door with complaints, and to make amends Amma immediately made arrangements to feed a few Brahmins so that the god would not turn things upside down in anger. Whenever prasad arrived from the temple, all the women in the house said "Thu, thu, throw it to the hens, it's impure." But Amma would set it down on one of the shelves and in a twinkling the children gobbled it up. Only then was she satisfied. Anyway, children can digest even stones and, who knows, maybe there was something propitious in the prasad.

And now she set out to serve Aunt Qudsia. Agreeing to everything anyone said, she organised incantations and invocations to get rid of jinns, spirits and demons. She also offered niaz in the name of holy saints and began treating Aunt Qudsia with undue regard. She was afraid of this new Qudsia. On the question of madness she was neutral; who knows, maybe the insane also held special powers. Someone with children and a family had to exercise extreme caution in order to avert the threat of danger from any source. And jinns were known to be temperamental; after all, God almighty made man from clay and the jinns from fire; if the fire was ignited who can say what the consequences might be.

It was quite obvious that the spirit or demon that possessed Aunt Qudsia was not the type that would instruct her to throw the shit around. No, she seemed to be under the influence of some very cultured, fashionable, extremely fanciful saint. Uncle Machu writhed when he saw the way Aunt Qudsia was pampered; true, God had not shaped him from fiery flames, but he must surely have used embers.

"I say, Qudsia Bano, what a clever one you are! You're fooling everybody, aren't you?" Uncle Machu smiled, but it was common knowledge that he was a worthless person and an apostate. Everybody cursed and rebuked him.

"The saint will convulse and collapse as soon as you administer three of Hakim Sahib's racking purgatives." He made poisonous remarks, causing Nani Biwi to beat her forehead in distress.

"May your tongue burn! That unfortunate girl has lost her senses and all you can think of is this gibberish." She felt very maternal towards her daughter these days. At the slightest provocation a lump would form in her throat and she would start reminiscing about Nana Mian. "If he were alive would the poor girl have had to listen to such nonsense from people?" she complained one day while preparing a fruit drink for Aunt Qudsia.

"Ah, I understand her wiles. Shabir Mian is the reason for…"

Aunt Qudsia, in the middle of combing her hair, turned to spar with him. She looked into his eyes and sneered.

"Why, did Mushtri Jan beat you with a shoe and throw you out of her house?" she mocked. Everyone was aware that Uncle Machu lived off the earnings of the nautch girls.

"Let's not talk about me, let's talk about you instead..."

"Qudsia, my child," Nani Biwi handed her the glass of sharbat and, turning her face away from Uncle Machu, said, "Don't bother with this wretch, he's a worm from the gutter and he thinks everyone else is like him." After the accident Nani Biwi had become extremely pro-Qudsia.

"The young lady is under the spell of a very powerful saint, he should, under no circumstances, be antagonised," Nani Biwi's Maulana from Lucknow stated emphatically. And Hakim Sahib ventured that in his humble opinion the purgatives should be postponed for the time being; it was important, he maintained, that emotions not be inflamed, otherwise more heat would travel to the brain. But how could you explain all this to Uncle Machu? Ever since she had become unstable, Aunt Qudsia had been enjoying a life of ease and comfort. It was as if she were living on a soft, cottony cloud. Like a princess she reclined all day on a bed that was draped with clean, sparkling sheets, and enjoyed the poetry of Zauq and Sauda; Uncle Shabir sat nearby and recited verses in sweet, melllifluous tones. Once in a while, just to make him uncomfortable, she asked him to explain a suggestive verse. He came regularly now as he had done in the past, and if he was even a few minutes late Aunt Qudsia became restless.

Uncle Machu frequently stooped to low tricks, but that day he went too far. Aunt Qudsia was holding the glass of sharbat to her mouth but hadn't taken a sip as yet.

"What a silly one he is, your Shabir Hasan. Now if it had been me..." He spoke softly in order to avoid being overheard by Nani Biwi.

"If it had been you...?" Aunt Qudsia ground her teeth.

"I'd run off with you," Uncle Machu said, stretching his long arms.

"You miserable wretch! Do you think I'm like Mushtri Jan?" Aunt Qudsia was like an unsheathed sword.

"There's a Mushtri Jan hidden in every woman, and when

the opportunity arises…"

Aunt Qudsia flung the glass of sharbat at his face and then, taking off her slipper, she attacked him.

If one can obtain the kingdom of heaven and earth by losing one's mind, who would be stupid enough to want to regain sanity? In the past if Aunt Qudsia happened to raise her voice she was immediately taken to task. Today she was hitting a six-foot tall man built like a giant, cursing him a hundred times in one breath, and everyone was silently applauding.

"Wait, wait, good woman, I was only joking," Uncle Machu said, trying to ward off her blows with his hands. This was the Uncle Machu who had once, for the sake of Mushtri Jan, lifted Sadeeq, the wrestler, and thrown him over a wall as if he were a bunch of flowers, not a man as big as an elephant. This same Uncle Machu was being beaten by Aunt Qudsia. We too were convinced that day that it wasn't delicate little Aunt Qudsia who was pounding Uncle Machu with the force of a wrestler, but indeed the jinn who was in love with her. And who could take on someone who is the beloved of a jinn?

In the twinkling of an eye the different domains of the house became disconnected like unrelated districts. The time for Urs was approaching. In addition to other festivals and celebrations, this too, was an excuse for visitors to appear. Relatives and distant acquaintances began showing up months in advance. But it didn't make much difference since no one was given separate bedrooms or bathrooms. Additional cots, beds and wooden divans were set out and that was all. The tablecloth was lengthened and two people were served in one plate. None of this was a nuisance, except that the atmosphere that prevailed was like that of a noisy, crowded bazaar. Which was a lot of fun. Our maternal camp and that from our father's side of the family were split into smaller groups. It was a strange spectacle. The women who congregated in Dadi Amma's camp were mostly elderly ladies who became agitated if you made the slightest movement in their presence. In Amma's camp were women of her own age, giddy and worldly. Those with husbands and nursing infants were cloistered in a far corner on two beds each, while young girls slept on the opposite side of the veranda, two to a bed. When they were not sleeping, these girls traipsed around like a herd, whispering in each other's ears. Children, hens, pigeons and dogs gathered in the centre of the courtyard and noisily jumped up and down on empty rope cots. If an accident occurred in one part of the house, it would be quite a while before everyone got wind of it.

This was why there were very few eye-witnesses to the beating Uncle Machu received at Aunt Qudsia's hands that day. By the time the females donned their shoes and, grabbing the folds of their pajamas, arrived on the scene, there was no trace of the accident that had taken place with the speed of lightning.

When everyone finally gathered, all they could see was Aunt Qudsia snarling, her face covered with her dupatta, and Uncle Machu ducking out of the door, laughing, as if he had just received sugary sweetmeats, not a sound beating.

"Is anyone listening? What is going on, girls, no one tells me anything." Dadi Amma groaned. All the tired, elderly women in her veranda turned over once on their sides and then continued dozing.

"What is it, what happened?" everyone was asking.

No one knew if smelly Pathani Bua had had an altercation with the cleaning boy upstairs, or if a snake had been spotted somewhere in the house.

"Who was beating whom?" they turned and asked each other again. Mothers were counting their children while Amma, oblivious of all this confusion, her pajama tucked in, had heard the bell on Abba's carriage and was off to meet her beloved.

"What could have happened? Lot of fuss about nothing, that's all!" Although she was one of the few eye-witnesses, Nani Biwi disclosed nothing. "Whoever tussles with these people will suffer," she added mysteriously. She was obviously not referring to Aunt Qudsia. That slip of a girl, so frail and delicate, where could she get the strength! All this was the doing of the saint.

*

It was a very melancholy evening. A thin layer of dust and fog stretched across the sky and swallows scissored the air. The qawwali groups were arriving, all day long workmen repaired large, sprawling marquees, and the shrine, spotlessly white after being whitewashed, looked like an untarnished tent that had been thrown open and spread out unevenly.

During this time we forgot about home and spent the better part of our days at the shrine. The sermon made us cry, but we found the qawwalis extremely enjoyable. We didn't understand a single word of the verses sung, but the mention of Mecca impressed us greatly. Somewhere along the line one of the spectators worked himself into a state of frenzied ecstasy which resulted in widespread commotion. At this time the qawwali singers got stuck at one verse, repeating it over and over again until the person dancing in ecstasy lost his momentum. Then the singers began with a new verse.

"What's the matter, people? Why don't you tell me anything?" As soon as we walked into the house we found Dadi Amma muttering in a confused tone.

Bua's sweepress was touching everyone's feet, begging, "Please come with me, Ram only knows what's happened to her."

"Now calm down, woman, who are you talking about?"

"What happened?" people were asking each other. Finally it was revealed that Bua had been running a fever for several days. The previous night she had left the house and in the morning was discovered lying face down in the cemetery. Since then her windpipe had been rattling.

"Tsk, tsk, the poor thing," the women said sorrowfully and returned to their chores.

"When I ask, no one tells me anything, am I a dog, barking away with no one to hear me?" Dadi Amma retrieved her sajdah gah from under her pillow and murmured her niyat. Nani Biwi was appalled by the manner in which she recited her intent and also objected to the way Dadi Amma bowed during prayers, claiming she looked like a frog ducking into water.

Aunt Qudsia, the only person who seemed to be in distress, ran anxiously from one corner of the house to another. "Will someone send for the doctor?"

The doctor responsible for cases at the shrine treated patients free of charge. No one was surprised at Aunt Qudsia's perturbation, and no one had the temerity to ignore her command. All night long Bua's windpipe continued to rattle. The doctor diagnosed her condition as double-pneumonia. The next morning we also went to see her, not out of concern for her health but out of curiosity. Stretched out on a worn-out rope cot Bua was struggling for life. The air was so putrid you couldn't breathe. It was only on the third day that the rattling of the windpipe ceased.

May God forgive us! Her body stiff in the white shroud, Bua looked so terrifying! How woebegone and miserable her face was–those half-opened eyes, the purple colouring, that pinkish fluid oozing from her nose and mouth. For years to come she appeared in my dreams to frighten me. I'd be scared to go in the dark, fearful that Bua might suddenly appear and devour me; as soon as it was twilight my spirits flagged and I'd be afraid to go out and pick buds. It seemed as if she was behind the mosque, standing under the banyan tree, dusting off sand from her slipper and I almost expected to see her appear suddenly, singing, "*Beat the drums/We'll meet in Meerut...*"

She was always cross with Bale Mian, but when he turned away from her the whole world rejected her. Bua suffered in this terrible manner and not once did he bother to turn around and ask how she was doing. Ah, poor, unfortunate Bua! The world polices dreams as well, the very reason for living becomes a sore point with people.

The terror of Bua's death hung over the entire household. Everyone's hands were stained with Bua's innocent blood. In order to rid the house of evil spirits, two maulvis were immediately stationed in the outer courtyard. All day they rocked while reading from the Quran, and then proceeded to stuff themselves with trayfuls of food.

Bua's death completely unsettled Aunt Qudsia. For two days she ate nothing. All night she paced about restlessly, stared at the floor in the veranda, in the dark, with her head lowered as though in search of a crack that she could disappear into. She gazed about her, wide-eyed like a starving bird, as if afraid that some bloodthirsty animal might spring at her and grab her throat. All around her she saw death. Nani Biwi prepared glasses of sharbat and left them with her and she emptied them into the spittoon when no one was looking. Holding the paan in her hand, she pretended to chew but later threw it into the toilet. She took a morsel or two only from Amma's plate. She no longer trusted anyone.

That evening Uncle Shabir came. For a while he sneaked glances around him like a thief, then, avoiding Aunt Qudsia's gaze, he handed her a copy of *Diwan-e-Ghalib*. After this he greeted Dadi Amma and then left without casting another look at Aunt Qudsia. Tightly clasping the book in both hands, Aunt Qudsia sat still, as though a cobra might leap out of it and devour her if she opened it. Nani Biwi was straightening her bedsheets. She lovingly arranged some flowers on her pillow and turned back the quilt.

"Here, daughter, why don't you rest for a while. I'll bring your food here, there's a lot of rubbish over there." She pointed to the crowd eating at the tablecloths laid out on the veranda floor.

"I'm not hungry, Amma Bi." Aunt Qudsia placed the book under her pillow.

"Why child? You didn't eat anything at lunch either, and..." She had no idea that her daughter was distrustful of her. After all, she was a mother. She had always doted on her favourite daughter, whatever she did was for her own good.

All at once Aunt Qudsia's heart jumped into her mouth. Uncle Machu was picking up the book. She felt as if she was in the grip of a fever. A tiny fragment of paper fluttered and fell at her feet. Before she could retrieve it, Uncle covered it with his shoe, bent down and picked it up, turned it over a few times, then handed it to Nani Biwi. Aunt Qudsia closed her eyes.

"What is it?" Nani Biwi took the fragment from him, glanced at it cursorily and threw it down. "Don't be silly!" Nani Biwi was illiterate, she couldn't read a thing.

"Wait a minute, this is a charm, don't be disrespectful." Uncle Machu took the paper and placed it on Aunt Qudsia's pillow.

"What kind of charm?" Nani Biwi asked in a serious tone.

"It's for getting rid of evil spirits."

"Hunh! I'm not your playmate that you should tease me." Muttering angrily, Nani Biwi left.

"And those who are playmates don't care either," Uncle Machu mumbled softly as he walked off to pay his respects to Dadi Amma.

"Amma Begum, please give me the Fatehpur land or, I swear by Imam Hussain, I'll become a Sunni."

"Some religion!" Nani Biwi grunted under her breath.

"If you give me the Amethi mango gardens right away, I promise I'll become a Sunni," he wrangled with Nani Biwi next.

"Goodness! Those are in Qudsia's name!"

"That's all right, I'll take Qudsia too as a gift, and I'll shut everybody up, don't you worry."

"Dust in your mouth!" Nani Biwi ran after him with her shoe and he shot off to one of our other aunts.

"If you give me these bracelets I'll cut the noses and plaits of all your rivals and place them at your feet." But no one gave him anything because everyone knew he had wasted his entire inheritance on dancing girls.

Nani Biwi woke up in the middle of the night for *tahajud* prayers and the hands that were raised for ablution remained suspended in mid-air. Aunt Qudsia's bed was empty. The flowers were still on the pillow, untouched, fragrant, not a petal out of place. The front door was ajar like a gaping hole, its latch still swinging. Nani Biwi's screams roused the whole household. She was running around from one corner of the house to the other, yelling Aunt Qudsia's name. Soon everyone picked up lanterns and began the search.

"Will you listen, what's going on, I ask?" Dadi Amma's whimpering query compounded the confusion.

Her arms around her as if she were a little girl, Amma tried to comfort Nani Biwi.

"What's happened?" The question came from all sides. Children began to whine, the hens started cackling.

"Oh, I think someone left the chicken coop open." In her state of drownsiness Dadi Amma came to the conclusion that the cat had made off with one of the hens.

The imprints of Aunt Qudsia's small, bare feet were traced to the edge of the large well, where they disappeared. On the left the path leading to the railway station was full of marks made by animals and people, but there were no signs of Aunt Qudsia's tiny, white feet. The well was searched thoroughly but Aunt Qudsia's body was not found. Had the earth devoured her, the sky swallowed her?

"My daughter was meant for heaven," Nani Biwi wailed, weeping uncontrollably on the third day of mourning.

"Why do you cry? May Allah bless her wherever she is," Uncle Machu said, drying false tears. What a vile man he was, our Uncle Machu!

"Amen." Dadi Amma proceeded to recite verses from the Quran under her breath.

In a few days some rather strange stories began circulating.

When Aunt Qudsia jumped into the well a window suddenly opened in its floor. She saw a vast expanse of open space. Absolute silence reigned around her and there wasn't a soul in sight. All at once a cloud of dust rose in the distance. When the dust settled she saw a golden throne arrayed with richly-embroidered cushions. Four fairies, holding the throne aloft, stood before her respectfully, their heads lowered. Aunt Qudsia was escorted to the throne which then ascended into the sky.

It was Uncle Machu who invented these tales. Some tactless people also suggested that she had run off with Uncle Shabir. Anyway, the mention of Aunt Qudsia's name became taboo in our house from that day on. As long as Nani Biwi was alive no one dared take her name for fear of a rebuke from her. Then everyone forgot everything because forgetting is profitable; your conscience doesn't torment you.

*

About two and a half months ago I received a telephone call.

"My name is Rafiah Hasan. I'm calling from the Victoria Terminus. Tomorrow I'm leaving for London by a morning flight. Do you think you could see me...I won't take too much of your time."

She was going abroad for her Ph.D. I didn't feel like seeing her. She was probably a literary enthusiast and she would reiterate the usual trite views and upset me: well-established writers don't give newcomers a chance, they only praise each other, etc. She would attempt to prove I was biased, that I was an opportunist.

"As a matter of fact…" I tried to hedge.

"I promise I won't stay long, just ten minutes will be sufficient." I could see she was clever.

When she arrived she smiled affectionately at me and for some reason I felt a burden lifting.

"I obtained your address with great difficulty. You probably don't know this, but you're my cousin. My mother, Qudsia Shabir Hasan, is your aunt."

"Aunt Qudsia? You're Aunt Qudsia and Uncle Shabir's daughter?" I stuttered like a fool. '*We'll meet in Meerut/The two of us.*' Bua's melodious voice rattled the doors of memory. So they did meet. Some people die so that others may learn how to live!

"And just then Ammi's courage gave out. She fought with Abba, accused him of trying to lead her astray, but Uncle Mustaqeem…"

"Uncle Machu!" He was not destined for heaven, but God works in mysterious ways.

"Ammi lost her nerve when she saw him. She was on her way to jump into the well and drown herself. But Uncle Machu said, 'You left your shoes behind, you'd better put them on or else you'll catch your death of a cold.'"

"Uncle Machu said that?"

"Yes, and took out Ammi's shoes from his pocket and gave them to her. But Ammi insisted she wanted to die."

"But the imprints of her feet?"

"How could anyone find those? Abba lifted her up in his arms." She burst out laughing. "Whenever I think of this story I can't help laughing. Ammi is so fat now. Well, from there they went to the railway station."

"And from there to Meerut." I was tormented by Bua's memory.

"Meerut? No, to a friend's house in Raduli."

"Raduli? Her in-laws. Well done!"

"Whose in-laws?" She was confused.

"Never mind, continue."

"Abba's friend, Abrar, was a lawyer. They tried very hard to obtain a divorce, but he said, 'I'll die before I divorce her'."

"And how could fate be so cruel–he didn't die."

"It didn't make any difference. He was never really alive anyway."

"You're right, it didn't make any difference."

When all efforts to secure a divorce failed, Uncle Machu's friend came up with the idea that there was a chance of getting a divorce if Aunt Qudsia became a Christian. A priest in Kanpur was consulted. But when he was given the reason for the intended conversion, he was furious. Also, if Aunt Qudsia reverted to Islam later the divorce would be nullified.

Uncle Machu, when he got news of this muddle, arrived on the scene and threw a fit. He threatened to kill everyone and run off with Aunt Qudsia himself. He also threatened to take Uncle Shabir to task. That same evening a maulvi was sent for and the nikah took place.

"'This is not a proper marriage,' Shabir Hasan's friend, Abrar, said. He was a lawyer."

"'Why not?' Uncle Machu was ready to twist Uncle Abrar's neck."

If Aunt Qudsia's husband had got wind of this he could have brought charges of adultery against them.

Aunt Qudsia and Uncle Shabir went into hiding like thieves for the rest of their lives. It's true, ordinary people generally lead anonymous lives but there's always fear, this despite the fact that Uncle Machu had warned Aunt Qudsia's husband that if he gave them the slightest bit of trouble he'd kill him.

"And how will I face God?" Aunt Qudsia used to say.

"You just fall down and faint when you're there, and I'll take care of the rest," Uncle Machu comforted her.

"And when the divorce bill was passed he and his English wife were in England. They had settled there after he obtained British nationality. Also, I wasn't a child anymore. My parents didn't think it was necessary to start a commotion all over again." She became pensive for a few moments. "When I think of Ammi and Abba's love, I feel like laughing at the importance that is attached to marriage and divorce. Perhaps this is because I'm not like everybody else."

"How do you know you're not like everybody else?"

"Because I think what Ammi and Abba did was what they should have done. I consider myself fortunate to be the fruit of their love."

She had come for ten minutes only. But the thought of wishing her goodbye had still not occurred to me and she hadn't mentioned leaving either. A few hours earlier I had had no knowledge of her existence. She was a stranger to me. After dinner we strolled on Marine Drive late into the night, hand-in-hand, like children. A fragrant flower blossomed between us and kept blooming.

"It seems as though we've known each other for years." We were both experiencing the same feeling.

"Sometimes one tiny moment becomes a heavy burden for the rest of life."

"For what crime did Ammi suffer so much?"

A silence hung between us for some moments.

"And why was Bua separated from Bale Mian?"

"Why do people snatch someone else's dreams and crush them?"

"Because there are no dreams in their own barren lives."

"And so they murder others? Why?"

"In order to get rid of their feelings of inferiority they scream and say, 'My country is great, my religion is the most supreme, my city, my house...my world are the best and of the highest order, my consciousness, my beliefs, my way of thinking are right."

"But forcibly?"

"Yes, forcibly. These are the people who regard freedom of action and freedom of thought to be the right of every individual, who advocate democracy, who use swords to stuff democracy down your throat, or call it a divine right, or force it on the pretext of some emotion or principle, some cultural or social standard. And if all fails, they blame spirits and demons."

At the airport the next day we embraced and she clung to me for a long time, as if she wanted to imbue my very being with a special message.

"There's only one thing I hope for."

"What?" The line of passengers was diminishing.

"That we should also have someone to love us with the kind of dedication with which Abba loved Ammi...and..."She lowered her eyes.

"And?" I stopped her at the stairs leading to the boarding gate. If she left without telling me I'd be tormented by the sharp pain of this unfinished sentence for the rest of my life.

"And Like Uncle Machu who..."

"Uncle Machu!" Uncle Mustaqeem, that crooked, devious Mustaqeem, the lecher, libertine, apostate, drunkard, liar, who was a running sore on the family's lustrous, elevated forehead, whom no girl in the family would allow to touch even her soiled hem. He had loved Aunt Qudsia, loved her in such a way that today her daughter held in her heart a longing for such a man.

"But he knew Ammi didn't care about anyone except Abba. Poor Abba, he was such a wishy-washy person. The entire scheme had been devised by Uncle Machu."

She left. Suddenly I was engulfed by an immense loneliness.

"Uncle Machu. Did you hear? Right now there must be little fireflies glittering in your grave."

When will people learn to recognize each other's true worth?

The plane shuddered like an irate giant, thundered, and flew off into the lofty sky.

Go, Rafiah Hasan, you can go without fear wherever you want to go. You have your own tape measure, your own weights, your own scales to plot and gauge life's values. No one will be able to cut you down, your dreams will never be crushed.

The Wild One

(*Ziddi*)

Puran

RAIN fell with unflagging tenacity. The sky seemed to have developed holes, but was it any wonder really that having been stretched taut for this long it should now come apart? It had rained several nights in a row and today, beginning early in the morning, it had continued to come down all day. It was as if oceans of water were being hurled with great force at the earth. Defenceless now, the mud walls of many of the houses had started collapsing from the impact of the water; roofs swung like soggy beards from the weight of the poles and bamboo rafters, forcing the inmates of these dwellings to seek shelter under trees. But the water appeared to mock them. The trees were not canopies of stone, so why should it not find its escape through branches and leaves? The sound of overflowing drains sharpened the mood of anxiety that prevailed, while darkness, fast approaching, threatened to further exacerbate the situation.

Asha was trying to give Amma a last drink of water. Her own mother had died early, while her father, a good-for-nothing fellow, was found dead some years later near the railway station. Since then Asha's maternal grandmother had been both father and mother to her. Btu her grandmother was also about to depart. She had been good to her, but now she was old and sick. It was true that at one time she had been Raja Sahib's nurse, and after he passed away she had continued to straddle his children on her shrunken, bony knees and sing the same old worn-out lullabies that she had once amused him with. But she was a servant after all; she hadn't been left with an endowment of land. As for her jewellery, she sold the pieces off one by one when she fell on hard times. She had always lived in Raja Sahib's palace, and anyway, who needs gold trays in one's old age? Slowly she crumbled away in a corner of the palace until finally, as an act of kindness, Raja Sahib ordered a subsidy for her and sent her back to her village. Whatever else might happen, she was glad that at least she would die in her own place. But it wasn't her village really, it was Raja Sahib's.

"He's not here? He's not here yet?"

Asha thought the old woman was referring to the messenger of death, but in fact she was thinking of Puran. Puran was Raja Sahib's younger son. He had slept in the old woman's bed until he was seven. Every Sunday he came to the village with his older brother and today was Sunday, wasn't it? Why was the old woman waiting for him? If it hadn't been for this, her breath might have abandoned her body a long time ago.

"Where is Ranji's mother?" The old woman came out of her stupor.

"Yes, Amma, shall I get her? It's raining."

"No … but she … shouldn't have left … like this."

Her own breath seemed to be strangling her. "Is it raining hard?" She was worried the rain might hinder the lighting of her funeral pyre.

"Yes." Asha nervously twisted a corner of her dhoti.

"And where is Ranji's mother, the wretch!" Why was she so preoccupied with Ranji's mother?

Ranji's full name was Ranjit; the 'Singh' had been added on to veil the stigma associated with the trader caste. But everyone called him just Ranji. His mother had been known at different times as Kirya's bride, Moti's daughter-in-law and Ram Bharosa's wife, and had changed roles quite often. All the men she had been associated with died one by one. Ranji was the offspring of one of these men, and as such his place in society was akin to that of a thor tree; he expressed no desire to be useful. As a teenager he joined a band of singing eunuchs for a period of time. This caused his mother to spend the better part of her day cursing and swearing at the people in her neighbourhood; persistent in her refusal to believe he had anything to do with the eunuchs, she kept telling everyone he was with a nautanki troupe. Whatever it was, after a few weeks Ranji returned to the village and, soon thereafter, gained notoriety for his singing. Also, he suddenly developed a defiant streak; whereas he had once been associated with eunuchs, he now kept company with the worst kind of ruffians. His mother, despite all this, went around the village with her head held high.

The old woman's anxiety bore fruit; Ranji's mother arrived under cover of a gunny sack.

"Where did you go?" the old woman roared like the angel of death.

"It's all right, I went to see if Ranji had returned. I stopped over at Lachmi's mother's place—I don't know where that wretch has taken off to!"

"Hunh! And what if I had died?" The old woman didn't want to frighten Asha by dying when the girl was alone with her. And she was justified in scolding Ranji's mother. After all, Ranji had professed love for Asha. The old woman's first reaction had been indignation. Then she examined her surroundings closely and realised there weren't any wonderful young men forthcoming. Also, although Ranji behaved like a scoundrel in his own home, he had certainly never had the courage to tease Asha. But then Asha rarely left the house. Like a snake the old woman had sat guard over her all these years. Whatever Ranji's mother did for the old woman was in the nature of a bribe. And whenever Ranji came over, he'd sit in a corner like a donkey with his head lowered. The old woman felt inclined to consider him for Asha, but she hadn't quite made up her mind yet. Anyway, Asha was still too young. It was only two years ago that she started wearing a proper dhoti; until then, dressed in a leh̃nga, she looked like a little girl. But Ranji's mother maintained that the lehnga or dhoti had nothing to do with anything—at Asha's age she had already had two miscarriages and was pregnant for the third time.

"It depends on how one is built," the old woman used to say, impressed by Ranji's mother's pluck. "My Asha is so delicate." And then she would take a look at Ranji's massive physique and shudder fearfully.

Ranji was not a bad man. But who was conducting a beauty contest? True, he was short and his teeth were slightly inverted; the lower line of teeth protruded while the upper row was pushed in, making his jaw stick out somewhat and when he laughed it seemed as though his throat had been turned upside down. His lips were flat, his nose was broad and bent, and the little hair left on his head was constantly bedraggled from lack of washing. But he had soulful eyes.

"Isn't Puran here yet?" the old woman asked, tired of hearing about Ranji.

"What? Do you think he's going to come in this downpour? Let me tell you, these high-class people don't really care about anyone."

If the old woman had had any spirit left in her she would have come down hard on Ranji's mother, forcing her to swallow her words. The blind wretch! Did she not see him come every Sunday? As soon as he came he would ask for pure butter and pickles. Pure butter in war time? Why did the war make butter disappear? They must be using it to fire their canons ... but why don't they use gasohol instead? People have to subsist on gasohol while the canons ... yes, these canons, these blazing canons ... no sooner do you speak than they start spewing flames, these white men! What is this? What do white men have to do with butter?

Anyway, Puran came every Sunday. Today the old nurse waited anxiously for him and the rain wasn't letting up.

"What do you know? Of course he will come ... look, is

that him?"

"No, that's not him." Afraid of having to get up and go to the door, Ranji's mother answered quickly. "Now, have you eaten anything?" she asked, making an attempt to change the subject. "Just look how weak you are." She tried to frighten the old woman by reminding her of death.

A few minutes later they heard Raja Sahib's car. The old woman perked up. She recognized the sound of the car well. When did any other car ever come to the village? In a few minutes Puran was sitting beside the old woman in the soiled, foul-smelling bed.

"Amma, you're not getting the proper treatment here," he said lovingly, "I've come to take you home."

The old woman was willing to go with him, but a hand stronger than Puran's was pulling her with increasing force.

"I'm going to be with Pramatma soon, son ..."

"What kind of talk is this? You're the one who used to say I'll bring home Puran's bride, I'll sing songs to his son, I'll get leave from Pratmatma if I have to ... Let's go then, let's go today. You'll get treatment like this!" he said, snapping his fingers.

"No doctor can cure me now ... listen, son ..."

"No, Amma, you ..."

"Listen, my dear child ... Asha, my daughter, she's a very good girl, I've taken special care of her ... take her to Raja Sahib, don't make her unhappy, find a nice boy for her to marry ... people are all the family she has now."

Puran failed to recognise the signs of death. "No, you have to come along."

"I'll go ... if only Ranji had been a decent ..."

"Ranji is making plans to start his own business with the village lender's help," Ranji's mother spoke up. "It will get going in no time." Although Ranji had made several attempts to run his own shop, the business lasted only as long as the goods in the shop did. When he and his friends consumed whatever was in the shop, Ranji would move on to another enterprise. He set up a dahi-bare stand and finished everything off himself; the paan and cigarette shop was done in by freeloading friends and acquaintances. The initial investment also went down the drain.

"Yes, if Ranji settles down he's not a bad sort at all."

"We'll see, Amma. First you must concentrate on getting well."

But the old woman was not the slightest bit interested in getting well, and even if she was death had no mind to wait any longer. Puran's request became futile when the old woman departed, leaving a sobbing Asha behind.

Ranji's mother let out a fearsome wail which frightened Asha into silence. Who was left to mourn like this? When the tree dried up, the leaves were scattered here and there. Asha got into Puran's car to begin a new life at Raja Sahib's house. All the way there she cowered in a corner, silently wiping her tears. Afraid that her sobbing might increase if he talked to her, Puran left her to herself.

But when Asha arrived at the palace, her wildly thumping heart quietened somewhat. Raja Sahib patted her head lovingly and Mataji made her sit next to her. But Bhabi—Bhabi clasped her to her bosom.

Asha was too young to grieve forever for an old grandmother. In a few days she forgot her pain. The company of the other servants, her own work, and the love she received from Bhabi and the children made her forget everything else as well. Soon she embarked on a simple, peaceful life.

Bhabi

Asha had no brothers or sisters so there was no question of having a bhabi. But whenever she saw the impish, good-natured daughter-in-law of this family, her heart stirred with love. Although petite like a doll, with hands that were small and helpless-looking, Bhabi was mischievous indeed! And how her laughter rang, like silver beads striking against each other. It was difficult to imagine she was mother to these children. Judging from her looks you would think she was only a little older than Nirmal. As a matter of fact, when Nirmal was born she didn't quite know how to wrap a sari. And Sheela! What a cow she was, the stout daughter of a dainty, slender mother. What she ate in one day her mother would not be able to consume in three. And the youngest, he was remarkable! Yes, it wasn't difficult to imagine him as Bhabi's son because he was the one she doted on the most. Such strange children, and then her husband, the image of Buddha! The more she laughed, the quieter he became. A bania's spirit seemed to have invaded his body; he appeared to spend most of his time managing the affairs of the estate. Yes, sometimes he smiled, but that was all. And Bhabi? She soared like a butterfly all day long. Although she and her husband were as different as the sky and earth, they got along well, just as the sky and earth have been getting along since eternity. He wasn't concerned with the fact that his wife was young and stubborn, or that she was temperamental and easily upset by some little thing her mother-in-law might say. She would shut herself up in her room and cry for hours afterwards, or complain to her brother-in-law, and she was such a favourite among her in-laws that her mother-in-law's alleged mistreatment of her was also reported to her father-in-law. As for Puran, she quarrelled with him constantly. He was the first one to win her affection after she was married and came to this house, and he was the one she fought with the most too. She had never learned to be timid.

This Bhabi, spirited and lively, began her day early in the morning with orders that the children bathe and dress. Then she supervised breakfast until she was out of breath.

"Mummy, my toast!" Nirmal screamed. Skinny little boy!

"Where's my milk?" All the milk she drank made Sheela

as round as a kachori.

And at this point the baby would emit a scream from some remote corner of his throat. Bhabi wrestled to keep peace between them.

"Look, Mummy, she took my papad," Nirmal bleated.

"Here, take your papad back, you beggar!" Sheela threw the papad at him.

"Mummy, look," Nirmal wailed.

"Dried insect!"

"Fat cow!"

"You dried up insect, the wind's going to blow you away one day."

"You fat cow, one day you're going to burst with a loud bang."

"Dog! Cow!" The two ended up scratching each other's faces. Before long milk spilled on to Sheela's beautiful embroidered frock and a piece of toast got stuck to Nirmal's elbow. This was when Bhabi yelled at them.

"Nirmal, what silliness is this?" Nirmal would receive a couple of smacks on his thigh and Sheela a wallop or two on her back.

And if by any chance Puran happened to wander in, all hell would break loose. He would make Nirmal choke on his food, tickle Sheela in the stomach and squeeze the baby's chubby cheeks until they were red.

"Get away, who do you think you are," Bhabi would protest, pushing Puran away with her small hands. "My poor baby, his cheeks are so sore from all this pinching."

But Puran proceeded to crush him and the baby continued to giggle.

"Look, Bhabi, he's laughing," Puran would say.

"He has no shame."

"Yes, he's like his mother." Puran would fling the baby in the air, making Bhabi's heart convulse.

"Puran, O Puran, my baby!" She would hold her breath,

but when Puran turned the baby's face around she'd see he was still smiling.

And if Asha were given a chore to do Puran would protest: "Asha is not our servant, Bhabi, why do you make her work?"

"Why, don't we do any work?"

"Oh yes, you really work very hard, smacking the children all day long. What else do you do? But Asha is not a servant..."

"You don't become a servant simply by working. And anyway, Asha has to get married one day, she's from a poor family, do you think she'll have servants in her home?"

"So what if she's from a poor family. Why does she have to be married to someone poor?"

"If she won't marry someone poor, then you had better find her a prince, Puran Singhji," Bhabi spoke in a loud voice so everyone could hear her. Puran lost his nerve.

"That's not what I mean, you're raising your voice for no reason. Why do you have such an enormous throat?" Puran muttered and took his revenge by turning again to Munna's cheeks and Sheela's stomach.

Chote Bhaiya

There was an old saying that if you eat fiery hot peppers while you're pregnant, your baby will have a peppery temperament when he grows up. Perhaps when Bari Bahuji was carrying Puran she had chewed on some hot peppers. He could not be still for a moment. There was no problem when he was away at college, but when he came home during the holidays, he brought a storm in his wake. Having finished college, he was permanently home now, preparing for the civil service exam. Who knows why he had taken this silly notion into his head. The family's land holdings and assets were enough for seven generations of comfortable living. But once boys go to college their attitude towards life in the village changes. Actually, the fault lies with the villages themselves.

What can they offer besides land cultivation and management to hold misshapen, dilapidated cottages, muddied paths, putrid streams, revolting rows of cow-dung cakes, sickly-looking livestock, and soiled children. How can one be happy there?

Anyway, Puran didn't have a quiet bone in his body. All day long he locked horns with Bhabi, teased the children, clowned around with the female help, and sneaked in sarcastic comments about Bare Bhaiya.

"Bhabi, I've heard that a black cat crossed our mother's path when Bhaiya was about to arrive in this world."

"Hunh! Do you think he should be a good-for-nothing like you? And stop tickling my daughter, her stomach's not made of stone."

"All you ever think about are the children. Do you give any thought to their father? It's true that the children can't be ignored, but what about your dear husband? He putters around with the accounts ledger all morning. I'm sure he laughs sometimes, perhaps when he's by himself ..."

"I am going to hit you, Puran, you wretch!" The idea of Bhaiya laughing in private proved to be so funny that Bhabi blushed.

Bare Bhaiya was not the only one who bore the brunt of his teasing. Puran went after the servants as well, especially Chamki, who often received a playful smack from him. Sometimes he splattered her face with shaving cream while he shaved, or tied her braid to the bedpost. All right, she was a young woman so she enjoyed his teasing, but what did he have in common with Bhola's aunt? Frail of mind, she lay in a corner of the veranda all day long like a pile of abandoned debris. In winter she covered herself with an old coat or sweater, but in the sizzling summer heat even her kurta became too much for her. Since she couldn't tolerate the humidity in her room she chose to doze on the veranda instead, fanning herself with a broken fan. Puran often went and sat beside her.

"Do you hear me, Bhola's aunt? Why throw your youth in the dust?"

The old woman glared at him in the hope that he would take her indifference as a hint and leave her alone.

"Do you hear me, you're still so young."

"Go away, boy."

"Now this is what I don't like, listen to me …"

"What do you want?" Bhola's aunt's voice was like that of an old man's.

"What I'm saying is, why don't you wear a kurta?" Puran said, unable to come up with any other criticism.

The old woman stubbornly ignored his remark. The young servant girl blushed at this, and Bhabi also pretended she hadn't heard anything.

"I'll get you something, if you like I can get you three or four blouses."

"Be off, you and your blouses!" There was no change in the old woman's bad humour.

"How many times have I said, Bhola's aunt, you should apply some mehndi and kajal." The young girls giggled and Bhola's aunt muttered coarse invectives under her breath.

"These witches are jealous of you, Bhola's aunt." And slowly Puran inched closer to the old woman.

"What is this? Get away, son."

"You're calling me 'son'?" Puran pretended to be seriously offended.

"Yes, brother, now be a good boy and sit over there, it's too hot."

"Now you're calling me 'brother'?" Puran feigned further indignation.

"Shouldn't call you son, shouldn't call you brother, so should I call you husband?"

And once again the old woman let loose a tirade of invectives.

"I suggest we get married. Now, how old are you?"

"Wretch! Don't court trouble, bastard!" The old woman roared in a heavy voice.

"Bhola's aunt, when you start swearing, I want to kiss you. Wonderful! Excellent!"

Finding that her swearing was ineffective, Bhola's aunt resorted to physical retaliation. All the young servant girls became involved in the scuffle, the old woman continuing to spew a torrent of such foul language that even Puran finally made off from there in embarrassment. When she took her complaints to Bari Bahuji, Bhabi teased:

"Well, why don't you, Bhola's aunt? He's not such a bad boy."

And Bhola's aunt retorted with something that made Bhabi bolt from the room.

Chamki

Chamki came from the same village as Asha. Her name was Chamki because every other girl in the village was called Chamki. If you saw a girl who had a squint, was small and dark, you would think her name might be Kallu or Radhu or something similar. But no, she would turn out to be Chamki. Chamki, however, was indeed Chamki; her cheeks shone, her eyes shone, and as for her hair, it shone like strands of polished steel. As a matter of fact, her waist shone too, as did her hands, and when she danced it seemed as though she was surrounded by dancing stars. Her voice was loud and melodious, not meek and cowering like Asha's which could put you to sleep. Her voice roused people from their dreams, and if she went out, all the orderlies, stewards and gatekeepers began humming; not only that, the dhobi's arms rippled with renewed energy and the sound of his humming grew louder. But she wore an angry look when she was out of the house and ignored everybody, so that if the Munshi, who at least had an F.A., ogled her, she abruptly turned away from him as well. Of course, when her back ached from Puran's pummelling, she seemed to bloom. And what a disorderly person he was! None of the menservants could keep his room in order. He turned the whole cupboard upside down when he took something out, and while looking for one pair of shoes, would toss out five or six others, scattering them all over the room. His books would be strewn about like a scattered deck of cards and his dressing table, always dripping wet and splattered all over with shaving lather. If Chamki cleaned his room he rewarded her by spanking her or tweaking her cheeks.

Like a diligent supervisor, she began making preparations to clean his room early in the morning. If there wasn't anything else to be done, and while Asha was busy helping out with rolling puris, Chamki would spend her time arranging fresh flowers in Puran's room so that it resembled a garden.

First these young women throw themselves before an oncoming train, then you have moaning and groaning followed by complaints that they have been disgraced, dishonoured and robbed. Thus they hold society responsible for their own weaknesses, and how strange that the world chooses to participate in their mourning and proceeds to join in their condemnation of society. So Chamki, too, threw herself before the train. Luckily this engine changed tracks and went its way. Puran's game didn't go beyond pummelling and occasional pinching. But thunder will bring down rain some day. Anyway, the other female servants in the house didn't approve one bit of Chamki's tomfoolery with Puran. Cutting remarks and comments were exchanged all day long:

"Well, haven't you seen a cat playing with a mouse, and the stupid mouse thinks it's just play?" Lata was very philosophical and why not, she was the mother of six children.

"Wait and see, she's always in there with him, she'll not

forget, these princes are no good ..." Bhola's aunt was not Chamki's rival.

Asha paid little heed to what was being said, but there was no doubt that she was afraid of Puran. She remembered that one day he had sauntered in while she was mending Sheela's frock and started a conversation with her.

"Work, work! I say, Asha, why don't you ever do something for me too?"

"What do you want me to do?" Asha bent over the machine.

"There are thousand of things to be done. For example, the dhobi brings back my wash with nearly all the buttons missing and I have to go around with my shirt-front open."

"What buttons?" Chamki interjected sharply. "I stitched on every last one."

"I'm not talking to you! You see, Asha, you've never done a thing for me. Anyway, why should you be working at all? Are you a servant?"

"Everyone has to work—you don't work, you don't eat." Chamki vied for Puran's attention, but he was only interested in Asha.

"You're so frail and thin and you have to do all the work. I'm going to speak to Mataji, I'll tell her she shouldn't make you work so hard, and ..."

"No, please ... I like working."

"And why don't the others do some work, too? This Chamki, for instance, such a cow, why isn't she sewing?"

Chamki was sitting nearby hemming Bhabi's sari. Asha cowered under the weight of Puran's burning gaze.

"That's enough now," Puran said, snatching the frock from her hands.

"No..." Asha wished she could disappear into the machine.

"I forbid you to continue sewing!"

"Sheela is going out, she's in a hurry."

"There's no hurry."

Asha remained silent.

"All right, there, go ahead and sew right over this." Puran placed his finger next to the needle on the machine.

"A curse upon these scissors!" Chamki flung her scissors down and left the room in a huff.

"What is that witch so worked up about? Here Asha, let me see, did she hurt your hand? I'll see to that miserable creature in a minute..."

"Chote Bhaiya, we'll never be done with the housework if you keep meddling like this." Chamki's defeat had amused Lata.

"What a grouse you are, Lata. Am I talking to you or..."

"I wish you had been outside, instead of sitting here wasting your time with these girls." It was Bare Bhaiya, standing in the doorway.

Embarrassed, Puran quickly busied himself with extinguishing his cigarette.

"For two hours Seth Tikka Ram ate my brains up and I couldn't do any work at all. If you had been there I could have gone to the office for a while."

"Bhaiya, I don't have the energy to take Seth Tikka Ram's nonsense," Puran said, making a face.

"Nevertheless, you had better come outside."

"There, that serves him right," smiling, Lata whispered under her breath.

On his way out Puran bumped into Chamki. She looked upset and angry. Puran reached out and pinched her in the ribs. She felt cleansed, she was shining again, but not with anger.

Flowers

"The dining room, the veranda, Bhabi and Bare Bhaiya's bedroom and ..."

"And what about me?"

Startled, Asha turned and saw Puran chewing on a match. She had been counting vases.

"You're not putting any flowers in my room."

"But Chamki is the one who puts flowers there..."

"That Chamki again! So what if she puts flowers there. You are arranging flowers in every other room except mine, I'm going to lodge a complaint."

"I'll take a vase to your room, too..." Asha quickly began sifting through the remaining flowers.

"No, not these dead white flowers that look like they belong on a corpse. I want those red ones."

So Asha took the red flowers to his room and arranged them in a vase. But all the while her heart thumped violently, as if she were stealing. Unless it was absolutely necessary she never stepped into Puran's room. What if Chamki appeared without notice?

During dinner Puran thanked her quietly for the flowers and she ran from there with the food tray in her hands. Later in the afternoon, when she happened by the veranda on the way to her room, she felt as if someone had kicked her; scattered about near the drain were the red flowers. She hastened to her room.

'This is the punishment for your boldness,' she scolded herself, lying on the floor as if some earthshaking event had taken place. Humiliation, anger at herself, and a host of strange feelings invaded her thoughts and left her troubled and depressed. They had wilted, who knows how long they had been lying near the drain and how they must have suffered the cold, she thought. All at once the sound of whistling startled her. Usually, because of all the work she had to do, she did not have time to see who was doing what, but from her place on the floor in her room where no one ever came except herself, she could peek at him through the chink in the door. What was that smiling, mischievous face like? She saw it a hundred times during the day, but she couldn't recall a single feature. Why? The reason was that she had never really looked at him closely.

She saw a pair of large, fair-skinned feet encased in sandals and topped by striped pyjamas abruptly come to a halt near the flowers. Asha held her breath. Two hands were lowered and the flowers were swept up. Asha's eyes closed and she clung to the earth on which she lay as though she wanted to be swallowed by it; after all this was the earth that had given birth to those red flowers.

"Who threw these fresh flowers here? This isn't a public garden," a voice said and the sandals disappeared.

For a long time Asha remained prostrate on the floor with her forehead glued to the earth.

In the evening when she was returning from a walk with Chota Munna in his carriage, Puran came up and started kissing the baby.

"Munna, oh Munna! I feel like swallowing up your cheeks, and you're so naughty, pretending to be so quiet, I know you well now. All this talk of work, work, work. I wish Bhagwan would take work out of this world. Why don't you ever talk to anyone?'

Asha, twisting the knob on the handle of the baby's carriage, stood quietly nearby.

Puran continued, "I know what it is, you think I'm not a very nice person, I'm an orge, I'll devour you."

Puran lifted his face and looked at Asha. She was frightened by the intensity of his gaze. "You think I'm a lion, I will tear you into pieces and swallow you?" He continued looking at Asha. "And who knows, if that's what you really wanted, I could indeed devour you this very minute." Asha's discomfort made his heart melt and he bent over the baby again.

"And, Munna, do you know that I picked up those flowers? Chamki's a wretch, isn't she? Yes, she is. Those beautiful red flowers, red just like Munna's cheeks, I've stashed them safely in my drawer. Well, you must have a lot of work to do, right? You may leave now, yes, please go."

When Asha went past the bush with the red flowers she felt they were smiling quietly, smiling with their eyes shut.

Holi

The weather never ceases to toy with humans. In summer you feel like jumping into a sea of ice, and if someone speaks to you, you can do little more than snap back in response. Scorching heat, a dull ache, and without a fan, the feeling that you're simmering slowly. And if the fan is turned on, your head swims. Oh God! And winter? Lethargy, lassitude, cold, cold, everything so cold. Even the heart turns cold. When spring arrives, everything blooms, all that has been lying dormant, stirs. For no reason at all you feel mischievous and playful, tickled by a strange restlessness. And then comes Holi and it's as if a volcano has erupted. If Holi didn't come around every year, this heart would break out of its cage in frenzied madness. How long can a river be held back by a dam? Only so long as the dam can hold. But why hold back in the first place? On the day of Holi Asha's spirits danced, too. Bhabi had been tormented all morning; she was like a little nugget of coloured powder. Already she had changed her sari thrice. It seemed as if the colour from the powder had penetrated her very skin. What does vermilion do? Does it contain some secret ingredient which affects you like alcohol? The more it is rubbed on the more delirious you become.

Today even Bare Bhaiya was not spared. His turn came after Bhabi's. Asha emptied bucket after bucket over him and also splattered him with vermilion powder. As for herself, so far she had managed to slip out of everyone's hands like a slithery snake. Puran, meanwhile, had succeeded in creating havoc. When Bhabi finally fell down in exhaustion, he turned his attention to Bhola's aunt.

"You bully, why do you lock horns with me?" she roared in her manly voice.

"Dear Bhola's aunt, we are fated to be together. In my past life you must have belonged to me, why else…"

Her shrivelled hair glittered and bloomed with vermilion-coloured flowers, while suggestive, full-bodied invectives rang out as further embellishment.

"Hey, Puran, here's Asha," Bare Bhaiya said, trying to get rid of Asha, "let's see if you can cope with her."

Everyone egged Asha on. She became nervous. Puran advanced towards her in all his glory.

She succeeded in emptying a glass of coloured water over him, but hesitated when it came to the vermilion powder. If her face hadn't been covered with dye you would have seen that her skin was glowing with the brilliance of stars.

Puran was not about to drag his feet. He left her helpless. Her vision was blurred from all the coloured water on her face and the ground under her feet was wet and slippery; suddenly she lost her balance and fell from the veranda.

"You'll kill her, Puran, you wretch!" Bhabi pounced on him like an eagle.

"Look at this swelling on the poor girl's foot," Bhabi said as she lovingly warmed Asha's ankle with cotton. At the same time she continued to reprimand Puran. "You're always losing control, aren't you?"

"Come, Bhabi, that's enough." Puran sat down beside her and began heating cotton for Asha's ankle.

"You should be ashamed of yourself. Do you realise what a hulk you are and how tiny this poor girl is? If you had been playing Holi with Mahesh instead, he'd have shown you a thing or two." Bhabi thought highly of her brother Mahesh.

"But, Bhabi, did you ever hear of men playing Holi with other men? Why would I be playing with Mahesh?"

"Well, you can only pull your weight with this helpless girl then, right?"

"You know, Bhabi, this is what you should do."

Bhabi became attentive.

"Take a knife and run it across my throat, all right?"

"Hai, Ram! But ..."

One of the children started crying just then and Bhabi dashed off to see who it was. Puran continued to heat the cotton pads.

"You made Bhabi scold me," Puran said, applying the cotton pad to Asha's ankle. Asha tried to wrestle the pad away from his hands.

"Let me do this, you want Bhabi to scold me again?"

But Asha covered her foot with both hands. "I'm all right now."

"Well, well, that was certainly quick."

"Yes," Asha answered hastily.

"Look ... listen..." He felt helpless. "I'm going to tell Bhabi..."

"What will you tell her?" Asha said nervously. Her heart grew sick with guilt.

"I'll tell her, I'll tell her that..."

Asha stared at his face in apprehension.

"That's better." He placed the cotton pad on her ankle again. "Here's what happened, you know..." He distracted her with small talk. Holding her breath, Asha listened intently as if he were about to reveal some terrible secret of hers.

"Listen, I'll tell Bhabi, I mean I'll say, that is, if you hadn't let me warm your ankle properly, I would have told her."

"What?" Asha said in an expectant tone.

"I would have said, 'Asha hates me'."

Bhabi returned. Asha rubbed her ankle fearfully. How that wound hurt! Hate? Asha had never learned to hate anyone. And Puran? Hate Puran?

Hide-and-seek

Puran wasn't the child Bhabi said he pretended to be. Of course he had always been treated as a child and was spoilt, and his mischievous pranks added to the childish demeanour he presented; he did go around the house clowning with the servants and the kids, often encouraging them to climb all over the furniture with no thought to their grimy clothes and soiled feet. Sometimes, the racket he created made Bhabi's head swim so that she would run after the children with a stick.

In two days Kamlaji was arriving at her father's house. Bhabi had turned everything upside down in preparation for her sister-in-law's arrival. The house had become a nuisance for Puran. There was cleaning going on everywhere; he felt stifled. His own room had also been taken over by Bhabi. Kamlaji's husband was coming with her as well, a prospect that made Mataji very nervous; he was a well-endowed landowner and then, of course, he was a son-in-law. But in addition to that there was a possibility that their connection with his family might grow; his younger sister, Shanta, was still unwed and Puran had also reached a marriageable age.

At one point Puran came into the drawing-room with the children in tow and a game of hide-and-seek commenced. Poor Asha wandered in to do some dusting and found the place in an uproar.

"Please leave the room, I'm going to do some cleaning here," she said in a matter-of-fact tone.

"So this room is going to be cleaned, too!" Puran exclaimed.

"Yes," Asha replied softly and began moving the chairs.

"What is this? All the rooms are being cleaned. No, no cleaning here, we're playing hide-and-seek. Why don't you join us, Asha?"

"Yes, yes, ..." the children clung to her.

"Oh yes, she'll play. She'll be the dai."

"No, please, I can't, I don't know how…"

But Puran took hold of her and pushed her into a chair. "All right, we'll start now. I'll be the thief." He sat down on the floor at Asha's feet and rested his head against her knees. "Now cover my eyes properly," he said.

"No, please, Bhabi said…"

"She didn't say anything. Now make sure my eyes are covered, quickly." He took a corner of her sari and placed it over his eyes.

"Chacha, no cheating." Nirmal was, after all, a businessman's son.

"It's your Ashaji who's cheating. Here, cover my eyes tightly, like this." He took Asha's hands and placed them over his eyes.

Asha became nervous. But the children hid and the game began.

"This is not fair." Asha tried to pull her hands away from Puran's face.

"Why, yes, I'm going to eat you up, aren't I? Why are you so afraid of me? I won't rest until I drive out this fear, Asha Devi—understand? Have I ever hurt you that you should be so afraid of me? Hunh? You chat with Bhaiya, have long talks with Bhabi, you even engage in such friendly chatter with Bhola's aunt. I'm the only one—tell me, why?" His eyes, in complete disregard of the rules of the game, were open. Asha was overwrought.

"Chote Bhaiya, please … all right, I'll clean the room later, you continue playing."

"I am playing." Puran looked more serious than Bare Bhaiya ever could. "You think I'm always playing games, don't you? All this is a game, my life, everything I say—you think all this is a game, don't you, Asha? You think I'm playing a game with you, too. How can I convince you I'm not?"

"Come and find us!" one of the children yelled.

"It's not a game, Asha, listen…" he chewed his lips

helplessly.

"Come and find us!" Nirmal called in an impatient voice. He was tired of crouching behind the sofa.

"Please don't think of any of this as a game, Asha ... for Pramatma's sake. You think I'm a child? If you hate me, tell me and I'll accept it. All right, now I know, you do hate me."

Asha had been sitting despondently with her head lowered. She glanced furtively at Puran. She was no child. Yes, unfortunately she was not a child. She had understood everything well, and not just what was happening today; for many days now she had felt the truth shake her soul.

"Bhabi will be coming here any minute," she said, trying to move Puran's head away from her knees.

"Chacha, you're not coming to look for us ... we're not playing anymore." Sheela grumbled from her hiding place.

"Just answer my question, do you hate me?"

For a while Asha couldn't summon up the courage to lift her head and face Puran; she couldn't bear to look into his eyes. Finally she mustered some strength, raised her head and gave her answer with one look. Then hastily, she lowered her head again and covered her face with her hands.

"Asha!" Bhabi was calling her.

Dazed, Puran sat as if trying to seize a dream. The seriousness that had haunted his face earlier was gone; for a split second he paused, then a river of joy and emotion gushed forth, he shouted, "Coming to get you!" and went after the kids. Asha pretended to busy herself with straightening things near the fireplace. She crouched low on the carpet fearfully, her eyes closed, as if feeling around for some lost object. She wished she could sink into the ground, deep into the bowels of the earth under her feet.

"What is this!" Bhabi screamed, her voice barely discernible over the din Puran and the children were making.

"Hide-and-seek, Bhabi!" Puran said joyfully, speaking like someone intoxicated. "Come and join us."

"A curse upon hide-and-seek! Asha, you call this cleaning?"

"Bhabi, we've been playing hide-and-seek, and Ashaji was playing with us. Come, Bhabi, you'll be the dai now." Puran lifted Bhabi in his arms and twirled her around.

"Puran, Hai Ram! Puran! Put me down!" The children forgotten, Bhabi tried to extricate herself from Puran's ticklish grasp.

Sister-in-law

Devar, the word is as lively as sister-in-law, devrani, is dull. Until the devrani comes along, the bhabi is the queen of the household and the centre of interest for the devar. But as soon as the devrani arrives on the scene the devar disappears. No longer whispering everything in Bhabi's ears, he now quietly listens instead to his queen's complaints about Bhabi, and slowly turns into a poisoned thorn. The very same Bhabi without whom a meal tastes bitter, who can be teased and then pacified by putting one's arms around her neck, must contend with just "Namaste, Bhabiji" after the arrival of the queen.

"There will be two of us then and more trouble than you can dream of," Puran said when Bhabi brought up the question of his marriage.

"Hunh! You could be two or four, it doesn't really matter. I'll give you both a thrashing when I see fit."

"But, Bhabi, you'll hit her? Won't you feel sorry for her?"

"She'll be punished if she's mischievous."

"But what if she is very innocent?" Puran cast a glance at Asha who was sitting some distance away on the grass with Munna.

"I hope Bhagwan will not give you a wife who is innocent. You won't let her live."

"Bhabi, what a thing to say! Do all of you think I'm a dog?"

"Anyway, we're searching for someone very pretty."

"Searching? How long will you search? At this rate you'll find someone when I'm an old man."

"Actually, there is someone … and she's beautiful…"

"Is that true? Well, I have someone in mind, too, and she's also very beautiful." Asha was attempting to hide behind Munna. If she had had a choice she would have run from there.

"Liar! You couldn't have seen her. Have you seen Kamla's sister-in-law?"

"No, I haven't seen Kamla's sister-in-law, but I've seen a kamal." Puran's gaze sought Asha's eyes, but she was looking down at the grass as if in search of a hole she could disappear into.

"Is Shanta coming as well?" Bare Bhaiya, who was sitting in an armchair nearby reading a newspaper, asked.

"No, she's not coming. But you've seen her, haven't you?"

"Yes, but she was very young at the time. I think she was in F.A."

"That's right." Bhabi's attention wandered to Munna who had crawled away from Asha. Just as Asha got up to leave Bhabi called her.

"Asha, will you take Munna?"

Munna stiffened when Asha tried to hold him in her arms and, freeing himself, climbed over Puran.

"You see, Bhabi, the more I tease him the more he laughs," Puran said.

"It's your doing that he's so shameless."

"Bhabi, find a devrani who resembles Munna." It seemed Puran found the word vastly amusing.

"Oh no! You mean like this little monkey?"

"Well, someone who looks like you then. Petite, delicate. Tell me, Bhabi, why is it that you have several vagabond brothers but not even one sister?'

Bhabi remembered her only sister who had died of small-pox as a child. Had she lived she would have made the best sister-in-law. Bhabi began talking about her, how she crawled, how she lisped when she talked, and how the two of them quarrelled.

"Bhabi, for goodness sake, of what use would a little lisping wife be?"

"Don't be silly, Puran, she wouldn't still be lisping. And she would have been twelve or thirteen years old now."

"No, this won't do. Why must Bare Bhaiya have such a nice wife? He's always been ahead of me. He came into the world first, and he also managed to find a nice wife first. Why couldn't I have been born before him?"

"Enough silliness, Puran," Bhabi was blushing and Bare Bhaiya, hearing his wife's praise, smiled sheepishly. Puran had such a habit of blabbing nonsense.

"No!" Puran yelled. Munna had taken out his pen and was pushing it into the ground. There was ink all over his face.

"Dear me! No wonder he was so quiet all this time."

"You bad boy!" Puran pinched Munna's cheeks and catching hold of his chubby legs, pulled him.

"Leave my child alone, Puran— "

"I'll kill him today, Bhabi—that was a twenty-one rupee pen."

"You can take his father's pen—he has two."

"I'm not taking anyone's father's pen. I'll teach him a lesson today." Puran sat him on his knees. "You little devil!" The little devil smacked Puran across the face with an ink-stained hand.

Bhabi rolled on the grass, helpless with laughter.

"Why are you laughing? You just wait and see what I do to him." Puran lifted the child up and flung him in the air. Then, turning him upside down, he swung him about.

"Oh no! Puran! My baby, oh, his intestines are going to turn over, oh my poor baby." Bhabi was about to cry, but Munna, his face smeared with ink, continued to giggle. And when Bhabi tried to take him from Puran, he clung to Puran's shoulder and wouldn't let go.

"What a stubborn one he is," his father said.

"He is not going to learn like this." Puran grabbed the baby's cheek and twisted it. Munna's face began to crumple, Bhabi screamed, and Asha snatched Munna away.

"You just wait, Puran. I promise I'll treat your children the same way—actually, they'll get worse from me."

"No, you won't. My children won't be nobodies."

"And mine are?"

"Maybe not. But you won't be able to beat my children."

"Oh? And you can beat mine all you want?"

"There will be someone to protect them—you won't be able to touch them. If your children can be protected, mine will be protected, too."

"Hunh! No one will be able to protect your children from my wrath. You've thrashed my children so much I'll—"

"No, you won't. Munna will protect them, or someone else will. Asha, you'll protect them, won't you?"

Asha busied herself with tying Munna's shoelaces.

The Fair

Asha had been living at Raja Sahib's for a whole year, and in all this time there had been no reason for her to return to her village. But the village fair came along and Ranji's mother thought of Asha. Ranji borrowed some money, had a new suit of clothes made for himself, and both mother and son arrived at Raja Sahib's. Asha was reluctant to return with them alone, so Ranji's mother coaxed Chamki into going along and the four embarked on the trek back to the village. On the way Ranji's mother stopped to chat with somebody and was left behind. Ranji took charge of Asha and Chamki and continued on.

The importance of the fair was evident from the way people

thronged the roads. A colourful array of dupattas, turbans and caps adorned the streets; trooping along hurriedly were hundreds of vendors carrying toy paper fans and birds slung on long bamboo poles; also advancing towards the site of the fair were carts laden with gazak, chaat, and sweets fried in oil, accompanied by the buzz of flies; merchants carrying colourful hair ribbons and beaded necklaces hurried along with the vendors; and adding to the festivities was a tumult of lost donkeys, sick cows and mangy dogs. All in all, it seemed that heaven had arrived on earth with the fair for a couple of days.

In addition to the decorative shops constructed with bamboo and coloured paper, there were expensive goods of all shapes and sizes strewn about in great number on the fair grounds. Among these were Japanese toys, clay idols, rubber balloons and bamboo reeds, which the vendors played to attract the public. One could also see a bear, a five-legged cow, a two-headed calf's cadaver, a fox with a man's face, a magician, and jugglers who jumped from bamboo poles with far greater alacrity than monkeys.

And in the midst of all this, Ranji was treating the girls to all these delights in grand style; already they had had potato chaat, dahi-bare and papri. The purple-edged turban glowed against Ranji's dark skin, the edges of his striped yellow shirt billowed with the wind revealing his charming pink underwear under his diaphanous dhoti. New plaid socks, held up with red rubber bands on his stocky, hairy calves looked quite jaunty, and the large gilt rings on his fingers, together with the red Japanese silk handkerchief, were enough to wrench one's heart. Kallo, the sweeperess, sneaked coquettish glances at him, Roopa's widowed daughter-in-law blushed when he ran into her, and a few of his friends teased him with profanities, but Ranji was in very high society at the moment; rolling his eyes, pulling in his pot belly, he moved on.

Asha, who had not only never been to the fair before but

who, in her grandmother's lifetime, had not even ventured to the shop down the street to buy oil, was bewildered by the crowds and the strange goings-on. She kept colliding into people, and every once in a while she was jostled or pushed by someone behind her. And when she glimpsed Puran in a hat, riding his chestnut mare in the midst of all this pushing and shoving, she nearly fell on her face. Suddenly, she wanted to hide. However, suffused with the importance of his position as a landowner, Puran rode past her haughtily without noticing her. Asha breathed a sigh of relief.

But moments later, while she was haggling over the price of bracelets made from melon seeds, Puran rode over to her side. Perhaps he had seen her, after all. But why wasn't he smiling if he had? Abandoning the bracelets, she hastily made her way through the crowds, but no crowd could forestall the stride of the chestnut mare. Not when she was watching the puppet show, nor when she was looking at some colourful ribbons later, nor even when she was gulping down a soda drink. And to make matters worse, just as she was demurring at Ranji's offer of a silver-coated paan, the mare seemed to hover over her. And the rider? He was still on the horse, but his eyebrows curved angrily and his face had turned red. The paan fell from Asha's hand and landed on the ground, its mouth split open. Well, there would be other paans; this wasn't real silver anyway, perhaps gilt or some such thing. And the worst of it was that Chamki was nowhere in sight. A minute ago she had been counting bangles with Lakshmi, and the next minute she had flown!

"Let's go home now. Where's Chamki?" Asha said, trying to repress an unknown fear that kept growing.

"So soon? There's plenty of daylight left," Ranji said, although dusk had already settled in the east. Today Ranji, feeling courageous, walked with an air of resolution. He exhibited a new image. Paan after paan had been consumed and he had successfully reduced several packets of biris to ashes. His gait was becoming more and more languid and the smoke from the biris darkened.

"Where is Chamki? Why didn't she tell me she was going off somewhere?"

"She's probably with Lakshmi. Let's go and see the wrestling match."

"No," Asha said, shaking her head vehemently. What a thing to see! Masses of naked flesh rolling about in the dust while the spectators, all good-for-nothing vagabonds, swore and offered revolting suggestions to the wrestlers. Asha shuddered at the very thought, and was shocked when she caught a glimpse of the inky-black, naked limbs of the wrestlers from afar.

"All right, let's go and have some sherbat then. We'll find Chamki. What are you scared of?" Ranji drew closer to Asha.

At the sherbat-wallah's Asha came face to face with a scene that robbed her of her equilibrium altogether. The men who were drinking sherbat loitered in the area of the shop with frightening expressions on their faces, while others rolled about in the dirt. A gramophone nearby blared away. No sooner had these two arrived than the men began ogling her with phlegm-coloured eyes. As if this were not enough, they proceeded to exchange obscenities accompanied by vulgar gestures. And then there was the smoke from the biris and the rank odour of the sherbat itself. Asha felt nauseated.

"Let's go," she pleaded tearfully. She had also glimpsed the chestnut steed and its rider. "Let's go this minute," she said and moved away from Ranji.

"Where are you going? Wait, I'll come with you." Ranji was intimidated by Asha and the obscenities were making him nervous. Also, a red-turbaned policeman had been eyeing him suspiciously for a long time.

"Wait here. I'll see if I can find Chamki." Ranji simply wanted to escape for a while so he could gather his wits. He knew Chamki wasn't lost and would come looking for them when she was ready.

Asha leaned against a bamboo jalousie and tried to still her wildly beating heart.

"So, this is what you have been up to."

Startled, Asha jumped aside; she could have been trampled by the horse if she hadn't moved so quickly.

"Who is the scoundrel with you?" Decency and jealousy don't go hand in hand, but Puran wasn't one to think before he spoke.

"Ranji," Asha murmured, picking at a splinter in the bamboo.

"Ranji—the name's certainly beautiful. I didn't know you were interested in the sherbat."

Had she even glanced at the sherbat? And what kind of sherbat was it that smelled like dog's vomit!

"Who gave you permission to come here by yourself?"

"Chamki—is here with me, too."

"But why did you come? And aren't you ashamed to be seen chewing paan and drinking tarhi?" Puran spoke in a controlled voice. It seemed that if he could have, he would have taken the whip which he was striking at the bamboo rods in the jalousie, and skin her with it. Asha wished he would, instead of speaking to her in this manner. She didn't know how to respond.

"You can do what you want, but remember everyone knows you are a servant in our household. Pitaji will get a bad name."

Asha was amazed that Puran should talk to her like this. Yes, indeed she was his servant, only a servant. Suddenly she was filled with a desire to scrape her hands against the bamboo rods till they bled or tear her heart out and sob unashamedly. How long had she carried a burden in her heart.

"And how innocent you seemed. One little question and you started quivering and shaking as if you were a little girl! I didn't know you at all!" Puran chewed his words, flinging them at her like stones, and her fear grew. The mare was stomping restlessly, and all the while the whip kept striking at the bamboo rods.

Suddenly the mare bucked and Puran dug his heels into her sides with full force. She reared, missing Asha by inches, and then galloped off. The chestnut mare was also punishing her.

Asha couldn't stay there any longer. The ruffians loitered around her, first coughing knowingly, then humming lines from film songs. She was so terrified she wanted to run from there. A few men, standing not far from her, lazily scratched their thighs and eyed her with syrupy looks. They had all fallen madly in love with her, it seemed. Walking away, making her way through the throng of men, she found herself next to a pole. Distressed, she stopped and looked around frantically.

Standing in the midst of friends, not too far from her, was Chamki. She giggled bashfully while saying something to the suave rider of the horse whose eyes were concealed under the rim of the hat, but whose lips, Asha could see, quivered in a naughty smile.

"Don't you want to see the fireworks?" Chamki said, surprised at Asha's insistence on leaving in such a hurry. "The fireworks are the best part of the fair. And Chote Bhaiya is here too, did you see him? He's so wicked!" Holding back a laugh, Chamki puckered her lips. "Right in front of everyone he said, 'Chamki, will you sit on the horse, you must be tired.' Hunh!"

But Chamki didn't see too much of the fireworks. There were fireworks going off in her own heart.

An anar thundered; a glittering gold cloud rose and there was light everywhere, then darkness. A fire-cracker went off, illuminating the very depths of being, and finally total, absolute darkness! How dull life appears afterwards, like the empty clay shell of a spent anar or the tail of a fire-cracker!

Hatred

When, tired and exhausted, Asha returned from the fair to her room, her body ached like a ripe sore. As she poured water over the blisters on the soles of her feet to wash off the mud, her muscles contracted sharply with pain and she broke out in a sweat. But what of the larger sores that mushroomed in her heart and in her mind? She wished everyone would fall asleep so that she could hide her face in her pillow and sob without restraint. Her temples pounded with the weight of emotions she had stifled, her forehead throbbed. The body is weak, but why was her heart so timorous? Her grandmother used to say it was because she had been a premature baby, but how was that her fault? She was in no hurry to come into the world; if her young brother had not slipped and fallen she would not have come at the appointed time.

During mealtimes she noticed that Puran neither teased Bhabi nor did he pinch the children's cheeks, and she didn't catch him laughing in his usual manner either.

"Oh my! How quiet you are today," Bhabi said. But God knows what held Puran's attention. Bhabi mischievously put a spoonful of salt in his soup and shook his shoulder.

"Are you asleep? The food won't be left here for you all night."

Puran began gulping down the soup. "All right Bhabi, one day soon it will be my turn." They were all laughing at him; Puran's discomfort became evident. Chamki gave him a fresh plate of soup and he pretended to be engrossed in eating. But things were not right today; Puran neither ate properly nor would he talk. When Asha served him his favourite dal, he said, "I don't want any." Actually he might have had some, but as soon as he saw Asha he looked away irately, and busied himself instead with the papads Chamki was serving. Scared, Asha moved away quickly.

"Puran, how can you scold my Asha? Is that any way to

speak to anyone?" Bhabi spoke angrily.

"Who am I to scold your Asha? I'm just not hungry, that's all. Excuse me." Puran rose from the table.

"But Puran, you haven't eaten anything." Bhabi looked worried.

"I don't feel very well." Puran left the table and went to his room.

Maybe it was just a coincidence or maybe it was the heat, but the next day Puran developed a high fever that left him floating in and out of consciousness for days. The fever persisted, occasionally subsiding just a little at a time, leaving Puran irritable and testy. Asha was afraid to go into his room, yet, as if propelled by some secret force, she would find herself at his door on one pretext or another. He had had a rough night and Bhabi was exhausted. When Asha went past the door she called out to her: "Asha, my doll, come and sit here for a while. I need to get some air, I'll be back in a few minutes."

Asha tiptoed in and sat down quietly on a stool near Puran's bed. It had been a long time since she had had the opportunity of looking at his face closely. How mature he looked, just like Raja Sahib. Two days of fever had left him pale, his lips were chapped and his hair tousled. Asha wanted to straighten every little lock, to move her fingers gently and lovingly on his forehead. Perhaps the soul is awake even when the body slumbers. Asha's scrutiny awoke Puran. He shut his eyes and opened them again and stared at her. She found his gaze disturbing. The fever had no doubt agitated his brain for he was flushed. All at once his eyes burned with life and his lips parted joyfully.

"Asha," he whispered, trying to lift himself on one elbow.

Asha got up hastily. She was at a loss, didn't know what to do. For a few minutes Puran continued to stare at her. Then his eyes fell on her wrist; he saw the bangles he had seen Ranji buy for her at the fair, and that necklace with the white beads. He fell back on his pillow as if someone had knocked his elbow. Asha rushed to his side but he was like a man possessed by a demon.

"Leave me alone ... where is everybody?" he looked around the room frantically.

"Should I get Bhabi?" Asha turned towards to the door.

"Hai Bhagwan! Where is everyone! Is everyone dead? Where is Chamki?"

"Bhabi was very tired, and Chamki—shall I get her?"

"Bhabi got tired and left you here? Why did she trouble you? Is there no one else in the house?" Puran spoke in a cutting tone. "I'm so thirsty, and this darkness..." He began thrashing about feverishly.

Confused, not knowing whether to give him water or call Bhabi, Asha simply stood before him like an idiot. But she was such an idiot!

"Ohh ... I can't breathe ... it's so dark ... pull the curtains away from the window..."

Asha ran to draw the curtains. It wasn't quite evening yet, but the room had darkened just a bit. Her hands trembled when she realised that Puran was still staring at her. When she reached for the curtain next to his bed she found herself close to his pillow; to avoid his searing gaze she bent over inches away from his face. The curtains fully drawn, she decided to get Bhabi, but when she looked at Puran she saw that his eyes were closed. She sat down again. After a short while Puran opened his eyes. She jumped from her seat.

"Shall I get Bhabi now?" she volunteered.

"Hunh! You can go if you don't feel like staying, I want to be alone. Where is Chamki? Why didn't Bhabi leave her here instead of you ... please go."

"Chamki was also very tired. She's taking a ... nap."

Asha was holding back her tears with great difficulty.

"Chamki is asleep, Bhabi is tired, you are tired, you can leave, I don't need anyone. Go."

The tears began to flow.

"There you go, crying now, what have I said to you? Who can say anything to you, you are free to go anywhere you want."

"Why ... what are you saying ... I..."

"What have I done now? Why don't you run to Bare Bhaiya and complain that I scolded you when I saw you with Ranji ... I don't care, why should I care..."

"When did I complain to Bare Bhaiya?"

"So now you're lying also. Didn't you tell Bare Bhaiya that I was angry with you? Why would I be angry with you, why?"

"I didn't complain to Bare Bhaiya! He asked me, 'Is Puran angry with you?' I ... I said, 'No', and then he said, 'Why is he, why is he like...'" Asha didn't know how to continue.

"All right, so you didn't say anything to him. But you're upset that I spoke to you so harshly. I shouldn't have said anything, I hope you will deign to forgive me." Puran's tone was caustic but he didn't sound angry any more.

"But I'm not upset," Asha made an attempt to be bold.

"Maybe not. But I'm sure you didn't like my interference in your affairs. Who am I ... you can see Ranji whenever you want to. It's foolish of me to interfere, you have the right to do as you please." Puran smiled.

"You're ... you're so cruel!" Asha burst into tears.

"I've heard that you are engaged to Ranji. It's my fault, Asha, I'm a fool. I scolded you for no reason at all. You like Ranji, don't you?"

Asha glared at Puran, making him break into a laugh. "And what about your ... Chamki?" Asha mumbled between sobs.

"Chamki? What? My Chamki? Who says? Hush!" He tried to get up. "What a silly thing you are."

"I know everything," Asha said in a child's voice.

"But who told you that Chamki..."

"And who told you that Ranji..."

"Asha." Puran gazed into her eyes. Her face was puffed up from weeping. "Asha, I'm a terrible person, my own dear Asha." He struggled to get out of bed.

"Please lie down," Asha tried to push him back.

"Asha, I'm so hasty, so hateful." He grasped her shoulders with both hands, but overcome with emotion and a wave of weakness, he tottered on his feet.

"What is this!" Bare Bhaiya, who came into the room just then, caught Puran in his arms. "What is this, Asha?"

What could Asha have done?

"Bhaiya, didn't you know better than to entrust someone as stubborn and unmanageable as me to Asha's care? How could she stop me?"

"You should have stopped him," Bhabi said. "Why didn't you call me?"

"Bhabi, my dear, do you think I would have listened to her? She tried her to best to stop me ... Bhabi, some water, please..." Puran fainted.

Commotion swept up the entire household but Asha was vindicated. The doctor explained that Puran's sudden weakness was a good sign, a direct result of the fever subsiding, and after a few days of bed rest he would recover completely.

In the days that followed Puran turned into such a clown of a patient that it was nearly impossible to keep him confined to his bed. He wanted everyone in his room, even Bhola's aunt. And Asha, from whom Puran's eyes had sought forgiveness a hundred times, also sneaked in with the others.

"Bhola's aunt, if you get angry with me once for some reason, will you never make up with me?"

"Be quiet, you crazy boy."

"No, I mean it. If I upset you, do you make up your mind to hold a grudge against me for life?"

"What?" Bhola's aunt had no idea what he was talking about.

"Bhola's aunt, look, we all make mistakes, don't we?"

"Who made a mistake?" she asked foolishly.

"You're so dense ... how will we spend our life together?"

"Spend your life with your mother and sister!"

"If you are Bhola's aunt, what will my relationship to Bhola be?"

Bhola's aunt proceeded to describe a relationship so disgusting that Puran was forced to hide his face in his blanket. How could such a patient keep still in bed for long?

This was the hatred that had burst like a storm in Puran's heart and in two swift jolts had weakened him to the bone. But now it was the same again. How does one develop such violent hatred and then poof! it evaporates like steam. He had decided this was it, the game was over. And within minutes he was clean, like the smooth surface of a clay waterpot. Good grief! Is this hatred? It is just another fanciful aspect of love.

The old pranks returned, the taunting attacks on Bhabi, Bhola's aunt's profanities. Asha's hide-and-seek, and the teasing of the children. Why do you become so light-headed when you're in love? Why do the body and the eyes dance with merriment as does the heart? And why does everything seem to be made for the purpose of gaiety? Where does sobriety take off to? And you have no thought of tomorrow. But a woman? How cautious she is. Her heart quivers fearfully all the time, if she laughs it is with trepidation, if she smiles she does so hesitatingly. At every step she is afraid her secret will be revealed. What will happen? How will it happen? And what if this comes about, or that? And then, the unfortunate creature also considers herself a fool.

Asha had just given Munna a bath and was now combing his hair. He twisted and turned and wouldn't sit still at all, tossing a box here, opening a bottle there, chewing on the comb, turning the surma-dani upside down. Asha was getting annoyed.

"You bad boy!" she said, snatching the surma pin from him.

"Who? Me?" Puran spoke in a frightened child's voice from the door.

"No, it's Munna, he won't let me comb his hair."

"Munna's very naughty, he's not scared of you, you're such a chicken yourself ... frightened off by a little baby frog!"

That morning Puran had surprised Bhabi with a tiny frog perhaps the size of a berry. Bhabi ran crazily all over the house.

"This won't do, Puran, tie it to a string and hang it around her neck." Instead of coming to her rescue her husband was offering suggestions on how to destroy her.

"Puran, my dearest brother, I beg you, on my life..." Bhabi was screaming now. Turning away from Bhabi, Puran threw the frog on Asha who had been watching this drama in amusement all this time. Asha fled from there as though she were being pursued by a lion. And when Puran slipped a fragment of paper in her lap, she began pulling and tugging nervously at a corner of her dhoti.

"Would it have devoured you, that tiny frog?"

"Frogs make me sick."

"But why did you run from the garden? Do I make you sick as well?" Puran took the brush from her hands.

Asha picked up another brush and continued combing Munna's hair.

"What is this, Asha devi?" Puran snatched the other brush from her.

"I had things to do."

"That's right, you have the whole world to take care of." Using both brushes Puran set to combing his hair.

"Raja Sahib must be home now, he'll be looking for you."

"There you go again, thinking of everyone else except me, and if I tell you to do something you start making one excuse after another. Just think, Asha."

Asha picked up Munna and made as if to leave.

"So, running away again," Puran said, grasping her hands with both of his.

"Let me go, Munna is hungry."

"Who is holding you, I'm kissing Munna... why, shouldn't I kiss Munna? Hunh?" And he began kissing Munna. Asha turned her face this way and that but Puran's hair covered her eyes and her cheeks, then her heart and her head.

"Puran, I wish you had time for more important things." It was Bare Bhaiya. "Come with me."

"Me? I'm coming." And Puran followed him out of the room.

Asha breathed a sigh of relief and rested her face against Munna's cheeks.

*

"I don't like this at all, I don't approve of your behaviour," Bare Bhaiya said in a serious tone.

"My ... what ... who?"

"Yes, your behaviour. I'm not blind, Puran Singh. This constant joking with the girls..."

"What jokes, Bare Bhaiya, I don't joke with them. As for Asha, I feel sorry for her, after all she's the granddaughter of our wet nurse, actually Grandfather's wet nurse."

"But your teasing is in very bad taste."

"Bhaiya ... you don't understand ... you're mistaken, I don't feel sorry for Asha ... I love her and ..."

"And? And? And nothing! Puran, have you ever known me to glance at any of the female servants? We are true princes, our honour does not permit such actions."

"But I want to marry her."

"You?" Bhaiya laughed derisively.

"Why do you laugh?"

"Because you won't marry her."

"How can you say that, Bhaiya?"

"I can, that's all. I don't make jokes, I don't have the time to laugh all day long, and this notion you have of marriage—some idea!"

"But why do you object? I'd like to know." Puran twisted the ends of his shirt front nervously.

"She's our servant, Puran. You are probably thinking these foolish thoughts because of some film you've seen. But you should be aware that life is not a film, life is reality, a very real reality, and you are not a child."

"I know I'm not a child, and that is why I must know why I can't do as I please."

"Yes, but who gave you the right to dishonour your family and break the hearts of your elders?"

"The family, hunh! The same old story. I know that Pitaji is not that old-fashioned."

"That's where you're wrong, you are mistaken. No matter how enlightened Pitaji is, he will never give you permission for such a horrible undertaking, and just think, what has Mataji or the children, your innocent nephews and nieces, what have they done to deserve being sacrificed?"

"What are you talking about? What sacrifice?"

"What place will they hold in society after this? Well, Uncle Puran married a servant girl. What decent family is going to ask for Sheela's hand in marriage, and what family will give Nirmal their daughter after his uncle's actions become public knowledge?"

"To hell with such society, with people who will reproach Sheela because her uncle married a girl from a poor family. It will be better for Sheela to remain unmarried rather than be married to someone with such despicable ideas."

"Of course. It's easy for you to say all this, to make plans for your own happiness while the rest of the family is destroyed."

"That's not true! All I'm saying is we won't marry our Sheela into a family which subscribes to such old-fashioned views."

"So you believe that I should look for someone related to Asha, a custodian, or a steward, for Sheela?" Bare Bhaiya was not a very talkative man, he wasn't stupid. Puran felt helpless in the face of his taunts.

"You're misconstruing everything I'm saying, Bhaiya," Puran said, defeated.

"Think well, you're wiser and more intelligent than I am. Anyway, let's drop the subject for the moment, your Bhabi is coming this way. I don't want this matter made known until it's absolutely necessary."

Bhabi arrived with her kids in tow.

"Look, did you see how Munna kisses my cheek?" Munna squeezed his mother's face with his short, stubby fingers and placed his flat nose on her cheek.

"He learns from copying," Bare Bhaiya hinted obliquely and Puran tried to conceal his embarrassment by turning to his usual pranks with Munna.

"Bhabi, I'm going to make him stand, he's old enough to learn now." Puran put Munna down.

"Hey, Ram! No Puran, no! He's too young to stand by himself yet."

"I don't care, he can do it, he's so fat, surely he can stand, he's just pretending he can't."

"I don't see how a ten-month-old baby can pretend, he just can't do it, that's all." Bhabi tried to wrest Munna away from Puran.

"I don't care, I'm going to let go of his hands." Puran wanted to frighten her.

"Oh, my baby! Puran!" She snatched Munna out of Puran's grasp.

"What are you worried about? Did you really think I'd let go of his hands? I'm not his enemy." With these words Bare Bhaiya's remarks echoed in Puran's ears.

The Blow

There is only one way life ends, with death. But we forget that every morning ends with night, slumber with waking, and laughter with silence. The beauty of sunrise would have gone unnoticed if it hadn't been for sunset, if the sun straddled the sky forever. And may God keep us from a sleep from which there is no waking. But the blows God has deemed necessary for lovers are a shade too many. One kind of blow, related to the appearance of the rival, leaves you frustrated, but no sooner do the clouds dissipate than the moon appears again and all is well; a little bit of unhappiness, like a full stop after a sentence, makes life interesting. Then there is another kind of blow your friends and well-wishers make ready for you. This is the backlash from society. If you're lucky you might leap across the ditch, but if you're not, it's right there in front of you. You can recover from other kinds of blows, but not the one society deals out. How both literature and films have dragged society into the mud, but like a hungry lion it leaps up, ready to attack. Actually, this is all just a front for something else. The collision is not with society but with people, with those you care about. And who would suffer more in a situation like this than someone as adventurous and carefree as Puran? Surely it couldn't be sombre, cautious Bare Bhaiya?

Puran's behaviour alerted the family members. Everyone's attention was trained like guns towards Puran and Asha. A change began to appear in the way Asha was treated. Instead of being placed with the other servant girls, she became a favourite of Mataji who coiled her presence around her like a snake. During meals she was made to sit beside Munna while Puran was seated between Mataji and Raja Sahib. Puran understood the reason for this close watch, but he had neither the courage nor the opportunity to get out from under. However, even if a thief can be prevented from stealing, he can't be forced to become honest. While leaning over Mataji's lap to get to Munna's cheeks, Puran did not refrain from sneaking a glance at Asha. And as if that was the reason for living, somewhere in the gallery, behind the drawing room curtains, you would find the honey hidden and the bees stuck to it in a stupor.

It was Munna's birthday. And Diwali was also just around the corner. The house was getting a thorough cleaning. Anyway, how long can flies buzz around for a kill? Asha was putting the curtains up in Bhabi's room. Puran arrived, pretending to be looking for something.

"I wish someone would tidy up and decorate my room as well," he said, standing close to her, one leg resting on a nearby chair.

"Your room is so sparse, what can one decorate it with?" Asha had learnt to talk back to Puran.

"Hunh! That's because I'm a poor man." His gaze travelled over Bhabi's silver things. "Bhabi's father is a millionaire."

"Don't lose heart, who knows, when you get married your wife will bring even more lavish things with her."

"I don't think so. What if my wife is poor?"

"Ram forbid that you have a poor wife."

"Why, is it a failing to be poor?"

"Of course. If it weren't a failing why would the upper class be so privileged?"

"But my wife-to-be *is* poor, she doesn't have money. She does have good looks, though."

"Oh my! But Chote Bhaiya, we'll be truly impressed if she has both money and good looks."

"I don't want money or good looks, I want..." Puran stammered. Asha continued to loop the curtains.

"Asha, is money everything? Suppose I lose everything, Pitaji doesn't give me a penny, will you, will you..."

Asha's hands trembled and the curtain rings slipped from her fingers and fell to the floor.

"Tell me, Asha, if I'm penniless and if Ranji..."

If only Ranji were dead, Asha thought. But she occupied herself with picking up the rings from the floor.

"And if Ranji has money, you won't think of me, will you?"

"What do you mean? Why should you become penniless?"

"Let's just say I do."

"Please don't talk like this," Asha pleaded.

"Why don't you take what I'm saying seriously, why don't you give me a proper answer? Hunh?"

"What can I say? You're going to be late for the match, you'll miss the train."

"Listen, I'm not joking and I don't have the time to listen to your excuses either. I've told you so many times how I feel and now I'm going to speak to Pitaji."

"No, please, for Pramatma's sake, don't do that."

"Why? Why shouldn't I tell him? What's the reason? He has often brought up the subject of my marriage."

"So why don't you marry?" Asha tried to change the subject.

"That's what I'm talking about. I'll tell him everything."

"No, please don't tell him anything. If you..."

"If I what? Go on. I'm going to inform him that I want to get married and that I don't need his money."

"No, you can't say that."

"Why not? Who will stop me?"

"I will stop you."

"What do you mean? You will say that ... that ..."

"Yes," Asha moved away from him quickly with the curtain.

"Asha, you're toying with my emotions. Why? Why are you doing this?" He caught hold of her arm.

"Because I want to."

"Because you want to? Don't you love me at all and..." He let go of her arm.

The curtains done, Asha started changing the slipcovers on the pillows.

"Say something, don't you love me? I'll never bother you again." He clasped her hand in his.

Asha tried to avoid his gaze. She could feel her eyes filling rapidly with tears.

"Just say once that you don't love me, that you don't love me as much I love you ... speak, say something."

"No!" Asha exclaimed, unable to hold her emotions in check any longer.

Puran let go of her.

"Oh," he said with a laugh, "liar, what a liar you are. If I die, Asha ..."

"That's enough," Asha interrupted him, "please leave now." She placed her hand on his mouth. "What can you get by teasing and taunting a poor woman like me? You and I are not suited to each other, you must be married to a princess."

"To hell with princesses, you're my princess. And who says we don't belong together? Look at that mirror, what does it say?"

Seeing herself so close to Puran, Asha forgot everything for a moment and rested her head on Puran's chest.

"I'll speak to Pitaji today, I don't care if he kills me," Puran began speaking softly in her ear, "and then, my dearest Asha..."

"Chamki!" Asha's eyes fell on the mirror and behind her she saw Chamki's face red with anger. Asha sprang away from Puran.

"Chamki? That witch is nothing. Are you still thinking of her, are you still jealous of the wretch?"

"No, she was here a moment ago."

"Oh, so she's spying on us. It doesn't matter, I don't care who else find out that I love Asha. I'm not afraid of anyone."

"Ah, such daring! Let me look at this valiant hero who's not afraid of anyone." Mataji's mighty presence loomed ominously in the doorway like a black cloud. At that moment Asha wished desperately she could turn into a fly, or turn to stone. As a matter of fact, she had already turned to stone.

"Mataji..."

"Silence! Aren't you ashamed, calling me Mata with the very lips with which you were licking filth from the gutter a moment ago?"

"But listen to me, please..."

"I've told you once to remain silent, Puran. I don't want to have anything to do with you. A person who has no regard for the honour of his family or his father's name can have no regard for his mother. It is this witch I must deal with." She moved towards Asha menacingly.

"But first you have to listen to me, then..."

"Tell me, you wretch, did we nurture four generations of your family so that you could poison us at the first chance you got? Speak, you ungrateful girl, answer me." She advanced. Asha's whole body quivered. In all this time Mataji had never cast a disapproving eye at her. Actually, she was not known to express disfavour with anyone. Her forceful personality and her air of authority were enough to strike fear into the hearts of those around her, and for the most part she stayed out of everyone's way, cloistered in her room, immersed in reading and worship. However, this was a matter of such immense import that she had been compelled to come down to earth from her heavenly domain.

"Asha, you are under my protection," Puran said, his heart wrenching at Asha's trembling.

"Oh? Let me see what kind of protection it is that you're offering. Puran Singh, you forget your place. Leave us. All I want to do is to ask this girl why she chose to repay our love and affection in this manner."

"Mataji, forgive me, please..." Asha fell at Mataji's feet.

"Forgiveness? You destroy my home and then ask for forgiveness? It's true, once you take in a low-class person, he will not be satisfied until he gets more and more from you. How did you even dare to do this?" When Mataji's anger was aroused she turned into Kali Ma. Taking hold of Asha's hair, she twisted her head back so that she was facing her.

"That's enough, Mataji, let her go." Puran pulled his mother away from Asha. "You're not listening at all."

"Puran, how can you do this?" Mataji's voice cracked.

"What's all this wrangling about?" The wrangling had brought Raja Sahib out of his hole as well.

"Pitaji..."

"Do you see, do you see your beloved son's antics? Did you see how he twisted my wrist? Ahhh, Bhagwan!" Mataji caught her head in her hands and moaned threateningly.

"Puran, come outside." Faced with his mother's wrath, Bare Bhaiya also shook with fear. "But first ask for Mataji's forgiveness."

"Mataji ... I ... forgive me, but remember..."

Bare Bhaiya didn't allow him to continue. "That's enough nonsense, Puran." And he dragged him out of the room as if he were a child.

This, in reality, was the blow Puran received. And what happened in the course of this collision is what happens when a hammer comes down on glass. But once smashed, broken glass scatters and wounds the soles of all those who walk on it.

The Verdict

There is really no need to say this, but the verdict was issued. The whole family assembled. Mataji was in the judge's seat and Raja Sahib, assuming the role of a puppet, was also brought in. Who would be interested in such a dull affair; the heroine weeps alone in a dark chamber, the hero paces about in his room wearing the floor thin. And how else could such a hero and heroine fare? To top it all, the court was ready. When summoned, Puran came in with his face lowered, his hair awry. From behind the curtain Bhabi watched him in this condition and sighed. But could the sighs do anything to diminish anger?

"Come in, Puran. What is this dispute, son?" Pitaji had not fathomed the nature of the dispute as yet.

"There you go again, encouraging him. If you hadn't been so soft, these children might have been worth more today." Mataji knew, however, that her husband was a gem.

"All right, all right ... yes, well, Puran, what's all this nonsense about? You had better return to college, enough preparation for the exam, I'd say."

"Pitaji, I'm not committing a sin."

"No," Mataji interjected, "this is no sin, it's an act of goodness, isn't it, smearing dirt on your family's name."

"Does one blacken one's name simply by getting married?"

"Marriage? You are not going to try and marry that low-caste wretch while I'm alive."

"Puran," Raja Sahib said in a conciliatory tone, "don't be so stubborn. Life is so short, why do you want to get into this? Let us suppose for a moment that you do marry that girl. Well, it will be a great mistake. Just think, do you imagine that your mother will let either you, me or that girl live in peace? Will she ever accept her?"

Mataji groaned. "I pray to Bhagwan I never have any kind of a relationship with her. Look here, ji, why are you beating about the bush, why don't you frankly say what you must say?"

"Because you won't let me get a word in. Now listen here, Puran, think carefully. How will she live here and then she, uh, she..." Raja Sahib liked to be thought of as a liberal. He hesitated.

"But Pitaji, you're a friend of harijans, how can you..."

"Harijans! It's these very harijans who have sunk our boat! You're not thinking, not reasoning. You had better return to your herbs and medicines, ji."

Poor Raja Sahib. Some years ago he had experimented with drugs that are known to increase virility and strength. He found it embarrassing to be reminded of that episode in the presence of his grown sons.

"You're angry with Puran and you're taking that anger out on me. I'll say whatever you want me to, but nothing seems to make you happy."

"Look here, Puran," Bhaiya spoke up, "you understand the matter very clearly. I've told you this before. Try and think of how all this will affect our lives. What will Kamla's in-laws say, and what will my wife's family think, where will we hide our faces?"

"You're very selfish, Bhaiya. And what about your father-in-law? All his life he's lived on interest and now ..."

Behind the curtain Bhabi trembled, then stepped back.

"Nevertheless, you will not be allowed to take this step."

"No one can make me do anything or stop me. I don't want anyone's help or interference. So Pitaji will deprive me of an income and I'll be penniless. Fine, I don't care about that at all."

Mataji retorted: "No, you don't care, but she whom you think of as a goddess, she will no doubt rush to marry you. Why, she won't even spit on you! Do you hear?"

"You don't understand her nor did you ever try to."

"I understand such base women well."

"That is enough, Mataji ... Pitaji, Bhaiya, here's my asnwer. I will marry Asha and make the impossible possible. I'll leave this house today so that no one can blame you for anything."

"Wherever you go you'll be held responsible for disgracing your family's name. And people will say 'What a greedy old man, and all because the girl was poor'."

"People are crazy, you know."

"So? Is there no way out for me?"

"No, you were born here and—"

"I wish I had been born in a poor man's house, then no

one would have taunted me. But let me tell you once again that I will leave today, and I'm sorry there's no way of saving you from dishonour." Puran left the room.

"There is ... you're still a child, Puran Singh," Bare Bhaiya muttered under his breath.

"Pitaji," he said to his father, "there is only one way. We must send Asha away without Puran's knowledge. If he leaves there's no doubt he'll be miserable, but worse, the family will suffer dishonour."

"Where can we send her?"

"I say we send her to Kamla's. We'll explain everything to her so that she can take care of things."

"No, not at all! I don't want to cause trouble for my daughter. Send her off to her village." Mataji knew that her son-in-law, Karan Singh, had a ready appetite.

"Then let's poison the witch!" Pitaji said in exasperation.

"Try and control your temper, please."

"Arup is right. Kamla will take good care of her and Puran will never know where she is."

And so the Asha who had been brought here with such love and care was swept up and transported hundreds of miles away to Kamla's house. She was ashamed of what Kamla might think, but Kamla was not accustomed to thinking too much.

When little Sheela informed Puran that Asha Didi had left, he got up with the alacrity of a snake. First he went to the village, and then he came to fight with Bare Bhaiya.

"I understand everything ... I knew from the beginning that you don't like your own sweet wife and have an eye for Asha ... that's why you were so worried about her." Anger drives one to madness.

"Puran! What are you saying, have you lost your senses? Whatever I'm doing I'm doing for your well-being, otherwise if it were in my power, my dear brother..."

"Your power? What power you have used, Bhaiya! You

severed my hands and feet, you've always been my enemy, Bhaiya ... you must celebrate my death, you will inherit everything."

"Stop, Puran! Don't say things you will regret later. You're not just my brother, you're like my own son. If I wanted the estate I'd have arranged for your marriage without permission from Mataji and Pitaji so that they could disinherit you. Puran, don't think of me as someone so low, please, for Pramatma's sake, don't break my heart." Arup's sombre eyes filled with tears.

"But where did you send her, tell me where she is, I beg you."

"I didn't send her anywhere, she went away of her own accord. She said she didn't want to ruin your life—Puran, she's a goddess, she also said she would die rather than have any contact with you."

"Bhaiya, why did she say that? Doesn't she love me any more?"

"No, Puran, that's not it, she's a goddess, didn't your hear me? She left you because she loves you. Listen..."

"But what will I do now, Bhaiya?" Puran mumbled like a child.

"You're a man, you shouldn't weep for a woman. She's gone, but she didn't take your reason and common sense with her, did she? Immerse yourself in the affairs of the estate, finish preparations for your exam..."

"But I'll seek her out..."

"You'll only cause her more pain, Puran..."

"Pain? Ahhh..." Puran broke down and started sobbing.

You Forgot

The world forgets. A knife wound heals and the thought of pain slips from one's mind. While giving birth a mother vows she won't have any more children and wishes she were infertile. The moment her pain passes she croons over the new baby, and before long she is yearning for another child. But Puran's forgetting was a proper forgetting. Asha's dead. They say the plague took her. The whole village was swallowed by the plague. Even a wrestler like Ranji was not spared; his old mother's back is broken. Asha died, and Puran's desires died with her. He forgot a great deal. He forgot to laugh. Munna was older and had become so naughty, and a second baby now clung to Bhabi's breast, but Puran had forgotten how to show his affection for them, to tickle them. If Asha were there he would have remembered everything. He would have shown people that he wasn't a coward, that he had more to his name than Pitaji's money; he would have shown them that there are many ways to live in this world. But why did Asha die? He even forgot Bhola's aunt. She tried to tease him herself, he smiled wanly in response and remained silent. The old woman's heart ached, she wilted.

"Puran, it's Sheela's birthday," Bhabi said in a playful tone, "what will you give her?"

"What shall I give her?" Puran asked, lowering his head.

"Let me see—here, Sheela, what would you like?" She whispered something in Sheela's ear.

"Auntie, right Mummy, auntie?" Sheela chirped.

"Yes, tell your uncle..."

Puran got up quietly and left the room.

"Why don't you marry, look how unhappy Mataji is." It was Bhaiya's turn.

"Yes, Bhaiya, everyone is unhappy on my account."

"That's not it, Puran, the doctor says marriage will improve your health."

"What? Bhaiya, marriage is not some medicine that can bring the sick back to health, and who said I was sick?"

"Puran, my dearest," Mataji said, placing his head in her lap, "will I take this longing with me to the grave? I have two sons, and one won't be married while I'm alive?"

For a while Puran said nothing. Who knows what emotions crowded his heart. He wanted to put his arms around his mother and weep. When he was a child and she took something away from him, this is what he did and she returned whatever she had taken. But it was death that had taken Asha away.

"My precious, your father is also getting old. Don't you think he longs for your wedding?"

The word 'wedding' stirred old memories; he remembered so much. But what a strange thing a mother is. She might cut you up into little pieces but you are, after all, a part of her body, and there was so much love in those eyes.

"Mataji, if you had any wish to see me married..."

"Puran, let bygones be bygones. A mother's mistakes are part of motherhood; it's maternal affection that makes a mother nurture her child with her blood, it's that same maternal affection that makes her destroy that child. But is she a demon? Son..." Tears flowed thickly from her eyes. "Do you think I'm happy?"

"Mataji, please, don't..."

"Say yes to marriage. When I see that you are happy I'll live a little longer, or else..."

"Do what you want, Mataji." Puran got up and went to his room. For some time he lay on his bed. Then, assailed by discomfort, he opened his drawer and took out the flowers. They were the same flowers, red, red like Munna's cheeks, red flowers that the earth had yielded, the very earth that had swallowed Asha. The flowers were black now, like congealed, dried blood.

When Puran's proposal arrived for Kamla's sister-in-law, everyone was jubilant.

"Do you hear, Puran is like our very own son," Kamla's mother-in-law, who had always looked down her nose at Kamla's family, said lovingly.

"Yes, Mataji," Kamla said, "Puran is such a pleasant

person, just like our Shanta."

"Yes, do what has to be done." The old woman was trying to hold back her excitement.

*

"Forgot, you forgot so soon, Puran Singhji," Asha said, falling to the floor of her little room.

If only she were in her village so that, like Ranji the wrestler, she too could have been consumed by the plague!

Flames

There is one kind of fire that burns day and night in a hearth, and then there's another kind which is ignited when someone foolishly sets dry thatch aflame and you can see everything flare up in a flash like paper. Now we hear there are fires caused and spread by bombs, fires that, within moments, demolish large dwellings.

But the little spark which, deeply embedded in hot ashes, smoulders slowly, that too is fire. It does not burn down any large mansion or house but the hot ash around it gradually becomes lifeless from its slow heat. And if such a spark finds its way into the heart and hides there, the body eats, drinks and performs other functions, but that slow warmth and that sweet pain make you restive.

Asha was helping with Shanta Bai's dowry but her heart, like her hands, was shrouded by the light and shade of memory. God knows, it wasn't that she had ever wanted Puran to lose his sanity, nor had she wished that he would remain single in her memory. She did not deliberately fall in love, and when she did she didn't expect to be patted on the back or congratulated for it. But still—what did she want? Even when she was alone she could not admit to herself what she wanted.

Puran could have done something, he would have said something; she wasn't so far away, she was at his sister's house. She did not know that sometimes what we long for is right beside us but we still can't have it.

"Asha, look you've got the cloth hanging here." Showing her a piece of fabric, Shanta jolted her out of her reverie.

"What? Oh, yes, Shanta Bai. That's the way the fabric is—I did my best."

"Your best? Nonsense! Stitch it by hand now. Your heart's not in any of this." Shanta flung the fabric at Asha and left.

"Oh, Asha Devi is sewing." Sham Lal's manner when he spoke to her was always ingratiating. She didn't know what it was that made Karan Singh keep him on. True, he was intimidated by Karan Singh and perhaps that's what Karan Singh found appealing. He was a distant relative no doubt, or at least pretended to be, but now his position in the household was that of a poor relative. When Asha arrived he treated her with deference, but whenever he found her alone he regarded her with sweet, timid eyes and conversed with her in a honeyed tone.

"So you're angry with us, Asha Rani."

"Munshiji, why should I be angry with you?" Asha replied with a scorn that was worse than anger.

"But you turn away when I talk to you. Asha Devi, do you know what's going on in my heart?"

"Munshiji, will you go or shall I call Kamlaji?"

"Hai Ram, such cruelty! Is it a sin to talk?"

"Why don't you talk with Shanta Bai if you're so fond of talking?"

"Oh my—well, but Asha Devi, I'm a poor man and it's not my habit to reach beyond my means..."

Sham Lal had heard the story about Asha.

"Have pity, Munshiji, or is there anything else you want to say?" His fake sarcasm drove Asha to tears.

"Well, all I'm saying is that people should tread their own

paths. Why climb over high terraces and end up falling on your face?"

"Yes, you're right, Munshiji."

"So, Asha, what if I talk to you..."

"Munshiji, there's something else ... I ... why don't you go from here?" Asha felt lacerated by his sugary voice.

"Yes, but now Shanta Bai is getting married and I've heard her groom-to-be is very good looking, isn't he?"

Sham Lal was very clever, but he presented a dumb exterior so that he often managed to say something extremely meaningful, making it slide down your throat like a lump of sugar so you would never know what hit you.

"There'll be two or three people accompanying Shanta Bai when she leaves for her in-laws' house. Why don't you go, too?"

If she could, Asha would have stuck the dog's tongue with needles. Instead she just sat there with her head lowered, but after he left she could not hold back her tears.

The wedding day arrived. Kamla's carelessness was not something new; there were many things that didn't come in on time, several sets of clothig that still hadn't been finished with gold and silver lace. As if she were a machine, Asha was entrusted with putting the finishing touches on the clothes.

The wedding procession was fit for a king; for hours the columns of people on foot kept approaching, then the elephants and horses appeared. Crowded together in the window with some of the other girls, Asha too was watching the show unfold.

"Get out of the way, you witches," Shanta Bai pushed some of the girls aside and stuck her head out.

"You get away, girl, we won't let you see the barat. Have you ever heard of a bride clamouring to see her own barat?"

One of them said: "Well, Shanta is a child. When I insisted on seeing my barat, my uncle pickd me up in his lap and took me to the window."

Another said: "And then the groom appeared on an elephant looking like a doll; you couldn't even see his face because of the way he was bundled up in fancy clothes!"

A picture of curiosity and interest, Shanta looked anxiously for his face. And Asha? That face had never been far from her vision. The wedding procession turned a corner and all the women ran to the other window. Lost in thought, Asha remained where she was. Where was she to go, anyway? Slowly her head fell on the window sill and she began to breathe heavily.

Away from the hustle and bustle of the wedding ceremonies, in a broken-down part of the house, Asha lay quietly on a small cot. For a long time she had vacillated between sleep and wakefulness; her heart sank, then seemed to receive a blow from somewhere, and she would awaken. The circling of the bride and groom around the sacred fire had already taken place. Fire-crackers and bombs were going off. Suddenly Asha felt at peace. Everything was done. As long as the ceremonies had not been completed she had nursed a tiny hope. But now that too was shattered. Her steps took her towards the door. What harm was there now? Had her eyes committed a crime that she should not see anything? And who would notice her in all the commotion, who would recognize her?

Quickly, keeping out of the way of the ropes extending from the tents, stumbling, she ran. The hall glittered with lights. The bride and the groom were seated next to each other. Tearing her way through the throngs, she found a place from where she could at least see Puran clearly. Forgetting everything, she had come to look at the bride and groom with the curiosity of a child. But the golden diadem looked so beautiful on his pale forehead, he was like a fairy prince! Asha had never seen him dressed in anything but his usual black and gray clothes, she had never seen him in such fancy, glimmering attire. He was a strange Puran today, so changed. Man takes on so many roles in the course of a lifetime. Sitting next to him was Bhabi, blooming like a flower, holding a bowl of water. Some kind of strange ceremony was in progress; the bride and groom were competing to see who was cleverer, who could find and retrieve the ring from the water. Puran had won several times; actually, it was Bhabi who was guiding his hand as if he were a child.

Right in front of the door, in a small clearing, a dance was in progress. Today, after a long time, Chamki was dancing. As soon as the ceremonies ended, people turned their attention to the dance. The crowds thickened.

Outside, fire-crackers were going off. A sparkler came and fell near one of the curtains which, along with a part of the door and the decorative paper cut-outs hanging from it, began smouldering. Chamki appeared drunk; her eyes flashed, and under the lights her cheeks glowed like flames.

Perched on a stool, Asha was trying to look over people's shoulders. The fire was surreptitiously advancing, low on the ground, and soon the carpet too was ablaze. The dance continued with the frenzied pace of death, like a pigeon fluttering its wings before being dashed to the ground. One of the girls tried to climb the stool on which Asha was standing. Asha lost her balance and screamed. The stool was quickly stabilised, but the game was ruined. Puran's gaze plunged into Asha's eyes and she became numb.

"Asha"! Puran sucked in his breath like a madman, like someone who sees a ghost approach from the cremation grounds and loses his senses. But within seconds Asha's stool tipped and she fell, just as if she had dropped into the very grave she had emerged from. A combination of shock and surprise made Puran's face turn a deathly shade of yellow. He stared wildly at that portion of the wall from where, moments ago, Asha's sorrowful face had slipped a message into his eyes and disappeared.

"Puran, what's the matter?" Bhabi shook his hand.

"Asha ... just now..."

"What are you saying, Puran? What kind of silly talk is this?"

"Bhabi ... she was here just now ... she was here."

"Puran, don't act like a child. How can she be here?"

"But Bhabi, this was no dream, she was right here," Puran said in a strangled voice. "She's not dead, Bhabi."

"Puran, my dear brother, don't be a child. She may be alive or dead, but think, speak softly," Kamla cautioned.

"But, Bhabi..."

"No buts, Puran. What does it matter to you now if she's dead or alive? You're married and..."

"Married? But is she alive?"

"Puran, come outside with me, you don't look well." Bhabi tried to cover up the situation.

But the fire was blazing, flames leapt from the carpet, the curtains and the door, and Chamki ... Chamki continued to dance. Flames flickered in her gossamer dupatta, but she was in a trance.

"Fire!" People started screaming. With one loud blast Chamki reeled, like a moth that flutters before crashing to its death on the flame, and then she fell on her face. "Fire!" Everyone saw her. Within seconds an electric wire caught fire. All hell broke loose. Puran glanced at Shanta's frightened face illuminated by the light of the flames. Overcome by the heat and smoke, she teetered. No one else was around and soon the flames were reaching up to the sky. Puran lifted Shanta in his arms and advanced in the direction of the room behind them. He saw the flames rising above the electric wire. He turned towards the veranda. Once again, in the half-lit darkness, his soul retreated from the world and found itself in the cremation grounds. Withdrawn from the tumult around her, resting her head against a wall, was Asha.

"Asha!" Puran whispered hoarsely.

Asha was stunned. But not for long. Seeing Shanta in

Puran's arms she began once more to sink into the river of despair; every fibre in her body became taut, the hot fumes choked her breath.

Puran put Shanta down and she watched these two with surprise; she too had heard some of the gossip.

Puran moved slowly. He was certain this was Asha's ghost which had risen from the earth for the purpose of turning the wedding parade into a funeral pyre. Afraid that she might disappear into thin air, he advanced cautiously.

"No!" Asha cried, clasping the wall. And Puran's being was touched to the core by this cry of anguish. Gently he touched her shoulder, sure that she was a figment of his imagination. But when his hand felt Asha's cold body he awoke.

"Puran." Sham Lal's voice fell into his ears, telling him he was alive, but Sham Lal hadn't seen the ghost as yet.

Puran made up his mind in an instant. Picking up Asha in his arms, he came out onto the veranda.

"Asha, you can't leave me now," he said, clutching her to his breast. "Tell me, was this a conspiracy? Now I understand, now I know! But the game is over. Asha, let's run away from this vile world, let us go." He made his way hurriedly along the line of trees.

Asha was lifeless like a puppet; Puran held her gingerly as if she were a child, a precious toy he had lost and found with great difficulty. She had slipped from his hands and was lost. Now he had dragged her from the cremation grounds.

"But wait, Asha, wait a moment. Bhabi and her children, I wonder if they are all right, wait here for me, I'll be back soon." He propped her up like a doll against a tree and left.

Puran battled with fire while Asha struggled with water, that water which is more forceful than fire and which will dislodge a solid rock from its place.

Sham Lal had been following them. As soon as Puran was out of sight, he approached Asha.

"I see, this is indeed a fine plan. Well, Asha Devi, you must be congratulating yourself for snatching the morsel right from the mouth." Who knows what Sham Lal was made of; no matter what the situation, his behaviour remained the same.

"Rani dear, this is all very well, but the sacrifice is not right."

Asha lifted her head at the word 'sacrifice'.

"This sacrifice of Puran Singhji's life—this is a rather high price to pay."

Asha said nothing.

"Have you thought about the fact that he is married?"

Asha felt as if someone had axed her, but she did not move.

"He's married, and his life is now tied to Shanta Bai's … Shanta Bai … what has she ever done to you? How strange that a woman oppresses another woman and then charges a man with the crime. Just think, Asha Devi, what will happen now? You'll go with Puran Singh, but where? Far away from the love of his mother and father, deprived of his inheritance? And you think you're so valuable he will forsake the whole world for you? And even if he does, you're also a woman…"

Once again a storm was brewing in Asha's breast, the same storm in which a great many weak people are swept away.

"And what will you get? You will only be known as a whore."

That was something Asha had not thought of.

"You'll be like a whore who forced Puran to lose everything." Finding that his argument was taking effect, Sham Lal became more forceful.

"Asha Devi, I know you're a goddess, a devi. Listen, although I'm a fool, I'm better informed on the ways of this world."

"What should I … what should I do?"

"Leave this place right now. If you go away Puran will

never be able to find you. He was told you are dead. He will create a commotion, but if he doesn't find you he'll settle down eventually. He's a simple person, such a person can't be trusted. It would not be at all strange if he were to tire of you, too. If you go away he'll not remember you forever. Hadn't he forgotten you already? He was getting married, wasn't he? Listen to me, in a few days he will have forgotten you again. If you don't believe me, test him."

Asha got up. "I'll go."

"Yes, you'd better hurry, there's the road, it will take you to a village, it's not far, you can take a train from there to your village. Do you need money?" Sham Lal handed her something from his wallet.

"Remember what I have said. If Puran doesn't forget you, you can hit me a hundred times with a shoe, all right? I'm doing this for your own good, hurry up now, before someone comes along."

Struggling through thorny bushes, avoiding ditches, Asha ran. In the distance she heard Puran's voice. "Asha, Asha!" He was calling her. She stuffed her fingers in her ears and clenched her teeth. The fire had turned cold, but the embers continued to smoulder.

Peace

If you grind something and dust it off, does it disappear? You whitewash the walls, but in no time the paint is peeling again. You put a silver coating on the brass, but before long the silver wears off and the brass is only brass again. And here's a wound, you swathe it in bandages, but does it cease to be a wound? Yes, it ceases to be a wound, it festers and turns into a sore instead.

Unable to find Asha, Puran stumbled and fell. And he fell at the right moment, or else he would have found himself taking the road on which Asha was dragging herself. The commotion resulting from the fire, the upheaval of emotions and the force of the fall he took on the cold earth on such a chilly night—all of this reduced Puran to a state of inertia which lasted several days. His fever, his headaches and the weight of his family's anxiety seemed to clog his brain like smoke rising slowly from a charcoal fire. Ahh, how foolish he was! He had become such a nuisance. He reviewed his behaviour again. Was there any difference between him and a madman? And so he decided that he would fall into the terrible chasm called the world and cease to offer resistance. He no longer trusted his own judgement, and he was tired of the ever-recurring lectures. Letting go was a source of such peace, he could feel himself becoming completely submerged in it. Whatever medication was given to him he accepted willingly; when someone made him laugh, he laughed, and when he was asked to sit, he obeyed. And thus, led by others, he began to live. It was as if he were floating alone in a calm, quiet river.

"Puran, why don't you read something," Bare Bhaiya suggested one day, and like a dutiful child he settled down with a book. Who knows how much he read. What an interesting book that was, what a great deal of information it contained!

Flowers, red, red flowers, fire, the frigid earth and buried in it that simple, pale face. Those sad eyes, the cremation grounds and that funeral pyre!

"Puran, you're reading the dictionary?" Bhabi asked in surprise.

"Let's play something, Puran, let's play a game of carom."

How the striker hits the checker, Puran mused, and whoosh! it falls into the pocket. And the striker is off again, racing across the carom board. 'Got it!' Black and white checkers, one that's red like a drop of blood—there, that's gone, too.

"You silly boy! You're hitting my checkers," Bhabi said,

laughing. But then her eyes fell on Puran's lost child's face, and she became sad.

He's like a checker that's forced into the pocket by the striker and then retrieved and replaced on the carom board. When a person is cremated, do the ashes drift away from the cremation grounds and return? And does she stare at him again with tired eyes? And why were they giving him one drug after another? Oh ... he was sick. He must be, or why else? After all, people must have his good at heart or they would not be making him take all this medication. How everyone loved him! And his wife? Oh, he had forgotten about her. He had circled the sacred fire with her at his side. That's right. But he didn't know what to do with her now. She was his wife, so what should he do with her? That's right, he will go to her tomorrow, yes, definitely and then, and then, he will go to her ... they had walked around the sacred fire, hadn't they?

But the memory of circling the sacred fire made his head spin. Why had they gone around the fire? Once he had longed to walk around it, he had even teased Bhola's aunt that he wanted to marry her. Bhola's aunt. Like the black and white checkers she had fallen into a hole and, along with her tattered garments, she had been burnt. But these souls return from the cremation grounds, and those loving eyes become suspended in the air right next to you, the same quiet, shy eyes which once chattered impishly with you.

Why did he go and sit by the carom board last night? Why did he stare at it? Unseen hands twirled the striker, hit the checkers with it, making them fall into the pockets while he watched silently. And how sweet their faces were, just like the faces of Bhola's aunt, Chamki, and Asha. Asha, who was afraid of a baby frog, the timorous, frightened young girl!

And he would go to the drawer and open it, the drawer where those flowers still lay, the colour of congealed, dried blood now, but within seconds they burst into flames.

Chamki's face, the one Puran had last seen glowing like embers, would dance among the flowers and he would fall into a chair, upturning it as he sank into it. And then, for no apparent reason, Shanta would start sobbing and he would be given more drugs, but there was peace. Complete peace, the kind of peace that sits upon the undisturbed waters of a putrid, stagnant pond. Peace, silent and weary like death.

Stubbornness

For a few days Shanta continued to be bashful, but gradually she started giving Puran his medication and said a few words like, 'Lie down,' 'Get up,' 'Eat something.' However, she said no more than this nor did Puran understand any more. He was not mad; he ate, he drank, he dressed. But every once in a while he did develop a fever, cough or headache. This was the extent of his illness. If he were deranged would he not turn violent? The same Puran, who at one time thundered like a cloud and stormed, was now a docile person. And people still complained? Did he ever harm anyone? Could he ever harm anyone?

"Puran, why don't you talk to Shanta?" Finding him in good spirits one day, Bhabi ventured to ask. This was the same Puran and she was the same Bhabi.

"Me? Oh … but I do, Bhabi."

"Listen. No man mourns in this manner. Women have the prerogative to jump onto the funeral pyre and burn, but a man must stand firm even when he is crushed from all sides. The rules are not the same for all of us."

"Bhabi, why should I be mourning? I'm married, everything has been done. It's just that I don't feel very well."

"No, you've been sicker than this in the past. And you're not really sick, you're only imagining all this. Puran, just look at Shanta, see how unhappy she is. She has a heart too, you know, and you never say a word to her."

"Me? I speak to her, Bhabi." Puran indeed spoke to her, but what Bhabi was referring to was something else. After all, why was Shanta unhappy? All any Hindu wife wanted was to have a husband, and she had a husband. So what other goodies did she require? He was not a philanderer, he wasn't absent from home at night, he didn't hit her, didn't sell her jewellery in order to buy alcohol, didn't have eyes for other women, so what spiritual anguish was he causing her? Why did she go about looking like the very soul of suffering? A woman is a dissembler by nature. Especially those women who think they have inherited the right to consider themselves pure and chaste. But wait until the husband becomes old or sick; the treatment meted out to him is reminiscent of the way a butcher treats a cow whose milk has dried up. These are the women who, at the slightest pretext, turn to prostitution and then ask for the world's sympathy. What a good custom that was when they were burned like bugs on funeral pyres, or else the world today would have been overpopulated with prostitutes.

Puran was punishing her, but this was such a Mahatma Gandhi-ish punishment that no one had the gall to reprimand him. They had forced him to marry, but making him laugh or cry was not something they could control, and actually he was sick. As he lay slumped on the cold earth on the night of the wedding, a chill enveloped and bound his whole body and now that chill had travelled to his lungs.

"If a person doesn't feel very well, how can you expect him to laugh for no reason?" Puran said evasively and pulled the blanket over his head.

"It's up to you, but you should pay some attention to her. She was at her mother's for almost three months and you..." Bhabi knew Puran was not listening to anything she was saying.

"Shanta, watch over Puran, my dear. Do you see how lost he looks?" Bhabi played her other card. Shanta lowered her head and remained silent. If there was sap in the leaves, would things not have been altogether different to begin with?

"The doctors have assured us there's nothing to worry about. A stubborn man always likes to have his way, it's just a matter of a few more days. You should try and talk to him."

"Bhabiji, he doesn't reply when I say something, it's as if he hasn't heard me. And if I speak too much he covers his face with his blanket. You don't know him." Shanta was a woman and all the weapons she had at her disposal she had used already. She wasn't a man so she wasn't going to climb onto Puran's chest and force him to listen to her.

"There's a letter from Mataji." Puran was silently looking at some pictures in the newspaper. Shanta treid to distract him. "She's written that we should come for Holi."

Puran was gazing at a picture of a goat balancing all four hooves on a small peg. Animals have more gumption than humans. "Hunh," he mumbled, whether in response to Shanta's query or as a reaction to the picture, who could tell.

"She'd like you to come also. She's written that we should both go." Shanta felt like screaming.

"Should I go alone?" she continued patiently.

"Hunh, hunh," Puran nodded.

"You're … always like this … what I have done to you that you should hate me so?" Shanta could no longer hold her tears in check.

"I … Shanta … I…" He was frightened by her tears and dropped the newspaper in alarm.

"It's not my fault that my parents burdened you with my person, but …" Her voice cracked.

"What are you saying? Shanta, I'm not well," Puran said shamefacedly. How could Shanta continue crying before a man who was so easily frightened? After she left, Puran returned to the picture of the goat. Suddenly he was engulfed by feelings of anxiety; leaning his head against the back of his chair, he sat unmoving for a long time. In the evening he developed a cold following an attack of sneezing.

What, after all, was the matter? He thought long and hard, but he was unable to come up with an answer. Finally he gave up thinking. The moment he focused on a thought his head swam. So he had chosen peace. What pleasure there was in this peace; we are lying here in contentment while people are tossing on live coals.

"Oh dear, Shantaji is hiding in her room again. Always hiding, isn't she?" Mahesh came in unnoticed and startled Shanta. She dried her eyes hastily.

"Ram, Ram! Tears? Are you crying, Shanta? There, I'm not speaking to you." Lowering his bulky frame into a chair, Mahesh grimaced.

"Why, you're always shedding tears ... I agree that ... but ..." He muttered to himself. "I wish I could shake up Puran and throw him out. Shanta, do you know how I feel when I see you cry? My blood boils!" And indeed Mahesh had gallons of blood in his body.

"It's my destiny to weep forever," Shanta said wearily.

"What? What kind of destiny would that be? Get rid of it, throw it into the fire, I say. Listen, you create your own destiny, do you understand?"

"No one can create their own destiny, that's a silly idea, Mahesh Bhaiya."

"Whether we create a good destiny or a bad one is a matter of choice. But Shanta, I can't bear to look at your mournful face." Mahesh gazed at her fondly through half-shut eyes.

"Then don't look," Shanta retorted playfully.

"I shouldn't look? What a thing to say! As if it's in anyone's control to look or not to look."

"Of course, if you think something isn't nice you should..." Shanta turned her face away.

"Shanta, are you pretending or don't you really know what's in my heart?" The colour receded from Mahesh's face. "Shanta, how can I tell you, oh, you..."

Shanta continued to silently count the flowers on the cushion in her lap.

If on such occasions women respond wildly like flaming fire-crackers, you should be aware that the move has gone awry. And if there's silence, then that silence is just silence. Shanta didn't have enough gall to glow like a fire-cracker, nor was Mahesh foolish enough to scatter seeds on fallow land.

Was Shanta going astray, then? Who knows what going astray really means. Sometimes we go astray and, without being aware, digress from the crooked path to the straight one; often the difference between the straight and crooked paths is barely discernible. As a matter of fact, the paths leading to heaven are usually tortuous and thorny, while on a straight road a person stumbles and wanders like a blind man without a guiding stick, and what's funny is that he doesn't even know it. Why do people always strive for the straight path? Straight paths are frequently dull, well-lit and flat. Taking this route even a donkey, if it isn't disturbed along the way, will arrive at its destination. But these crooked paths, littered with unseen pits, hidden thorns, sharp stones, pain, heartache, where does one encounter these?

Shanta too was faced with two paths. One on which she was walking, on which she was rolling along like a true Hindu wife who worships her husband, as a good daughter, a chaste and pure woman, rolling along like a ball of loose dirt. Actually, like something worse. She had been burning in this cold funeral pyre for nearly a year. If only she, like Puran, were afflicted with a malady. She was afflicted, but what kind of affliction was this that constantly excited her being, making her body even more voluptuous, her eyes more unrestrained? Why did she quiver when she set eyes on Mahesh's body? Why did she feel as if that bulky figure was an engine threatening to crush her very being? But not crushing her so as to destroy her soul. Instead, it was like a pestle crushing a piece of sandalwood on a stone slab to make it more fragrant. Her soul, her mind, her heart were being pounded and poured into new moulds. Mahesh was not a philanderer, a profligate or an immoral person; he had never had a liaison with a low-caste woman, he had a wife and two children, and he was a family man. Then what force was this that pulled Shanta towards him? Just as your nostrils flare when the aroma of delicious food enters your nose and you inhale that fragrance so deeply it reaches all the way to your stomach, so the doors to Shanta's soul opened as soon as the sound of Mahesh's footsteps reached her ears. And she gathered into the depths of her heart his every utterance and every nuance of voice.

Just as Radha was compelled by the sound of Krishna's flute to forsake everything, pick up her pitcher of butter and run to him, so Shanta, driven by the same sacred and pure emotion, was driven to Mahesh. And like a burdened corpse, Puran's being drowned in oblivion.

Some things happen so slowly. The new moon appears silently, on tip-toe, like a tiny, insignificant thorn and gradually, a little bit at a time, it becomes a full moon. No one sees it grow. Puran's eyes failed not only to see the moon, they also failed to see the flames that blazed around his own person. And if he had observed the flames he would not have understood their significance, or perhaps he saw and understood but feigned ignorance. Who knows how many deranged people there are who, under the guise of madness, laugh at our folly.

Mahesh was not a scoundrel so he had no reason to be wary of Puran. He would sit with Shanta and talk to her for hours in Puran's presence. But he spoke to her in a language that only the discerning can understand. Puran didn't pay too much attention to them. And why should he have, anyway? Once, only once, he saw something that struck him as odd. Mahesh was helping Shanta take off bangles that were really tight on her wrists, and suddenly a bangle broke and made her bleed. Mahesh didn't do it intentionally, but Puran was surprised to see him bend over and suck the wound clean. His face resembled that of a hungry dog, and Puran felt he was going to suck all the blood from her body. But when he saw that Shanta, instead of looking pale and weak, seemed to have bloomed, he was relieved. Another time he was caught by surprise when he chanced to see Mahesh and Shanta in the drawing-room. Shanta had been lying on a sofa with her face down. Suddenly Mahesh flipped her over and then scooped her up in his arms as if she were a flower. True, Mahesh's hands were large and long, but ... Puran examined his own hands; the skin was blotchy, and how crooked his fingers looked. He sat down on the sofa just to test something. First he gently turned the cushion upside down and then quickly lifted it up like a flower. His face glowed; slowly he put the cushion back in its place and gazed at it lovingly. He didn't like it when he caught his old servant, Lachman, staring at him oddly. Upset, he hurried to his room.

Puran's eyes had been blinded but others could see, and as for Lachman, he had eyes in his head that darted in all directions.

"Chote Bhaiya, there's something I've been wanting to say to you for a long time, I couldn't get a chance to say it before, but today I thought I'll say it," Lachman came and sat down at the doorstep.

"Hunh, what is it?" Puran said, counting the lines on the page before him.

"What can I say, master, don't you see? Don't you see how weak you've become?"

"Yes, Lachman, and I am taking my medicines regularly."

"Medicines? What medicines? I say something is wrong with Chote Bhaiya."

"What?" Puran was counting lines again. "It's the wrong medication? Well, why don't you suggest something then."

"You're asking me, master? Do you know what's happening in your home?" Lachman spoke in a loud voice.

"My home? Yes I do, Lachman, why?"

"Nothing! You know nothing!"

"All right, so I don't know. But is it necessary I should be aware of everything? And I admit you know everything. Now go and bring me some tea."

"Why not? If you won't pay any attention, someone else has to..."

"Lachman, bring me some tea. And don't make it too strong, don't make it jet-black like you did the other day."

"Chote Bhaiya," Lachman spoke with restraint, "do you know that you and..."

"Lachman, bring me my tea!" Puran threw his book down on the table like a stubborn child. He wanted to scream. Lachman had no idea what was going on in his heart.

"All right, master, all right, but..." Lachman left.

How much can anyone take? One day Arup Singh arrived in Puran's room.

"What are you doing, Puran?" Arup Singh intended to stay for a while so he took off his coat.

"Me? Nothing really, Bhaiya," Puran assumed a jovial tone.

"Puran Singh, you've been married for nearly two years now, but there hasn't been the slightest change in your behaviour. The doctor says you're not sick."

"The doctor's an idiot, Bhaiya," Puran said with a smile.

"He says you're feigning, that is, you're superstitious. Puran, come to your senses. Lachman was saying ... you're an intelligent man." He stopped suddenly.

"What was Lachman saying?" Puran was feeling better than usual.

"That ... that ... Puran, aren't you ashamed? You're a man, how can you tolerate all this?"

"Yes, Bhaiya, I'm a man. Who says I'm not? Look, these hands, these feet..." He extended his hands mockingly.

"Look, I eat, drink, what a big man I am, I got married and now, if Bhagwan so wishes…"

"Oh, Puran! Don't you have any shame?"

"Shame?" Puran broke into a laugh. "Why should I feel ashamed?"

"Listen, this has crossed all limits. I don't approve of Mahesh's visits and his association with Shanta."

"Why, Bhaiya?"

"Because Shanta is drifting towards sin."

"Sin? You mean because she's in love with Mahesh?"

"How easily you're saying this, as if it's no big thing," Arup said in surprise.

"If she loves Mahesh, let her, Bhaiya, please let her."

"Puran!"

"Listen, Bhaiya, she's in love, right? Let her be in love." Excited, Puran got up. "You have never loved, you have never loved in a way that … that you were consumed by. You loved, but how? When Bhabi's love was delivered into your lap then you learned to love, and…"

"Isn't she your wife? Tell me, isn't Shanta your wife?" Arup felt he was losing ground.

"She's my wife according to the pandit's mutterings, but …"

"Then stop her!" Arup thought that wives were like bicycles that could be stopped merely by applying the brakes.

"Stop her? No Bhaiya, if I can't give her love, how can I stop her from asking for it from someone else?" Puran was changing his aspect today. He was speaking in a slow, deliberate manner, saying all the things he had been thinking about for a very long time. He sat down to catch his breath.

"You've gone mad!" Bhaiya thundered.

"Yes, I've been mad for a long time." Puran seemed bent on taking his revenge.

"The family's honour is not dear to you?"

"I have no honour or shame, Bhaiya. I have lost the

capacity to feel. Nothing is dear to me anymore." He smiled bitterly and began drumming his fingers on the carom board. Once in a while, from the corner of his eye, he stole a look at Arup who was pacing the floor like a wounded cobra. Puran piled the checkers on the board. Today the feeling of victory was making him restless. He was taking his revenge with such passion. Sometimes a wounded sparrow innocently becomes the attacker. A calf must be sacrificed in order to ensnare a lion. Puran had given up his life in order to win the battle today—the calf lost its life but the lion was irrevocably snared.

At that moment Lachman came in and handed Puran a note. Taking it up to the light, Puran read it. If you suddenly receive the news that India has gained independence, complete independence, and you've been chosen president, how would you feel? Or if the British hear that a large chunk has fallen off from the sun and landed on the entire German army, burning it to a cinder, and Hitler has been torn to shreds by a ferocious bear, how would they feel? That is exactly how Puran felt. But he wasn't a mean-spirited man. He read the letter silently, and saying, "Here, take this," he put it down before Arup and lit a cigarette.

His hands shook but a smile played on his lips, as if he had just received the disturbing results of an important exam.

"*I'm leaving … I am nothing to you, but still … Shanta.*"

The paper fell from Arup's hands. It annoyed Puran to see that although it was his wife who had run away, it was Arup who was flustered.

"It happened finally … she left … Mahesh!" Arup held his head in his hands and shook from head to foot. Only he knew how he and his wife would be brought to task because of this incident. He glanced at Puran. In a flash the whole story unspooled before his eyes like a film reel: Puran's face which was like a blooming flower, his eyes wild with merriment that he longed to see again. He observed him closely: this was the same Puran, his younger brother, Bhabi's favourite brother-in-law, Amma's spoilt son, the children's beloved uncle. He had become a smelly, rotting dose of medication. If he hadn't been spoilt would he have been so obstinate? It was true that ever since his childhood he had been used to having his way and this was why he now clamoured for the stars in the sky.

"Shanta is an intelligent girl. Why would she have continued to seek pearls in a mound of dirt?" Puran broke the silence. He was attempting to curb his sense of victory.

"What are you saying, Puran? What has happened to you?" Arup didn't know what else to say.

"He's dead, your Puran has been dead for a long time. Now it's this dead Puran's turn. You can say whatever you want, Bhaiya, but the soul died ages ago. Now only this dead clay is present, if it can be of any help, please use it. But remember, Bhaiya, this body is hollow, there's not an iota of life in it." Puran smiled triumphantly.

"I ... always regarded you as my child, Puran, and you talk as if I did everything deliberately..."

"But Bhaiya, have I complained? Whatever you did was all right. Not one but a thousand Purans could be sacrificed to save the family's honour." Puran hadn't forgotten how to be sarcastic.

"Puran, my child..." Arup choked with emotion.

"Bhaiya, what's there to cry about? Be grateful that the family has been saved from dishonour. However, your son is growing up now, just make sure he doesn't make the kind of mistake I did."

You can make any numbers of sacrifices, but God doesn't budge. Why does He have such an insatiable appetite? His stomach is like the pit of hell, it's never full. Every day He devours thousands, those sick from cholera, those chewed up by tuberculosis, still others dying from the plague. But nothing happens to Him; His demand remains unchanged, He does not even suffer from indigestion. Now, what had poor Raja Sahib ever done to harm anyone? Whose cow had he snitched that his daughter-in-law should run away? What crime had Arup's innocent wife committed that she should cry and go without food for four days and grey hair should suddenly sprout at Arup's temples?

Arup held his head between his hands. As a matter of fact, the whole family held its head between its hands; everyone was trying to make sense of what had happened. What now? What will be the fate of Arup's children? The family's name had suffered dishonour in the eyes of the sisters in-law as well. What a terrible thing this honour is; the more you serve it, the more difficult it becomes. A pox on it!

As if in vengeance, Puran became seriously ill. He spat blood again and again during the course of the day, and there came a time when all of them forgot about Shanta and tried instead to snatch Puran back from the jaws of death. The mother's forehead was lowered innumerable times at Bhagwan's feet and Arup, the commander-in-chief of the family, concentrated on protecting the castle. But the castle, it seemed, had resolved to bring destruction upon itself.

When I was a little girl I once saw a small shrub growing on the roadside. 'I'll plant it in my garden,' I said, and tried to pull it out with all my might. The weak and tiny roots shrieked, the trunk stiffened, but I succeeded in finally pulling out the shrub. The stubborn roots remained in their place. I brought the shrub home, planted it in my garden and nurtured it, giving it bucketfuls of water, but it soon dried up. Puran's family had also severed the roots, but just imagine their obstinacy! They were bent on replanting the tree and making it bear fruit. There is a special kind of tree that one can plant with its roots absent, but Puran was just an ordinary, weak plant. Then! Suddenly someone remembered the roots and a graft was suggested. Everyone convinced Arup to go to the village and bring Asha back.

After stumbling from place to place, Asha had finally found refuge in her village. When she returned to her old, crumbled dwelling, her first instinct was to set the house on fire and burn herself with it. But soon the people in the village got word of her return and her friends came running to greet her. She was assaulted by questions. She felt as if she had just awakened from a long dream. When she thought of Puran, it was as if she were thinking of the shiny moon stuck to the soaring heavens. She didn't like moonlit nights any more.

Ramu's mother once again began showering her with attention, while Ramu strutted about with his hair generously oiled. Asha observed his behaviour and remembered Puran's bright, untarnished face, his hair which was always clean and shining without the aid of cream or oil, his fragrant, unblemished hands. And here was this pickled, plastered down hair, hands roughened and afoul with the odour of cheap tobacco, and his vile desires! If a frog decided to make eyes at a nightingale, people would be sure to remark that the frog was out of its depth.

"Puran's condition has worsened," Arup said without mentioning the drama involving Mahesh and Shanta. "Mataji is alone and your Bhabi..." He blushed.

"Is Shantaji well, Bare Bhaiya?"

"Yes, but ... for Puran's care..."

"I have no objection to coming, but Ramu's mother can't see very well and..." Asha was making excuses. If Shanta was there and certainly there was no dearth of servants, why did they suddenly want her? Someone eats the mangoes while Asha is left counting the leaves.

"Shanta is ... at her mother's..."

"Oh? Is she ... expecting?" Asha's heart lurched.

"Yes, that is, her mother is sick," Arup fumbled. "You

come home with me and you'll understand everything. Asha—" he cut himself short.

When Puran heard that Asha was coming, he became inflamed. "How long are you people going to play games with me?" he muttered. "Won't you even let me die in peace?"

But Bhabi silenced him with a stare. In the evening his fever soared and he became delirious. "Such fire! Red, red flames … Bhabi, draw the curtains, these red flowers are like thorns in my heart … tell Chamki my head is swimming, tell her to stop dancing so wildly, tell her not to open my drawer, she's not coming back, why should she come back? Will I eat her up?"

He smiled to himself. "Such a frail little girl, Bhabi, don't make her work so hard, tell Mataji not to make her work so hard."

"Be quiet, Puran, the doctor says you shouldn't talk so much." He frightened Bhabi with his ravings.

"The doctor is an idiot, what does he know? The bastard, he won't let me speak. Bhabi, what will she say when she sees me? Don't tell her I'm sick, do you hear … what will she think?"

"Asha is here, Puran."

A flush spread over Puran's lifeless face. Bhabi was teasing him. The thought of Asha again filled his heart with a sweet and timorous feeling. He felt as if his dead self was being slowly tickled back to life. He glanced at his scrawny hands: how ugly they were! But why were his feet so smooth and healthy in appearance? He was disturbed by the sight of healthy feet attached to his thin, spindly legs; their roundness revolted him. He came to life when Bhabi left the room. She was so naughty! He got out of bed and stumbled to the mirror. He felt as if the roof had caved in on him; skin and bones, a corpse from the grave, he looked like the dead body of a madman that had been propped up in front of the mirror. The mischief that had earlier danced on his face at the thought of seeing Asha confronted him now like a frightening ghost arisen from the cremation grounds.

He examined nature's handiwork closely. Cautiously he touched the veins in his temples and his neck. There were so many toiletries on the dresser, but there wasn't one thing among them that he felt he could use to adorn this corpse. He picked up the comb but found it impossible to struggle with his hair which had become thick and unmanageable. There was a sound at the door and he turned swiftly.

Asha saw the frightening vision and held herself back with great difficulty. But she ran forward when she saw him stumble. With his thin, reedy hands he grasped her like a hungry animal, his protruding ribs jabbed her chest like knives, but she summoned up all her strength and drew him closer to the bed. He thought she was trying to get away from him so he began crushing her savagely.

This was the same Puran whose slightest touch set Asha's body afire, making it glow. But today it seemed as though someone was enflaming her body by lashing it with icy whips. Forgetting everything she clung to him without shame. The time for modesty and diffidence was over. She embraced his bony, lifeless hands, and placing her head on his hollow chest sought some signs of warmth there. She felt as if an engine inside that skeletal frame was being set in motion; stifled, choked heat, a quiet tumult like molten fire inside a volcano that snarls like a wounded cat, and then violent tremors which seemed to have decided to upturn everything. In one jolt all order became chaos, the molten lava burst and, startled, she stood up. Her head was swimming, she felt she had been swung around several times and then flung on a flat plain. She didn't try to steady herself. Instead, she quickly went to the door and bolted it from the inside and, picking up the bottle of massage oil from the table, she gulped down its entire contents. Coughing and spitting, she quickly tidied the bed.

Then she pushed all the chairs and tables around the bed, pulled out clothes from the closets and spread everything on the chairs and tables. As she slipped her hand into the middle drawer of the dresser she felt she had been stung by a snake; the dessicated red flowers were still there, wrapped in a white cloth. She picked up each petal lovingly and arranged the flowers on Puran's chest. After this she picked up the night lamp from the window-sill and sprinkled kerosene from it on the clothes that were strewn around the bed. Then she climbed onto the bed like a new bride. Ahh ... there was no time for modesty. She was not even repelled by the wetness of the lifeless blood that had trickled down his chin. She felt as though someone was raking her heart with sharp nails. Her hands shook. She put a lighted match to the kerosene that surrounded them and lay down in Puran's embrace, next to the dried out flowers that danced on his chest like a bed of red tulips.

Obsession
(*Saudai*)

Buzdil, *the film starring Kishore Sahu, Premnath and Nimmi, produced and directed by Ismat's husband Shahid Latif, is the basis for this novel.*

1

CHANDAR slid down the banister and landed on the floor with a loud thud. As always, Masi's heart lurched.

"You wretch, if you miss your step you'll break your bones," she said, striking her forehead. But Chandar didn't listen. He slithered down like a turtle every day and every day Masi's heart took a plunge.

"You troublemaker, one day you'll fall on your face and all your teeth will break and get stuck in your throat! Nobody listens to me, what am I to do?"

Chandar curled his upper lip until it was touching his nose, then with a hissing sound he swooped down on the dining table.

He loved teasing Masi. He had also made Pimo's life miserable. She was a year and a half younger than Chandar, but she regarded him as her guru. And what choice did she have? He dragged her by her tiny braids, tripped her again and again with his foot, pounded her dolls, and ordered her to obey his every command.

"Hold your nose and say salaam to me seven times."

"Walk on one leg and fetch me a glass of water! And I will not speak to you ever again if you spill a single drop."

Not speaking meant that he would give her a wallop every time he passed her and jostle her with his elbow, or pinch her nose. Experience had taught her that she couldn't win with Chandar. The only person he was afraid of was Barre Bhaiya. He regarded him as the world's greatest, most esteemed and most brilliant human being. Barre Bhaiya was a full fifteen years older than him and was so virtuous, so superior that it was impossible to utter one word against him.

That's why his name was Suraj. And when the rays of the sun fall on the moon only then does the moon begin to shine. If the Sun God was driven to anger, the face of Chandra would turn black like soot.

That was why Masi performed aarti before Suraj every morning and evening, because he was a god, and that's why she called Chandar a demon. Suraj had never beaten anybody or teased anyone, nor had he ever lied or stolen, and he had never played gulli danda or kabbadi with the boys on the street. His mother knew that there was not a single boy in the neighbourhood fit to socialise with Suraj. His companions were not people, they were princes and sadhus and other holy men who existed in fairy tales and fables.

Masi always sang Suraj's praises. It was common knowledge that she had decided he would marry her daughter, Usha, and that was why she toiled ceaselessly to mould him into the best of all sons-in-law. Constant praise had made him think so highly of himself that even if he wanted to indulge in any mischief, he would worry about losing his reputation, afraid that he would be regarded as an ordinary human being and cease to have praise piled on him. Masi would no longer perform aartis, Chandar and Pimo would stop being terrified of him, and then what would be left in the world for him? At this young age, respect was the only thing he possessed. He wasn't going to let anyone steal his treasure.

On her deathbed Mataji had held Pimo's and Chandar's hands and said to Suraj: "My son, you are now both father and mother to them, don't do anything that will make them stray from the right path. If the honour of the family is tarnished, my soul will never find peace."

Pitaji had passed away a year before that. He had rejected the rules of the world and lost everything after becoming involved with a woman of loose morals. Then he quarrelled with her, got drunk and was killed in a road accident.

Masi was a dear friend of Mataji. Her husband had also abandoned her and the two unhappy friends constantly poured homilies into Suraj's ears about virtuous living.

Masi was of the opinion that Suraj's father, Tarbhun Nathji, had not been raised properly. To begin with, his parents had loosened their reins, then he was married to a woman who lacked spirit and could never really control him which was why he had died young. For fifteen years Suraj was the only and most beloved child. Fearing her husband's lack of attention, the mother dug her claws into her son. Then fortune smiled on her and she had two more children, but neither received the same love as Suraj. Chandar and Pimo were raised by the servants.

Sermons were not considered enough to keep Suraj from going astray, so Maa had Suraj betrothed to Usha Rani and both she and Masi embarked on a campaign to nurture a blessed union. But before they could arrange the wedding, death overtook her.

When Maa died, Pimo was a year-and-a-half, Chandar was three and Suraj had just completed his eighteenth year. Burdened with such immense responsibility at such a young age, Suraj began to mature before his time. He had never been naughty, but now he became a complete sadhu. Afraid that he might fall into bad company in school, he was tutored at home. Maa had been dead for three years now, but not a day went by when Masi didn't tearfully recount the events surrounding her passing. Several times during the day she would repeat Maa's sayings. Chandar and Pimo had forgotten Maa, but Suraj felt her influence still and was also weighed down by Masi's authority.

Along with supervising Suraj, Masi kept a vigilant eye on Usha as well. She was to be the queen of the house some day, destined to be Suraj's Yogiya. Masi kept her busy with studying and embroidering. Someone who has been burnt by boiling milk learns to fear even the froth on the surface of buttermilk. Men are like monkeys; no matter how much you train them, teach them, the minute they get an opportunity they will climb back up a tree. And she wanted to teach Usha special tactics so that her husband would not be able to climb the tree, would stay on the straight and narrow. Compared to her mother, Usha was like a cow, she went in whichever direction her mother steered her.

Masi was not a dishonest person. She nursed her love for her friend with great dedication. Looked after her during her illness more diligently than a sister would. Even though she was mistress of everything in the house, she took nothing for herself. She did the work of four servants. Actually, the affairs of the bank and management of the estate were handled by Sitaramji. He was a very gracious, honest man who had devoted his life to religious exercise, austerity and celibacy, and was raising these three children as his own. But the rest of the belongings in the house and all the jewellery were in Masi's charge. Except for the jewellery the dying woman had placed in Masi's hands, there wasn't a single strand she had touched — what need did she have to, anyway? Maa had left all the jewellery for Suraj's wife. When Chandar and Suraj grew up she would see to their needs, why worry now? Suraj would handle everything. Who else besides Usha was Suraj's bride! Why did Masi need anything?

From a very young age Usha had begun to regard Suraj as the god of her heart. Ever since she was twelve or thirteen she had been taking care of Suraj's needs like a good wife. Without waiting for instructions from Masi, she would get hot water readied for his bath, supervise his change of clothing, and at mealtimes, arrange delicious morsels of food in his tray. Without his saying a word she would know whether he needed salt, a hot chilli or a glass of water. She embroidered chikan kurtas for him, knitted new styles of sweaters, and embroidered bouquets on his handkerchiefs.

It was her house after all; if something broke or was misplaced she scolded the servants just as the mistress of the house would.

By now Suraj had become used to being waited upon by her and regarding her as his, never questioning the attention she showered on him. But unlike other young men, he never teased her or looked at her amorously.

"He doesn't like behaving irresponsibly, he's not a vagabond, nor is my daughter a girl without morals," declared Masi. And if someone pointed to Suraj's lack of feeling towards Usha she would brush it off, saying, "Why, he's just like his mother."

It was Chandar who took after his father: restless and stubborn. It really didn't matter if he suffered an ill fate. Satwanti's womb wouldn't have been damageed if he hadn't been born — Suraj, equal to a hundred children, was present, wasn't he? When the time came everything would be taken care of. Masi was confident of her ability to keep things in order, and she was aware that, if and when the need arose, she would be able to teach Usha the art of ensnaring her man. As a matter of fact she was already doing her best.

"My child, even Bhagwan, when you serve him, will look kindly on you, and Suraj is just a man."

Masi herself had never truly waited on her own husband. That poor man was not her match anyway. Even if he had been a police inspector or a deputy instead of a clerk, he wouldn't have been able to save himself from her clutches; she would have outshone Sati-Savitri as the dutiful wife.

As was his custom, Chandar jumped over the furniture and attacked the dining table.

"Hai, hai, Chandar!"

"What is it, Masi?"

"Where are you sitting?"

"On the chair, Masi."

"Arre, whose chair are you sitting on?"

"Oh, on Barre Bhaiya's." Chandar leapt up as if he had tainted a god's throne in a temple, and plonked himself on the chair next to it.

Masi looked respectfully in the direction of the staircase from where the Sun God was about to descend.

"Stop, Chandar!" Masi admonished when she saw him reaching for the fruit. "Wait for Barre Sarkar, you good-for-nothing. How greedy you are!"

Stand at attention, ready to pay your respects!

Mahabali approaches.

The atmosphere was imbued with the power of his presence. Receiving a signal from her mother, Usha quickly jumped up and, pulling her dupatta over her head, stationed herself like a puppet at the bottom of the stairs. First the sound of footsteps was heard on the stairs, then the Sun God raised his head in the east.

Big, deep set eyes, thick wavy hair of which a lock trembled on the forehead, a sharp nose. Dressed in a foamy white dhoti, a loose kurta of heavy silk, a brown pashmina shawl draped on his shoulders, he made a radiant appearance at the top of the stairs. (He had borrowed this mode of dress from the Bengalis.) Then, with measured steps he came down the stairs.

"Namaskar," Usha's soft voice rustled.

"Namaskar." He looked past her in the distance and joined his palms together, brushing the lock of hair on his forehead with his hand as he did so.

"May you live long, my precious son, may you live a thousand years!" Masi rushed towards him to ward off the evil eye, but he cleverly evaded her grasp for fear that she might disturb the lock of hair which he had arranged carefully, standing before the mirror for a long time, but which gave the impression of having carelessly fallen over his forehead.

Every morning it was this very lock that Masi threatened

to fix and this really made him angry. But he never allowed his anger to show because gods don't get angry.

Chandar was starving. As soon as Barre Sarkar sat down he pounced on the food.

Which was when Pimo hopped in, made a face at Chandar and dropped into a chair.

"Pimo Rani."

"Ji?"

"What did you forget to do today?"

"Uhh… "

"All right, say namaskar first," Masi ordered and Pimo immediately put her palms together and like Chandar, proceeded to stuff her mouth with food.

Masi quickly picked up the plate of ladoos and placed it in front of Suraj.

"Let Barre Bhaiya eat first. My dear boy, I'll bring some fresh pooris for you. I don't trust the servants, I'll make them myself. Actually, Usha is the one who makes them every morning. Here, girl, peel a pomegranate for Sarkar."

Keeping in mind the future relationship between them she discouraged Usha from calling him Barre Bhaiya.

"But why do you have to bother? Have all the servants died?"

"Arre, my son, what bother? Hai, how much you think of me! My dearest child, if your Sati Savitri mother had not taken care of me, where would we be now?" Masi immediately began sniffling. Her weeping always amused Pimo and Chandar and they burst out laughing.

"Here, have an orange," Masi said when she saw Chandar reaching for one. Her tears had disappeared.

"No, he'll cough at night." Suraj pushed Chandar's hand away.

It amused Barre Sarkar to see her change gears like this, and he would quickly place a handkerchief on his nose that would begin to twitch in anticipation of the laughter that threatened to erupt. How could he possibly laugh?

Masi left to fetch fresh pooris, Usha bent down to tie Pimo's shoelaces while Pimo fed Tommy biscuits under the table. For one moment it was all clear. There were fresh, fragrant ladoos on the table. The child hiding in Barre Sarkar's heart leapt out and he snatched up two ladoos in a flash. Just then he heard Masi's footsteps — no time to pop them into his mouth and not possible to put them back on the plate, so he deposited them in his pocket.

"Hai, Chandar!" Seeing that some ladoos were missing Masi began beating her chest. "Why, you scoundrel! The doctor has forbidden you to eat sweets and you gulped down not one but two ladoos!"

"I didn't eat a single one!" Chandar protested.

"And now you're lying, you bad boy! Show me your hands."

Chandar shoved his hands under Masi's nose. She recoiled.

"Open your mouth."

After a thorough search she concluded that he had swallowed the ladoos without chewing them first. She grabbed his ear.

"That's enough, Masi, he made a mistake. Forgive him, he won't do it again," Barre Sarkar said.

"I'm being blamed for nothing, Masi, I didn't take the ladoos."

"Then Pimo must have eaten them." Barre Sarkar glared at Pimo.

"No, Barre Bhaiya, I didn't. Ask Usha Didi."

"Usha Rani certainly didn't eat them, so where did they go?" Barre Sarkar turned his large black eyes towards Chandar and glowered at him. Fearfully, Chandar lowered his eyes.

"You see? You see how guilty he looks, the wretch! Here my son, eat." Masi pushed the plate of ladoos towards Suraj.

"No, Masi, you know I don't like sweets," Suraj said, lovingly caressing the ladoos in his pocket. "Chandar, if you do something so inexcusable again – well, I won't tolerate it."

Chandar and Pimo exchanged knowing glances and quickly slipped away. Masi and Usha brought out the ledger containing the daily accounts.

"Pudina, three annas, lauki four annas… tori …" Masi rendered an account of every little item in order to impress Barre Sarkar so that he would see how profitable this relationship with her and Usha was. But Barre Sarkar only wanted to claw her face.

"Ginger, one and a half pao… garam masala —"

"Oh…" Barre Sarkar suddenly and dramatically seized his head with his hands. Masi jumped up.

"Ai hai, my child, what's the matter?"

"Headache … I have a headache."

"Arri, Usha, don't stand there like — tell Munshiji —"

"No, don't send for the doctor. Get my pills from my drawer."

"Go, you silly girl," she pushed Usha out and quickly began to fan him with a corner of her sari.

"Wa … ter," Barre Sarkar said, tossing his head. Masi ran to get a glass while he calmly retrieved a ladoo from his pocket and dropped it into his mouth. Closing his eyes, he began chewing it with pleasure.

When Masi returned with a glass of water, panting and out of breath, and Usha arrived with the bottle of pills, he gave them a startled look as if he didn't know who they were.

"Your headache … pills … water," Masi reminded him.

"Water? Pills? Oh, I see. No need any more."

And he turned casually to the paper. Both mother and daughter were left baffled by his behaviour and were sorry that they had lost an opportunity to serve.

Barre Sarkar took great pleasure in frequently tricking them like this. He was so clever that he could hoodwink anyone and then, remembering what he had done, would laugh heartily and feel very pleased with himself.

2

"It's true. If you dig a hole with your finger a dwarf will come out of the earth." Chandar made up a story.

"Hey, Ram! Then he'll play with me, Chot Bhaiya?"

Pimo had barely scratched an inch of earth with her tiny finger when her nails, filled with dirt, began to hurt.

"Chot Bhaiyaji."

"What?"

"Have you ever seen a fairy?"

"Many times."

"Oh, you haven't, you liar."

"It's true, I swear."

"Well then, show me too."

"You're a fool, you won't be able to see a fairy."

"Why?"

"Because I said so."

"Chot Bhaiya."

"What?"

"My finger hurts."

"I told you, didn't I, that you wouldn't be able to dig a hole."

"Unhuh … fairy, Bhaiyaji."

"All right … look over there."

"Where?" Scared, she edged closer to him.

"There … there … on the pomegranate tree. See it?"

"Ohh…that's just a pifon."

"Not a pifon silly, a pigeon. In reality it's a fairy."

"A fairy? How do you know?"

"Well, I just know, that's all. It's a fairy. Be very still and you'll see that the bird will flip around and turn into a fairy."

But unfortunately Pimo sneezed just then and the pigeon flew away.

"You see, you silly girl! Why did you have to sneeze? If she had become angry she would have waved her wand and turned you into a mouse."

"The fairy?"

"Yes."

"She turns people into mice if she gets angry?"

"Of course."

"Chot Bhaiya."

"Yes."

"Let's go home, I'm scared." Pimo began whimpering. "I don't want to see any fairies."

But Chandar was staring at the pile of leaves next to the tree. There was a tiny pink hand lying among the leaves.

"A hand!" Chandar darted across but Pimo stumbled and fell and started bawling. Chandar stopped to help her up and his fear diminished. Mistaking it for a flower, a butterfly had alighted on the hand.

"Look, Pimo," Chandar said, grabbing her.

"A hand? Who left it here?"

"Definitely a fairy. Left it here by mistake," Chandar said.

"Where is the fairy?"

"She flew away."

"But left her hand here?"

"That's what it looks like. She forgot it. Pick it up, Pimo."

"No, Chot Bhaiya, let's go home." Pimo was terrified.

"Arre, don't be afraid, you fool. Wait, let's see."

Chandar picked up a twig and cautiously touched the hand. A tiny finger moved and with a loud croak a wild duck suddenly flapped out of the pile of leaves. Terrified, they both fled, but Chandar bravely returned and moved the leaves with a stick. Brown curly hair and a fair-complexioned face emerged, and a pair of large, frightened eyes opened. Tiny lips quivered. A two or two-and-a-half year old girl, dressed in rags, rose to her feet, brushing off leaves from her body as she did so. The two children froze.

"You're a fairy, aren't you?" Chandar asked apprehensively.

The girl nodded.

"You see!" Chandar turned to Pimo triumphantly.

"Where are your wings?" Pimo asked, emboldened.

The girl looked around her timidly and then began to whimper.

"You fool, now see what you've done, you made her cry. Here, fairy, do you want a toffee?"

The girl shook her head.

"Oh, the poor thing is hungry." Pimo's eyes brimmed with tears. "She doesn't have wings, Chọt Bhaiya, how will she fly?"

"Don't cry, the poor thing has lost her wings, but new wings will sprout."

"Don't cry, fairy."

"What should we do now?"

"Let's take her home. Fairy, will you come with us?"

The girl shook her head again but the two children dragged her with them. Rani, the potter's wife, started screaming when they returned.

"Hai, Masiji, Chote Bhaiya has brought home some girl!"

"Girl? Have you lost your mind? It must be one of the milkman's daughters, get her out of here, the wretch."

"Ai ji, they won't let me throw her out, they're hitting me, the two of them."

"Arre, which two?"

"Ai ji, Bua, it's Chote Bhaiya and Pimo. Let them be, Masi, tell the police and they'll come and take her away."

But the children set up a real commotion. Clung to Suraj's feet and started weeping.

Masi ground her teeth and said, "Well, I'll see how Chandar stops Thanedar Sahib!"

"We'll beat up the police, too!" Chandar declared, waving his hockey stick in the air. Like a brave knight he was bent on protecting the fairy.

"You'll be handcuffed, my boy."

"We'll break the handcuffs!"

But when the police arrived and made inquiries they discovered that the girl didn't belong to anyone in the village. Who knows who had abandoned her in the woods.

"She must be illegitimate," Masi decided, "take her to the orphanage."

"Let her stay here until we find someone who claims her," Barre Sarkar said, "and when the children get tired of her she can be sent off to the orphanage."

But the girl was indeed a fairy. No one came to claim her and she continued to live at the house. Usha Rani was still playing with dolls so she cut up old clothes and stitched shiny garments for her. For a few days she slept with Rani, the potter's wife, in the small room next to the kitchen, and then started sleeping on the floor in the children's room. A few nice words to Didi, and the children were able to have new clothes made for her. Sometimes Masi would get upset and exclaim, "Who knows whether the wretch is a bhangi's child or a chamar's offspring, eating at our table with us." But the girl not only gained Chandar and Pimo's devotion, Usha Rani too had become very fond of her. And so the children's demands continued to be met. Suraj did not object to her presence, but she was terrified of him and ran to hide in some corner the moment she saw him. Or she would seek refuge behind Chandar or Pimo, or bury her face in Usha's dupatta. If she was crying and he appeared, she would be stunned into silence, and if she was laughing she would clamp her hand on her mouth. When Barre Sarkar saw the overwhelming effect he had on her he swelled with pride.

Usha dressed her up in beautiful clothes as if she were a little she-monkey and named her Chandni. Chandar's Chandni. After all it was Chandar who had found her.

Chandar and Pimo were crazy about her. Sometimes they would pass their fingers over her shoulders gingerly to see if she had sprouted wings — she might fly away if she had!

Despite Masi's opposition she continued to receive an education because she was always with the children.

"I don't know why my heart is filled with fear," Masi would heave a long sigh and say. "It's not a good omen that rubbish from the wayside should fill one's eyes. Who knows what trouble this girl will be when she grows up."

Barre Sarkar was a person of superior qualities so it was just him and his books of philosophy. The only time he left the house was to ride or swim. The estate was large. The canal was theirs, the woods were theirs as well, and the lake, too. If only Chandar had been closer to him in age he wouldn't feel so terribly lonely. How close Chandar and Pimo were. Sometimes he felt such an urge to laugh loudly like them, climb trees and run about, but his overly mature self came in the way of all that.

He never quite understood Usha. Bashful, she seemed to have no other use except to steal furtive looks at him. The thoughts that arose in his mind when he saw her growing up scared him because he thought they were dirty. He began to be annoyed by her presence. Chandar was such a fool. Didn't like studying, was naughty and harassed everyone, especially Masi who couldn't handle him at all. She was convinced he would grow up to be a bandit, and given half a chance would squander the family's wealth.

One day the children were playing ball in the garden. Chandar was beating the girls at the game and suddenly the ball slipped from Chandni's hands and landed close to Suraj's feet. He picked it up quietly and slipped it into his pocket. When the children came looking for it he pretended he was reading the newspaper. As the children looked in the bushes for the ball, the dormant youth in Suraj suddenly awakened. He took the ball from his pocket and gazed longingly at it. He looked around, then threw the ball in the air and kicked it hard when it came down. The ball went flying through Masi's window, shattered it, and hit Masi's head hard. Masi had been deeply engrossed in reading aloud from the Gita. When the ball hit her she let out a shriek, glared wrathfully at the ball, then marched into the garden, screaming and yelling. Chandar was still searching. Masi grabbed his ear and dragged him towards Barre Sarkar. Chandni saw Chandar being mistreated, suspended herself from Masi's wrist and dug her tiny pointed teeth into her.

"Punish me, but leave her alone," Pimo begged and took the entire force of Masi's pounding on her own back. Suraj was watching all this and couldn't help laughing at Masi's foolishness. When the case was presented in his court he pretended to be engrossed in his paper. Masi felt a surge of love for him.

"So Chandar, you've become very naughty," he scolded Chandar. The Suraj who couldn't resist a ball a little while earlier had disappeared; the Barre Sarkar who was like a god remained. He was afraid to admit that both these beings were actually the same. The despicable Suraj was not Barre Sarkar, he was someone else; if he could hide after committing an offence, he had nothing in common with his other self.

"Barre Bhaiya, I'm telling the truth, I didn't throw the ball," Chandar stammered.

"And now you're lying. Come on, ask for Masi's forgiveness."

"Forgive me, Masi." Chandar laid down his weapons and Masi accepted his apology.

3

Moments flowed into each other to become years. The tiny jamun plant that Chandar and Pimo had planted on the banks of the lake now swayed like a massive tree. Suraj's authority also grew like a giant and permeated the entire household. The children respected him more than they would their own parents. Chandar was still afraid of looking him in the eye.

Pimo was favoured because she was young, but she too didn't have the courage to talk back to him. The darkest shadow lay on Usha Rani's heart and mind. The giant had incapacitated her completely. She was ruled by Barre Sarkar. She circled mechanically around the Sun God. Gave him breakfast, uncovered the bread basket for him, sprinkled the right amount of salt and pepper on his eggs, buttered his toast, then cleared the dishes herself. There was neither joy nor discomfort in this service anymore.

She is Barre Sarkar's fiancée and this is what the fates have decreed for her. There was only one man in the world for her and that was Suraj. One day she would be married to him, Barre Sarkar would lift her veil.

Munshiji had come to this house as a teacher for the children. He had wasted his youth waiting for Usha Rani's love. What could he do except see her and sigh soulfully? If she appeared while he was tutoring the children, he would flounder helplessly. Usha loved making him uncomfortable, would deliberately laugh sweetly and say things to tease him.

"Munshiji, if someone falls madly in love with you, what will you do?"

"I ... I... well..." Munshiji would break out in a sweat.

"I mean anyone ... for example, if a girl is loved by a very special man, what should she do?"

"She...she should have pity on him." Munshiji began to wipe his face with his dhoti.

"Should she say without any hesitation that she loves him?"

"Yes ... yes ... if..."

"Why if? She's a girl from a high caste, not some low class, dimwitted girl, and he too is of a good caste, very talented and handsome."

"Oh?" Munshiji began to feel the conversation was not about him.

"But he never says anything." Usha Rani would then look

sad. "Perhaps because it's not proper to do so. Is that true, Munshiji?"

"Yes ... yes, I think so ..." Munshiji would become more dejected.

"That's why she worships him, considers him her guru, considers making a life for herself at his feet, but he doesn't know this and that's why he says nothing. This is what it is, isn't it, Munshiji?"

And Munshiji would see the fate of his love revealed to him clearly. Usha Rani's beauty and youth were a punishment for him. He had no relatives who would arrange his marriage somewhere else so that he could forget her. He would pass his life as an unhappy rejected lover and burn like a cinder. If a drop of water keeps falling in one place, it creates a dent even in a stone. His suffering on account of his love for Usha had created many a dent in his heart and he had grown accustomed to this pain, but of late his passion had begun to develop a bitter taste.

Once in a while Barre Sarkar became irritated with Usha and scolded her, and then he would give her some false hope in order to assuage his remorse. Smile at her, and flowers would bloom in Usha Rani's heart.

Masi would try to advise her. "My child, why do you allow these irrational thoughts to trouble you? If he didn't like you, why would he feel obliged? Wouldn't he have asked to marry someone else?"

Sometimes Masi lost her patience. Was there something missing in Usha that she didn't appeal to Barre Sarkar? She insisted that Usha Rani dress well, wear the latest fashions, and she herself kept her close to Suraj on one pretext or another.

But Masi had been right in saying that Chandni would grow up and make trouble. When she reached womanhood she was like a fragrant flower in full bloom. Such vivacity could not exist in a girl from a respectable family. She must be the child of a harlot.

Chandni was so confident of her beauty that she became fearless. She even stopped being afraid of Barre Sarkar. The moment he arrived on the scene everyone fell silent, but she would continue to chatter.

"Why should I be quiet? I wasn't swearing. Arre, you're afraid of him for no reason. I'm not. When he glared at me yesterday with his big eyes he thought, this wretch will die of fright!"

"Hai, O mother, Barre Bhaiya glared at you?"

"Yes."

"Then?"

"Then what? I made a face at him," Chandni laughed.

"You're lying!"

"I swear."

"And then?"

"Then what? I ran off."

"And what if Masi had seen you?"

"Arre, who's afraid of Masi? She just barks, she can't bite!"

"All right, so if you aren't afraid of him why do you call him Barre Sarkar?"

"What else shall I call him?"

"Why don't you call him Barre Bhaiya?"

"Oh, stop it."

"Why?"

"Rani teases me. Is he your brother-in-law already that you call him Barre Bhaiya, she says. That's why I'm shy."

"But one day you'll have to call him Barre Bhaiya."

"Stop, or I'll hit you," Chandni said, acting coy.

Chandni was extremely impish. She enjoyed being a tomboy. Masi's cobra-like head would be raised in vigilance, making sure no girl and boy became too free with each other, although she did send Usha to Barre Sarkar's room again and again. Maybe, if something happened, a marriage would become inevitable. But Barre Sarkar was made of stone. Masi was afraid that Chandni might ensnare Chandar in her net, but she was quite sure she didn't have the power to rid Chandar of the love and awe he had for Barre Sarkar. Even now one look from him would make Chandar weak in the knees. He might be good for nothing, but he was ready to sacrifice his life for his older brother. Then it occurred to her that if he blackened his name through his association with the girl, he would no longer have the courage to ask for his inheritance.

But Chandni's feistiness came to an end the day she became suspicious of Barre Sarkar's intentions. If it had been some other girl she wouldn't have given it another thought. But because she had no inhibitions herself she immediately understood. Chandni was bathing and suddenly a sixth sense told her that someone was peeking at her. She had taken off her clothes, had already put some herbal soap in her hair when she felt there was someone at the window that opened onto the lawn. That witch, the washerman's daughter, she's a wicked one, always sneaking around. Chandni quickly draped a towel around her. A glance at the shadow on the glass pane of the door established that it wasn't a child. The shadow moved; the dark spot on the polished glass was erased and light shone through. It was not a dark spot. Someone had scraped off the polish on the glass in order to look through it. It was the gaze of a person with a filthy mind, someone who had run away when she was alerted to his presence. Humiliation and shame made it difficult for her to continue bathing.

She asked Usha to cover up the spot the next day, but a few days later she found a pea-sized hole scratched out on the other pane. She started bathing in Usha's bathroom, but Masi made such a fuss that she stopped.

Chandni decided that she would somehow catch this person who had been peeping through the hole. She went in one day and started to run the water. She unlatched the bolt on the door opening onto the garden and fixed her eyes on the glass pane. Whoever peered in wouldn't know that a light shadow could be seen from the inside. The moment an eye appeared at the scratched spot Chandni opened the door wide. Barre Sarkar was standing in front of her and his eyes were filled with all the filth of the world. She was transfixed. Then she fled to her room and fell on her bed like a wounded bird.

She couldn't believe her eyes. It was as if she had seen Bhagwan devouring cow-dung. If she mentioned this to anyone, a storm would break and she wouldn't be able to stay in this house for another minute. So all she did was to tell Pimo that the glass panes should be covered with paper so no one could look in. From that day on Chandni avoided Barre Sarkar. Leave alone looking him in the eye, she wouldn't even glance in his direction. It was the worst at dinner time — she sat cowering like a mouse between Pimo and Chandar and after quickly swallowing a few mouthfuls of food, she would dash off from the dining room.

For several days after this incident Barre Sarkar remained confined to his room. He didn't eat, didn't change his clothes. All night he smoked one cigarette after another and paced about restlessly. He abused this wretched Suraj who had behaved so dishonourably. He would strangle him if he could. He didn't want to see anyone. Masi and everyone else in the house was completely surprised.

Everyone except Chandni knocked on his door, but he told them off. After several days of atonement, and when he was sure that Chandni had not said a word to anyone, he felt somewhat encouraged. Soon he reassured himself that there was no way Chandni knew what his crime was. He had just been standing near the door, what was so bad about that? This was his house, he was the master, there could be a thousand reasons for his presence there. Chandni would never muster enough courage to misconstrue his intentions. After confidently arriving at this conclusion, he emerged from his room. That very day Masi had tied a ribbon on the trellised grate of Sarna Devi's shrine and made a vow. Seeing the arrow hit its mark she immediately fell at the Devi's feet.

"Oh, my son, I have been so worried. What is the matter?"

"Nothing at all, Masi. I wasn't feeling very well and thought I should fast for a few days. All of you start worrying for no reason at all. I also had to look through a few books on philosophy to write up some notes."

Chandni disappeared the moment he came out of his room. After this it became routine — the moment the sun came out the moon's light was extinguished. The matter was soon forgotten, but the chase of the lion and the doe had begun. The doe sprinted away the instant she smelled the lion's presence.

Often at night Chandni would have a nightmare and would start sobbing, felt as if she had landed on a heap of dry leaves somewhere far away, in a desolate forest, completely alone, surrounded by a frightening silence. There was no one around, no one. She was running, two eyes emerged from their sockets and crawled towards her, making her stumble! Long serpentine eyes entangled her entire body, a strange fear slowly grounded her. She couldn't breathe, her lungs had collapsed, she would keep falling like this, one lifetime after another. She would wake with a start, draw a deep breath and begin weeping, stifling her sobs so that she wouldn't wake Pimo who was asleep next to her.

Where was she born? Did she have a mother? A father? If yes, then why had she been abandoned? Perhaps a fairy had dropped her on earth and then forgotten all about her.

Every single particle of her being was trapped in the bonds of the Thakur family. Indeed they had picked her up from the dirt and turned her into a princess. And Chandar — how can there be moonlight without the moon? How sad and dark the world would be without a moon. She was Chandar's shadow, wasn't she? She had longed to be part of him ever since she was a little girl. How accepting his love was! And she was his … he had found her, hadn't he?

Pimo! Who knows what good deeds Chandni had performed in her previous life to get a friend like Pimo as a reward in this one. Pimo's friendship, her sisterly love, her maternal affection, call it what you like, it was her life's most beautiful gift. Pimo was not a human being, she was the avatar of some goddess who always protected her.

And she couldn't say enough about Usha Didi. She's Usha Didi, isn't she, the queen of the household. No one can find fault with her. She's loving towards everyone, takes care of them all. Her heart is filled with love, isn't it? But her god is a real slab of stone, doesn't lift his gaze to see that the devotee is a flesh and blood creature not a mound of sandy soil! She doesn't ask for anything. The fire in her heart lit, her forehead touching the ground in worship, she sits waiting, waiting for her god's eye to open, and then the flame of her love will ignite his heart, and her life will be fulfilled.

Her palms pressed together Chandni pleads with Bhagwan: "Hey, Bhagwan, when will you yield? When will Usha Devi find happiness? How long will the little bird wait to slake her thirst?"

But Masi just barks, she doesn't bite. Her husband died when she was young and ever since she has devoted her life to Usha, determined to serve the entire household in the hope that one day she will be the queen of this house. She wasn't interested in food or clothes; all she ever wished was that Usha's destiny would awaken one day. Was this wish so complicated that Bhagwan was having a hard time fulfilling it? This troublesome situation is all due to the fact that Bhagwan does not accept this offering. O you who nurture us, your godliness will not be marred if you fill his heart with Usha's love.

One day she attempted to casually broach the subject with Chandar.

"Chandarji?"

"Hunh."

"What will you do if Chandni dies one day?"

"The moon has to drown before the moonlight can die. Are you scolding me?" Chandar looked at her through half-shut eyes.

"Hai, curse my mouth, why would I scold you? But you know, life is uncertain, people do die."

"Stop it, you silly girl. Why all this talk about death at this time?"

Chandni sighed deeply and placed her cheek on his palm. "Well, what if someone snatches me from you?"

"No one can snatch you from me. I'll shoot him."

"Your Bhaiya can't snatch me either?"

Suddenly Chandar pushed her away violently and stood up. His eyes blazed. "How dare you mention Bhaiya's name?"

"Chandro –" Chandni let go of his hand in fear.

"You wretch, he's like my father!" Chandar said in a voice choked with terror.

"I made a mistake, Chandar, I spoke without thinking, I didn't really mean it."

"I'll smash your face in if you say something like this again! He loves me so much, and who do you think you are, you bhangan?"

"I'm the dirt at your feet, Chandar – your shadow." She edged towards him.

"Get away from me, I'm very angry. You insulted Bhaiya."

"Then beat me, Chandar – slap me hard," Chandni said, her eyes filling with tears.

"All right, enough." Chandar softened.

"I just said it without thinking. He's my master also, just as he is yours. What I meant was – if he turns me out of the house and ..." Chandni tried to change her position.

"Then I'll leave the house as well, but that will never

happen. Bhaiya is so good, never in his life has he refused me anything."

"But who knows anything about me – who knows who I am, and you're the son of a Thakur."

"You're Chandni and I don't know anything more than that." Chandar took her into his arms and squeezed her so hard she could hardly breathe, and they both rolled on the cool grass. Chandni grabbed Chandar's hair to steady herself but trembled when she realised that she seemed to be losing herself in him.

Suddenly there was a rustling in the dry leaves and the two of them drew apart hastily. They glimpsed Barre Sarkar with a gun in his hands, casually gazing at the sky. Chandni quickly hid herself behind the trunk of a tree. Barre Sarkar glared at Chandar who, looking guilty, was still sprawled on the grass. There were serpents glinting in Barre Sarkar's eyes. Chandar got up quickly and brushed off the grass from his clothes.

All of a sudden Barre Sarkar broke into a smile and said gently, "You're lying on the wet grass, you'll catch a chill. Go inside and put on a sweater."

"Yes, yes, Bhaiya," Chandar said, trying to escape.

"Are you studying for your exams?"

"Yes, Bhaiya."

"This is a nice place for studying, but where are your books?"

"Err… they're … in my room."

"Well, that's all right. But as a matter of principle, you should be sleeping in your room and not here."

"Yes, Bhaiya."

Suraj sat down on a wooden log, opened the chamber of his gun, retrieved the blank cartridge and blew into the opening of the barrel to clean it. Chandar was still standing. Barre Sarkar looked up at him with his large eyes and Chandar bolted from there.

Barre Sarkar inserted a new cartridge and clicked the chamber shut. Chandni was so startled that she jumped as if a bullet had just struck her chest. Suraj leaned against the tree trunk. As the tree moved, Chandni stumbled and almost fell on her face, but steadied herself quickly. First she saw the barrel of the gun appear, then a hand and shoulder moved from behind the tree trunk. She tiptoed to the other side, but the barrel of the gun moved just as quickly and came back in a circle to face her. Chandni was shaking, sweat poured down her body. She turned swiftly with the intention of fleeing but became rooted to the ground, motionless as a statue. The barrel of the gun was pointed at her like a cobra's head.

Two deep wells, at the bottom of which were bullets. She tore her gaze away from the gun's barrel and looked fearfully into something even more dangerous – eyes, poisonous, like steel rods — and saw flames of hate and anger leaping at her. Despite her efforts she couldn't free herself from the vortex of his gaze.

She was stunned when the hissing snakes suddenly lowered their heads. Barre Sarkar's forehead was covered in sweat. The barrel of the gun was lowered. It seemed that a mountain had toppled over Barre Sarkar. His tall, thin body swayed, his shoulders drooped, his legs seemed to have turned into crunched-up paper, and he almost crumpled as he bowed before her.

If a hunter becomes helpless in the presence of the doe he has been stalking, then she too forgets her readiness to take flight. But in the next instant Chandni roused herself, jumped over the barrel of the gun and bolted towards the haveli.

4

"Nothing will ever come of it, Masiji. Give up hope of ever growing flowers on this rock."

Munshiji continued with his jibes. Masi was arranging Barre Sarkar's breakfast. When she called out to Usha the girl came running, dressed as she was. This behaviour will definitely help you become a queen! She was immediately made to turn around, go back and change. Munshiji laughed sarcastically and continued teasing Masi.

"Keep barking, you wretch — now even you think you can give yourself airs," Masi said angrily.

"But I'm saying all this for your own good. Why are you letting your daughter's youth wither away? Will you suspend her from the branch for the rest of her life? Parrots and birds will peck away at it the fruit until it is hollow."

"Look here, Munshiji, don't meddle in my affairs."

"But I have to say there's something strange going on. I swear I have been standing guard here for seventeen years and nothing has happened yet."

"You wretch, what gibberish is this?"

"You're a woman, what can I say? But tell me the truth, have you ever heard that Barre Sarkar has teased the cleaning girl or pinched the washerwoman's bottom?"

"A curse on you, you wretch, do you think he's depraved like you? Will a Thakur's son flirt with the cleaning girl and the washerwoman?"

"Well, dear lady, don't say that. We all know about the nobility of the Thakurs. You remember the time of Barre Thakur? Not a single street was neglected."

"That's why he rotted away. My Suraj is not like that. You won't understand him, Munshi. Men with such devoutness and piety don't have any deceit in their hearts." Masi drew a long sigh.

"Well, all right, let's forget the cleaning girl and the

washerwoman. Take our Usha Rani, beauty that would make the gods drool, but has Barre Sarkar ever flirted with her?"

"How dare you take my daughter's name? Bastard, get out of here!" Masi picked up her slipper and Munshiji ducked hastily.

"All right, all right, don't get so angry, but I still say something is wrong. What kind of piety and devotion is this, anyway? Does our Usha Rani say anything to any of her friends? Dear lady, this Vishwamitra looks like a wooden owl to me. Why are you praying to Sarna Devi all the time? She has no sway over this devotee."

The slipper hit his ankle with a whack and, screaming and cursing, he dashed out.

"Hey Ram, I'm dead," he howled in pain.

5

"Keep your wits about you, Munshiji."

All dressed up, Usha Rani was walking in from the other direction and thought Munshi was trying to tease her again.

Munshiji became enraged. "To hell with these slippers!" He kicked the slipper with force. "You will have to pay for my patience, mother and daughter, remember that!" And limping, muttering angrily, he left the room.

Dressed in pink, Usha Rani looked graceful and beautiful. Not twenty-seven years old at all. The glow of shyness and reticence on her face only enhanced her beauty.

Carrying a heavy breakfast tray she tiptoed into the room to find Barre Sarkar bent over his table, a hunting knife open in his hand. Before him lay a badly damaged picture of a naked woman. Usha screamed and the tray fell from her hands.

Startled, Barre Sarkar spun around to look at her. Usha saw that the person in front of her was not the god of her heart's temple, but Satan. His fang-like teeth sticking out, his eyes filled with a wild madness.

"Why are you here?" Barre Sarkar threw the knife down violently on the table and crushed the picture.

"Break … fast…," Usha stammered. Trembling and hiding her face in her hands, she turned to leave.

"Usha." He got up apprehensively. Usha stopped.

"Usha, come here," he said gently.

"Yes," Usha said, turning around.

"You … you … why do you take all this trouble?"

"But what's wrong? Whether I bring it or the servant, it's the same thing."

"I don't like it."

Usha did not respond and, wiping her tears, walked towards the door.

"Listen."

She stopped again.

"You're not upset about what I said, are you?" Barre Sarkar asked, looking at the waste-paper basket from the corner of his eyes.

"No, what is there to be upset about? It was my fault that the tray fell from my hands."

"Actually, I was very worried. This picture …"

"Yes?"

"Chandar's behaviour has left me very distressed. I don't know why his head is full of all this filth, where he gets these obscene pictures from."

Oh! He must have confiscated the picture from Chandar. Once when she was tidying up Barre Sarkar's desk she had seen some among his papers. She felt very angry with Chandar. The wretch! Barre Sarkar was right, such pictures should only be cut up and thrown away.

After Usha left Barre Sarkar collapsed on the table. The scratches made by the knife on its surface rose and quivered like hot flesh. His entire body was drenched in sweat.

Exhausted, he clenched his fists against his temples and broke into sobs.

6

Panting, gasping, Chandni fell on the bed and started crying. She felt as if her whole body had been bloodied. There was not a scratch on it but the feeling that she was taking her last breath stroked her heart with icy fingers.

What if someone had come, had seen?

If Chandar had seen them she would have died. That would be the end.

Luckily, just then the horse escaped from the stables and appeared on the lawn and all the servants ran after it. If that hadn't happened, the red flowers of her blood would have been blooming all over the pure white carpet in the lounge. She was running down the stairs, her foamy dupatta flying behind her. She had books in one hand and with the other she was trying to keep the dupatta in place, but as she gave it a tug it escaped from her grasp. When she turned around to pick it up, her hand flew up and the books fell from her other hand. On top of the stairs stood Barre Sarkar and her dupatta was fluttering in his hand.

Long snakes uncoiled from the sockets of his eyes and began to envelop her. There was a hunting knife in his hand, and with a slight twist of his wrist he was twirling her dupatta around it.

"Are you very frightened?" he asked, bending over her and touching the button on her shirt with the tip of his knife. Slowly he took her hand and placed the edge of the knife on it, but instead of going through her palm, the knife began to crawl over her wrist. Then, travelling up her arm, its tip rested at her throat.

The sharpness of ice shot all the way to Chandni's soul. She stood still, her eyes lowered, her breath held. The knife moved expertly and the top button of her shirt snapped and rolled down the stairs with a pinging sound.

One by one all the buttons were snipped off with a light movement. Huge tears kept falling soundlessly down her cheeks. The strength of her hands hanging by her side had been sapped. The icy tip of the knife halted exactly at the beating of her heart. A fiery drill tore through the depths of her soul. Silent explosions began going off in her head.

Before the volcano could erupt and she was reduced to ashes the horse escaped from the stables and began to create a commotion on the lawn. Suddenly it was as if the world had awakened. Drained, Chandni crouched on the stairs. She didn't see where Barre Sarkar had vanished, didn't know whether it was actually him or his ghost, whether all this had been manufactured by her troubled thoughts, a trick that had vanished in an instant.

Whom can she tell? And what will she say? How can an ant accuse an exalted god? Who is her witness and who her supporter? Pimo was her friend, she adored her, but would she be willing to tolerate this insult to Barre Bhaiya?

Barre Sarkar hates her because he is afraid that Chandar might develop a relationship with her and besmirch the name of the Thakurs. She is a lowly creature, the result of someone's sin no doubt, which is why she had been abandoned on a rubbish heap.

Once again she felt a bullet hit her chest. In front of her, in the big hall, Barre Sarkar's photo in the golden frame was sparkling. In front of the picture were flowers and the fragrance holder with cold embers. Every day Usha Rani would pick fresh flowers and place them before the picture, take the offering with the oil lamp, circle the room, then place it at its base.

Chandni wanted to pick up a large stone and hurl it at the picture. Her mouth became dry with anger and hatred, as if it was filled with ash all the way down to her throat.

Suddenly it seemed to her that the picture was smiling, that the poison-filled eyes were dancing. She turned around and ran, speeding down the stairs, and bumped into Chandar.

"What's the matter, ji?" Chandar steadied her.

"Hai, Chandarji." She placed her lips on his chest and burst into tears. Chandar immediately took advantage of the situation. There was such pleasure, such sweetness in his love — Chandni melted.

"Hey Ram, Chandru, devour me, let me drown in you." The intensity of her love made her tremble. Sparks flew in her head when she was close to Chandar, but that was also when she felt really angry with him. She had no control over the desire to simultaneously sink into him and run away from him. The fifteen year-old Chandni became terrified when she couldn't find the answers to many of life's questions. An unknown fear impelled her to flee from the joy of Chandar's love, but when she was apart from him her heart was filled with longing.

Very soon Chandar made her laugh. The frightened Chandni of a few minutes earlier was quickly transformed into a coquettish beauty. Sprinting like a doe, laughing freely and taking shortcuts through the lawn, she clambered up the veranda to the dining room. It was dark inside, a dim light streaming through the windows. Chandar stumbled over a flower-pot and fell, but ran laughing towards the gallery. She spun around to look and knew from the sound of Chandar's footsteps that there was no escaping him, he would certainly catch her. The moment she turned to move towards the staircase two powerful hands manacled her. She felt a burning cobra mouth on her lips and the poison, hissing and spitting, seeped into her being … down… down … She felt as if she had reached the absolute bottom, would never get her breath back. In the distance the sound of Chandar's footsteps was slowly fading away. Chandar … Chandar the moon … with every ounce of her being she pulled herself up from the abyss, dashed towards Chandar and fell on her face in front of him.

"Arre, what happened?" he said, alarmed by her terror-stricken expression.

"There ... he..." Her eyes were wide open and her voice suffocated.

"What is it, you silly girl?" Chandar went in and looked around the gallery. Leaning against the column was Barre Sarkar. The devilish look on his face startled Chandar as well.

"Arre, Barre Bhaiya, she's crazy, this Chandni, took fright when she saw you!" Chandar laughed sheepishly and pushed Chandni away from him. Then he began scratching his head like a fool. He had a cigarette in his other hand which he quickly thrust into his pocket.

Chandni tried to say something, but seeing the look on Chandar's face she turned and ran, sobbing. When Chandar tried to slip away as well, Barre Sarkar said in a very sombre voice, "Chandar."

"Yes." Chandar flinched.

"I have to talk to you. Please come with me."

Chandar trembled at the severity of his tone but said nothing and followed him obediently.

"Sit down." Barre Sarkar gestured and then started pacing back and forth restlessly. Chandar was sweating, he wanted to sneak out and not show his face again for many days, and surely afterwards Barre Sarkar would have forgotten everything.

Suddenly Barre Bhaiya stopped pacing and stared intently at Chandar, as if he would devour him whole.

"Here." He offered Chandar his cigarette case in a surprise gesture.

"Ji ... oh no ..." Chandar stammered.

"Well, as you please. Perhaps it's more fun to smoke surreptitiously." When Barre Bhaiya was angry he would adopt a more formal mode of address.

"Do you love Chandni?"

"Ji... ji... no ... ji ... " Chandar cringed. He was unprepared for such a frontal attack.

"Don't make a fool of me by lying!" Barre Bhaiya roared. "Your behaviour is becoming increasingly intolerable." This was something else he did when he was angry, he resorted to speaking in English.

Chandar's head dropped further with each word. Barre Bhaiya was delivering his lecture without pausing. The idea that he was in love with Chandni was not new to Chandar, Pimo teased him constantly about it. Masi had also taunted him, and as for Usha Rani, she had nearly sealed the matter. But he always made light of it and avoided speaking about it seriously.

He had not yet felt the need to marry. But hearing Barre Bhaiya bring up the subject so abruptly unnerved him.

"What have I done wrong, Chandar?"

"Ji?" Chandar was so distracted he hadn't heard what Barre Bhaiya said.

"Have I ever done anything that would bring harm to you, to Parmila or any other member of this household?"

"No, Barre Bhaiya."

"Have I not fulfilled my duty faithfully? Have I done you an injustice of some sort? When have I given you reason to complain?"

"No, you've never been unjust, Barre Bhaiya."

"Then what crime are you punishing me for?"

"Me? I, Barre Bhaiya ..." Chandar whimpered and started thinking of ways to make his escape.

"Do you know how this despicable action of yours will affect the family? What will the world say? You ... love her, don't lie. She has taken control of your brain and your heart like an evil spirit, you've lost your senses, and you're quivering like a fish caught in a net. A lowly ant has compelled a mountain to lower itself at her feet. Do you know the family you belong to? You are Surya Vanshi and she … she's an unidentified, base creature about whose parentage nothing is known, who in all likelihood is the fruit of some ignominious person's act. Do you want to stain the family name by marrying her, are you blind, don't you know how all this will end? You will become mad … mad … ma…"

Suddenly Barre Sarkar jumped back … he was foaming at the mouth and standing in front of the mirror, chastising himself. Filled with dread, he turned to look at Chandar and saw that the chair was empty. Who knows when Chandar had slipped out of the room.

"Oh, Bhagwan! Bhagwan!" He held his head in his hands and slumped to the floor. "What have I done to deserve such an awful punishment?" Who knows how long he smouldered alone in the conflagration his mind had created, how long he suffered its turmoil.

7

A wave of hot blood surged in Barre Sarkar's head, the pen shook in his hands and the red embers in his eyes began to dance.

"You … you like her?" he asked Munshiji in a choked voice.

"Ji … ji, Sarkar. The girl is a firecracker, strikes you on the heart with a loud thud. And then I have eaten your salt, and even if you make shoes with my skin and wear them I will consider myself fortunate. Chote Sarkar is getting out of hand." He placed more papers in front of Suraj for his signature. "You will not have to worry and I …" Munshiji spoke as if a rasgulla was dissolving in his mouth.

"And you …" The veins in Barre Sarkar's neck became taut like steel, his temples throbbed and his nostrils flared.

"Ji, Sarkar, how long can I carry on alone! In three or four years she'll be strong like a she-goat and then there'll be trouble. Masiji is already losing sleep over her. If Chote Sarkar makes some kind of a slip there will be no help for it. And it's not his fault. The girl is full of wiles, she can make the best of them sweat, Sarkar, and Chote Sarkar is so naïve. That's why I thought, when else will I be of use? Ram knows whether she's the offspring of a bhangi or a chamar, but Sir, I am your very loyal servant so what does it matter if …"

"You want to … marry her?"

"Ji … the matter will end here, no one will have the audacity to say or suggest anything."

"You are … you like her?" Barre Sarkar ground his teeth, demons began dancing in his eyes, his mouth tightened. Suddenly Munshiji's laugh froze on his lips. He drew back with a start, but like an angry lion Barre Sarkar leapt up and grabbed his neck.

"Sir, I made a mistake, Sarkar!" Munshiji freed himself from his grip and, falling on his feet, he began begging forgiveness right there. Suddenly Barre Sarkar retreated in shock.

"I understand, I understand, Sarkar … How would I know …" Munshiji got up and, fixing his dhoti hastily, put his hands together.

"Know what?" Barre Sarkar turned around and hissed.

"Nothing, Sir, nothing at all."

"What do you understand, you wretch?"

"Nothing. Sarkar, I understand nothing. What can I know? I … I …" Flabbergasted, Munshiji ran from the room and bumped into Usha Rani on his way out.

"Arre, a curse on you!" he swore at the long folds of his dhoti which were getting entangled between his legs. "Ram, Ram, hey Shri Ram, what unkindness!"

Usha had witnessed only the scolding, and that made her happy. She laughed and said, "Arre, Munshiji, have you lost your mind, do you want to die? Why else would you try to get familiar with him?"

"To hell with getting familiar! Ram Ram, this is too much. What a – Bhagwan … one can't even trust sadhus and saints anymore, I swear."

"Arre, what happened?" Masi asked, "Barre Sarkar has never lifted a finger against anyone. This dog must have said something really terrible to make him lose his temper."

"What could it be, a curse on you!" Munshiji muttered angrily.

"All right, that's enough. You had better pack your things and get ready to leave."

"Arre, death to those who will pack and leave! I say, think about yourself now. Forget all your dreams of becoming the mother queen. What queen, consider yourself lucky if you find a place in this house that will provide you a roof over your head."

"What is all this nonsense, are you mad?"

"This is not nonsense, my queen, listen to me and think about your well-being. Arre, he's the lord and master and can do what he wants and no one can question him, but I have to say the girl is a poisonous thorn."

"Which girl?"

"Arre, please don't ask me, if you have eyes, see for yourself. Hey Bhagwan, the signs are not good, everything will be turned upside down, a violent Mahabharat will take place, brother will devour brother."

"Oh, you are so disagreeable," Usha Rani said angrily and went inside.

Drenched in sweat, Barre Sarkar sat with his head down on the desk. His whole body was wracked with sobs. Usha Rani was badly shaken, seeing such a dignified man shattered like a broken toy. The maternal instinct that had lain dormant in her was aroused, she felt like taking his sorrow-laden head to her breast, but shyness and reticence stood in her way.

Barre Sarkar lifted his head. There was an ocean of pain raging in his eyes. His lips began to quiver like a defeated, whimpering child. He looked at Usha like a beggar scorned, then became agitated. He wanted to fling himself at her feet and say: "Usha Rani, save me. Save me from the cobras in this terrifying cave. Place your pure lips once on my throbbing forehead and all my sins will be washed away."

But Barre Sarkar had learned to conceal his pain. At the place where he had arrived there was no companion, no friend, just him and his isolation. Immediately he became conscious of his status. Flexed his neck and spoke arrogantly, "What is it?"

"What are your wishes regarding Munshiji?"

"Munshiji? Give Munshiji two hundred rupees for some winter clothes."

"But …" Usha Rani was speechless.

"Tell Gopal to bring me my tea on the terrace," he said curtly.

"This … the … Munshiji …"

"What do you want to say about Munshiji?"

"I mean that …"

"Are you upset at the way I treated him?" he asked brusquely. "If that is the case, I'm sorry. I thought you didn't like him."

"Yes."

"But it appears that I was wrong." Barre Sarkar started acting.

"I … I don't understand."

"He wants to marry you. If you're willing, then …"

"No!" Usha Rani exclaimed, holding back her tears.

"But if you want to, then …" He enjoyed upsetting her, he felt this gave him some relief from his own misery.

"No, of course not!" Usha Rani burst into tears.

"Oh. Well, that's what I thought and that's why I scolded him, but I got angrier than I should have."

"You did the right thing," Usha Rani said passionately.

"No, I didn't do the correct thing at all. I have no right to place obstacles in the path of your marriage." Barre Sarkar continued to mislead Usha Rani and she quivered like a fish that has swallowed the bait. As if she was a football and Barre Sarkar was playing with her emotions.

"Give him the money in cash and take these papers as well. Tell him he can do what he thinks is appropriate. I'm not feeling well, I lose my temper easily at the slightest thing." When he had had his fill he changed the topic with careless indifference.

Hey Bhagwan! My lord is so great. Hai, is there anyone who feels so sorry for having beaten a servant, especially a pig like Munshiji, who doesn't know when to hold his tongue.

In the meantime, while Usha Rani went to find out what Barre Sarkar had in mind for Munshiji, Munshiji had not retreated. He stood with his ear to the door, but hearing Barre Sarkar's instructions, swore roundly and became giddy with joy. When Usha Rani appeared at the door he put on a serious face and asked, "Raniji, what's my punishment?"

Usha threw a furious look at him and, incensed, walked away.

Munshiji constantly mourned Usha's wasted youth. He was unmarried and knew well the taste of solitude. He was Barre Sarkar's age, had no family of his own, and had never taken any interest in getting married. His salary, every single penny of it, had been saved. He had been admiring Usha from a distance for a long time, but after hearing Barre Sarkar's remarks, felt his courage return.

As was her custom, Masi completed Barre Sarkar's aarti and then, holding the tray in her hand, sat down on the floor near him.

"My son, Usha Rani is getting older, it's time you did something about her marriage."

"Of course, of course. We shouldn't delay any longer. You can do whatever is best. What is the young man like? Don't worry about money, the groom should be suitable."

"But ... but my son ... your mother wanted her to stay in this house," Masi stammered.

"When did I say she shouldn't live here? All the rooms in the west wing are vacant, bring a son-in-law who will be willing to stay with his in-laws. What does the young man do?"

Masiji couldn't restrain herself and burst into tears.

"My son, you are everything for Usha, I have pinned all my hopes on you."

"Oh, Masi, I'm so sorry, I have been remiss, and you know how useless I am, I don't meet anyone, don't go anywhere. It's not easy finding a husband for Usha Rani. The man should be decent, worthy. By the way, Masi, what do you think about Munshiji?"

Barre Bhaiya skirted the issue with such skill that Masi was left in a state of complete shock.

"Munshi? That worthless upstart! Is he the only one left for my daughter? I would rather fling her into a well! Whoever marries my beautiful, gracious girl will be blessed with good fortune. My son, the special attachment Usha has for this family is no secret. How she has adorned and organised this house. It is her house, that's why."

"I know, Masi. All right, don't worry. By the grace of Bhagwan, all will be well. Let me take care of the harvest first. This year we haven't had enough rain. Arre, Munshiji..." He tried to dodge the issue again.

Munshiji, who had been eavesdropping, appeared immediately. "Ji, Sarkar," he said smiling coyly like a bride.

"Just check that new tractor, it's not working properly. Aali is so incompetent, he doesn't understand anything, he's also very lazy."

"No, Sarkar, he's not lazy, he's scared. He says if the bosom of the earth bears so much weight, how will anything grow on it."

"What nonsense! And the oxen and the plough have no

weight? The fool … Munshiji."

"Ji, Sarkar."

"Can you recommend a boy?"

"Ji, Sarkar, for cleaning and dusting the house?" Munshiji was befuddled.

"No, no, not for cleaning and dusting, to marry, for Usha Rani."

Masiji didn't wait to hear the rest and stormed out of the room. Barre Sarkar felt exhilarated. He heaved a sigh of relief and broke into a smile, but the moment he noticed Munshiji smiling too, he assumed a stern look. "Yes?"

"Ji … ji, Sarkar!" Munshiji said, bemused.

"What is it?"

"Ji, Sarkar, you called me."

"Oh, I did call you, but that doesn't mean that once you're here you have to remain here like a ton of bricks on my head!"

Munshiji retreated hastily like a dog that has received a beating from its master. Barre Sarkar regarded his behaviour as a mark of his superiority over others. He had developed a dislike for Masi. He wasn't really interested in Chandni, he had just begun to feel that life without a woman was barren and so had thought, if not Usha Rani, then Chandni would do. She was an Untouchable no doubt, one doesn't find the children of goddesses lying on heaps of garbage, but at least she was a woman. Today's events put a seal on Munshiji's suspicions.

Hai Ram, who knows what is about to happen in this haveli? Will the sun and moon clash? There will be a terrible explosion. This girl must be a niece of Menaka, which is why she has come to destroy Barre Sarkar, a man of Vishwamitra's stature. Here he is, a god, and she a sinful woman.

"Just stop, your god be cursed," he muttered, and looking around, swore heavily at many others as well.

Masiji, Barre Sarkar, and life's drab solitude.

8

"No, no, Pimo Rani, I feel shy."

"Now stop, you silly girl, what's there to be shy about?" Pimo said, patting her lovingly on the head.

"But no one knows the correct date of my birth."

"Look, the day we found you is the day of your birth. You probably don't remember, Usha Devi made such shining new clothes for you. There hasn't been a year since then that we haven't celebrated your birthday, so why make such a fuss now?"

"It just doesn't seem nice. I've been treated so well, isn't that enough?"

"Chandni, you're very mean, you're always talking about being brought up here. I've been raised in this house as well, Chandar and I don't always keep complaining about that."

"But you're the children of this family!"

"And Usha Didi?"

"She has been doing the work of ten people since she was a young girl. I'm useless."

"If she works, it's not as a favour to anyone. After she gets married to our brother she will become the mistress of the house."

"By Ram's grace, may she get married to Barre Sarkar soon." Chandni began praying fervently. "I bend my forehead before Gori Mayya every day and pray for this to happen."

"And you don't pray for your own wedding? You wait, I'll tell Chot Bhaiya that Chandni doesn't love you one bit!"

"Arre, what? Of course I do!"

"Ram, Ram, what a shameless girl, telling me openly that you're crazy about my brother."

"Stop it now, why would I be crazy about him?"

"But he's crazy about you…."

"Look, Pimo, stop teasing me. What about you — all day long you're writing letters to Prakash ji."

"Unh! How can one trust a man who is thousands of miles away? What if he finds someone to fall in love with there?" Pimo had got engaged to a doctor who was now in England. "Leave my story alone, did you remind Chot Bhaiya about the necklace?"

"Arre, the poor fellow can't afford it, Ram only knows how expensive it is."

"So what? It will always be in his wife's possession."

"Don't tease me, please, you'll make me cry."

"Why? Where will the moon's moonlight go and –"

"She'll die, the wretch!" Chandni collapsed face down on the bed.

But Chandar was running around in a state of consternation. Fulfilling the demand for a two hundred and fifty rupee necklace was no joke. But he had a share in the family's wealth as well, surely Bhaiya wouldn't refuse? He felt awkward asking it for Chandni. He asked Usha Didi, but she could spare only a hundred. He had about fifty or sixty. A hundred and fifty was not enough.

Finally he was forced to approach Bhaiya.

"Bhaiya, can I have some money?" he said, standing behind him.

"Money?"

"Some rupees."

"How many rupees?"

"About two hundred or two hundred and fifty."

"Why do you suddenly need money?"

"I … I ordered a tennis racket and I have to pay the freight … and…"

Barre Sarkar seethed at Chandar's lie. He had eavesdropped on the conversation in the house about the necklace. Pimo said if Chandar didn't buy the necklace Chandni would not talk to him for the rest of her life. Well, forget the rest of their lives, if this laughter and hilarity, this kissing and hugging in corners was interrupted for even a few days it wouldn't be such a bad thing.

"I have about ten or twelve rupees with me and the bank is closed now," he replied curtly.

Chandar wiped the sweat from his forehead and departed.

After Chandar had left, Suraj got up calmly. The safe was stuffed with bundles of rupees that had come in for land taxes. Picking up a fat wad he slipped it into his pocket and came out looking very dignified, asked the driver to bring the car around and getting in, drove off.

Chandar sat down on the stairs with his head between his hands. What should he do? Pimo won't give him a penny. And if Chandni found out that he was collecting money from here and there for the necklace, she wouldn't speak to him. Actually, she herself had been telling him not to get it, it was Pimo who insisted, saying Chandni didn't have any real jewellery. She or Usha Devi would force her to wear something of theirs on festivals. Pimo taunted him so much that he was determined to demonstrate his gallantry. It would be a real disaster if the necklace failed to materialise now.

Pimo was all dressed up and ready for her dance practice. Chandar grabbed her on the stairs.

"Arre, Pimoji, I saw someone do something extraordinary today."

"Who?"

"A magician."

"Magician?"

"Yes, he came to our college. I learned a trick from him."

"Oh?" Pimo started walking.

"Do you want to see some magic?"

"No, no."

"Why not, you silly girl?" Chandar got annoyed.

"Arre, my tonga is waiting, I'll be late."

"All we need is two minutes." He pulled Pimo to the stairs and made her sit down.

"Now, take out a note."

"No."

"Arre, come on, I'll turn it into two."

Pimo finally took out a one-rupee note.

"*Come on Kalkatte-wali, may your attack not fail, ant-sant, bijli basant* ... here blow." Pimo blew gingerly, Chandar opened his fist. Instead of one rupee there was a ten-rupee note in his hand.

Pimo screamed. "Oh my, Chandar Bhaiya!"

"Come one, let's quickly change all of them."

"No, no, that's enough." Pimo calmly put the money into her purse and got up.

"Arre, arre, where are you running off to?" Chandar pulled her down again. "You'll regret it later, I swear, come on, take out the money." Chandar clicked his fingers.

Pimo took out the ten-rupee note.

"Why are you dawdling like this? I can't sit here forever and keep blowing the magic words one by one on ten-rupee notes. Give me a hundred rupee note and I'll change it to a thousand."

"Really?"

"Oh, yes."

"A thousand?"

"Of course. And if it's a thousand, I'll change it to ten thousand."

"I don't have a thousand rupee note."

"All right, let's have the hundred." Chandar got hold of the money and began blowing on it quickly. "*Kali Kalkatte-wali, chal chaal,* come on blow, do it properly, what's this *phoo, phoo,* remember if you don't blow properly the whole thing can be reversed."

Pimo blew on his fist with all her might. When Chandar opened it she saw a fragment of paper on his palm.

"You see?"

"Hai Ram! My hundred-rupee note."

"What can I do now? I was telling you, silly girl, blow

properly, blow properly please, but..." Chandar roared.

"I don't care, I want my money back!"

"Ahaha, you didn't blow the right way and the magic worked backwards, so what can I do? I'm getting late, out of my way." He pushed her aside and tried to leave.

"Oh no, how will I pay the dance master? Give me back my hundred rupees. Here are your ten rupees."

"Arre, I performed my magic right in front of you and now you're complaining. My dear, this is magic, sometimes it works and sometimes it fails." Chandar assumed an innocent expression and took the ten-rupee note as well. "Don't worry, I'm going out for just a while. When I come back I'll change all your money and make it grow ten times over."

"You wretch, I'm not going to be deceived by your tricks again." Pimo understood Chandar's tricks very well, but if he had asked openly for the money she would never have given him a penny.

9

The haveli was lit up with electric lights. Everyone knew that Chandni's birthday was just an excuse. The inhabitants of this haveli would even celebrate the birthday of a dog. Life's monotony and weariness are banished for a short while, there's a bit of excitement, Usha Devi gets a chance to show off her cooking skills, an effective way of impressing Barre Sarkar.

Chandni was pacing restlessly in her room, waiting anxiously for Chandar. When she saw his bicycle coming around the bend towards the gate, she dashed out.

"Chandarji, my necklace!" She was startled to see his sad, forlorn face. "What happened?" She shrank back.

"The necklace was sold."

"It was sold?"

"Yes. Someone came and bought it half an hour ago, but the jeweller has promised he'll make the same necklace in about fifteen days."

"Fifteen days!" She became tearful and turned to go.

"Listen, Channo..."

"I don't want to listen," she yelled. "I've been telling you it's going to be sold, but you wouldn't listen."

"A second one will be made ... then ..."

"I don't want a second, third, fourth or fifth. If you get it, I swear I'll smash it with a stone!"

"Chandra Rani ..."

"Don't you dare call me Chandra Rani! I'm not a rani, I'm an orphaned girl left on a pile of garbage. If I had been a rani you wouldn't have dared to not get the necklace for me. The person for whom somebody else has bought the necklace is the real rani." Her face was streaked with tears.

Barre Sarkar stood observing this poignant drama and was overjoyed. No one noticed his smirking. He had been turning the necklace around in his hand for the last two hours.

Every year he used to hand out money on birthdays through Munshiji. How was he going to give Chandni the necklace? He paced for hours trying to figure out a way to do it. What would he say? How would he say it? Should he give it to her in front of everyone or in private? All he wanted was to see her smile light up her face when she saw the necklace.

Chandar, who thought of him as a father, whom he loved more than his life – how much he loved him! And how much he hated him! In his waking and sleeping hours he dreamt about his death. Chandar falls from the horse, his brains are crushed, he has lifted up the broken, sorrowing Chandni to his parched lips and – and he would wake up! His throat dry, bathed in sweat, he would shiver in exhaustion. How many times had he killed Chandar in his imagination? Trampling over his blood-soaked body he had entered the bridal chamber and … and then he would awaken, his heart would sink, he would sob bitterly. Chandar … his little brother!

"My dear son, you are now father to both Chandar and Pimo, don't ever cause them pain, otherwise my soul will roam forever restlessly," his mother had said on her deathbed, and from that day on he had sacrificed his childhood and donned the prickly garment of maturity and responsibility. But nature was determined to ruin his plan, an unknown power was making him dance like a puppet, his entire life's piousness and goodness were being annihilated in one stroke.

At night he was woken abruptly by frightening nightmares. Turning the lights on he would search frantically for blood stains on his clothes. When that didn't reassure him he would go to Chandar's room and look at his sleeping form, trying to ensure he didn't have any wounds, that he was breathing normally. Seeing him alive and well he would fix his blanket, tuck his mosquito net in properly. If Chandar woke up suddenly he would joke, "Oh Bhaiya, I'm not a child!"

"There's malaria spreading in the wetlands. You're very careless."

When the two brothers sat next to each other, they spoke affectionately, reminisced about the loving care of their parents. This was when Chandni was far from their thoughts and Barre Sarkar would make plans for Chandar's grand future, estimate Pimo's wedding expenses, generously dole out money to Chandar, as if he were applying a balm to wounds that he had inflicted on him, although these wounds cut just as deeply into his own heart.

But right now, he was anxious to witness the interesting drama of Chandar's defeat and his own victory. When he came down with the necklace the scene before him was quite unexpected. The same Chandni who had been so enraged a while ago was melting in Chandar's arms.

"My Chand Raja, your arms are my real necklace. A curse on the necklace! How stupid can I be? Wah, Chandar Raja will one day put a diamond-studded necklace around my neck. Yes, Chandar?"

"But to this day I've never given you anything." Chandar sat with his head lowered in shame.

"You gave me my life, you silly boy. You gave me what Bhagwan had snatched from me – this house, happiness, a friend like Pimo … what else do I need? And when you look at me like this, my being is clothed with pearls. Don't look at me, Chandar." She placed her hand over his eyes.

A fire flared in Barre Sarkar's being, he began to breathe heavily like a wild boar, poisonous arrows swam through his eyes and pierced his temples, the necklace stung his fingers like a snake. But before he could attack his rival like a wild animal, someone's footsteps behind him stopped him.

Usha Rani was coming down the stairs slowly, all dressed up.

"Usha." He swallowed the bitterness in his throat and called out to her in the sweetest of tones.

Ahh! Hearing her name on his lips, Usha felt as if a bullet had struck her bosom. Pulling herself together she said, "Ji."

"Please come here," he said, greatly enjoying her discomfort.

Usha felt life slipping from her. Like a new bride, she walked towards him. Hey Bhagwan, he had uttered her name today!

"Look what I've got for you."

"For me?"

"Yes, a small little gift." He dangled the necklace in front of her.

"The most beautiful adornment of my life," she said softly and spread out her hands.

"Unhun. I'll put it on myself."

"Oh, so you bought this necklace?" Chandar spoke up before Chandni could stop him.

"Yes. Why? Don't you like it?"

"No, no, I mean, yes," Chandar said tonelessly.

Suddenly Masi arrived on the scene and burst into tears. "Live long, my beloved son, live long always, may you have my life too," making the gesture for removing the evil eye. Then she embraced Usha and began crying loudly, as though the bride's palanquin was ready and she was about to depart for her in-laws'.

A storm of anger and hate raged in Barre Sarkar, but he controlled himself.

"Oh yes, Ushaji, please tell Munshiji to give Chandni money for her birthday, whatever she got last time," he said coldly and walked towards the library.

"I don't want any money," Chandni hissed. For a while their spirits fell, but they soon forgot everything and got busy with the birthday revelry. Boys and girls were making a racket on the lawn, the place echoed with the tinkle of laughter. A new kind of glow shone in Usha Rani's eyes today. Again and again she gently caressed the necklace and then blushed.

Masi was in a strange frame of mind. On the one hand she was burning with jealousy because of the attention Chandni was getting, but at the same time she was happy that Chandar was completely overpowered by her. The moment he marries her Barre Sarkar will cut him off from the family's assets. He is the master, everything is in his name.

Barre Sarkar was alone in all this commotion. Rancour and malice rained on his thoughts, disappointment and misery stifled him, the desolation in his heart grew. Like an idiot he pinned his gaze on Chandar and Chandni. Every joyful gesture of theirs lashed his emotions like a whip.

Suddenly he noticed the necklace glinting in the grass. It had probably slipped from Usha's neck after its clasp came undone. He bent and picked it up and was about to give it to Usha when he paused, as if held back by something. Then he got up. Chandni's purse was lying on the table. He opened it quietly and slipped the necklace inside.

10

Chandni lay motionless on a pile of dead leaves under the molsri tree. She would come and sit here whenever she felt her heart was breaking. This is where Chandar had found her. This is where she would lie until she dried up like the leaves and the gardener would sweep her up with his jharu made of brambles and burn her with the rest of the garbage. Her ashes would permeate the air and fly from one lifetime to another.

In the past whenever Chandni was upset, Chandar would quickly appease her. But this time when he saw her lying on the leaves, he ignored her. He had never been so angry.

When Usha Devi's necklace came out of Chandni's bag in the presence of all the guests, Chandar felt like sinking into the earth with shame. He slapped Chandni so hard in front of everyone that her face was still swollen. He wouldn't let her say one word in her defence.

"She must be the child of a thief or a bandit," Masi said, apologising for carrying out a search among the guests.

"Let it be, Masi," Barre Sarkar tried to intervene, but she wasn't one to stop.

Barre Sarkar said, "Uff-oh! Please let it go. It's human to make a mistake. Usha Rani shouldn't wear this necklace now."

"Why not?" Usha Rani trembled in trepidation.

"Give it to the person who likes it. I'll buy you another one."

"Why should she give it? Who does the girl think she is to want the necklace? I'll forfeit her any day. She's been raised on our leftovers and she tries to deceive us!"

"Masiji, I'll swear by anything you want me to, I did not touch the necklace." Overcome by shame, Chandni began to weep.

"Stop it, you wretch, who do you have in the world, dead

or alive, by whom you can swear? If you had anyone, would you have been thrown on a rubbish heap? My daughter treated this bitch like her own sister, made all the arrangements for her birthday celebrations, dressed her up, and this is how she is repaid?"

"Chandni!" Pimo was sobbing. "You loved this necklace so much that you weren't afraid of stealing it? Chot Bhaiya!" She ran into Chandar's arms.

His eyes moist with tears, Chandar glanced at Chandni. She felt completely crushed. "Chandar, don't you trust me?"

And that was when Chandar slapped her hard and thrust her from him.

"Look, you are all making too much of this. She liked the necklace, she took it, what's so terrible about that? Chandar, you're being unfair." Barre Sarkar added fuel to the fire and as a result Chandni received further scoldings.

"You know, if someone likes the necklace so much that she has to steal it, then I don't want that necklace to be given to Usha. Usha, let Chandni have it."

"Oh, if I have to lose my life I will not give this necklace to anyone!" Usha said, choking, as if someone was stealing not just the necklace but her marital bliss.

"Yes, why should she give it away?" Masiji shouted. "If this wretch asks for someone's life should the great lady's wish be granted?"

The party broke up, the guests made hasty exits. It was as if someone had died. Chandar's tender heart had never suffered such a blow before. As for Chandni, she felt she no longer had reason to live. When the moon is covered by dark clouds, why will the moonlight not be extinguished?

Pimo argued, "If Chandni is a thief why doesn't she steal the jewellery that is always lying on my dressing table?"

"She stole to cover me with shame," Chandar said, swallowing hard.

"She's always coveting other people's things, she wanted

to hurt me, she can't bear to see anyone happy," Usha whimpered.

"No, you don't know this miserable wretch!" Masi spewed out more poison. "She's actually jealous of Barre Sarkar. If she had her way she would have all the family wealth transferred to Chandar's name. He's crazy about her, isn't he?"

The only one who didn't scold Chandni was Barre Sarkar. He was a noble man, after all! How much compassion there was in his heart! He kept saying, "Such a terrible punishment for such a small transgression. This is unfair on Chandar's part."

He was a god. To forgive was a sign of greatness. Those whom Chandni regarded as her own turned out to be so cowardly, and he whom she regarded as her mortal enemy was trying to save her. Overnight her heart was washed clean of all the bad feelings she had nursed against him. If she hadn't been so scared of him she would have fallen at his feet this very instant.

My Sarkar, I misunderstood you, I'm a sinner, please forgive me, punish me as you see fit, but tell Chandar not to destroy me like this. I won't even be able to die without his love.

Ah, in this house where everyone had treated her so lovingly, there was no one now who wanted to look at her. Several times Pimo tried to approach her, but Masi made such a fuss that she didn't have the nerve to do it.

"You will be ruined in the company of this thief, this low caste girl," Masi shouted, and then threatened to move her bed to Usha's room. But Pimo felt stifled in Usha's room, and she couldn't stay away from Chandni either.

"Chandni, you wretch, why did you steal the necklace? I want to beat you to pulp." She couldn't restrain herself.

How much love there was in this reprimand! Chandni burst into tears. "Pimo Rani, I swear on your life, if I have touched the necklace I should be stricken with leprosy, I should die, I should be blinded."

"No, no, please don't talk like that. But this Chandar, he's such a killjoy. We had plans to go for a picnic on Sunday and that's all ruined now. One would think it's not a necklace, it's some spectre – the house looks desolate. I feel so depressed."

So saying she went to Usha's room.

"Yes?"

"Please forgive me, Rani Didi."

"Forgive you for what?"

"That necklace of yours? I … I took it," Pimo said, rubbing her eyes.

"You took it?"

"Yes … and then …"

"And then?"

"I slipped it into the purse."

"Chandni's purse?"

"Of course. My purse was in my room."

"You're lying."

"Arre, it's the truth, my dearest Didi."

"Don't talk nonsense. Why would you steal it?"

"I did it for fun, I didn't steal it."

"Then why were you lying about it?"

"I picked it up, it was lying on the grass. I picked it up and put it in the bag. You weren't there."

"Hai Ram! Why didn't you tell me?"

"I … I was afraid that everyone would think I was a thief. Masi was so angry … I had gone to the bathroom and when I returned I saw that … Chandni had been accused of stealing," Pimo started stuttering.

"You're lying, didn't you also scold Chandni?"

"Well, what else could I do? Usha Didi, I was confused, I didn't know what to say."

"Hai Ram, this is terrible. All right, you witch, you stole the necklace and Chandni got the scolding for it. Why didn't you say something?"

"Well, Chandni had been quarrelling with me since that morning."

Chandar was livid when he was told. "And so you trapped her? Come on, you witch, let's go to Barre Bhaiya." He pulled her by her plait. "You'll see how I make him give you a thorough beating," pushing and pummelling her. Pimo kicked and struggled and then sat down, refusing to budge. Chandar lifted her up in his arms and dumped her like a gunny bag in front of Barre Bhaiya.

"Bhaiya, look what this witch has done!"

"Chandar, are you in your senses?"

"How can I remain in my senses? She's the one who stole the necklace and poor Chandni got the blame for it!"

"Parmila, what is all this?"

"Barre Bhaiya … I…"

"Stole the necklace and …"

"Chot Bhaiya, don't interrupt me. Barre Bhaiya, I put the necklace in Chandni's bag."

"You're a liar!" Barre Bhaiya shouted.

Pimo started weeping.

"But, Barre Bhaiya, she has admitted this herself."

"She's lying." Barre Bhaiya's eyes blazed in anger.

"No, Barre Bhaiya, she's saying she did it. Just think, is there anyone else who can be so stupid?"

"Yes … but …" Barre Bhaiya lowered his eyes.

"Please forgive me, Bhaiya. I hid the necklace as a joke. But when the situation became serious I got scared and kept my mouth shut."

"Pimo!"

"Ji, Barre Bhaiya."

"Come here."

"Ji, Barre Bhaiya."

"You know that lying is a sin."

"But Bhaiya, I can swear that Chandni didn't steal the necklace."

"Then who stole it?"

"I did." She lied, but there was not the slightest hint of hesitation in her clear and innocent gaze.

"No."

"Then who did it?"

"I did," Barre Sarkar said.

"You? Oh..." She burst out laughing. "Go on, Barre Bhaiya, you ..." She couldn't control her laughter.

Chandar went and told Chandni that Pimo had admitted her crime, that she was the one who had placed the necklace in her purse.

"Pimo?" Chandni was startled.

"Yes. Probably because she was jealous that your birthday was being celebrated with such pomp."

"Ram, Ram, what are you saying, Chandarji! Pimo jealous of my happiness? She *is* my happiness. Bhagwan took away everything from me, gave me Pimo and I got everything back. This is the greatest wealth of my life."

"Arre, you don't know her, she's a real witch."

"No, no, she's lying."

"Arre, wah! What will she get by lying? A scolding?"

"Because ... you don't know her, Chandarji ... because she is as innocent and soft-hearted as a child, she's taken on all the blame."

"Then that means ... you mean she didn't steal it and you did?"

"No, I didn't steal the necklace, but what difference does it make? You had already decided I was the culprit and punished me accordingly. What's the use of investigating now?"

"Chandni..."

But Chandni turned and walked away.

"Listen, Chandni." Chandar caught hold of her arm, but she shook him off.

"You won't talk to me for the rest of your life?"

"No." Chandni bit her lips.

"All right, we're not speaking to each other ever again?"

"Never."

"So you won't marry me?"

"Only if I wanted to die, would I marry someone mean like you who would never give me any respect!" Chandni made a face.

"So who will you marry?"

"Whomever I want."

"To hell with what you want! I'll shoot the bastard."

"Oh, who do you think you are to shoot anyone?"

"Watch what you say, Chandni — whom are you calling stupid?" Chandar shouted, advancing towards her.

"Yes, stupid!" Chandni turned and jumped over the drain.

"The worst kind of stupid person?" Chandar tripped her.

Chandni fell into the sludge flowing in the gutter. Gritting her teeth she picked up a handful and lobbed it at Chandar. Within a few minutes the two of them were grappling with each other in the muddy slush.

"What is going on?" Barre Sarkar asked. He was standing on the steps.

"Union!" Usha Rani broke into a laugh and extended a glass of orange juice towards him. Chandar got up and scooted from there like a drenched cat. Chandni slowly edged her way towards the bathroom.

"Usha Rani."

"Ji."

"You should drink this orange juice, you have a great need for it. Look how you are drooping."

"Me?"

"Yes, you're ageing. Arre, your hair is already graying at twenty-three? You're always pestering me, why don't you look at yourself in the mirror? You look so haggard."

The glass of juice slipped from Usha Rani's hand.

11

"A face like Bhagwan's, and the temperament of a devil."

Chandni was passing remarks on Barre Sarkar's picture and was very pleased with herself. Then, feeling lighthearted, she took the pen clipped on to her neckline, wrote 'devil' on the picture, and was busy drawing horns when suddenly all hell broke loose.

"Hai Ram!" When Chandni turned around she felt Masi's resounding slap with such force that stars danced before her eyes.

"You wretch! Treacherous creature! Thief!" A storm of Masi's wallops and slaps rained down on her. "You make a hole in the very plate you eat from! Vile creature, born of a harlot!"

Chandni's screams brought everyone rushing. When she tried to wipe the picture with her dupatta, Masi pushed her away violently and stood in front of it like a police inspector who has found the body.

"Look at this, look at the misdeeds of your beloved girl!" she said, shoving the picture in Chandar's face.

"You … you wrote this?"

"Chandarji …" Chandni stammered fearfully.

"Yes, yes, go ahead, say you didn't write it, you daughter of a whore." The minute she saw Barre Sarkar emerging from the library, Masi let go of Chandni and rushed towards him.

"I tell you, dump this feckless creature in an orphanage. Look … just look!" Masi burst into tears.

"Wonderful!" Barre Sarkar smiled generously. He was tired of being worshipped by the entire household. Instead of feeling angry with Chandni, he found a kind of sweetness in her mischievousness. "But Masi, if someone has a particular idea about me what is there to feel bad about?" and he walked way laughing.

"A curse on her ideas! This base-born creature!"

"Chandarji, it was ... it was just a joke."

"Do you have the kind of relationship with him that you can make such jokes?" Chandar shouted.

"Chandarji, I beg of you, I made a mistake, I fall at your feet."

"It won't do to beg me and fall at my feet. Go and ask for forgiveness from the one you've insulted." Chandar pushed her away roughly.

"Oh ... no ..." Chandni winced.

"So you won't ask for forgiveness? I swear, you'll get such a beating that ..." Chandar growled angrily.

"Then beat me."

"Get away from me! And if you ever try to talk to me in future you'll be in trouble."

"All right, I'll ask forgiveness, let's go."

"Why should I go?" Chandar settled down on the easy chair.

"Hai, so should I go alone?" Chandni said.

"Will someone devour you if you go alone?"

"But ... I ..." Chandni couldn't proceed. "Pimo Rani."

"No, my dear, I don't want to get involved in this. Anyway, I have to go to class."

"Hey Bhagwan! I pray to Ram that I should die this very minute. Pimoji, just come with me up to the door ... my dearest Pimoji ..." Chandni tried to sweet-talk her.

"All right, I'll come up to the door with you, but I'm telling you right now I will not go inside," Pimo said.

"But you wretch, why did you do this? Oh my God, calling Barre Bhaiya a devil! He cares so much about you."

"You don't know –"Chandni broke off suddenly.

"Arre, I know. He stares at you and you think he hates you. No, Chandni, he's not angry with you, he's angry with Chandar and that's because he's thinking of the family's prestige. But you'll see, he'll agree in the end. Here, go in now," she said as they reached Barre Sarkar's door.

"Pimo, you come too …"

"I'm not listening."

"But wait … just see what he is doing."

"He's reading — a book," Pimo said, peeping in.

"What is it?" They heard Barre Sarkar ask.

"She … Chandni … Barre Bhaiya …" Pimo was trapped.

"Yes?"

"She … she wants to say she's sorry."

"Oh?" Barre Sarkar could not control the beating of his heart. "Let her come in," he said, wiping the sweat from his forehead.

"You come too, Rani," Chandni grabbed Pimo's shirt.

"Parmila, tell Durga to bring tea," Barre Sarkar ordered. Pimo extricated herself from Chandni's grip and ran off.

Chandni tried to make her escape as well, but then, finding it impossible to exit, entered the room gingerly. Barre Sarkar was sitting at his desk with his back to her. She turned to go.

"So you've come to say you're sorry?" He turned around but kept his eyes on the book in his hands. Chandni felt encouraged.

"Come, sit down."

She came forward timidly and rested her body against the chair as if she was a bird ready to fly off at the slightest disturbance.

"So what are the sins you have come to ask forgiveness for?"

"Ji." Her lifeless voice caught in her throat.

"Yes." He sighed. "I'm being punished for the sins I committed in my previous life," he added, as if speaking to himself.

"I made a mistake, I want to ask your forgiveness," she said and turned to leave.

"But I haven't forgiven you yet," he smiled roguishly. "Sit."

But Chandni remained standing.

"No one answers my question," he muttered.

"Ji?" Chandni didn't understand what was happening. An unknown fear seemed to be suffocating her. She looked at him questioningly.

"When you look at me like this my head begins to explode." There were evil spirits raising their heads in his gaze.

Chandni lowered her eyes, Barre Sarkar broke into a laugh.

"This is even worse," he mumbled.

"Should I go?"

"But answer my questions first." He got up from his chair.

"Me?"

"Yes, you – do you want to make a spectacle of me?" Suddenly he looked very angry.

Chandni hastily dropped her eyes.

"This is even more cruel," Barre Sarkar protested.

"Shall I … shall I go?"

"First answer my questions! What has happened to me?" He gripped his head between his hands. "I'll go mad."

Chandni tried to run out quickly.

"Wait." He leapt up and grabbed her arm. The moment he touched her it was if explosives had been detonated in the air, a silent blast took place, and Barre Sarkar's body began to shake. The veins in his neck became taut, a river of sweat poured from him. Imploring, he placed her hand on his heart. It seemed as if a monster was jumping in his bosom. Suddenly he was no longer conscious of what he was doing. Like a wild animal he tore off her clothes, ripped them to shreds. A stifled scream emerged from Chandni's mouth and countless snakes began to sting her lips.

There was a loud clanging noise as the aarti salver shattered the stillness of the air.

"You harlot, you witch! May you die!" Masi clawed her own throat with both hands as if there was something stuck in it. Suddenly she stumbled and hit the chair. Her face turned blue, as though stung by a snake, her expression became deathly and she collapsed on the floor.

Hearing the crashing of the salver and Chandni's screams the entire household rushed to the scene.

"Doctor, for Bhagwan's sake, call the doctor..." Usha placed her mother's head in her lap and began to sob loudly.

Pimo, stunned by the sight of Chandni glued to the wall in this awful condition, quickly pulled off a blanket from the bed and threw it over her, and Chandni darted from the room.

Chandar sprinkled water on Masi's face.

"No!" Barre Sarkar screamed loudly, and then seeing everyone staring at him in surprise, recovered quickly, "I will call right away."

While he was dialling the number he realised that if Masi survived, the veneer he had covered himself with would be stripped and he would never be able to live with this dishonour.

"Yes," the doctor was saying on the phone, "Hello."

But Barre Sarkar looked around him guiltily like a criminal and put the phone down.

Masi was a longtime heart patient. It was not necessary for Barre Sarkar to have burdened his conscience. Even if the doctor had been informed, she would have died before he arrived.

Masi wanted to say many things before she died, but she had lost her voice. She tried to place Usha's hand in his, but he pretended not to notice, just sat next to her and kept weeping. Who knows whether he was crying for Masi, or was mourning an end slowly creeping up to his own existence! Everyone believed Masi had beaten up Chandni in anger and subsequently suffered a brain haemorrhage.

Barre Sarkar did not feel the need to confirm this and Chandni could not bring herself to speak.

Silence hung over the house for many months. Barre Sarkar isolated himself completely. Staying in his room by himself, lost in a world of his own thoughts, he felt more disoriented than ever. As for Chandni, she made every effort to keep out of his way.

The responsibility for the entire household now fell upon Usha Rani. She acquired the demeanour of a housewife, a wife whom the husband has forgotten about after depositing her somewhere with all the goods and chattels of his household.

The season was abuzz with new life, the forest was ablaze with tesu blossoms, Barre Sarkar looked somewhat agitated, but the atmosphere was calm.

Chandni was carelessly floating down the stairs like a butterfly. Today, feeling tired of his seclusion, Barre Sarkar had finally emerged from his room and was at the piano in the lounge, slowly strumming the keys. The moment he saw her the embers that had lain low all these months stirred suddenly and his fingers played feverishly. Startled, Chandni tried to make a hasty retreat.

"Listen!" His voice sizzled like the hissing of a snake.

The hair on her body stood on end and she was rooted to the ground.

"Come here."

Two black cobras emerged from his eyes and wrapped themselves around her body. Pulled by some unknown power, she advanced slowly towards him. The air was still, the surrounding atmosphere motionless. Barre Sarkar's gaze pierced her body like red-hot steel rods.

Slowly he grasped her tiny waist between his hands. Little by little his hands began to move upward. Up, further up. Her arms hung loosely by her sides, she trembled like a wounded bird. With a slight tug of his hands she fell against his chest.

Chandar came running noisily down the stairs. Suddenly the atmosphere resounded, Chandni hastily released herself from Barre Sarkar's hands and fell into Chandar's arms.

"Chandarji, Chandar..."

Barre Sarkar dropped his hands on the piano keys and put his head down on them.

Chandar was very annoyed with Chandni for seizing hold of him like this in Barre Sarkar's presence.

"Arre, arre, Barre Bhaiya is sitting over there, you silly girl."

Chandni jumped away from him and walked to the steps, her feet dragging.

"What's the matter, Barre Bhaiya?" Chandar was worried, seeing Barre Bhaiya with his head down like this. "Do you have a headache?"

"Hunh? Oh, yes."

"Uff-oh! You read all day, that's why. I'll fix it right away."

"Chandni," he called her from the bottom of the stairs.

"What is it, Chandarji?" Chandni replied tonelessly.

"Could you bring the bottle of almond oil from Didi's room," he said. "Barre Bhaiya, lie back on the chair comfortably." Settling him in the chair he began to untie his shoelaces.

When Chandni appeared with the bottle of oil he said, "Would you put a little oil on Bhaiya's hair," and began massageing Bhaiya's feet.

"I? Chandarji?"

"Yes."

"I have work to do … you … why don't you do it?" She became tearful.

"Arre, I have to go for tennis practice later, my hands will become oily and the racket will slip from my fingers."

"Wash your hands before you go."

"Don't talk nonsense. You won't faint if you put oil in his hair."

Although he was afraid of confronting Chandni in private, in public he always showed his bravado.

"It's all right, Chandar, it will go away in a short while," Barre Sarkar moaned as if in pain.

"Arre wah, how can it go away by itself? Chandni!"

Unnerved by the roughness in his voice, Chandni started applying oil to Barre Sarkar's hair. He was soon enjoying her discomfort.

"Chandar, where is today's newspaper?" he asked, pushing the paper under his arm. Chandni broke into a cold sweat.

"It must be in your room."

"No, it's not there."

"Maybe it's on the veranda. Should I bring it?"

"Please."

"And I also have to pay for the racket."

"The wallet is at my bedside."

"I'll be back in a minute." Chandar bounded up the stairs.

"Chandarji," Chandni's voice stuck in her throat.

A sneer spread over Barre Sarkar's face, his nostrils flared, the veins in his neck throbbed. Pretending to scratch his neck he groped for Chandni's fingers. Terrified, Chandni pulled her hand back.

Her eyes were pinned to the staircase, waiting for that fool Chandar, wondering when he would bring the newspaper and she would be free to leave. If only she could have spoken when Barre Sarkar hid the paper under his arm – but how could she muster such courage? In the meantime Barre Sarkar was continuing to play with her fingers.

Chandni's prayers were answered. Usha Rani was returning from the kitchen. If someone else did Barre Sarkar's work, it was an infringement of her rights. She came in quietly and moving Chandni aside, began to pat Sarkar's head. Suddenly Barre Bhaiya opened his eyes and peacocks danced joyfully in his heart. He again tried to stroke her hands. When he felt a return pressure, responding to his touch, he was intoxicated. Usha blossomed like a fragrant flower. Finding no resistance, she surrendered her trembling fingers to his. Barre Sarkar gently dug his nails into her palm. Quivering with happiness, Usha closed her eyes. Emboldened, he placed her hand on his cheek. With only a slight tug, Usha Rani fell into his lap like ripe fruit.

The heavens seemed to have fallen on Barre Sarkar! He shoved Usha aside and stood up quickly. Her support gone, Usha Rani fell with a thud on the floor. Because of the sudden interruption in her enjoyment she couldn't grasp the situation fully and stared wide-eyed at the anger blazing in Sarkar's eyes. She trembled in fear.

"Oh. I see." She understood immediately what had happened and shook her head.

"What do you see? You understand nothing. If you had the ability to understand then …"

"Then what?"

"Then … then it wouldn't be necessary to say … that … that …Uff-oh!"

He melted at the sight of the tears flowing down Usha's face.

"You don't like anything I do?"

"But why are you always pestering me? Why don't you do other things in the house?"

"My touching you displeased you so much, but she … she…"

"Who?" Barre Sarkar roared.

"You know who! You held my hand because you thought it was hers!"

Usha Rani couldn't tolerate this humiliation and began to sob uncontrollably.

"Stop this nonsense! You idiot … do you … do you want to dishonour my name? You …" He shook her violently by the shoulders. Weeping hysterically she fell at his feet.

"Please don't do this, for Bhagwan's sake, I'll die, please don't turn me away like this."

"Usha Rani, it's better that you die rather than insult the name of women like this. For Bhagwan's sake, don't force me."

"You'll regret this, what you are doing is so unfair."

Suddenly he began to feel sorry for Usha Rani.

"Why should you care, why do you care so much about me?"

"Because ... because ... you know yourself that one cannot help something like this."

"Oh! Please stop aggravating me ... go now."

"I ..."

"Go, I say!"

Usha Rani stifled her sobs and turned away swiftly.

"Usha ... Usha ... for my sake..."

Usha halted in her tracks like a wounded deer.

"You know, you're so silly ... I was joking and you started crying!" he said, gently touching her chin. Usha gaped at him like a fool.

"Chandar made her put oil in my hair, I couldn't refuse. Then you came and I knew immediately it was you. I don't know what came over me but just to tease you ... I was joking, and when you fell I became nervous ... just think ... I thought you would pull your hand away."

"Oh." That this was all her fault made Usha turn red.

"If you were offended, please forgive me, I made a mistake."

"But ... but you don't like me to do anything for you."

"No, I don't like it at all. My blood boils when I see you working. What are all these servants for? It's just that when you're stubborn I lose my temper and say things I don't mean. Afterwards, I feel sorry. Can you forgive me?"

"Arre, you've scraped your elbow. I'm a very bad person."

No ... No, I'm not hurt."

Poor Usha had no experience of lovers, and thought in her heart that this was how they behaved. She continued to smile. Chandar came in just then.

"I couldn't find the newspaper anywhere. Arre, it's right here."

When Barre Sarkar had got up in panic the paper slipped from under his arm and fell on the floor. "You always dash up the stairs in such a hurry, I called after you but you didn't hear me."

Chandar, embarrassed, turned to leave.

"Arre, Chandar, come here," Barre Sarkar said, "pick up the paper and bring it with you." After that he had a long discussion with Chandar on the subject of sports.

Silently cursing Chandar and heaving a sigh, Usha left. She had been afforded a small chance, a reasonably hopeful love scene had been in progress and this wretch had to show up just then. The occasion lost its momentum. But that was all right, for when her dreams were woven tonight the feel of his hands, the brief interlude in his embrace, the touch of his fingers on her chin – all of this would come to life and light up her solitude.

Instead of gradually diminishing because of one setback after another, Sarkar's ardour for Chandni began to assume strange forms. If he had been an ordinary mortal circumstances might not have taken such a delicate turn. He would have fallen in love with Usha or developed an intense dislike for women, or he would have taken an oath to remain celibate for the rest of his life. But he was slowly losing self-control, his obsession was growing. At night he would pace unshod on the roof in the cold air. If he succeeded in finally falling asleep the ghouls and spirits that inhabited his thoughts would find release and start creating a commotion. He would have no strength left then and his unconscious would become its own master. Sometimes, when he woke up, he would realise that he had walked to Chandni's room and was standing at her threshold, banging his head on her door, weeping uncontrollably. When he came to he would flee from there, weak with feelings of shame and humiliation. In the silence of the night he would wander deep into the woods. He was now terrified of falling asleep as well because once, while sleepwalking, he found himself on the turret leading to a window in Chandni's room. Only a narrow ledge connected it to the window. His desire for Chandni was pulling him towards her like a magnet. His weakness and fear had become subservient to his sixth sense, an unseen ghostly power was the only thing that was wide-awake.

A heart-rending scream pierced the silence, dashed against the hills and recoiled, a star fell and disappeared, and Barre Sarkar was awakened by a loud explosion. He saw that he had arrived at the window. His hand was bleeding profusely from having smashed the glass. All at once his sixth sense abandoned him. When his gaze travelled to the khud below the whole world began to rock. Everyone wants to live, and right now Barre Sarkar was not a god but an ordinary, frightened human being. He clung to the wall and closed his eyes.

Chandni's continuous screaming woke everyone up.

"There … he …" Chandni kept pointing to the window like someone who had lost her mind. "Barre Sarkar … Barre Sarkar …" And she collapsed in Chandar's arms. Handing her over to Pimo, Chandar rushed to the window. Usha Didi was already there.

"Who was it?" Chandar tried to open the window.

"No … no one." Usha screamed and grabbed the window casement with both hands.

"Let me see, please. If someone was there, he can't have got away that quickly."

"No!" She pushed Chandar away. She knew that if Barre Sarkar's secret was revealed he would not be able to live. Before she closed the window she had seen his bloody hand with his ring and knew it was him. She had nursed suspicions for a while now — how long can the beloved conceal what is in his heart from his mad lover! But she was not his lover, she was his devotee.

"No, Chandar, if it's a thief he will cut your throat!" Pimo screamed.

If he slips he will die, Usha thought, gritting her teeth, but at least his honour will not be sullied. She was trembling violently, in fearful expectation of the accident that was about to happen. She listened closely in the silence for the sound of Barre Sarkar's footsteps as he slowly drew back. A stone fell and kept banging against the wall all the way down into the khud. Usha stifled a sob.

"There is someone out there, let me see please." Chandar tried to move her out of the way but she tensed and screamed with such force that he withdrew nervously.

"Chandar Bhaiya, why do you want to put your life in danger?" Pimo was able to avert a very delicate situation with her characteristic innocence. "Usha Didi, don't let him look."

"Everyone return to your rooms. Pimo, take Chandni to my room."

"Should I sleep there as well?"

"Yes, you sleep with her and I'll sleep here."

"No, Usha Didi, what if he returns?"

"No, my dear, the thief will not come again," Usha said tonelessly.

"Chandni, did you see the thief with your own eyes?" Pimo asked.

"It wasn't a thief … it was …" Chandni stopped in mid-sentence.

"Not a thief? Then who was it?"

"Nobody," Chandni said annoyingly.

"Then why did you scream?"

"It was a dream, I got frightened."

"But … who broke the glass on the window?"

"Stop pestering me!" Chandni burst into tears.

"Arre wah, I'm just asking." Pimo's face fell.

"Don't ask, just go to sleep, Pimo Rani," Chandni said affectionately.

"Chandni," Pimo asked before falling asleep.

"Yes?"

"You called out to Barre Bhaiya."

"I did? No, of course not."

"Yes, when I woke up you were screaming, 'Barre Sarkar, Barre Sarkar!" Pimo imitated her.

"Really? I don't remember."

"But he must sleep very soundly, he didn't get up."

"Hunh." Chandni covered her face with her dupatta. How could she tell Pimo? But there would never be a better time. She sat up.

"Pimo."

"Yes."

"Will you believe what I say?"

"Yes, why not?"

"If I swear on Chandarji's life, will you believe me?"

"Yes, what is it?"

"That glass..." She could say no more, Usha was standing in the doorway. By the light of the candle she saw that there were flames blazing in her eyes.

"So what were you saying?" Pimo hadn't seen Usha.

"If you want to talk rubbish at two in the night you can both get out of here," Usha scolded.

"But Usha Didi, in Chandni's room there's a ..."

"Yes, go there. It'll be great if the thief throttles you both. Tell me, how could Chandni see anybody in the dark, and who could it be? The khud is full of thieves and crooks."

"But how did the thief climb up?" Pimo cross-examined.

"I don't know how he climbed up! We'll find out in the morning. Everyone go to sleep now without another word, understand?"

She retrieved the first aid box from the cupboard and left, locking the door behind her so that Pimo couldn't pursue her out of curiosity.

"Who's injured?" Pimo asked.

"Shush ..." Chandni turned on her side.

"One would think Usha Didi is related to the thief, she's defending him so much!"

"Go to sleep, Rani," Chandni begged.

"You know what?" Pimo suddenly jumped up.

"What?"

"It must be Usha Didi's sweetheart! He must have come to declare his love for her but ended up in the wrong room."

Despite her apprehensive mood Chandni burst out laughing. "Come now, you silly girl."

"Really, that must be it, that's why she's constantly coming to his defence. She herself leaned out of the window and started scolding Chandro Bhaiya when he tried to take a look. If he had done so her sweetheart would have been caught."

"Pimo, if you don't stop talking rubbish I will strike my own head," Chandni warned angrily and Pimo finally stopped talking.

She fell asleep at last but Chandni remained awake, staring at the ceiling. She was afraid to close her eyes. Again and again they travelled to the dimly-lit windows, as if a stranger was standing next to each one and she felt that the minute she closed her eyes, one of them would come and land on her chest. Her helplessness drove her to tears and also made her angry. Why had she been born, wretch that she was? Would the world have ended if she hadn't been?

Usha ran with the first aid box first to Chandni's room. Her heart beating violently, she opened the window and flashed a torchlight; there was no one there. He hadn't fallen for if he had she would have heard him falling. Then she saw that there were bloodstains on the wall he had leaned against. She heaved a sigh of relief. This meant he had reached the turret safely.

She rushed to his room. As she entered she found him rummaging through a drawer in the closet. When he turned at the sound of her footsteps she saw that he had a pistol in his hand. Usha acted as though she had seen nothing. She put the box gently on the table, sat on the stool nearby and calmly took out spirit, cotton and bandages.

"Where are the scissors?" Usha opened a drawer and retrieved a pair of scissors.

"You can sit here on the bed," she said casually.

The blood had congealed in Barre Sarkar's eyes, his cheeks had sunk in, he looked as if he had been ill for a long time. There were thorny bushes on the turret which is why his clothes were in shreds. He advanced towards Usha with the gun and stared wildly at her. The muzzle of the pistol rested close to her temple but she neither trembled nor experienced fear. She wasn't afraid of dying, it was as if in the midst of life's awful bitterness death had lost its lustre.

Their eyes met and for a few minutes they exchanged glances. Barre Sarkar's eyes were filled with hate, loathing and unfulfilled longing, but in Usha's eyes there was the sweetness of abiding love, tenderness and affection.

Barre Sarkar's eyes fell! The pistol slipped from his hands and in the next instant he dropped his head in Usha's lap and began to sob like a child.

"Usha Rani, save me … save me, Usha, marry me, now, this moment … Usha … or else… or else I will go mad, my head will explode. Usha save me!"

For one second Usha recoiled, as if someone had plunged a knife all the way into her heart. She wanted to ask:

"Do you really hate me so much? Have I committed such a great sin by loving you that I can atone for it in no other way? But at this time there's neither love nor hate for you in my heart, just a void! Perhaps because I have partaken of your salt all my life, it now inhabits every vein in my body."

But she said nothing. She just looked at him with tired eyes and a poisonous smile spread over her face. Quietly she lowered her head and concentrated on bandaging his hand. When she finished, she put everything back again neatly in the box and, closing the door behind her, left.

Usha spent that night pacing the veranda. How solitary her fate! How lonely her world! Especially after Masi's death she felt she was a calf roaming around without its mother. She hadn't learnt to place any kind of blame on Barre Sarkar, had always regarded him above reproach.

The heavens are testing him. The gods are displeased with him because he is greater than they are, he is superior to the ordinary worms crawling on earth. That is why Chandni has been sent by them in the form of a beguiling woman to destroy him. In truth he was not so low as to cast a lustful eye on a mere child. All the satanic powers had collectively taken the form of an unknown girl and were enticing him. He alone had the ability to silently suffer the torment of earlier lives. If it were someone else he would have fulfilled his desire and then destroyed the girl who had been sent to destroy him. The sun god is special because he blesses the particles of dust with heat, he doesn't pick up the dust and cover his face with it. That is why Barre Sarkar is putting his life on the line, to battle what the fates have in store for him. And Usha's place is at his feet. He is her venerated god, her master. Who knows what sins she had committed in the previous life to have been rewarded with this life-threatening love for him. His rejection of her is her honour. Who knows which form that the god takes is real and which the disguise he has assumed to destroy Chandni. But he doesn't love anyone! If he does, then it's this devotee of his that he loves! If he is suffering from an illness, is it not her duty to sacrifice her life in order to save him?

When her legs became heavy with all the pacing and her mind wearied with all the thinking, then Usha picked up a book of Meera's bhajans and found an echo of her pain in them. Her being was finally at peace.

Girdhar Gopal is mine
No one else.

She kept reading it in a low voice, swaying with the words. The entire world was asleep, a woman was burning the lamp of her sorrows in her heart, but the night was still dark.

She stopped suddenly as a thought crossed her mind. Without worrying about taking someone along, she draped herself in a shawl and started walking quickly towards Sarna Devi's shrine. She did not feel the darkness of the dense woods. Tigers had been seen here, snakes and scorpions were known to frequent the dark areas, but Usha Devi's love had illuminated the entire universe and the path shone like the Milky Way. In the distance somewhere jackals were howling, owls were hooting in accompaniment, but Usha Devi kept walking, intoxicated like Sati Savitri with the desire to safeguard her beloved.

12

Chandni screamed as if it wasn't Chandar she had bumped into in the gallery but an evil spirit.

She couldn't sleep in Usha's room. All around her the new surroundings took on strange and terrifying shapes to frighten her. The doors and windows had been bolted from the inside but her gaze still strayed towards them. She tried very hard to distract herself, but no sooner had she stopped feeling tense about the doors and windows than she would feel that the wall was slowly splitting into two, dark shadows were emerging from within and would seize her any second.

She was afraid of falling asleep. She got up, splashed some cold water on her face, changed her clothes and came out. The long corridor was isolated. In the bluish late-night light shadows leapt from all sides to attack her. Taking quick strides she came to the end of the corridor and that was where she bumped into Chandar and screamed.

"Arre wah, you silly girl, you're scared of me now?" Startled, Chandar laughed at her.

"Chandarji … hai, I will die." She placed her head on his chest and began to sob violently.

"You've gone mad. I thought I heard someone opening the front gate and I came to see if it was you."

"Chandar, I'm afraid, the walls of the house scare me, they will devour me. Take me away from here or I will suffocate."

"What kind of talk is this, Chandni?"

"If you don't take me away, I'll go alone." Angered, she pushed Chandar aside.

"But what's the reason for this? How cold your hands are." Chandar blew on them, holding them in his own.

"Reason? I can't tell you the reason. All I can say is that if you don't take me away from here this very minute you will see my corpse tomorrow."

"Chandni, don't talk like that. I'll die with you." Chandar pulled her into his arms.

"But I don't want to die! I'm alive in the hope that one day you will put sindhur in my hair. Then I will put my head on your chest and die. Take me away from here, Chandar, don't let me die."

"Who is killing you? Let me take you to the doctor tomorrow."

"The doctor doesn't have the cure for my ailments."

"But –"

"No ifs and buts, or you'll regret this. Take me far away from here and then I will tell you everything. If my suspicions are unfounded, you can come back."

"You won't tell me here?"

"I'll tell you on the way."

"But let's wait until the morning."

"No, I may not have the strength to stay alive until then."

"All right. Here, take the key, put on your coat and sit in the car. I'll bring my coat."

She took the key, returned to her room and put on her

coat. A glance at the sleeping Pimo brought tears to her eyes. She gently kissed her head, came down and got into the car to wait for Chandar.

"You took so long," Chandni said, playfully slapping the key in his hand when he came. The burden weighing on her heart was already feeling lighter. Chandar didn't reply and quickly started the car. Suddenly a pedestrian in black clothes appeared in front of them, but instead of slowing down Chandar accelerated. Chandni screamed and clung to him as the man barely escaped being run over.

"You're angry, aren't you Chandarji," Chandni said, hugging his arm. She didn't know where to start. Looking serious, Chandar was staring ahead at the road. His face was hidden by his hat and the upturned coat collar, but there was a strange kind of tension in the air.

"Chandarji, are you angry?" she touched his hand anxiously. "Are you?"

"No." Chandar's voice sounded gravelly.

Chandni stammered out the whole story, one incident at a time. Chandar didn't seem at all furious and Chandni felt encouraged. The speed of the car increased.

"I swear on my life, Chandar, Masi saw everything with her own eyes, that was why she had a haemorrhage, she was so angry. If she hadn't died, the secret would have come out. Usha Didi also knows everything. You and Pimo are the only ones who are so innocent you know nothing. Munshiji was the first to figure it out. The wretch taunted me. I tricked him: the young one is useless, everything is in the hands of the older brother, he is the master of everything. Hunh! The very sight of his face makes me sick. What a demon! And what a saintly air he puts on! I would die rather than even spit on his life, my stupid fool is good enough for me."

Chandni draped her arms around his neck. "I don't want a raja, Chandar, I'm yours and will always be yours. Whether you marry me or keep me as your servant, in this life I am already yours."

A tremor passed through Chandar's body and he lowered his head. Agitated, he accelerated.

Suddenly Chandni was gripped by fear. Why doesn't Chandar say something? He's angry! He adores Barre Sarkar, he worships him – he hasn't lost his mind because of all this talk, has he?

"Chandarji, you don't believe me? Please don't drive so fast. Look at me, please," she implored, pulling Chandar's face toward her.

Then Chandni's eyes opened wide, fear rendered her speechless. Like a wounded pigeon she tried to open the door and jump out, but Barre Sarkar broke into a savage laugh and, grabbing her waist, pulled her in roughly.

13

Wearing his coat, muffler wrapped around his ears, Chandar arrived in the garage and was thunderstruck. There was no sign of the car. The door of the other garage was locked. Puzzled, he came out, wondering if Chandni had left without him. He was rushing to get the key when suddenly Usha Didi, covered with dust and dirt, stumbled in through the gate.

"Arre, Usha Didi! Where have you been?"

"He … he has left!"

"Who?"

"He … Barre Sarkar has taken Chandni."

"Oh, well in that case there's nothing to worry about, but –"

"You fool! Don't stand there staring, go and get the other car out! Bhagwan only knows what is about to happen today. Hurry up, Chandar." She pushed him towards the garage.

"What's the matter, Sarkar?" Some of the servants gathered.

"Keys to the car!"

"I have them," the chauffeur said and quickly went towards his room to bring them.

"Hurry up — no, you stay here," Usha took the keys from the chauffeur and dragged Chandar. "Hurry up, Chandar, hai Ram, if something happens to them ... He ... he ..." Usha couldn't bring herself to say anything. She covered her face with her hands and started sobbing.

"Usha Didi." Chandar became very worried.

"Drive faster, Chandar..."

"I am, Didi, why are you so scared?"

"Go fast, my brother."

"How can I go any faster? A winding road, rocky terrain on one side and steep ravines on the other. Don't you see the boulders? But Usha Didi, where has Bhaiya gone at this time of night?"

"You'll find out, you'll find out everything. Just drive!"

"Usha Didi?"

"Yes."

"Is Bhaiya angry with me?"

"What?"

"He is upset that Chandni and I ..."

"You and Chandni! Yes, yes, why shouldn't he be angry? The wretch, a poisonous weed, she's become a real nuisance for everyone."

"But Didi..."

"If you had been in his place and your younger brother who was dearer to you than your own life did something as low as this, would you have patted his head in approval?"

"Am I committing a sin?"

"He loves you so much. If you make a mistake doesn't he have the right to –"

"But if he had talked to me I would given him an explanation."

"But why would he talk to you about such things?"

"Didi, if he does something ... he won't treat Chandni badly, will he?" Chandar suddenly became fearful.

"Chandar, if you want Chandni and your Bhaiya to be safe don't waste time talking. Today he will take his own life and hers. The witch, how she has ensnared him in her magic!"

"Why do you keep reprimanding her? It's my fault too, I should also be punished."

"You too will receive a punishment that you will remember for many lifetimes. You planted such a poisonous seed in the house that you will not be let off lightly."

"Is he threatening her life?"

"If she doesn't listen to him today then both his life and hers are in danger."

"But who is he to make or destroy my life! I can obey his every command but he will have to listen to me where Chandni is concerned."

"So will there be bloodshed between brothers because of this harlot? Hai Ram, Chandar!" She still couldn't bring herself to speak the truth. But there was no need to tell Chandar anything. Sarna Devi was going to grant Usha's wish today, everything was going to be all right.

In the distance they spotted the car standing at a bend in the road. Chandar pressed the accelerator and the car jumped forward. When they came closer they saw that the headlights were on, but the car was empty.

14

It became so difficult to manage the steering wheel as Chandni was scratching and biting like an angry cat. Unable to continue, Barre Sarkar stopped the car. The moment it slowed down, she slipped out of his grasp and, opening the door, fell on the road. Then, in the next instant, she got up and began to run wildly.

Seeing her running towards the river with the bamboo bridge he leapt after her but, making a detour, she started clambering up the rocks. Her shoe fell off somewhere and her dupatta flew off. He caught up with her several times, but she was able to free herself from him. Finally there was only one recourse left; she could either jump into the river or submit to Barre Sarkar. She ran towards the water, but the rocks were slippery and she kept losing her footing. And then, when she was about to get up, she saw that Barre Sarkar was right in front of her. She made an effort to stand but he grabbed her, seized her foot with his hand and tightened his grip.

Clutching her foot he was sobbing and kissing it wildly. "Chandni, I can't live without you, have pity, I'll go mad, Chandni."

A huge storm of hate and anger rose in Chandni's heart, she bent down and picked up a heavy stone to crush the head of the snake, but suddenly saw Chandar climbing up the rock. She felt an immense wave of relief and dropped the stone. Covering her face with her hands she began to cry. Finally Chandar had seen her plight.

"If you have decided then that's all right, but don't forget, my hands will be tainted with Chandar's blood," Barre Sarkar was babbling on and on. He was not at all aware of Chandar's presence.

"Are you listening to what your brother is saying, Chandarji, the brother who is like your father? Come and see for yourself."

"Bhaiya!" Chandar called out and started scrambling up hastily.

Suddenly it was as if all the strength in Barre Sarkar's body seeped out. His grip loosened and sweat drenched his body. Like a beaten dog he cowered in a corner. As he raised his head the demon that had been baring its teeth a few minutes earlier disappeared. In its place was the brother like a father, the old gentleness in the eyes, the same seriousness, the same tenderness of tone. Barre Sarkar, who was a humble human being, and a magnificent fraud.

"Have pity, Chandni, have mercy on me. If you want the family wealth you can have it, my share and Pimo's well, but for Bhagwan's sake give up Chandar. I promised my mother on her deathbed that I would take care of Chandar, and if I have to give up my life to do that I will feel I have done my duty."

All colour drained from Chandni's face, her throat was parched and her tongue became glued to the roof of her mouth. Eyes wide open, she stared in horror at this masquerader.

"Bhaiya, what are you saying?" Chandar sounded remorseful.

"I'm begging Chandni for your life. My brother, how young you were – our mother placed your hand in mine and said, 'Promise me that you will look out for Chandar.' If Maa's soul is troubled what reason will I have to live then?" Barre Sarkar was being melodramatic.

All at once Chandni pulled her foot from his grip and running to Chandar, grabbed his shirt.

"He is a fake, Chandarji, don't listen to him! This is all a farce, lies—just moments ago he was threatening to take your life, he is a liar, Chandarji—this villain has—"

"Chandni, have you gone mad?" Chandar said, frightened by the wild look in her eyes. He was not used to hearing such dreadful things spoken about Barre Bhaiya.

"I'm mad and you're very clever! Chandar, you absolute fool ..."

"Don't talk rubbish, Chandni, or I will slap you so hard that your face will be bent out of shape ... you have no control over your tongue!"

Chandni looked once at the godlike form of Barre Sarkar, then turned to look at the innocent, naïve Chandar and broke into hysterical laughter.

"I'm mad and you're not mad. I'm a sinner and you are all gods. Because of me one brother is ready to kill the other, because of me the forehead of Suraj Vansh is about to be tainted." Chandni's sigh ended on a sob. Dawn was breaking, the sun was about to rise. In the far distance, on the banks of the river, the moon's visage was turning pale yellow, moonlight was taking its last breath.

Chandni bent down to pick up a pinch of dirt at Chandar's feet to put in her hair. For one moment she stood before him, looked long and hard at him, then turned around and ran towards the river. Usha Rani tried to stop her, the guard at the bridge shouted, "The bridge is falling apart," but she flashed past everyone with the swiftness of an arrow. The bridge swayed dangerously, its bamboo shafts began to split and fall into the river below.

Like a madman Barre Sarkar got to his feet and dashed after her.

"Stop her!" He panicked when he saw her walking into the jaws of death.

"What are you doing, Sarkar! It won't be able to withstand the weight of two people, stop for Bhagwan's sake!" The guard tried to grab him by the waist, Chandar tried to pin him down, but he was filled with extraordinary power. He pushed everyone aside and jumped onto the bridge.

"What are you doing, Chandni, come back!" he shouted. A bamboo shaft split under Chandni's foot, her leg fell through the gap all the way to her knee. When she tried to extricate herself, the wood began to splinter. Seeing Barre Sarkar approach, she managed to get her foot out and crossed to the other side in one big leap. She hadn't quite regained her footing when, along with Barre Sarkar, the ancient bridge, creaking and growling, plunged into the river below.

"Barre Bhaiya!" Chandar knew he couldn't swim. The current of the river swept Barre Sarkar along with the rotting remains of the bridge and surged forward – despite warnings by the guard, Chandar threw off his coat and jumped in.

Barre Sarkar wrestled with death for a week. Chandar had risked his own life and saved him. Sarkar had received several stitches in his head and on his face. The fever was slowly abating. The doctors had said that he was out of danger, but Usha Rani remained constantly at his bedside. If she became drowsy she would lean her head against the bedpost and sleep for a while. With great difficulty Pimo and Chandar forced her to eat something. She wouldn't let anyone into the room except for the doctors. Once in a while someone would come in for a few minutes but if Barre Sarkar became agitated, she immediately threw them out. No one except she and Chandni knew the truth. She didn't think Munshiji was important. She had warned Chandni sternly not to utter a word to anyone. She was not interested in anything except Barre Sarkar's life at this moment.

Chandni was badly shaken herself and could barely think, had secluded herself from Pimo and Chandar.

When Usha was satisfied that Barre Sarkar was feeling better, she began coaxing Chandni, using hints and innuendo, that the time had come to repay her debt to this family. But Chandni was not as strong as Usha Rani. The clever woman drew pictures of the splendours of heaven, provided reassurances by presenting images of a peaceful existence in the next life, lectured her on making sacrifices, but Chandni was not ready to die.

"I'll go somewhere, far away from here."

"Chandar will come after you."

"Is there nothing but death written in my fate?"

"This is not death, you silly girl! You will become eternal. If something happens to Him, will Chandar continue to love you? Will he be able to marry the woman responsible for his brother's death?"

"No … but …"

"If his brother lives he will spend his life worshipping you."

"And Chandar will love me?" Chandni said with a sob.

"Yes."

"He will worship me, he will be in pain when he thinks of me, my memory will make him sad."

"Yes."

"Then I will die."

"I know, Chandni, you're not some low-caste girl, you're the avatar of a goddess."

"Yes, I'm the avatar of a goddess, but Didi … I was so scared of falling into the river when I was on the bridge. I went there to die, but couldn't. The knife will hurt very much, and I don't even know how to use it. Didi …"

"Yes?"

"Why don't you plunge the knife into my heart or ask Chandarji to strangle me," Chandni began to weep.

"It's a sin to kill anyone." Usha valued her own life.

"But it's also a sin to kill oneself."

"Killing yourself is a sin, but sacrificing yourself is a good deed of the highest order, Chandni. I have a nectar which will make you fall into a deep and satisfying sleep."

"And then?"

"Then you will never wake up."

"Who gave you this nectar, Didi?"

"Sarna Mayya. After Mataji passed away I was very depressed and unhappy, I thought it's better that I join her rather than be alone like this. All my sorrows will cease," Usha Rani made up a story.

"But you didn't drink the nectar?"

"No. That very night Mataji appeared in my dream and said, 'It is your duty to serve my Barre Sarkar. Your life and your death are at his feet.'"

"All right Didi, tell me something."

"What?"

"If I drink this nectar will I go to my mother?"

"When you die you will meet everyone."

"Then give me the nectar. I will go to my mother, I will place my head in her lap and close my eyes and ask her, 'Ma, what sin did I commit that you abandoned me on a rubbish heap? Clasp me to your breast.' But Didi, how will I recognize her? I've never seen her."

"You can recognize everyone when you meet them after death." Usha retrieved a tiny vial from her purse.

"But who knows, maybe my mother and father are still alive and I will be wandering alone."

"If they were alive, why would they have abandoned you and disappeared?"

"No, they couldn't have abandoned me. I'm sure I got lost and some thug or robber left me there. They would have wept and wept hopelessly. Who knows, maybe they're still looking for me. Didi Rani, can we look for them? Maybe I also have brothers and they are looking all over the world for me. Hai Didi, my heart says I have a brother somewhere, he doesn't know that his unfortunate sister is living somewhere, crying over her fate." Chandni's weeping turned into loud sobs.

Usha got tired of her rambling and left. Chandni clutched the vial in her fist and continued to weep silently. Hearing Chandar's voice, she felt her heart take a plunge. He was looking for her. His call awakened her desire to live. Oh, the days they had spent together, days of love, life's melodious moments that were so far from death, days that had become a dream and had vanished. Chandar called out her name again, then left. She crouched in a corner of the gallery. The entire household was sleeping peacefully, she was the only one awake.

Why is it that one person suffers so much but no one is aware of the pain?

At any other time she would have started screaming if

she so much as saw Barre Sarkar's shadow. But now when she saw him slowly approaching the gallery, her heart did not beat violently nor did she cry out. He came closer and stood before her like a criminal, his arms dangling by his sides. Suddenly Chandni became aware of her own power. She was noble, was going to make a sacrifice. She had the nectar of eternal life in her hand. She had nothing to do with anyone, either with Barre Sarkar's love or Chandar's hate, she had nothing to do with anyone anymore.

"Do you love me?" she asked boldly.

"Yes." Barre Sarkar's voice rustled like the air sweeping through the cremation ground. His whole body began to shake. Closing his eyes, he leaned against the wall.

"Will you promise me?" she said, grinding her teeth.

"Yes." He held his head between his hands.

"So do it." Chandni's voice was flat and expressionless.

"You … you ..." Barre Sarkar starting tearing at his throat with both hands.

"Yes, I've decided."

He touched her shoulder cautiously, perhaps to see whether she was real or a vision. From her shoulder his hand travelled up to her wet cheek. He flinched as if he had placed it on live coals.

"You … you … you're playing a game with me." He looked at Chandni in fear. The same Chandni who used to cringe and recoil when face to face with him was looking at him serenely. She opened her fist and gazed lovingly at the vial of nectar and broke into a smile. Barre Sarkar stared at her in surprise for a while, then pulled her close and searched for the answer to his question in her eyes. But there was nothing in them. Exhausted, he lurched forward.

Seeing him like this Chandni's heart melted. What was Barre Sarkar if not a masquerader? Filled with a strange kind of maternal feeling, she put both her icy hands on his burning temples and pulled his head down to rest against her bosom.

"Chandni." Chandar blinked like a fool as he saw this strange drama unfold. Chandni did not turn to look at him but Barre Sarkar jumped back. Seeing a reflection of the crumbling image of his superiority and piety in Chandar's eyes, he lowered his gaze in shame and began shaking like a leaf.

"Chandarji, we are getting married." Chandni took a life-threatening chance and teased Chandar. In one stroke she had changed from a naïve young girl into an old woman. "Have you seen the bridegroom?"

"Have you gone mad?" Chandar shook her by the shoulders but she darted out of his grasp.

"Don't touch me, because this palace of sand will collapse in a minute if you do. Why are you staring at me like this? Why are you meddling?"

"What's happened to her? Bhaiya, you –"

"Yes, I … I am the sun." Barre Sarkar swayed as if intoxicated. "And she … she is the moonlight … did you … did you see? How the world lies when it says the sun and the moon can never unite! All this is nonsense because … because my real name is not Suraj, it's Chand … Chand."

"Bhaiya, you're not feeling well."

"I'm perfectly well … because my … my name is not Suraj any more."

Usha Rani swooped down screeching like an eagle.

"You ungrateful wretch, you shameless boy, you are insulting your older brother for this worthless girl? Look at the state he's in, how can you bear to see him in this condition? But you're bent on taking his life."

"Didi!"

"Don't say another word! What has he not done for you? He wasted his youth for you, he said until Pimo and Chandar are independent I won't sleep in peace. If it had been someone else he would have plucked you out like a fly in the milk and thrown you aside. But he never looked at you in anger, never raised his voice, and you are crossing all limits?" She supported Barre Sarkar, gently propelled him to a chair and helped him sit down.

"I ... what have I done?" Chandar felt that he too, like the others, was losing his mind.

"What did you not do? You brought this witch into our house. Weren't you the one to bring her here?" Usha thought this was the only way she could keep Chandar in check. "At your insistence we raised this she-cobra, what did she ever lack? She had greater comforts than the family's real daughter, and today this shameless creature is paying everyone back by pitting brother against brother. But as long as I'm alive I won't allow this family to be destroyed, even if I have to make a sacrifice of my own blood. I, too, have eaten the salt of this house and I will not be disloyal. Nor will I permit betrayal."

"Uff-oh Didi, listen to me. I came here and saw—"

"Go away, don't call me Didi. What can someone who has no compassion for his defenceless, god-like brother do for an orphaned, helpless girl like me?" Usha broke into tears. "Everyone has complaints against him. Ask Chandni."

"I don't want to ask anyone anything," Chandar said hatefully.

"Chandarji." Chandni had never seen him look so grave. He was about to walk away when he paused.

Usha glared at her threateningly, signs of life stirred in her eyes and then began to dissolve. Wearily she dropped her head to one side.

"Yes, Chandarji, ask me—but you're still very young, you haven't learnt to be scorched by love yet continue to smile. What will you understand?"

"You ... Barre Bhaiya ..." His voice wobbled.

"Yes, who doesn't love the nectar of life?" She opened her fist and kissed the tiny vial.

"Then why did you keep me in the dark for so long?"

"Life itself is a deception, all I know is that everyone will meet after the sweet slumber of death, then I will sleep … I'm so tired."

"And you fooled me by saying how scared you were of him, that he hated you, wanted to kill you." Chandar's voice was filled with bitterness.

"Does anyone know the secrets of love and hate? No one can erase what destiny has in store for us. Nobody has any control over what is fated to happen."

"Don't use fate and destiny as an excuse. Why don't you admit you wanted to be a queen and your wish has now been fulfilled. I … I am a fool, of course … a coward, afraid of everyone. Do you think anyone will die because of you?" The blood racing in Chandar's veins was passionate and proud.

"You're right, I want to be a queen, so I'll become a queen before morning. And yes, you're a fool and a coward. You cower in the presence of Barre Sarkar. You're not fit to be the dust at his feet, and I would be insane to reject the sun god and go with the moon that shines in his shadow. He … he is a god, an exceptional man, and you? You're nothing." She wanted revenge from Chandar for her own unhappiness.

"You witch, you're going too far, now that you have everything that belongs to Bhaiya. Masi was right, if you stumble into a gutter your entire body will be covered in filth. You're getting married, I don't care what happens to you anymore." Chandar turned to leave.

"Here are my blessings," he stopped suddenly and gave her such a resounding slap that the half-dead Chandni fell against the wall.

"Hai, you fickle man!" Usha's heart was not made of stone after all. Barre Sarkar who had been in a state of semi-consciousness suddenly got up from his chair, but Usha restrained him.

"Let him be, Didi, I'm glad he hit me. Now he will cry when he remembers me and will be filled with regret and sorrow." Chandni began to sob.

"I remember you, you worthless creature? I won't even spit on you."

"Don't say things you'll regret later, Chandarji, things that will make you hold your head and mourn." Usha was overcome by remorse. "If she does something reckless because she is upset, her blood will be on your hands." Usha found a way to shift her own wrongdoing onto Chandar's shoulders. In the morning when Chandni's dead body was discovered everyone would think she had killed herself because she had fought with Chandar.

"It's you who were born to hold your head and mourn, Usha Rani. I don't want to call you sister and insult this sacred relationship. You're not a woman, you're the crushed corpse of society's customs. You've been told only that serving your husband is your religion, but he is not even your husband! You've just been thinking of him as a husband since you were a little girl."

"Chandar!"

"You are the true daughter of Bharat, you will sacrifice your life for the person you think of as your husband, you will keep worshipping at his feet whether he cuts you up and feeds you to the dogs. You're not a woman, you're a bondmaid." He turned to go.

"Wait!" He was conditioned to being startled by Barre Sarkar's voice. He stopped reflexively.

"Ask Kiran to forgive you," he said sharply.

"Kiran?"

"Yes, this is not Chandni, her name is Surya Kiran from now on."

"Ahhhaha – this is great!"

"Don't be rude, or else…"

"Or else what?"

"You will have to leave this house."

"Do you think I have any desire to live here now? But

don't think for a minute that I'm leaving because I'm afraid of anyone. No. It's because this house is driving me mad."

"Kiran, forgive Chandar, he's very foolish."

"Chandar is very foolish, you're very wise."

"Chandni, go to your room, you should rest," Usha said.

"Yes... Usha Didi is also very wise, she knows what has to be done, what time one should wake up, when one should sleep, who should live and who should die," she muttered as she turned to leave.

Barre Sarkar looked greedily at the dazed Chandni. Her dupatta had slipped from her shoulders, a sudden breeze made her clothes cling to her body. He lunged towards her.

"No ...!" Her old fear returned. Hearing Usha's muffled sob she felt like clawing his face. Why was Usha so crazy about this wretched animal? "Make preparations for the wedding, everything should be ready, should be perfect," she said and left.

When she returned to her room she heard Chandar and Pimo talking in the corridor outside her room.

"Chot Bhaiya, listen," Pimo was running after him.

Pimo would also hate her now. Chandni went to the window and looked at the rocky peaks in the distance. Pimo came into the room quietly and stared silently at her. Pimo was her friend, her confidante, but she adored Chandar.

She couldn't say anything. Quietly she began packing her suitcase.

For a split second Chandni was overcome by the desire to put her arms around Pimo and tell her everything, because when she died who would explain the real reason behind her death to Chandar and Pimo? And Chandar wouldn't worship her, he would forget her. She wouldn't even be able to hold on to that in the valley of death.

She glanced at the vial in her hand, then put it into her purse. No, she couldn't die just yet. For a long time she kept writing on a piece of paper and kept erasing what she had written with her tears.

"Chandar, everything will be all right, when the time comes you'll understand everything," Usha said, putting away his clothes in his suitcase.

"There's nothing left in life that can be all right."

"Very soon you and Pimo will be back."

"I won't come back even when I'm dead."

"Is it possible for brothers to be separated forever? You don't know how ill he is right now. What I say is …"

"I've never understood what you say and never will. You're not a human being, you're a stone. He treats you so badly and you continue to worship him, and today you really went too far. You're handing him over happily to another woman."

"I've not handed him over to anyone, and as long as I'm alive no one can take him from me. I brought him back from the jaws of death, but how can I tell you … one day all will be revealed… the family's welfare is paramount. Here, take this cheque, Chachaji will have it cashed for you. I'll see that the car is brought around. And listen, make sure Pimo doesn't feel too disheartened. If she sees you getting so upset she'll curl up in a corner and cry."

"Didi, I'm terrible, I've been saying such terrible things to you, can you forgive me?" Chandar grabbed her feet.

"Arre, what are you doing, my brother! Are you crazy? How can I be offended by anything you say?"

"Maa left us when we were children, you were the one to give us all the comfort a mother gives her children. I had thought that one day you and Bhaiya … Didi, my blood boils to think … but I'm helpless, what can I do? What will you do here now?"

"This is my house," Didi smiled.

"Listen Didi, you won't be happy here, come with us, we'll all live happily somewhere else."

"Now only my funeral bier will leave this house. My dear

brother, trust me, but listen, if you hear some bad news don't lose heart."

"What kind of news, Didi?" Chandar looked worried.

"News of the wedding," Usha laughed.

"Arre, I'm repelled by the very sight of her face."

"No, Chandar ..." she stopped in mid-sentence.

"What?"

"Nothing. I will send your breakfast."

Finally Usha hugged Pimo, instructed her to take care of Chandar and said goodbye to them.

"Pimo ... Pimo..." Chandni ran after them as the car left the house. It stopped, Chandni leaned in through the window hesitantly and placed her hand on Pimo's cheek. Pimo's tears streamed down her face and she quickly turned away. Chandar asked the chauffeur to start the car.

"Pimo, Pimo, look at me once ... you won't see me again, Pimo..." She began running alongside the car, stumbled and fell on the gravelly road. The string of wax beads that Chandar had given her on her birthday instead of the necklace broke, and the beads scattered everywhere. She stared wildly at them. All at once they dissolved and became pearls. Her head dropped.

Silence reigned over the haveli, as if a death had taken place. Chandni stayed quietly in her room. She was no longer afraid of anyone. Seeing Pimo's things spread all around her heart sank, going into Chandar's room made her feel depressed – the past rushed at her.

No, she was not going to die so easily. She was alive only because she wanted Barre Sarkar's real self revealed to all. In addition, there was still a tiny ray of hope that glimmered. Maybe Chandar would believe her when he read the letter she had slipped into his pocket, and then she would gladly breathe her last in his lap.

When Usha reminded her of her promise, she lost her

temper. "Didi, I've never played the dying game before. Don't remind me again and again, let me die on my own. But if you want, you can strangle me yourself or pour the poison down my throat."

When she saw Usha looking worried she broke into a laugh. "You don't want my blood on your hands because they've been made to be decorated with henna. After I die and everyone has forgotten me, you will marry Barre Sarkar. But don't worry, I am destined to die."

And Usha Rani remained silent in order to appease her, but would sing the glories of sacrifice, of giving up one's life, sang melancholy bhajans so that there were times when Chandni felt like ending her life without waiting for Chandar. But then somewhere far away she would hear the whistle of a train and hope that Chandar was on it, that everything was going to be all right.

How many friends did Barre Sarkar have? Those who were his age were now planning their children's weddings. Who knew that he would get married at this age and that also to an unknown young girl? He was quite overwhelmed by the wedding arrangements. Usha Rani was in charge of everything. As the wedding day approached, she started getting very worried. What if Chandni went back on her word? If she turned her out of the house where would she go? Whom would she turn to for support?

The fire that had been burning in her heart had abated. Romance had turned into a simple question of food and shelter. Masi, while she was alive, had been such a great support. Always instructing her to turn to Bhagwan for succour, she had trained her in such a way that she had learnt to restrain her desires. But the need to survive and her self-respect were still alive.

Wedding celebrations began and there was no sign of Chandar. Usha responded to all of Chandni's appeals with silence. Chandni felt her hopes falling into slumber in the lap of death.

The fire at the mandap was being stoked. Chandni was decked out in all Maa's jewellery. Usha went up to her on the pretext of fixing her sari's pallu.

"The time for the lagan is approaching," she said tearfully.

"I know, Didi, don't worry."

"I have to worry."

Chandni saw Barre Sarkar dressed as a bridegroom and fell into a chair with a deep sigh. The time for the last train had passed. No one came and no one was going to come!

Usha poured a glass of sherbet from the jug. Chandni took the vial from her purse and emptied its contents into the glass.

"Are you satisfied now?"

Usha lowered her eyes.

"You will tell Chandar and Pimo everything, won't you?"

"Ye... Yes..." she promised. "Come, hurry up now."

"Why the rush? The ceremony won't begin for a while," Barre Sarkar said, pulling up a chair to sit on.

Colour draining from her face, Usha stood up with a stricken look.

"Is everything all right? What's happened?"

"Nothing." She turned to leave.

"You look very nervous," he said with a smile.

"No, no, not at all. The guests are arriving, I ... I..." Usha stuttered.

"Yes, of course, you should go and take care of the guests. Make sure the ice cream doesn't melt, and I think we'll need more sweets."

"No, we have enough."

"You have to do all the work, Usha."

"No, no, really..."

"Why no? You've made such excellent arrangements. No one except you and Masi had the capacity to do this." He stressed each word.

"Yes..." Usha stammered.

"Everything will be all right, yes?"

"Yes ... yes, it will ..."

"And you won't have any complaints left?"

"No, I won't," Usha said impetuously.

"Then go and take care of the preparations." He smiled, then glowered at her.

She left hastily, bumping into people as she walked out.

After Usha had gone, Barre Sarkar sighed deeply and gazed at Chandni with the same melancholy look. She sat quietly, her eyes on the glass.

He filled a glass with sherbet, then put it down and cautiously placed both his hands on Chandni's hands. As if stung by a snake Chandni pulled away quickly, then covering her face, broke into sobs.

"Arre, still so bashful? Wah!" He smiled wickedly. "You're happy today, aren't you?"

She gathered up all the hate in the world in her eyes and scrutinised him from head to toe. "Yes, I'm very happy." Then she picked up the glass in front of her and put it to her mouth.

"Arre, don't drink so quickly, it will go down the wrong way," he laughed, then picked up his own glass. "What's the rush?" he asked, taking a sip.

Intoxicated with a sense of victory, she pushed away his hand and, closing her eyes, began to gulp down the sherbet.

Usha Rani was with the guests but her mind was elsewhere. She wanted to be happy, but she was trembling all over.

After emptying the glass, Chandni broke into loud laughter and kept laughing, forgetting even to wipe the tears streaming down her face.

"Yes, Barre Sarkar, I'm yours now." She spread out both hands towards him.

But he fixed his eyes on her, kept smiling and continued drinking from his glass.

Suddenly Chandni clutched her throat with both hands. Standing in front of her was Chandar, looking dishevelled and worried.

Chandarji! When she realised that her eyes were not deceiving her and that Chandar was actually there, she stumbled across the room and clung to him.

"You're late, Chandarji, I'm leaving, Raja, I've drunk the poison, look there's your Surya god."

"You've come, Chandar." Barre Sarkar's voice resounded with the ring of victory and he drained his glass in one gulp.

Chandar was late. He would have been here six days earlier but he and Pimo had gone hunting with Mamaji, and it was only when they returned and his coat was being sent to the laundry that the note was discovered.

"But who can fight the fates, Chandarji?" Chandni said, touching his face with trembling hands. "Hide me inside your bosom, Chandarji, my heart is sinking." She became unsteady in his arms.

Chandar quickly put her down on the sofa. Pimo placed her face upon hers and began weeping. There was a commotion among the guests.

"Munshiji, please call the doctor, quickly." Chandar wiped the sweat from her forehead with his lips. "Please hurry."

"It's all right, Munshiji, we don't need a doctor." A twisted smile danced on Barre Sarkar's face, he was sipping the sherbet with relish, seated calmly in his chair, as if Chandni were an insect and not a human being.

"You wretch, you coward, you've taken the life of an innocent girl and you're sitting here, laughing like the devil!" Chandar leapt and grabbed Barre Sarkar by the throat and shook him violently. "But how will you escape me?"

Sarkar pushed Chandar away roughly, his face suffused with extreme anger. The Chandar who had always feared this look cowered before him for a moment.

"What kind of silly talk is this?" Barre Sarkar said gently. "Have you ever heard that a bee strangled a blossom, or a moth extinguished a flame?" He walked up to Chandni, the picture of dignity, and gently stroked her tousled hair.

"The silly girl – she thinks she has drunk the poison …"

A heartrending scream issued from Usha's mouth and she ran to snatch the glass from him, but he drained it in one last swallow.

Usha stared at him wildly, then fell down and clutched his feet.

Chandar pressed his temples, failing to comprehend what was happening.

Chandni moaned and opened her eyes. When Barre Sarkar placed a hand on the sofa to steady himself, she shrank and clung to Chandar.

"Yes, Chandar, save her. The moonlight fades away in the presence of the sun. Usha, get up, your tears are making the poison even more bitter." He tried to lift her up. "Forgive me, Usha Rani. I did not value your love, I have hurt you badly – and for that I'm being punished today. You wasted your entire life for me."

"My lord, serving you is my life." Usha placed her head at his feet. "Why did you do this?"

"I know that whatever I have done was not right. I loved Chandni. If I had loved Bhagwan as much I would have found him by now, but Chandni and Suraj cannot be one." He became dizzy and was about to fall. Chandar rushed forward and caught him in his arms.

"Bhaiya! Arre, Munshiji, have you called the doctor?"

"The doctor can't do anything now, Chandar."

"But Bhaiya, why did you have to do this?"

"There was no other way, Chandar. Usha, don't make me a greater sinner than I am by touching my feet. In trying to transform an ordinary human being into a god you turned him into the devil. Tiny lies grew into terrifying sins and … and …" He winced in pain and vomited blood.

The doctor ripped through the crowd of people to get to him, but he stopped him.

"Doctor, these last few moments of life are the most precious I have left, don't snatch them from me. You won't be able to save me. Even Bhagwan cannot avert death now." Then, driven by pain, his eyes turned inward, the bridge of his nose shifted, and in a few seconds his breath became laboured. He gazed at Chandni standing in the distance. As death approached, his eyes danced for the last time, and with a blood-soaked smile he said playfully, "Look at the silly girl, she's crying! But why are you shedding tears from afar? Come here, Chandni! Place your hand lovingly on my bosom just once … or else this heart will remain tormented for all eternity."

Chandni felt her heart sinking and she fell on his chest.

Barre Sarkar took her in his embrace, and for the first time Chandni did not resist.

"Ah, if death is so beautiful then why should one not want to be born and die a thousand times," he said, intoxicated with death and love, and placed his lifeless lips upon her forehead.

Chandni was filled with anguish. If only his chest would burst open and she could drown forever in its unfathomable depths.

"Don't cry, my love! It's your wedding today. Look, the sun is setting, today the moon will hold sway and there will be radiant moonlight everywhere."

In the west the last ray of sunshine sobbed and was silenced, and the soft, shy light of the moon spread like the shroud of a newly-wed bride.

Wild Pigeons
(*Jungli Kabutar*)

CRADLING her head tightly with her hands, Abida sat motionless in the half darkness of her room. The night was slowly filling it like black smoke, but more than the atmosphere it was the deep sadness that was stifling her desolate heart. Dry-eyed, she felt as if there were sand rankling between her eyelids. In the bungalow next door the phone shrilled continuously. Perhaps the owners had gone out. From the servants' quarters came the muted sound of their conversation and the tinkling of pots and pans.

She reached out with her hand and straightened the crease in the bedcover. If only there was enough power in one's hands to smooth layer after layer of wrinkles in one's heart. Drained by a sense of anguish she turned on the lamp. One half of the bed lit up, the black and green blossoms on the bedcover came to life ... part of the bed awakened but the portion where Majid had slept remained engulfed in tomb-like darkness. The lamp on his side of the bed was beyond her reach but she also knew that its light would not pierce the darkness that had swallowed him.

Six months had passed since the period of *iddat.* Amma had said innumerable times, "Child how long will you continue to ruin your life living in this desolate house?"

But Abida had turned her grief into her life. She didn't have anything else to remember him by, did she? She felt an otherness in that grief. She knew his side of the bed would never come to life, that the sudden touch of her hand could not make his body start and offer her the invitation of an embrace. The special fragrance of his cigarettes would never permeate the room, no one would potter around noisily early in the morning in the bathroom and hum songs that were out of tune, no one's bristly cheek would ever scratch her chin again.

Right next to the window the birds on the tangled vines of the Chameli were creating a real racket. A bullock-cart was creaking its way down the road. Abida got up and tiptoed her way to the almirah, opened it, and taking out one of Majid's shirts, crumpled it in her hands, carefully threw it down on the floor, then carelessly draped his pants and tie on the chair. After this she took out a cigarette and lighter from the drawer, lit the cigarette, turned on the lamp on Majid's side of the bed, and placed the lighted cigarette on the lip of the ashtray.

The desolation in the room was dispelled instantly. Abida sat down calmly on the rocking-chair and began knitting Majid's sweater.

*

Among the wedding guests at Makkan Baji's wedding she had spotted Majid Bhai laughing loudly. He was a distant cousin from her mother's side. She had never seen him before but had heard a great deal about him. He is a flirt, he has had several successful and unsuccessful romantic liaisons. Every year it was reported that Majid Bhai had married some actress. Then one would hear that yes, he was getting married, but to a friend's divorced wife. Once it was rumored that he had become enamoured of a lady doctor and a civil marriage was about to take place; the schoolteacher with whom he had had an ardent relationship was threatening to commit suicide. A lot of glamour attached to Majid Bhai's name because of all this talk. Young women loved to have long discussions about his amorous adventures.

After Bajia's wedding Abida got a chance to see Majid Bhai at close quarters. He was not at all the epitome of the young

Prophet Yusuf, but when you met him you realised that there was indeed something that made for a special excitement, something that tickled your heart.

"Oh, so you are Abida," he said pointedly, the moment he met her.

"Yes. Has someone complained to you about me?" Abida retorted.

"Uhh... no, no one has complained. Did I say that?"

"The way you asked me made me think that perhaps you had."

"Well, you're very perceptive."

"Yes, thank you!" And with that she turned on her heels and walked away to help Khala Jaan in the drawing room. She was angry because her heart was beating wildly.

"My dear, could you sprinkle some pistachio slivers on the kheer in the bowls? I can't imagine what embellishments the girls are busy with," Khal Jaan said, arranging onion rings on a dish of seekh kababs.

Abida saw five or six girls engrossed in decorating the kheer by writing Bajia and her bridegroom's name on it with bits of pistachio. She looked down to see what they were writing and at that moment Shabana slapped a piece of silver paper on her lips. Shabana was Majid's younger sister and she teased every young woman by calling her 'bhabi'.

When Abida walked past Majid Bhai while the food was being served he quipped, "People are disposing of the delicacies under the pretext of serving others."

"Oh, so now you have knowledge of the unknown, or is there an x-ray machine in your specs which enables you to see what's inside people's stomachs," she snapped.

"No need for an x-ray of the stomach. Mouths are speaking their guilt."

That was when Shabana broke into giggles. Even after Abida had rubbed her lips vigorously, a trace of silver paper remained.

But when her gaze fell on the bowl of kheer in front of Majid Bhai she thought she was going to die. Someone had written "Abida/Majid" on it with pistachio flakes.

She thought she would switch bowls but when she extended her hand towards it, Majid Bhai stopped her. "This is mine."

"I ... I ... well, I'll get you another one," quickly spreading her fingers to cover the kheer.

"Why? Leave my bowl alone." Majid's fingers covered hers. Abida quickly drew her hand away.

"Oh!" Majid Bhai coloured when he discovered the secret of the bowl. Abida felt the blood draining from her body. She hastily began pouring water in the glasses.

Later she would laugh about this incident, but that day she let Shabana have it until the girl's face was swollen from weeping. And she also put Majid Bhai through the wringer, something he would never forget because Shabana, the wretch, reported everything to him.

"What did you gain by making Shabana weep like this? There were other ways of showing your dislike of me, although there was really no need to make such a production of it. I'm not an idiot." He took the opportunity to say this at another party.

"I ... that is ... actually, I was angry and ..."

He was upset that she had been so angry with Shabana. "She's young, she thinks that all girls are as crazy about her brother as she is. She likes you, she likes you very much. As far as she was concerned she had made a very affectionate joke. She didn't have the slightest idea that she had done something you would find extremely offensive."

"I ... I'm sorry. I don't know why I felt my tongue burning and I scolded the poor thing so badly." Abida wanted to disappear. What was happening?

"Listen," Majid stopped her just as she was turning to go and said, "do you believe everything anyone tells you about somebody without first checking and asking?"

"Of course not."

"Then why did you insult her?"

"I ... I don't know what happened to me at that moment ... I'll ask her to forgive me."

"And think about asking me to forgive you, too. If someone had said something as objectionable about you I would never have believed it for a second."

"Why wouldn't you believe it? How do you know that ..."

"I know."

"What do you know?"

"I know you ... my sisters give me all kinds of information about you in their letters, including details like what you were wearing on a certain day."

"Oh!" Abida began feeling angry again, but this time with herself.

"All right, so tell me what other flaws I have besides being a vagabond, and a base and dishonourable fellow?"

"None," she said lamely.

Majid Bhai turned away and began talking to some other people.

And then he left. He didn't come to say goodbye. He went in to say his salaams to Ammi, while she stayed hidden inside. He never asked about her.

But within a week his proposal arrived. Bajia told Abida that he wanted to know if she was agreeable to the match and that Ammi had already said yes. "So this is just a formality."

"And what if I refuse...?"

"Ai hai, are you crazy? He's such a nice young man."

"I don't care. What if I don't like him?"

"Oh, come on, don't pretend. You're speaking nonsense, go and take a look at yourself in the mirror."

And feeling helpless, Abida burst into tears.

"Ai hai, what's wrong with him? You've given him your

heart, not your honour."

"Bajia … I'm scared."

"But why?"

"I don't know."

"All right, that's enough, now don't be a fool. And in any case you're not getting married tomorrow. Majid Mian has asked permission to first correspond with you."

"No, no, and anyway, what difference can writing letters make?"

"Do you want a courtship then? My dear, you're so lucky you're getting a chance to correspond. I just saw a glimpse of your dulha bhai from a crack in the door of the cowshed. And by God, just that one glimpse made me break out in a sweat. All night, all day, it felt as though he was here, sitting in front of me and staring, teasing me with his eyes. Oh God!" Bajia rocked with laughter.

*

"I'm attracted to pretty women but no one has stolen my heart yet," Majid wrote, "and I can't promise that after marrying you I will become a dull and pious man. You are the one who will have to decide whether to take your gift back and then allow it to be given to someone else."

Abida wrote, "I don't regard the heart as something that one gives or takes. Whatever the heart is, it will always be yours. If you wish you can distribute it here and there, but remember that I can't become a person who shares with anyone else."

"You argue so stubbornly, you know. This means we can't be married," Majid wrote.

"No, that's not what it means," Abida wrote back after thinking long and hard.

*

After the wedding Abida realised how subjugated you feel when the person who has won by writing letters actually appears before you in person. Not only had she never been in love, she had never even entertained the thought of a man in her heart. She saw God's light in Majid's love. She gathered her world with both hands and let it drown in his being. But she didn't abandon her feminine pride. If Majid was ever late coming home, she would roam restlessly, staring tearfully at the door. But the moment he entered she would still the beating of her heart, appear casual and busy herself with some silly chore. When he pulled her passionately into his embrace she would restrain herself and sprinkle cold water on his ardour.

"Arre ... arre ... look at the carpet, is it alright?" And Majid would stop to look at the carpet, his passion cooled. She would involve him in some very dry economic or political issue just to give him as few opportunities as possible to be amorous.

And that was not all. She didn't even take off her armour on the double-bed.

Because she was afraid of him.

He was false, wasn't he?

She would often think that she had relinquished her entire existence into his hands and if he betrayed her, what would she be left with? She wouldn't want to live. And so she kept reminding him that there were other more important things in life than him that were of interest to her.

*

But one incident shattered her strategy. What she was afraid of finally happened. She wanted to forget Majid's past but it pushed ahead and grabbed her by the throat.

One day a stranger called and asked that she send Majid to the hospital immediately. His wife had delivered a baby in Room 6. The baby was fine but the mother was dying. J. J.

Hospital.

Majid entered the house and became extremely agitated when he saw Abida. She was still sitting next to the phone. The colour of her henna still shone on her nails, but her body was cold and her face was ashen.

"Your wife has had a baby," she said with a smile.

"Arre, but it's only been two months since we got married. That's great." He heard her speak, was filled with relief and swept her into his arms.

"Don't joke. Are you a man or a beast?" She pushed him away. "A helpless woman has been a victim of your dastardliness and you..."

"Abida, what are you saying?"

"I called you everywhere..."

"But..."

"In J. J. Hospital ... the baby is healthy, but the mother is dying." She became hysterical.

"What is wrong with you? I swear I don't have any other wife except you."

"So, did you divorce her? You beast... the mother of your child!" If she could have had her way she would have strangled him with her bare hands. Majid tried to calm her but she scratched his face, tore his clothes and then, burying her face in her hands, began sobbing bitterly.

"Abida, for God's sake, please listen to me."

"Don't touch me! You think I'm crying because I'm feeling let down by my fate, but that's not it. By God, I'm crying for that unfortunate woman whom you have betrayed."

"Oh God, what is all this?" Majid collected his thoughts and called J.J. Hospital.

"Can you please tell me the name of the patient in Room 6?"

After several inquiries it became clear that Room 6 was empty.

"Ohhhh ... so the poor woman has died ... Oh my God, you're a murderer ... you killed her ... and your son ... what will happen to that unfortunate child ... he will be raised in an orphanage ... no ... he won't be raised in an orphanage... he didn't get a mother's love and his father is a devil."

The situation became unmanageable. With great difficulty witnesses were produced to swear that no one had delivered a baby in Room 6 and no woman had died there. A patient, Lalaji, suffering from indigestion had been admitted to the hospital and he too had left two days earlier. Then finally the riddle was solved. Majid's friend who was responsible for this tasteless joke, had thought Abida would be greatly amused by his prank. Several arguments later it was agreed that this was the stupid friend's fault, and Abida's own way of thinking had contributed to her state of mind. The story faded away, but Abida couldn't forget what had happened to her after the phone call. Again and again she was tormented by a nightmare in which she had had a baby in the hospital, she was dying, and Majid's new wife was looking everywhere for him. And Abida finally breathed her last in Room 6.

But ten years passed and the dream was not realised. The doctors finally gave up. Both are healthy. There's no reason not to conceive.

*

"Please come back, for God's sake." Majid's latest letter lay before her. Telegrams and letters were pouring in. "Ammi Jaan is not well," she would reply. Majid's mother had suffered a second attack of paralysis. He and Abida had come to see her and Abida had stayed back to nurse her. Now the old lady neither died nor recovered. "How can I leave her alone? Why are you in such a state? Find someone to fall in love with for the time being, it will help you pass the time." She wrote all this just to tease him and Majid would get riled up in response.

"Why, have you forgotten all your tricks in ten years?" she tantalised him. "You poor thing."

"You're asking for it," he replied irately.

Eventually Ammi Jaan improved but then Makkan Baji arrived to deliver her sixth baby. Abida was the only one without children, everyone else was busy tending their offspring.

"Should I leave Baji alone here in this condition?" she wrote to Majid.

"No, there's no rush, but for God's sake come back immediately after this," he replied wearily.

Six months passed in all this back and forth. When she returned she found Majid looking very glum and unhappy. But Abida got busy with tidying up the house. No linen in sight, no towels, plates and dishes a mess, half the pots and pans on loan to the neighbours.

"For God's sake, just buy new pots so we can put an end to this," Majid snapped, worn-out by all this talk about pots, pans and cutlery. But Abida had only one thing on her mind. Until she got the house in shape again she could not rest.

After fixing the bedroom, drawing-room and kitchen, she turned her attention to clothes. Half of Majid's clothes had disappeared. Her own saris were not all there. Except for the simple and very expensive ones, nearly all the others were missing.

And she was worried the most about Majid. Half of him had disappeared as well. His face looked sad and he appeared somewhat lost. Busy with getting the house in order, Abida had failed to notice this at first and he had been quiet as well.

"You're back, but still far away," he protested.

"Do you see that the house has turned topsy-turvy? My tin of talcum powder has also disappeared. I don't know what to complain about any more."

"You hated the smell of the powder."

"I didn't hate it. You're the one who made a fuss about it. Anyway, I don't care that it's gone, I want to know who cleaned out the house like this."

"I did," Majid said guiltily.

The cigarette ash fell on the tablecloth. In an instant she ran back to the room from the past. This long journey had tired her out. She placed the sweater she was knitting on the arm of the chair. When it was completed she would hang it up next to the sweater she had finished last week.

She gave herself up to grief and stretched out on her side of the bed. Tears flowed down her cheeks and wet her hair. She placed a hand gently on the pillow next to hers and turned back to the past. She had repeated each incident so many times in her mind that now she didn't need to make an effort to remember.

*

"She works at the canteen?"

"How many times will you ask?"

"As often as you say you don't love her." There was the stillness of death in her voice.

"Well, in that case this discussion will never end."

"You still think I shouldn't leave the house after this?"

"Yes."

"What will I do in this big rambling house after you've left…"

"No."

"But…"

"I can't live without you." Majid spoke like a stubborn child. Abida felt like clawing his face but she only smiled. Majid avoided her gaze.

"I'll leave by the morning train," she said determinedly.

"You won't be able to leave by the morning train, it won't

be possible to make arrangements for the funeral that early in the morning."

"The same threats again! Just think about what you're saying. I'm not made of steel."

"That's what I thought. I wish I could break down the wall of your restraint! I wish you would scratch my face like an ordinary woman. But you're not an ordinary woman, you're Abida, I didn't even have the courage to fall at your feet and ask forgiveness for my sins."

"There's no point in making these depressing comments. It's your duty to be fair. I don't want you to betray her as well."

"Abida, the softness of your voice is paralysing me. The only reason I haven't done what I should have done till now is that I had hoped, since you are different from other women, that you would think about my mistake objectively."

"What is it that you should have done and haven't done till now?"

"I have no right to live. If a man who is deficient cannot be forgiven then there's only one recourse left."

"In other words, suicide."

"Absolutely."

"Why do you entangle me in these romantic notions," Adida said wearily.

"Abida, if I've picked up an ember by mistake should I hold it in my palm and fan it forever?"

"This is a ridiculous example. You've always played with fire. For ten years you lived an unfamiliar and unnatural existence, and the minute you got a chance you returned to your true self." Abida's tone hardened. Majid felt encouraged.

"Abida, if you had committed such an error I would never have punished you like this. Do you really think that I can spend my life with this empty-headed, illiterate woman?"

"If she was really so uninteresting how did she become your precious beloved?"

"But if one enters a toilet to urinate should one be

incarcerated there? Can one spend one's entire life in such a place? I never claimed that I was an angel. You know perfectly well that I'm a weak, deficient human being, but I don't deserve such harsh punishment. Just think, if I could tolerate her what was there to stop me? I wouldn't have needed your insistence, I would have left you without a qualm. Would you have stopped me?"

"Absolutely not."

"You are definitely pushing me away with both hands. If I had the slightest bit of self-respect I would have left immediately."

"What if I had made a similar mistake?"

"By God, I would have smashed your bones, but I wouldn't have punished you for living with a wild beast."

"What do you want?"

"I want you to punish me as you see fit. If you're revolted by me, I promise I won't touch you without your permission. We can live like two friends, can't we?"

"But why must friends live with each other? She needs you, how will she battle life alone?"

"You're feeling very sorry for her."

"She's pitiful. And what will become of that innocent child? You will have to marry her."

"Abida..." Majid got up and started pacing restlessly. "I am ... whatever you decide, I am ready to do, except marry her. Don't give me this clichéd, worn-out punishment, I won't be able to endure it. You don't get married because of some compulsion or pressure."

"But an innocent –"

"I'm not refusing monetary assistance, and there will be all the publicity to deal with as well."

"Monetary assistance? I didn't know you regarded money as being so important. Will monetary assistance atone for everything?"

"I hate the idea of saving face. To get married just to

protect one's image would be a betrayal of my conscience. I cannot embark on a long journey with this girl."

"Don't be so dramatic, I understand only too well. But if you weren't so concerned about her, why did you give her my saris?"

"Only because I hated them and so I threw them away," Majid said listlessly. "Abida, have I committed a sin that has never been committed before? Has no one ever been guilty of such stupidity? I've explained to you several times, I was troubled. I wrote you numerous letters, sent you telegrams, you didn't come … I wrote in clear terms that I needed you. Pick up my letters and read them. I even said that my life and my convictions are being threatened, for God's sake save me."

"How could I leave Ammi Jaan, and then there was Baji's pregnancy …"

"So if I had died you would still not have returned? Compared to my mother and sister, I am nothing?"

"God forbid, if you were ill…"

"You mean to say I wasn't ill?"

"This is not an illness."

"My love, this is the world's most horrible illness. It has caused the greatest of saints to become weaklings."

"Uff! You're just trying to make a case for what you did."

"Abida, I don't at all expect you to forgive me and clasp me to your breast, although by God I'm ready to give up three-fourths of my life for such a miracle. I know I cannot regain the place I once had in your heart, which I have now lost. But I do beseech you, please meet her once and then decide. If you still want to stick with your decision after that, you will get what you want."

"I know I can never win with you. I will have to change my principles. You can marry a second time, you have my permission."

"Marriage is a sacred vow, it can't be made with anyone who happens to come your way, nor can it be undertaken again and again."

"You can fall in love with anyone who comes your way?"

"If someone falls into the gutter it doesn't mean they have fallen in love with filth. If the union of bodies doesn't involve the soul, you can't call it love. There's a difference between love and lust."

"Oh my God!" She clasped her head between her hands. She was surprised by how casually she was talking about the most horrible accident of her life. Her heart was devoid of all emotion.

"I won't beg for my life any more." What would she have done if he had come down to using force like other men? "I've said this before, the girl has no substance."

"But her body is not without substance," Abida taunted.

"Her body, too … has brought so much anguish for me that I'm now revolted by it. Abida, I thought a hundred times that I should get rid of her before you come back. How will I look you in the eye? But without hearing the verdict from your own mouth I couldn't even die."

"Oh dear, the same juvenile threats. Do you ever think of Ammi Jaan's advanced age? Let her die peacefully first. To inflict the grief of an only son's death on her would be the worst kind of cowardice."

"There's no room to move, no way to go forward."

"If you're thinking of the child … give her a divorce after the nikah."

"If a deficient man like me is forced to become a father, what pride will the child have in me? He will become an orphan before he is born. This marriage and divorce game is not something I can manage."

On this double-bed hearts had throbbed with a love and passion that became life's single purpose. Here they read books together all night and made love, then talked and made love again and chatted again – they never tired of each other, never once felt the ache of childlessness.

On that same bed now, two strangers sat together till it was morning.

A hazy light hung about the room. The sound of a child's whimpering carried over from the cook's chamber. Husband and wife's wretched faces were as pale and lifeless as dust. This was not the wakefulness of the wedding night, it was that night of eternal despair, dark even in the light of the sun. There were blue circles under Majid's eyes. The ashtray was heaped with cigarette stubs. Both were exhausted and had squeezed themselves into their respective spaces on the bed.

On Majid's forehead sparkled burnt silver strands. Abida wanted to forget everything and place her parched lips on his unshaven chin and let the tears that had been dammed for many lifetimes flow unchecked.

Then this horrible nightmare will end and she will wake up.

*

Making every effort to protect her sandals from the sludge in the gutter, she drew her sari pallu in front of her nose and kept going. At the doorstep of a house an old woman suffering from acute asthma was blowing her breath through the pipe in her bosom, in the hotel the radio was blaring away, naked children sat astride the gutter, a kitten was seriously attacking a scrap of paper. The news of her arrival was spreading. People were leaning over their balconies to look down at her.

Mona opened the door, gazed at her through half-shut eyes and then, leaving the door open, walked back in. This was meant to indicate permission to enter. Sitting on a high uncomfortable chair, Abida thought, why did I make the mistake of coming here? Why didn't I believe what Majid had said?

Mona was an attractive girl with a filled-out body. At this

moment it was more filled out than it should be and she was also walking stiffly, as if wanting to remind Abida that, 'the blessing for which you have been consulting doctors for ten years has been forced on me. I have to endure your torment.'

"Do you ... want him to marry you?" Abida's mouth was dry, something seemed to be moving with a loud thump at the back of her throat, and her temples throbbed. She shouldn't have come into the war zone after a whole night of wakefulness and emotional turbulence.

"Is there a medal for marriage that you received and that I will get, too?" She lit a cigarette, drew on it, then blew the smoke out slowly through her mouth and nose. Abida liked the fragrance of men's cigarettes, but this one was stifling her.

"What do you want then?"

"I want to find a cure for this nuisance." She threw the cigarette on the floor, stubbed it with her foot, clapped her hand to her mouth and made a dash for the bathroom.

The sound of her vomiting shook Abida to the core. What if it reached Ammi Jaan's ears? Once, because of indigestion, she had vomited early in the morning and seeing her, Ammi Jaan had been led to believe that distributing sweets was in order. Mona returned from the bathroom, wiping her eyes, and fell wearily into her chair. There was silence for a time.

"If you want to get rid of this nuisance, rest assured arrangements can be made." Majid's child! The entire family's most wanted child! She would raise it herself.

"And you will take care of the business in the meantime?" Mona said with a smirk. Abida held back her anger and frustration. This holding back was becoming second nature to her.

"Yes," she said good-naturedly. "You're concerned with money, you'll receive your payments every month."

For a while Mona looked at Abida pityingly. "You're barren?" she asked quietly. "How fortunate you are."

"One's fortune is not in one's hands."

"Don't you hate your husband?"

"No."

"And what about me?"

"What will hating you get me?"

"Damn what you get or don't get, but if you had snatched my husband I would have killed you."

Abida wanted to tell her she would never do that, but she ignored her impulse. Why engage with someone who is bent on being belligerent.

"But you really are an angel," said Mona softly. "I lose my temper easily these days. People in this neighbourhood are very mean. My landlady is a vile woman. If I miss even a month's rent she will throw me out on the street. I've lost my job because of your darling husband. They were teaching me typing and shorthand. I didn't know he was so inexperienced that he would get me into trouble like this."

'If you like, I can find you a place to live. I have a friend in Poona." Abida changed the subject.

"Your friend? She'll let me stay with her?"

"Of course she will. We don't have to give her all the details. Anyway, she's in England these days. She won't be back for a year."

"I'll die if I live there alone."

"I'll live with you."

"You?"

"We'll hire a servant. I'll tell him you're my sister."

"You really are an angel," she said mischievously, as if she was actually saying 'You are a fool and an idiot.'

*

Abida was packing and Majid was sitting in the armchair, his eyes closed. He couldn't even take her to the station because Mona would be there. She was becoming more and more bad-tempered with each passing day, not enjoying nurturing her pregnancy in this isolated place. Abida sewed tiny frocks for her, and napkins. Sometimes, watching her so engrossed, Mona would flare up and blurt out her nastiness.

"It would be better if it dies."

And Abida would tremble fearfully, as if someone had cursed her own baby.

"Do you love that bastard? Aren't you furious? Why don't you leave that rascal?"

She would hold Majid responsible for all the problems she had faced before she became pregnant. "Arre, you're still young, I swear you'll find a nice husband. Have you never been in love? Slept with anyone? I mean besides that vile man!" And then she would start scratching her drum-like belly.

"We have olive oil, why don't you use it? It will reduce the itching," Abida would say kindly, and Mona would fly into a rage and begin cursing.

"Put it in yours!" Then she would burst into tears and fill the entire universe with foul language. Head lowered, Abida would continue knitting the baby's sweater.

"I will wring the neck of that wretched baby," Mona threatened. Or she would say, "I won't give you what's mine, I'll turn it into a muddle like myself. And if the wretch takes after his father he'll be hoodwinking all the women he comes across. How can you tolerate that awful man? You are a Sayyed, you won't even touch anyone's left-over food. Don't you feel repelled?" She began comparing him with snakes and scorpions. Abida felt paralysed. As if her blood had stopped at her brain. Except for Majid and a very few close friends, no one suspected anything. Mona had grown up in Lahore. After completing eighth class in Lucknow, her inclinations brought her to Bombay. She kept taking up minor jobs on one pretext or another. The unfortunate girl was quite stupid. Instead of occupying a sixty-rupee-a-night room she could have stayed at the Taj. She looked unrespectable. Wasn't interested in household chores. But she dressed well and frequented high-class hotels.

Right now, wearing Abida's dressing gown, she looked like a large ball of cotton. Abida's maternal uncle had brought her the gown from Paris. She was trying hard to cope with this wretched creature. Once she signs the papers handing the baby over, the rest can be seen to. Mona had guessed as much and kept threatening her.

Abida suffered half the labour pains. The contemptible woman cursed non-stop, calling Majid all sorts of names. When Abida tried to placate her she pushed her away with such force, that if the nurse hadn't been there to grab her she would have taken a bad fall.

She didn't send Majid a telegram about the birth of the girl because she wanted to tease him, but circumstances had shaken her to such an extent that she could no longer think. The girl had taken after her father's side of the family. Majid's blood and hers, too, was coursing in her veins. It didn't seem as if she was a stranger. Because of the family resemblance she could pass for her own daughter. And if she lived with them she would absorb some of their ways. Abida suddenly began experiencing strong maternal feelings towards her. People say that if such feelings are genuine a woman will start producing milk.

When she returned home with soup and pure ghee she was stunned to see Mona nursing the baby.

"Ohh ... she bites!" Mona whimpered and then broke into a laugh.

Abida felt as if someone had plunged a knife in her heart and twisted it. In two days they would be discharged from the hospital. She tried to take the baby from Mona so that she could place her in the cradle.

"Let her be. We'll wait for the nurse," said Mona.

"Why, can't I pick up a baby?"

"Oh yes, you've had hundreds of babies, haven't you?"

Mona tone was confrontational.

"How many babies have the nurses had? They take care of them."

The nurse came in just then and the matter was shelved.

*

"What kind of name is Sabiha? Catherine, Cathy … that was my mother's name."

The name Cathy made Abida feel sick. She had decided, before she was married, that if she ever had a daughter she would name her Sabiha, and if it was a boy, well …

But when Mona flatly refused to leave the baby, saying a little thing like that couldn't survive without her, Abida said the baby would be given a bottle.

"She'll die if she gets milk from a bottle."

"Why will she die? The nurse is already giving her Ostermilk."

"That's because I'm not producing enough yet. The doctor has suggested a medicine."

"But if we have to wean her then why the pills…?"

"Why should we wean her? Mother's milk is good for the child." She avoided looking directly at Abida.

Abida's heart sank.

"Why are you looking at me like that? What I'm saying is correct."

"But you … you … will you raise the child? You …"

"I'll hire an old woman, or get an ayah who won't cost too much."

"So you've decided?"

"Decided what?"

"You said you wanted to get rid of this menace."

"I wanted that once, but now she is my life … my doll … Cathy darling!"

She began drooling over the baby, then looked up angrily

at Abida and said, sounding frightened, "You want to take away my daughter. I won't give her up! I'll never, never give her up. Whom can I call mine except her? You don't have to pay the hospital bill, I'll work hard and pay the last penny. I don't want your clothes, I don't want anything." She started sobbing loudly.

"Mona … think carefully. You're overwrought right now. Think about this child if not about yourself. What kind of life will you be able to give her?"

"Why should you care? Are you the world's caretaker? I know why you're saying all this. So that your conscience won't prick you. You'll take my daughter and make your husband feel you've done him a favour by attaching such importance to his sin. He'll worship you for it, the stupid fool. I'll give her up to an orphanage but I won't hand her over to you … … Yes… that's why you've been so thoughtful, making all those clothes … you want to fill the emptiness of your womb by taking my daughter. What woman would be so concerned otherwise about looking after her husband's bastard offspring?"

Abida felt as if the passages in her lungs had dried up, as if the blood was no longer flowing to her brain, and in a few minutes she would start smouldering like dry wood. She closed her eyes and leaned back.

Suddenly Mona realised her callousness. She jumped up and grabbed hold of Abida's feet.

"Sorry, Didi … please forgive me … Take the wretch. I'm despicable … you did so much for me. Please forgive me."

Abida wanted to abandon the wretch that very minute and leave, but realised it would be better for her to suffer this indignity quietly. She pacified Mona and helped her back to bed.

"Have you made up your mind?"

"About what?" Mona asked wearily.

"About the child."

"You're very cruel." Mona started sobbing again.

"Why are you getting so agitated? If you have to give the child away, then it's best to sever the connection quickly so that your milk can dry up easily. And if you're not giving it away, then there's no need to cry, is there?"

"I don't know what to do. I feel my heart is being slashed. I'll be able to see her, won't I?"

"Of course, whenever you want."

"How will she know who I am? She'll think of you as her mother. Will she see me as one of her own?"

"Auntie, or you ..." Once again Abida felt she was being stifled.

"My daughter will call me Auntie...!" She set off again. "And she'll call you Mama, and him, what about him ... she'll call him Papa, won't she?"

Abida had decided that the child would call her Amma and call Majid, Abba. She hated Mama and Papa. But she didn't think it was appropriate to engage with this packet of poison.

The days spent in the hospital were like being hung on a crucifix. Mona kept changing her mind. Sometimes she would say the girl would be nothing but the bane of her existence, then suddenly threaten to kill herself if she were separated from her. Or she would start swearing at Abida and heap curses on Majid and his family.

Abida wanted a decision to be made before they left the hospital. Her friend was returning from Europe and she didn't want everyone in the family to get to hear the story. On the last day she left for the hospital, her mind made up that the situation had to be resolved one way or another, but when she arrived there the ground slipped from beneath her feet.

Mona had left with the baby. Left behind her bangles and a locket as a guarantee in the office and gone off in a taxi. In her haste she had picked up just one set of clothes and one blanket for the baby, leaving everything else behind. Abida quietly picked up the jewellery, paid the bill and returned home.

Majid opened the door when she got back. Seeing her empty-handed he didn't understand what was going on because she was beaming with joy. He thought perhaps she had found an ayah.

Abida was talking at top speed. "Hai, she's so sweet and her mouth is so delicate, the eyes I think are gray, but the nurses said that all newborns have eyes like that, maybe they'll turn brown, because her hair is brown, soft, like silk … in the beginning the hair is always silky, after the *aqiqa* it will be thicker, she looks bald like Abba Jaan but the doctor says …" She stopped suddenly.

First Majid was smiling at her excited chatter, but when she kept on talking he began feeling a little sheepish. She was giving him details about the baby as if she were describing her niece, a blood relative. She was still smiling, actually once in a while she would break into a laughter. Majid didn't have the courage to question her about anything, he was feeling quite uneasy. Abida had brought back everything she had taken for the baby. So where was the baby?

"And pink really suits her. Light pink looks good on every baby, but bright colours like yellow and red won't suit Kitty." She was rummaging through the clothes in the suitcase.

"Kitty?" Majid gaped at her foolishly. How tired she looks, he thought.

"Yes, Catherine is a nice name … Mona's mother's name was also Catherine."

Majid was staring at the designs on the carpet. Abida was out of breath. Majid began feeling apprehensive.

"Sabiha is really a very old-fashioned name." She was trembling violently as if she had been running a great distance. "There are such nice new names now." Her words ended on a sob. "Catherine is a beautiful name, isn't it?"

"What happened?" Majid whispered.

"Arre, didn't you get my telegram? A pretty little doll has been born. You didn't get my letter either?" She seemed to be looking for something in the depths of the suitcase.

"I got it." Majid felt weighed down by a sense of guilt but "... You didn't send the adoption papers ... and so..."

"I changed my mind."

"Oh."

"It's cruel to separate a baby from its mother. I'm not so selfish that I should snatch up her baby just to fill the emptiness of my womb. She doesn't need anything from me and these clothes don't suit the baby at all. She looks good in pink." Abida was beginning to feel light-headed. Majid kept looking at her in stunned silence.

She quivered like a dry leaf and fell face down on top of the suitcase.

The news about Abida's illness brought about an onslaught of relatives. Anyone who saw her pale yellow colour and felt her cold hands, sympathised. Hai, the promise born after such a long time ... and lost before it could come to fruition.

Majid was shocked when Abida made no attempt to rectify this misunderstanding. If people thought she had had a miscarriage why shatter their happy delusion? Actually she was feeling as if she had indeed buried a child born of her womb.

Because of so many guests in the house husband and wife didn't get a chance to talk much. Majid was quite relieved. It would have been very strange to see the fruit of his stupidity in Abida's lap. Like a noose around his neck all the time. Mona had done him a great favour by refusing to give them the baby.

Like any ordinary husband he became rather nervous when a letter from Mona arrived at his office. There was no way he could hide it from Abida. She seemed a very loving wife in the presence of their guests, but talking to her when they were alone gave Majid the jitters. She was slowly putting the tragedy behind her and there was no point in reviving it. But when he came home he couldn't look her in the eye. Asked how she was in a serious tone, then started complaining about the heat. Then she gave him a long look and he felt as if there were needles pricking the soles of his feet.

"What did she write?" Abida asked, lovingly. For a moment he was transformed into a block of ice. How did you know, you magician? But he remained frozen.

"No, no, is everything all right?" she said quickly, when she saw him rummaging through his pockets.

Mona had asked that he beg his wife's forgiveness on her behalf and say that she was not a mother, but she had read so many books and so she must surely have some idea that she was not well-educated but that she was a mother after all. 'How can she think that I will turn the baby into someone stupid like myself? I swear by Holy Mary that I will raise her to be decent and virtuous like a respectable girl. I will get a job as a typist in the factory. Please don't bring your wife into all this. She is a very noble woman. I'm afraid of her.'

As Abida read the letter a smile spread over her face, and Majid felt as if he were being clobbered and insulted. He had thought that the matter would be laid to rest, that the burden his conscience had to bear would be lifted. Abida would become cheerful and chatty as she had been once. He would be granted forgiveness.

"Is it easier to send a draft or a money order?" she asked pleasantly. Majid's face fell. Is this a woman or a rock? If she clawed his face like any ordinary woman, cursed and reprimanded him, he wouldn't be sitting here like a dumb idiot. Instead of feeling grateful, he became angry. "Don't be idiotic. She's calling you names and you want to send her a money order?"

"She's doing her duty, I'm doing mine."

Majid wanted to scream, *This is not your duty ... it's my sin. Why are you taking it upon yourself?* He took the letter from her and started shredding it.

"Arre, arre, let me take down the address." She snatched the letter from him and slipped it under her pillow.

"What will you do?"

"I'll hammer my head."

Those who had come to see Abida were busy sightseeing in Bombay. Plans were made for picnics at Elephanta, film-shoots to attend and film stars to meet; food parties were the order of the day, everyone was busy chatting and socialising, and no one was aware of the mental and physical turmoil the husband and wife were going through. Throughout this commotion and carrying their respective crucifixes, the two of them continued to smile fake smiles and pretend to be an exemplary couple. But when they lay down in their double-bed at night a stony wall rose between them.

One night, believing this wall to be an illusion, Majid tried pulling her towards him, but she was so startled that she let out a stifled scream. He turned on the lamp and saw such hatred in Abida's eyes for one fleeting moment that, stunned, he quickly drew back.

"I must have dozed off." Her smile returned the next instant and she relaxed. If Majid had wanted to he could have drawn her into an embrace, but his hands were numb.

In the days that followed, whenever he made an effort to take his wife into his arms, she would hesitate for just a few seconds and then soften, but eventually bring up Mona and Kitty, which was when Majid's last reserve of strength would give out.

"Are you still angry?" he tried to restore his old banter.

"Uff! Don't be so sentimental, it disgusts me." She too resumed her old style. "Why would I be angry?"

"You avoid me."

"Allah! Why would I avoid you? I haven't stolen anything from you, so why should I avoid you?"

"I'm the one who's done the stealing … and you're the

one being punished for it."

"Don't be so melodramatic. Go to sleep now. The house is full of guests and look at you, acting silly like this."

"You just need an excuse."

"You're imagining things, that's all," Abida said in irritation.

"Tell me truthfully, how many days has it been since you kissed me?"

"All right, here..." Leaning across the rocky wall Abida placed her cold lips on his lifeless mouth. "Happy?" For a long time afterwards the two of them carried on a meaningless discussion about this delicate and fleeting touch, until their throats were dry and their eyes began to hurt. When, exhausted, they finally fell asleep they continued to sigh restlessly and kept reaching for each other.

One by one their guests were leaving. Finally, only Raffan Baji was left. Seeing Abida looking so despondent she suggested she come home with her. Abida agreed.

"Why are you going?" asked Majid resentfully.

"Baji is insistent, and I was thinking Ammi has been alone for so long."

"I'm also alone."

"You're going on a tour next month and then I'll be alone here. Farida's birthday is also approaching. I was thinking, I'll have a suit made for her with that green Chinese brocade you brought for me. I had kept it for Janee's ... Kitty's birthday. Now I think..."

It sounded like she was talking to herself. Majid felt a snake had sunk its teeth in him but he didn't give up. "The house will be turned upside down again."

"This time I will put away all the good dishes and give you the keys for the few things you need every day."

"Will you also put me under lock and key?"

"You I will lock up in my heart and take you with me," she said mischievously and, pretending she hadn't seen

Majid's hand coming towards her, got up quietly and started pulling out the suitcase under the bed. Like an idiot Majid pretended to be looking under the pillow for something. His fingers closed on a piece of paper. He picked it up and saw that it was Mona's receipt for the money order. His blood ran cold.

"Arre, I've been looking everywhere for this." She took the receipt from him, opened the drawer, took out a beautiful file and placed the receipt in it.

That night Majid was suddenly woken up by Abida sobbing violently in her sleep.

"Abida, Abida, what's the matter?" Majid shook her and she awoke. "What is it?" she asked with a start. Her voice betrayed no sadness.

"You were crying in your sleep. Was it a bad dream?"

"No, I wasn't dreaming."

"Then why were you crying?"

"I wasn't." She ran her fingers over her face. "Arre!" She began laughing when she felt the tears on her cheeks. "But I swear I wasn't dreaming. I haven't dreamt for ages," offering all sorts of justifications.

"You must have forgotten, some dreams are not recalled."

"But I'm telling you I wasn't dreaming. You're blaming me for no reason." She got upset.

"It's not a crime, everyone dreams."

"But if I were dreaming why would I lie about it? Is there a tax on dreams that would make me lie?" raising her voice.

"Uff-oh, but…"

"I swear by the Quran. May I be blinded if I was dreaming …" She became hysterical.

"Abida, for God's sake … I didn't mean anything by saying what I did," Majid stammered in bewilderment.

"But why did you say it? Do you think I pretend, that I'm a liar?" She began crying.

"Abida, please lower your voice … please…" He took her

in his arms and tried to comfort her as if she were a child. "My love… I'm sorry… I made a mistake… your nerves are …" She was as stiff as an arrow in his arms.

"But…" she suddenly became limp.

"Shhh… I said I made a mistake, alright?" Majid tried to hold her close but it seemed they couldn't remember how to hold each other in an embrace. They, who would once be bound to each other in a minute, could no longer manage it. It was as if suddenly a profusion of elbows came in the way or some important pieces of a puzzle had been lost. When he tried to kiss her mouth, he and she both found themselves in an awkward posture. His leg became numb, he pulled a muscle in his thigh, and Abida's neck twisted at an odd angle. Embarrassed, they drew apart and started massaging their respective muscles and nerves. For a while Abida sat looking drained, twisting her hands. Majid inhaled so strongly on his cigarette that his chest felt ready to burst. Then, enclosed in their separate desolation, both quietly stared at the ceiling.

"I've stopped dreaming," she said finally and, turning on her side, stared at the blank wall.

Having come to the conclusion that once the guests had left and the house was empty Abida would go mad, Majid did not discourage her when she started packing. He felt that in her mother's home, the constant hustle and bustle of relatives coming and going would help her become normal again. Her health would also improve. Ammi Jaan was going to Nainital for the summer. There, surrounded by fun-filled activities, her anger and sadness would diminish.

"All the world's children are ours." He had never fretted about being childless. There was such a profusion of children in the family that everyone admired those who remained childless. The beautiful life that these two had shared would never have been possible had they had children. That is why people called Majid his wife's slave. The only ones who knew the secret were the couple themselves and one or two close friends who were even more cautious than them. Despite all the mental and emotional anguish and all this distancing between them, their act was intact and they were regarded as the exemplary lover and beloved.

Abida's letters reassured Majid that she was immersed in parties, engagements, weddings, celebrations for newborns, films, and picnics. She also wrote spiritedly:

"*Ammi Jaan has no idea that her wish has been fulfilled. Some astrologer told her that you are not fated to have children. She wept bitterly. How my blood boiled. I wanted to claw the astrologer's face. What a thug! But what a tragedy, I say, that she is deprived of this happy news.*"

Then she would joke and start poking fun at their lives:

"*My love, I've forgotten to put a lock on the box with the china. Well, it's foolish to lock it. Let the wretched dishes and plates break. We can get more. Don't forget to send the money order.*"

"*Abida, Abida, my love, when will you come back … when will you bring your soul back with your body? I can't tolerate this dark chamber. I saw you in a dream last night. You were holding a bowl of kheer on which Shabana had written Abida/Majid with pistachio flakes and you were getting angry. I was laughing. You won't believe this, but when I woke up my face was covered with tears. I'm very alone. Please come back now.*"

"*Your letter made me laugh. All this sentimental, romantic talk is boring. It seems as if you first read* masnawi zehr-e-ishq *and then sit down to write your letters. It hasn't even been a full month and already you are asking me to come back. And listen, before you go, give Bhai Siddiq the cheque to mail. If you don't take care of the expenses I'll keep worrying. Tani is already walking. Baji insists I adopt her and is threatening to make it legal. I laugh. All children are mine as well. A daughter is not something you trade. Just thinking about this gives me the jitters. Shabana and Manzoor are expected soon. Everyone is insisting that I take care of them. I've become an expert at taking care of deliveries. Knitting a sweater now, and the rest of the clothes are all ready. Some Baji will hand down. She writes that if it's a girl she'll call her Sabiha, and she'll leave her here and go to England. It seems that Allah's believers are more generous than He is."*

Sting, sting, sting. Majid was tired of these poisoned barbs. His bags were packed for the tour, but he wanted to go straight to Abida give her a slap and say, "You're my wife, you're my life's desire, I have rights over you, don't make me beg any more, come into my arms … come."

And she came! When he opened the door he saw her standing on the edge of the stairs, smiling. In the mysterious misty darkness of the evening, the silver dots on her cottony-white sari twinkled faintly.

She walked past him, pressing against him lightly, threw her purse on a chair and sat down on her special chair, looking serious, as if she had always sat on that chair, had never left it. Her body had filled out a bit, her complexion had bloomed and motherhood had removed the hardness from her face.

"What are you doing here?"

"What a stupid question. I felt like coming so I did." She shook her foot casually.

"Look … you…"

"Uff-oh, stammering like a virgin again."

"…" Majid picked up the purse from the chair and thrust it into her hand.

"Thanks." She slipped off her sandals, crossed her legs on the chair and, taking a mirror from her purse, began examining her half-open mouth.

"Look, Mona, if you want to make a laughing stock of us, that's a different matter…" Majid's throat was dry.

"When did I say that you had deceived me?" She was trying to hold back her laughter.

"Our friendship…"

"Friendship?" She batted her eyelashes, smiling.

"Whatever... that was... was." He corrected himself quickly. "I never promised to marry you."

"Arre, do you think I'm here to get married to you? Wah!" She burst out laughing.

"Then... you can leave."

"I can leave, but why should I?" she snapped. "Am I stealing something from you or asking you for anything? You should have asked me why I'm here." She became tearful.

"All right ... so tell me why are you here?"

"I will tell you," she replied, but "why are you scolding me? Am I your wife that I should be afraid of you?"

"My wife ... don't talk about her. Tell me what you want."

"You're making me nervous. Why don't you sit down?"

Majid sat.

"Do you know Saran?"

"No."

"He knows you very well ... no, no, by God, I haven't told him anything, he knew everything already."

Majid's face turned red. "And so?"

"So I met him in Sholapur."

"Vinod Saran, Shakuntala's husband?"

"Yes, the same."

"Your friend's..."

"So? Shakkan is my friend and that's why ... he takes such good care of me."

"You came here to tell me this?"

"Yes." She lowered her head and fixed her gaze on the shiny stars on her sandals.

"That he is your friend's husband ... or that he takes very good care of you, I don't know why." Majid's tone became bitter.

"Yes, that's why I came, to tell you this."

"But why do you need to tell me?" said Majid, feeling stifled.

"Because you also took very good care of me."

"I still take care of you ... I was about to send you your

cheque." He took it out from the drawer.

"Oh, thanks."

He thought she would throw it in his face, but she took it quietly and put it in her purse. Majid was disappointed.

"What was I saying? Yes, that you take very good care of me, and more than you … it's your wife who takes care of me. I have to say, she's a remarkable woman." Suddenly her tone hardened. "A woman of such patience… suffocates me! Anger, revulsion, these one can cope with… but… her smile drives me mad. It would be fine if she yelled and screamed, but the way she smiles makes me feel so low and unclean."

"Weren't you leaving? I have to get up early in the morning," Majid said curtly. Mona's conversation was agitating his mind. He didn't want to admit anything even to his own conscience.

"So, what is your opinion? Is Saran untrustworthy?"

"I don't know," Majid replied roughly.

"Unh! Maybe he's a scoundrel, but what can he do to me? He says I shouldn't live in that filth. He has a flat on Peddar Road and another one in Santa Cruz. I like the one in Santa Cruz. It's far from everything else. What do you think?"

"I don't know anything." Feeling nothing but intense dislike, Majid turned away.

"Uff-oh, what airs you put on. I know you don't want to give your opinion, but whatever I'm doing I'm doing for Kitty."

"You receive money regularly for her expenses."

"And I have no expenses? Should I survive on air? How can a mother, daughter and one servant manage in Bombay with your Rs. 300? If you were giving us 500 it would be different."

"Yes… but Shakuntala… your friend…"

"She is my friend and the poor girl did a lot for me when I really needed help. Why, don't you see, if I don't accept

Saran's offer he'll get someone else?" She laughed mischievously. "And my sacrifice won't make any difference."

"I can't offer an opinion."

"Uff! You weren't such a bore once. Tell me truly, don't you miss me at all?"

"Our relationship was temporary and physical."

"Is there any other kind of relationship between and a man and a woman?"

Yes, there's an intellectual relationship as well, a kind of … a kind of meeting of minds."

"And I, unfortunate creature that I am, have no mind at all. Just this clay body." She looked at him in a strange way. "And the body has no memory, your body doesn't even remember, doesn't miss." She was slowly advancing towards him.

Majid moved to the drawer and busied himself looking for cigarettes.

"My body doesn't forget … whenever I see Kitty, it remembers." She edged towards the door as she spoke.

Majid lit a cigarette to hide the shaking of his hands.

"I don't know why you are not like the others. When I'm with you, for some reason I feel as if I'm not committing a sin, as if our relationship is sacred. You've given me a strange something that can't be found anywhere else. May the Holy Mother forgive my sins. I sit in front of her for hours and beg … Mother, bless me with peace."

"Don't place sin on the same level as worship."

"Majid." Suddenly she placed her head on his back and broke into tears. Then she put both arms around his waist and tightened her grip.

Majid broke into a sweat. He squeezed the lighted cigarette in his fist, closed his eyes and in one violent jerk, unclasped Mona's hands from his waist and pushed her towards the door.

Her face was wet with tears. Her hair had swung loose

and hung to one side.

"I'm sorry," she said haughtily as she wiped her eyes and nose with the back of her hand. "Sometimes when I see you in Kitty's smile, I feel like wringing her neck." Then, seeing Majid in this agitated state, she softened.

"Forgive me, Mona… I'm an exceedingly imperfect human being… I …Abida …"

"I know," she whispered philosophically. "I'm a prostitute, and if there had been another man in your place right now I would have chewed him alive, but… in your case, I'm also an imperfect prostitute." Her sheepish laugh masked her sadness.

The door swung shut behind her… there was a kind of sadness in the light drizzle outside as well. Majid felt needles pricking his scorched palms.

"*Abida, Abida … are these the rules of friendship? I'm here and you're there, playing carom with Baji's children.*"

Excusing himself at dinner, he retired to his room. For half the night he tossed and turned. Got up and drank some water, walked about, tried to read, but the unravelling of the brain and the call of the body could not be erased. Before his eyes there were stars twinkling on cottony-white clouds. He tried many times to loosen the hands from his waist but it seemed as if his body was being squeezed inside a steel clamp. He had changed his shirt, but the spots where her tears had fallen burned holes in his skin. The breeze was blowing in gusts, the chameli vine against the window was dancing.

To hell with the tour. He sat up with a start and lit the bedside lamp. Suddenly he turned and saw the pillow where Abida rested her head, one hand under her chin. It seemed as if she had just got up and left … he began thinking he had gone mad. Where could she go? She couldn't run away from him. She was his wife, she had destroyed his peace of mind, but she must be sleeping peacefully. Perhaps she has had a nightmare and is sobbing, but on waking will deny altogether that she had been dreaming.

I have stopped dreaming.

Can anyone stop dreaming? Dreams sustain life. Can anyone give up living? Actually her dreams have been shattered. He will mend her broken dreams. He will kiss her eyes and fill them with stars again. Then life will return. This loneliness will disappear. Once again their two names will be illuminated on silver paper.

He dressed quickly. He had left the car keys with the driver because he was going to take him to the airport, but it doesn't matter. He will take a taxi.

He forgot to take his raincoat but the downpour had diminished. He could see, in the muddied light on the road, a shining layer of tar stuck to the surface. His only companion was a wet, solitary dog.

He was soaked by the time he reached Opera House. The taxi driver looked at him suspiciously but he had got in already.

"Duncan Road." Where was this voice coming from?

He surrendered himself to some unknown power that was crushing him from all sides like a giant cobra. He is not at all an intellectual. He's a stupid, third class, deficient creature. He will set fire to the source of this deception. He and Abida are not compatible. He will send her the divorce papers in the post first thing tomorrow. He has no right to be in this elevated position.

Unmindful of the filth and dirt, he took long strides and turned into the street. When he took out his handkerchief to wipe his face, a tiny piece of paper fluttered like a wounded bird and landed on muddy slush. He bent down and saw it was his card. His name, address, designation, telephone number. For a moment he was exasperated. Who is this idiot?

Then, like footprints slowly sinking into the mire, the realisation sank in – he was this idiot. What is such a respectable and virtuous man doing in this muck? His eyes darted back and forth, from the card to Mona's door.

Where has he come? Where was he going? Bewildered, he turned back. The night had deepened. All the poverty and nakedness of the neighbourhood collapsed over his head. It started raining again, and leaving behind the filthy, muddy, congested streets, he fled from there.

Once he was back in the civilized world he looked at his watch in the light of the street lamp. It was 2:45, he had to catch a plane at six... there was no sign anywhere of a taxi. He kept walking. Away from the filth, away from stupidity and recklessness, towards the world of perfect men. He was not ready to leave his world, his place in it, at any cost.

He finally got a taxi at Flora Fountain, and when he reached home he was so exhausted physically and mentally that he didn't have the energy to change his clothes. He stretched out on the settee to rest. His flight was not for another two-and-a-half hours.

When the alarm went off at 4:30 he felt too weak to stretch out his hand and turn it off. His head was heavy and cramps had gripped his legs. He got up with great difficulty but then collapsed immediately. He felt so sorry for himself that he began to cry.

Heat. He wanted to thrust the blanket of flames from his being but he kept sinking into white, feathery snow up to his nostrils. At the base of his neck hung a heavy bell that struck against his temples with every breath he drew. Sometimes from the right, sometimes from the left. Strung around his spine were sinuous, rustling snakes ... cottony-white slush filled his eyes ... the spray of stars was rankling in his eyes like the ash of diamonds.

Wrapped in the colour of dry onion peels, Abida had spread her wings over him and was crying. On the other side bottles of milk were moving in an orderly fashion and melting icy needles were coursing through his veins...Abida... Abida... he tried to call out, but his mouth had been fastened with metallic bolts that had rusted.

When he opened his eyes and saw Abida bending over him he thought it was a dream... Abida who had stopped dreaming but had assumed the form of a permanent dream herself. He was too exhausted to confront these dreams.

But when she placed a trembling hand on his forehead he was fully awake.

"You... you... how?" He tried to get up.

"Don't get up ..." She was sobbing.

"Why... why are you crying?" He ran a finger down her wet cheek and closed his eyes wearily.

When he opened them again it was morning. Abida's pink gharara and dupatta were wrinkled. A lock of hair had fallen over her forehead, but tears were spilling from her eyes.

His fever had abated after ten days. What he did in those ten days, what world he inhabited, he remembered nothing. He was terrified that he had lost ten days of his life.

"What happened?"

"Rheumatic fever."

"When did you come?"

"Shankar sent me a telegram and when I came..." she was laughing and crying at the same time. "Hai, you... you scared me." Abida lifted his hand and placed it on her cheek.

"Will you leave me alone again?" Majid said, stroking her lower lip.

"When did I leave you alone? My heart was always here, with you."

"In your letters ... it didn't seem that way."

"Arre, I wrote those letters just to torment you." Abida's eyes were filled with loving sweetness.

"If you scold me any more, I'll be burnt to a cinder, by God."

"Forgive me God, forgive me..." Abida tapped her ears and smacked her cheeks. "My love, I'll never make this mistake again."

Once more, the joys of the early days of their married life

returned. Friends visited all day long, flowers, fruit, sweets and books arrived in such quantities that they didn't know what to do with them. There were so many letters and telegrams that Abida piled everything on trays and arranged them on the shelves next to their bed.

During his illness Majid had been transferred to the guest room. Taking care of a patient on a double-bed poses problems. When he was able to walk with some support she brought him back to their bedroom, but she changed its appearance entirely. There is little light on rainy days so she removed the heavy drapes from the windows and replaced them with pink netted curtains. Everything in the room was either white or light and dark pink so that the effect was pleasing to the eye. The white candlewick bedspread reminded one of snow-covered ground.

A dull pain in his joints persisted in Majid's body. Constant fatigue and apathy overwhelmed him. Abida tried to keep his spirits up as if he were a little boy. Her love, like a pink canopy, shaded him. Lying in this cool shade, eyes closed, Majid pondered his good fortune. He had found Abida again after a close brush with death. The nightmare had ended. Life's journey on a smooth road had begun again.

Gradually the constant stream of well-wishers ebbed, then ended. Majid had extended his leave by another two months. The doctor had instructed extreme care. Rheumatic fever affects the heart, dietary restraint was essential. Abida cooked special foods with her own hands and insisted on feeding him herself. However, excessive displays of affection in the presence of guests were now considered unnecessary and so abandoned. And she was very strict on the matter of restraint. If Majid tried to embrace her she stopped him immediately. Kept herself busy with elaborate arrangements to avoid the slightest bit of intimacy. She would change into her night-suit after he asked her to do so many times, but instead of her attractive nightdress, she began wearing long-sleeved kurtas and loose pajamas.

Majid protested loudly. "I don't like this old-fashioned stuff, it bothers me."

"Night dresses are just so showy. I gave them all to Shabana."

"Then have new ones made."

"Why?"

"Because I want you to."

"Why do you want me to?" Laughing mischievously. "I never complain. You always wear kurta-pajama and I think you look sexy."

"But you used to wear them earlier."

"That was before. I used to crawl then, even sucked on a pacifier once."

Majid felt he had nothing to say.

"And the truth is that this juvenile behaviour no longer suits us in our old age."

"So you're old now?"

"Almost old. A difference of about ten years…"

Majid's heart sank. No … Abida had not forgiven him, and she was never going to.

"Let's stop talking about clothes. Oh, I forgot to give you your orange juice." She got up quickly and left.

Yes, what difference do clothes make? If a slab of ice is draped in brocade will it become a bride? And the slab of ice on his chest kept getting heavier and heavier.

Physically he was back to normal. He had resumed going to the office, but Abida insisted on providing nursing care round the clock. She tried to do everything to make him submit to her ministrations.

"Abida." He couldn't stand it any longer and decided to confront the issue.

"Yes," she replied lovingly.

"Am I seriously ill?"

"God forbid. Why?"

"That's what I'm asking. Why then?"

Abida didn't answer. She was tracing a vague design on the bedcover with her fingers.

"Answer me."

"If there's no answer, what should I say?" she said listlessly.

"Does our marriage have no meaning?"

Abida lowered her head.

"Abida, for God's sake give me an answer."

She raised her eyes slowly and turned her gaze to look for something outside the window. She was extremely pale and tired. Her eyes filled with tears.

"Abida, my love!" He tried to take her in his arms, but felt that in his arms was not his beloved wife, but steel wires that lacked flexibility, had no elasticity.

"Uff!" She had pulled a muscle and started rubbing her neck sheepishly.

"Are there thorns in my hands?"

"No… but… I…" She was evasive.

"What…? But…?" He caught her hands and pulled her down on the bed.

"Oh," she moaned.

"Sorry… but what were you saying?"

"Your hands…" She hesitated again.

"What's in my hands?" he said wearily. "Are there thorns in them?"

"Why do you ask these ridiculous questions? There's nothing in your hands… maybe there's nothing for me."

"What do you mean?"

"You… when you touch me… it seems as if you're under duress… you're forcing yourself…"

"What rubbish is this?"

"Majid, it's no use… Majju… this drama should end now." A strange kind of cruelty flashed across her face. "This relationship cannot be forced, it must come from the heart."

"In other words, I'm under duress when I touch you…

what are you talking about?"

"Yes... and the reason is very clear... it's obvious. We have both made a mistake."

"Mistake?"

"Look... Majju, try to understand. If an electric wire is snipped and attached to another wire, the current stops going through... and if... the wire is cut from the other side, the fuse goes off and one receives a terrible shock."

"Severed wires can be joined together again."

"That cannot be achieved by our coming together."

"What do you mean?"

"When wires are severed between husband and wife, it's the children who become the solution that keeps them together."

"Uff! You'll drive me mad. Abida, my love, I'm yours, my heart is yours."

"But your body is not mine."

"Abida... please."

"And no marriage can survive a division. These two parts of you are no good for anyone. The body that doesn't have a heart and that heart..."

"Abida..."

"I've thought a lot about this... thought so much that I'm exhausted. There's no other alternative. You can't live by dividing yourself. For this reason you will have to become whole again."

"You're confusing me. All right, let's say I accept your theory. Still, my heart and mind are yours and my body has worshipped you for years. If it strayed for a moment because of a tiny lapse, you won't accept it back to lie at your feet?"

"Don't insult the body like this. I need your body in my arms, not at my feet, but I know this better than you do. Your body is slave to your mind and I'm not in favour of actions that are forced."

"And my mind is slave to my body."

"Every man's mind is overpowered by his body. That's nothing to be ashamed of. It's the result of centuries of training. And it's better to come to terms with this rather than to keep feeling guilty all the time."

"In other words if my body is ready to wallow in filth I should also throw my mind into the gutter."

"It's not fair to weigh a person on the scales of intelligence and education. For example, Mona is a better woman than me. The assets she has… I don't have. For this reason filth is sometimes more desirable than sandalwood."

"What are you saying? You're blinded by a sense of inferiority."

"I'm right, otherwise she wouldn't have been able to lure you away like that."

"That's rubbish. No one lured me."

"Not your whole being, but she skimmed off the cream." Abida laughed hysterically. Her eyes had an odd glint in them. Her face was flushed. The tips of her fingers had turned icy and her palms were wet with perspiration. This cruel combination of fire and water had caused a kind of hysteria in her.

"So what is your advice?" Majid asked bitterly.

"You should marry her… Look… look… listen to me with a cool head. If you sat on hot coals and said that her body is not beautiful, I wouldn't believe you even then."

"There are thousands of women in the world whose bodies are more interesting than hers. That doesn't mean that I can shut out all common sense and continue to exist. You don't have any right to issue this royal decree. Just think for a minute how cruelly you're rejecting me. If that's how it was going to be, why didn't you make a decision when…"

"When a woman's ego comes forward and confronts her, that's when my thinking became clouded. I thought I had a right over you and this prevented me from realising that I couldn't win you back, that I wouldn't have you whole.

Finding you incomplete, I have understood that it was my selfishness and meanness that made me agree that you should be split in two. I was really selfish then and I thought that losing you would be a blot on my womanliness, people might reproach you but at the same time they would pity me. Uff Allah! How could I allow the world to pity me? A false and stupid arrogance. The loser uses the worst kind of weapons. I was confident that I could flip a coin that had landed on the wrong side, that you would still be mine, and by being mother to your daughter I would in some way compensate for the injustice I had caused by being infertile."

"So, basically, you are trying to atone by flogging yourself."

"It's possible. Why not? Physical flogging is better than the blows suffered by one's conscience."

"So you've decided that in order to save yourself from the blows of your conscience and for your peace of mind, you will sacrifice me."

"Not happily. I've made these preparations after a great deal of analysis and thought."

"So now you're fully prepared to give me up."

Abida fell silent, seemed to be lost in thought.

"Is there no other way? Is there no place left in your heart for me?"

"It's the opposite. There is no place for anyone except you in my heart, nor for any other thought except that of you. For the last one and a half years it has been just you all around me. I've hated you, loved you, been angry with you, felt sympathy for you, just you. The links of every thought in my head reach back to you. And you say there's no place left in my heart for you! If I had devoted so much thought to God I would definitely have become a prophet by now. But inspite of all this I couldn't make you mine."

"You couldn't make me yours because you had never lost me in the first place. All right, you say there's anger in your heart for me, and love. This means I still live in your heart.

So how can you decide to bury what is alive? Abida, my love … does your body not yearn for me?"

"Not yearn for you! My body aches for your touch."

"So then, when I touch you…"

"I… I don't know what happens. Perhaps my body becomes paralysed by my feelings of inadequacy!"

"Abida!" Majid was tormented by the strange look in Abida's eyes. "Come to me, come here…"

She was standing at the window, her back to him.

"Sometimes I think that if I had been strong everything would have been all right." She was talking to herself. "If I had died then…"

"Abida!"

"Everything would be fine."

"I couldn't have lived without you."

"You would have said this and would have wanted to kill yourself, but everyone would have comforted you by saying that nobody dies along with those who are dead, and eventually you would have come to understand. If I had died then you wouldn't have been forced to split your life into two, and you would be truly alive. You, your wife and your daughter."

"For God sake, stop this nonsense. What is wrong with you?"

She sounded remorseful again. "And it wouldn't be surprising if Mona were grateful that I had given her a chance to improve her life. And perhaps she would have called her Sabiha instead of Kitty."

Majid's head was spinning and brightly coloured spots danced in front of his eyes.

"When I first discovered this I went to the ocean with the intention of killing myself but I lost courage. My foot slipped on the sand and I fell into the water and splashed about, and my mouth was filled with sand and water and that's why… I was terrified. Not of death but of having to go through the stages of dying."

God knows what she was looking for outside the window. Perhaps the reflection of dreams that had been shattered. There was an expression of extreme weariness on her face. Overcome, Majid closed his eyes and fell back on the pillows.

*

Her dupatta fluttered like a pink butterfly, she slipped from his vision and was falling into a distant abyss.

"Abida!" he called from the depths of his being, but no sound emerged. Startled, he opened his eyes. Abida's body was draped over the windowsill.

"Abida!" His body shuddered once but in the next instant he had seized her in his arms.

"What's the matter, Majju?" She was frightened by the wild look in his eyes.

"You... you... from this window..."

"From the window..."

His brow was covered in perspiration.

"Oh, you thought I was going to jump out of the window and kill myself!"

"Yes. I was scared to death, Abida ... you..."

Once again the suppleness of her body turned into steely rigidity.

"But this window is not even three feet from the ground! There's no chance even of a twisted ankle if I fall from here," she said laughing.

Poisonous thorns dug into Majid's hands.

"And if this window had been at a height of thirty feet instead of three?"

"Oh, my God! Then you would have pushed me down." Abida spoke affectionately.

"Abida."

"And people would have thought I was heartbroken and

had committed suicide." A smile played upon her lips.

"You... you think that..." There was no remonstration in his voice, only a deep weariness.

"I don't want to think this Majid, but I've lost." She laughed. "You're well, now... why am I hanging around here to cause you distress?" Her voice was filled with tenderness.

He stared at her, heavy-eyed, silent.

"Hamida is going to stop here on her way to Nairobi. I'll write and tell her that Ammi Jaan needs me. She'll be here a month earlier. Her presence will liven up the place."

He remained silent.

"And then you can go and visit Ameena Khala for a few days in Bangalore."

"And then?"

"Ammi Jaan is very uncomfortable during the rainy season."

"Do you want to go?"

"The house needs repairs. I'm thinking that if Barre Abba's house can be sold... then Shankar's and the doctor's loan can also be paid off."

"Give me an answer first. Do you want to go?"

"I... I think that..."

"Why?"

She silently straightened the creases in her shirt.

"Are you afraid? Like heroines in American films, you think I will kill you and..."

"I'm not afraid of dying... I... Majid... I'm beginning to distrust my mental state. My nerves are very...very... oh, how can I explain that I don't feel anything?"

"Are you beginning to distrust your mental state or me?"

"Both things are related, Majju my love. The period we are going through is very critical."

"Yes, I know. What you are going through no woman has ever endured." Majid's face was flushed.

"I can't say anything about that, but perhaps I'm not

perfect like other women. I am not generous in spirit, I hold grudges."

"Abida, I have admitted my crime, I have asked for forgiveness."

Abida wearily picked up the glass on the table nearby and dropped it. Glass shards scattered on the floor like a scream.

"If I now admit my mistake will these shards become whole again?"

"So you want to go. Whether the shards become whole or are thrown in the garbage."

"Time heals all wounds. Perhaps because of your illness some scabs came off."

"Abida, do you know what I used to think once?"

"What?"

"That if you were ever unfaithful I would strangle you and then shoot myself, but now…"

"But now…"

"Now I pray that you falter and betray me, then the scales would be balanced. That you would be as sinful as me, then this distance between us would be obliterated."

"That's why I say we shouldn't be together, because something terrible that shouldn't happen might happen." She was suddenly out of breath, as if she had run a great distance.

"Tell Hamida to bring my warm clothes, it will be chilly in Bangalore." Majid turned on his side to face the wall.

Abida quickly started counting plates and cutlery and began putting them away in cupboards. Whatever extra linen there was she packed with her own things. Who knows how long she would be away. People are not to be trusted; even the brooms will be stolen.

Abida always wore hand-dyed crinkled dupattas. The ones with trimmings that her in-laws had given her lasted a whole year. When the colours faded she would dye them herself and make them last a while longer. But of late she had only been using white dupattas. And then one day she took off her gold bangles saying they bothered her. Majid observed all this quietly and his heart sank. He wasn't dead yet, why was Abida mourning him already?

"Where's your ring?" The ring his mother had given him to present to Abida on their wedding night.

"Which ring? Oh… the stone was loose, I gave it to Shankar to get it repaired."

"What ring? Bhabi didn't give me any ring." Shankar was baffled when Majid asked him.

"Oh… she must have forgotten." But asking Abida for a clarification was an insult to his ego.

He came across the empty frame that had once held their wedding picture lying on a shelf in the almirah; it had always been on the dressing-table. He quietly put it back. He found shredded fragments of that part of the photograph containing Abida's picture in the waste-basket. His own picture had disappeared.

This time Abida was severing all her connections before she left.

Then one day the plates and cutlery were laid out once again on the sideboard. Towels and blankets came out of the large trunk. And the polishers for the copper pots were summoned from Shankar's house.

But the rings and bangles didn't return.

Abida swooped like an eagle when the mail arrived. Leaving Majid's correspondence on his desk, she immediately shut herself in the bathroom. One day he saw fragments of a fancy envelope on which the address had been typed very stylishly, floating in the toilet. Abida would emerge from the bathroom looking distracted and then he would hear her opening and closing the locker in the Godrej almirah.

"I'll be back in a minute, just going down to the corner."

Majid was becoming an expert at espionage. She wasn't going down to the corner, she was going further, to the post office.

"Perhaps she's planning to work," Majid told himself. The pain in his hands and feet had returned. He had taken time off from work, without pay. Abida's mother had sent them a draft for two thousand that seemed to have grown like wild flowers. He always handed over every penny of his salary to Abida. He had sent in a request for his full salary for leave due, but only half had been approved.

"Did you get a letter from Hamida?" he finally asked after being patient for ten or twelve days.

"No."

"Why?"

Instead of giving him an answer she went into the next room and began to discuss the different colour schemes for various rooms.

"What did I ask you?" Majid called out as she passed through the drawing room.

"What?" she asked archly. "I don't know."

"What do you mean?"

"Look, stop bothering me. The painter says lilac won't be suitable for the bedroom."

"Lilac?"

"The colour, light purple."

"What is this craziness?"

"All right, if not lilac, then let's go for light beige." She completely ignored Majid and continued arguing with the painter.

For some reason Majid was overcome by a sense of relief. He was reminded of his bride of twelve years ago. She would wake up startled from deep sleep and say, "Light brown curtains in every room would be fine, but the divan should definitely have a brown cover."

And he would make fun of her domestic preoccupations.

"Do you think I should take a course in interior decoration?" she would ask eagerly.

"Oh, no."

"Then cooking lessons maybe? I'm wasting my time doing nothing all day."

"Nonsense."

"So which course would be suitable in your opinion?"

"Intercourse!" he would grab her and say teasingly.

"Please..." she would blush and turn her face away. "Always thinking of dirty things."

"You're referring to the most beautiful thing in life as a dirty thing."

He drew a deep breath. Would Abida's dreams ever be revived again?

"All right, what were you asking? This painter is such a nuisance, always shirking." She came and plonked herself on the chair next to his bed.

"Did you get a reply from Hamida?" He didn't really want to know.

"No, I didn't write to her so why would I get a reply? Oh, my God, that's terrible!"

"What's happened?"

"I must be going mad. Well, I'll have it dyed."

"What is all this nonsense?" Majid was irritated now.

"The bedroom curtains are pink, so I think dark beige will look better, or pistachio green." She seemed to be talking to herself, as if Majid was not in the room with her.

"For God's sake!" said Majid, exasperated.

She began laughing and laughed so much that tears ran from her eyes. Then she looked at him fondly. "Why don't you just ask if I'm going or not."

A cotton ball seemed to have got stuck in Majid's throat. "Tell me..."

"What?" She had decided to be playful.

"Are you going?" Majid asked, his heart racing.

"Naa..."

"Why not?" he asked in a stifled voice. Was he hearing

her right?

"Because that's what I want."

"And… the shards of glass?"

"I've thrown them in the garbage."

He kept looking at her through half-shut eyes.

And what about the torn fragments of the envelope, the trips to the post office, closing of the latch on the locker?

His head was exploding. Someone was pumping his heart from below. Whirlwinds of dry sand began to dance in his lungs.

He extended his arms. Abida's dupatta slipped from her shoulders like an onion peel.

*

The bihishti's wife was wiping his eyes with her smelly, dirty dupatta, but the tears in his eyes had dried up. Sweat was trickling down and being absorbed by the dirt floor of the small room where firewood was stored. She was laughing at his inexperience.

But Abida didn't laugh.

Outside a light rain was falling. Crumpled like a heap of cloth, Majid was sobbing. His eyelids were sore from Abida's starched dupatta.

Just as a muddied dawn was breaking the two of them fell into tormented sleep.

"Where is your jewellery?" Majid asked her one day.

"I left it with Ammi Jaan." Abida was changing a cushion cover.

"Not that, what you wear all the time. Your earrings."

"I have them."

"And the bangles, the ring?"

"I have them all. Why do you ask?"

"Why don't you wear them?"

"They bother me. But I'll wear them if you want me to."

"Wear them now."

"Why? Don't I look nice without jewellery?"

"You don't trust me any more."

"There you go being silly again. By God's grace, you're the father of a daughter now, how can anyone not trust you?"

"Abida."

"Hmm."

"Divorce me."

"Why? Is the worm crawling in your head again?"

"You asked for a divorce once and I refused. Now I think I'm dead."

"Majju darling, I asked Veenaji. She said this happens after what you went through. Everything will be all right."

"And what if it isn't?"

"Majju, marriage is not just one kind of emotion. The bazaar is open to satisfy the emotion you're talking about. I have no complaints. But if you think that this is all a hoax, that I'm... that I'm the reason for your pain, then how can anyone stop you from letting another woman bring you back to life?"

"No one can bring me back to life, not a second woman, or a third or fourth – I don't need a woman."

"Then do something for me."

"What?"

"Don't think of me as a woman, think of me as a friend, a companion, anything you want. I'm also related to you, so think of me as a relative."

"You're impossible."

"No doubt. Now stop this nonsense."

"Abida," Majid asked after closing his eyes for a few minutes.

"Yes, my love."

"I don't think this job is going to last much longer."

"Well, you can still take ten more months of leave."

"Without pay."

"Well, we'll die of starvation then."

"You'll die of starvation."

"Well, I died once for you, now starvation will kill us both. Anyway, you took care of me for twelve years, now it's time for me to take care of you."

"You're impossible."

"Is there any doubt about that?"

"But adorably impossible."

"Which is why I'm not getting a divorce."

"You've turned me into a cripple."

"So you won't run away!" She laughed lightly.

"Abida."

"Uff-oh! What more do you want to say?"

"Stop wearing this pink dupatta."

"Here, I'll take it off." She removed the dupatta and threw it at him. Majid shot up and pulled her down onto the cushions.

The bell rang with the sound of paper falling into the mailbox. Abida tore herself from his embrace. Picking up the dupatta that lay like a pink onion peel on the floor she ran towards the door.

She returned with the letters, put them in front of him and walked to the kitchen.

"Forgot to give instructions about the soup."

But Majid knew she was lying, that she was hiding something.

He concluded that the answer to his dilemma lay in the locker of Abida's Godrej almirah. She wouldn't leave the key lying around even for a minute and Majid didn't have the courage to ask for it.

But if he didn't open the locker he would go mad. For several days he had been wondering how he could get to it without creating suspicions. Abida would be walking around the house, keys swinging from her hand and Majid would feel he was losing his sanity. What was she hiding there?

One day, fate came to his aid and he saw that the bunch of keys was peeping from under the pillow like a mischievous lover. He lay down on the pretext of feeling unwell. Unaware of his sneaky plans Abida sat in front of the mirror combing her hair. Perhaps she was planning to go to the post office, which is why she was wearing a sari. After getting ready she went up to the door, then feeling the absence of the silver key-ring on her waist she turned around.

Majid felt life ebbing from him. He pretended not to notice. For a while she stood near the pillow, pondering over whether to remove the keys from under it. Majid's heart was pounding so violently he was sure she could hear it.

After she left he remained still for a few minutes. When the sound of Abida's footsteps receded he got up, his body shaking. He didn't even know which key opened which lock. His body was racked with shadow pains, his left arm felt inert, and there was a heaviness in his shoulder. This could be a heart attack but he was putting his life on the line, trying desperately to fit one key after another into the lock. Finally, the cupboard opened. There was nothing in the locker. A few artificial gold bangles studded with stones in one corner, some pieces of cosmetic jewellery, a cheque book and electricity bills.

He staggered back when he saw a thick file in the other corner. How heavy it was for an ordinary file. He picked it up and walked over to the chair with great difficulty.

It wasn't a file. It was a record of Majid's misdeeds. Every single letter from Mona had been filed neatly and in order in it. In addition, every single penny that had been spent on her had been accounted for. Hospital expenses, tips to the nurses, taxi fares, the cost of their stay in Poona, details about the money spent on clothes for Kitty, on yarn, on knitting needles. Three hundred rupees a month had been agreed upon, but in every column there was an addition of another fifty to a hundred. But the receipt for the last amount that had been received a few days ago was for five hundred rupees. He had never imagined that a minor indiscretion would have such serious consequences. People committed heinous crimes, indulged in adulterous pleasures, and just walked away at the end of them. In the old days an adulterer was stoned, but the tiny stones that rained continuously on him had turned into a mountain. And yet he was still breathing.

Mona's most recent letter differed from her earlier ones. The paper was beautiful, smooth and fragrant. The address was also not that of Duncan Road, it was Omar Park. In this latest letter she had written that because of her increased workload she urgently needed an ayah. She had a woman from Mangalore to do the baby's work, but she wouldn't wash her diapers, so a maid had to be hired. The rent for the flat alone was three hundred and forty, but she couldn't burden Saran with the baby's…

A spear sank into Majid's shoulder. Needles seemed to be pricking his brain.

In the end she had written that if things continued to be so difficult she might have to send the baby to an orphanage; the receipt for the five hundred that Abida had sent her to take care of the situation was secured neatly to the letter.

"So now you've started stealing as well!" Abida snatched the file from his hands. Majid hadn't heard her coming in.

"By 'as well' you mean along with my depravity…"

"All right, please stop talking like this." She let go of the file and turned guiltily to the almirah.

"How did letters addressed to me get to you?"

Her back to him, she continued rummaging through the locker casually.

"Answer me," he roared.

"Shankar sent them to me."

"The bastard! Why did he forward my letters to you?"

"It's not his fault. I asked him to."

"Why?"

"Because you had entrusted the matter to me."

"Is that why you dash off to the post office every chance you get?"

"I don't dash off at all, I walk very slowly. I swear to God." She closed the almirah and turned to smile at him.

"Another five hundred after the first three hundred. Who gave you permission to send it?"

"I gave myself permission."

"She kept blackmailing you, and you? You didn't think it was necessary to mention any of this to me."

"It would just have distressed you further. You need a lot of rest after this illness."

"You didn't think that when I found out about it, I would …"

"I thought you would never find out. After you handed the matter over to me you never asked about it. You never enquired about anything. I was sure you would never find this file, and I never imagined in my wildest dreams that you would become suspicious and start searching through my almirah."

She ran her hand, which was dry as paper, over his forehead. Incensed by her touch Majid became even angrier.

"There's a limit to everything." He pushed her hand away. "I admire the hard work you've put into preparing a list of my crimes."

"List of crimes." Abida's colour drained. She quickly began straightening out the wrinkles in her dupatta.

"Afraid that I might forget and renege, you have…"

"No, no, Majju, I swear on your life… I have… I…" The muscles of her face quivered. "I didn't want to keep reminding you, but I never thought you didn't love your offspring, or that you don't have a relationship with the child's mother. Your relationship with me will last as long as we are alive, but your relationship with your daughter, then with her children and their children, that will stretch on and on."

"Your generosity is admirable. You're a goddess, a goddess. Let me worship at your feet." Majid aimed an arrow at her dramatically.

"You can say even crueller things if you want."

"And you will tolerate them so that the burden of remorse weighing heavily on my chest becomes heavier."

"Keep saying what you want, spew out all the poison. Actually, I should be weeping and whining and creating a commotion since that's the way decent women are expected to behave. But when you shared your secret with me you thought of me as your friend, not your wife. You did something unusual, I responded in an unusual way. You know how organised I am. I don't do anything haphazardly. This file is not a list of your crimes. Anyway, let me throw this damn file into the fire. Satisfied?"

"Why did you suddenly change your mind about going away?"

"Majju, after having spent twelve years with you I've got used to you. I consider your burden mine, your illness is mine, if you eat properly I feel full, if you have pain in your joints, my heart aches. I still don't believe that there's no place for me in your heart. Yes, go ahead and say I'm insufferable, I'm old fashioned, I'm one of those women who worships their husbands. So tell me, what will you do if I regard you as mine even after we're divorced?"

"For God's sake, don't put me on such a high pedestal, I feel as if I'm suffocating. I won't be able to tolerate such a great burden." His face became distorted.

"Oh God, Majid… my love." Abida began cracking her knuckles nervously.

"This is not love, this is suffocation. If I touch you the blood in your veins seems to freeze … I'm terrified of this kind of love. Only corpses love like this. I'm repelled by this dead body." He began to pace restlessly. Then suddenly he grasped both her hands in his and said, "Don't drown in the well that I have dug, Abida, escape from this spider's web."

"How can I escape? Is there a way out?" She covered her face with both hands and sighed.

"I will arrange for a ticket right away." He got up.

"The time to leave has come and gone."

"What do you mean?"

"If I hadn't listened to you and had left in the very beginning, everything would have been fine. But I couldn't go. My selfishness and weakness placed chains upon my feet."

"I stopped you."

"But why did I stay? Because I wanted to."

"Your reasoning will drive me mad."

"Her life was destroyed because of me. She had to turn to Saranji for help because the doors of this house are closed to her. The rights are all in my name. I'm Mrs. Majid, and even though she is the mother of your daughter she has no legal status. This is not law, it's a joke."

"If someone vomits in a filthy drain and maggots begin to crawl in it, will one marry the drain?"

"You think you're doing me a favour by calling Mona a drain and the child a maggot, but I'm not such a shallow person. I've seen Mona more intimately than you have. Yes, yes, you slept with her, but we've spent many grief-stricken and hopeless nights together, and together mourned your infidelity. Do you know, she used to feel great pity for me. She didn't believe for a second that you were abandoning her because of a dull, uninteresting person like me. She thought you were fickle by nature and that I would cover up your depraved deeds for the rest of my life because this is a barren woman's duty."

"You joined hands with a prostitute and created a front against me."

"How could we miserable women fight you? We were wringing each other's necks behind your back. Sometimes you kick and sometimes you rub your nose in the dirt to get your way. All right, I'm ready to get a divorce from you on the condition that you marry her. Do you agree?"

"The same stubborn arguments! I've told you before, there's nothing in common between us."

"Because she has been used by other men besides you? Then admit that we have nothing in common either, because you too have been used by others but I have always been devoted to you alone. Yes, go ahead and say that I'm arguing for the sake of arguing, but this ploy won't work."

"You're being irrational. Pleading her cause is a waste of time."

"Majid Sahib, have you ever thought … when Kitty grows up … what kind of decisions will she make about herself? After Mona's lovers have dispersed one by one, won't she lead her daughter down the same path? I'm comfortably settled in my house – won't my conscience trouble me? After Saran …"

"There's no question of 'after Saran' yet! He'll live for another forty years at least. He's healthy and in very good shape."

"Well, the fact that he is in very good physical shape is the problem. He can mourn and move on easily. Saran changes his car every six months. There's no need for him to take a break between women. As I was coming out of the post office yesterday I saw him leaving Grand Bazaar in the company of a beautiful young woman, both of them carrying packages. They looked very nervous when they saw me. He said she was the daughter of one of his friends, in Bombay for a visit. She is staying in Saran's executive suite at the Taj."

"And where did you get this last bit of information?"

"I got it from where I should have got it." She smiled a little secret smile.

"One won't find many wives who are generous enough to be taking such good care of their husband's girlfriend's lovers." The bitterness in Majid's tone became venomous. Abida could only stare at him with a wounded look. Every move she was making seemed to backfire.

"My love, you're very tired. Rest for a while." She tried to give him her hand him but he turned away from her loving gesture. There was a storm raging inside his head, his ears reverberated with a constant buzzing. He placed his head on the pillow like a defeated player and closed his eyes.

*

Majid closed the door behind him and entered the drawing room through the dimly-lit passage. Abida was standing on a stool, lovingly cleaning the imaginary dust from Ammi Jaan's picture with a corner of her pink dupatta. She craned her neck to see Majid but the words froze on her tongue. Their eyes met and locked.

"Mmm… Majjan…" She stepped down from the stool.

Seeing Majid stumble as if he were drunk, she reached towards him like a fluttering butterfly but didn't have the courage to touch him. Majid's body was taut like an arrow strung on the bow and his eyes were burning.

"Here you are," she said as if from a great distance.

"Yes," Majid replied from even further away.

"Why did you leave the house when you were so tired?" Abida asked reproachfully. "Come, sit down." She brought his special chair forward but he kept looking through her.

"Shall I ask for tea?" She turned to go to the kitchen. The look in Majid's eyes terrified her. When she returned with the tea-tray she found Majid standing where she had left him. His hands hung helplessly by his sides as if they had forgotten what their function was. Abida put the tray on the table. Then she sat down on the carpet.

"What did she say?" She spoke abruptly.

"She said she would decide after talking to you."

"Oh." She put two teaspoons of sugar in the cup. Picking up the teapot with a corner of her dupatta, she started pouring. "You wouldn't have missed the train if you had waited till Sunday. Why did you go to her? Why did you have to beg before a base woman like her?"

"Well, you're an expert in fixing things that go wrong. When the matter is entrusted to you, it will automatically be resolved."

"That ungrateful woman! How dare she treat you with such disrespect." Abida felt her blood boil.

"Just the opposite! She's buried under the weight of your kindness and cannot take a single step without your consent."

Abida was at a loss for words.

"I don't know if I put sugar in your tea or not." She touched the sugar pot with shaking hands.

"Every single pore of her being is trapped in the mesh of your benevolence and generosity. Your devotion has erased the black stains of my infidelity. I gave her unhappiness and disrespect. But you gave her a mother's love, a sister's sympathy and a friend's sincerity. You became the oar of her sinking boat and saved her from a life of perpetual uncertainty. You sent her money in my name, but she knows perfectly well that you sold your jewellery and..."

"Damn the wretched jewellery." She started stirring the tea rapidly.

"She's seen many lovers but this is the first time she's had to deal with a lover's beloved like you. She's extremely scared of you." Majid was smiling impishly but Abida's heart lurched when she saw that the look in his eyes reflected sarcasm not devotion.

"I... I..." she said nervously.

"If you want, my destiny can be reversed. If you order her to take pity on your beloved husband as a reward for all your kindnesses and your generosity, tell her that he will be destroyed and his unfortunate heart, which is actually your heart, will be shattered otherwise."

Placing his hand on his heart, Majid continued dramatically. "I am your beloved Majjan. I am yours, my heart, my brain, my kidneys and lungs, are all yours, the morsel in my mouth reaches your stomach, if I can't digest my food, you have to vomit, if my veins are slashed it is your blood that flows. You, you, you are all of me... and I'm just an illusion, a complete fantasy."

Abida's lips moved but no sound emerged. She was staring at him.

"If you put in a good word for me she will gather me in her embrace, I will have your permission to take her into my arms, and with your best wishes she and I will..."

"Majid... what are you saying?"

"You covered up my sin. I won't be able to deny your benevolence for many lifetimes." He was out of breath.

"Majid, you're exhausted... please." She seemed to be looking for something in her lap.

"I won't rest."

"Listen, Majid..."

"No, I don't have time to listen... it's your turn to listen today."

"Say what you want... I'm listening." She looked at her hands as she turned them upside down.

"Did you know where I had gone?"

"When you didn't get back from the office on time, I thought..."

"And you knew what answer I would receive."

"I... I had..." she stammered.

"You know what's unknown. Why did you have to ask then?"

"I... well... Majid, you..." Her lap was empty. She felt as if she had stolen something.

"Because you believe in playing every single chess piece on the board."

"Allah!" There was nothing in her hands.

"And this was your last assault. You had been pushing me for several days. There's deception in a woman's temperament – I don't want to repeat this hackneyed sentiment nor do I believe it. But Abida, you were not honest with me."

"You're not in your senses, wait until you are feeling calmer, more peaceful..."

"Peace, peace, peace! I'm repelled by this word." The veins stood out on his forehead. "The time for peace has passed. I've barricaded all of the enemy's trenches. My resignation was accepted today."

"But you could have asked for more leave..."

"It seems that the time for my leave-taking is not that far." The congestion in his lungs meant he couldn't breathe properly.

"Majju, I beg you." She began sobbing loudly.

"Even if I wanted to live, I can't now." He stared wildly at the walls around him. "I can't become a puppet for someone's entertainment. You are probably praying to God that I should become a cripple so that you can be my hands and feet, become my tongue and serve me for the rest of your life."

"God forbid! I beg of you, Allah..." She was trembling from head to toe.

"And perhaps I never loved you. I saw you and I thought my life would be incomplete without you. This is not love, this is selfishness. I acquired you to make my life complete. And you... you heard stories about my waywardness and resolved to possess me. You were fond of domesticating wild pigeons, weren't you? Wild animals fed from your hands." Words became entangled with each other and fell one upon the other.

"Oh God... Oh God... I will die."

"No, you won't die, your heart will continue to beat in your chest, and after I'm gone my heart will also beat in your bosom… I… you have gathered my entire being into yours, now it… it will never be dispersed… never fall into an abyss. With the heights of your being it will soar higher, higher still … higher than my reach… my breath will sob on your lips, the light of my eyes will shine in yours." Nonsensical words began to fall from Majid's lips, his eyes bulged and his face became burnished like burnt copper. He began to scratch it with both hands.

And just as Abida was trying to hold him up, he fell face down.

The air around them stilled. As if Bombay's soul had been seized. Abida's ears were blocked. The darkness in the room thickened. She carefully brought Majid to the divan and straightened his body. With her cold hands she closed his wildly staring eyes, tied her pink dupatta around the jaws that kept dropping and meticulously positioned his hands by his sides. Pulling off the ribbon from her ponytail she bound his big toes together and then, like an obedient child, sat down on the stool.

For a moment there was a slight movement in Majid's half-open eyelids. He looked at Abida through the corners of his eyes, a smile quivered on his lips, a huge laugh became a storm in his chest… and then the world stood still.

Majid's last look told a story.

"How diligent you are, you've readied me even before I am dead. I hope that in your prayers you will have made arrangements for me to be comfortable in the next world too."

Weary with the weight of her bridal bangles, Abida's wrists slumped, and like a shooting star she found herself drowning in a void.

*

The doorbell rang again and again… all in her imagination.

She heard bells ringing for no reason. Perhaps the husbands in the flats next door were returning from work. Her doorbell would never ring again, no one would take her in his arms the moment the door opened, never kiss her dry lips again…never kiss her again… she was lying in a grave, there were people all the way to the top… tears were falling …thick clouds of grief descended, the world was full but her life was empty… her wrists were as light as flowers, her white unstarched dupatta was drenched in the terrible odour of camphor and frankincense.

The bell rang again, sounding like a sick child's whine. As if in some other world, a faraway world, she carefully rearranged her scattered dreams and locked them in the almirah, placed the half-knitted sweater in the drawer, pushed the slippers under the bed with her feet and picked up the socks and stuffed them in a corner.

When she got up and opened the door to make sure she was not dreaming, she saw Mona turning to leave. She came back when she heard the door open.

"I dozed off."

"Uff, your daughter is so heavy." She was out of breath.

"Don't say things like that. Give her to me," taking the girl from her.

"I won't take her back then!" She laughed a phony laugh.

"All right, that's enough. Where are you headed?" Abida sat down on the sofa with the child.

"It's the last race in Poona. After that we were planning to go to Mahabaleshwar for two days. But she will be a lot of work for you."

"Thanks for your sympathy… is Saran ji well?" she said to change the subject.

"He's well. His divorce will be final in October."

"Oh, well, congratulations."

"I'm… I'm so selfish. Whenever I need to I dump her on you. And now I don't know what to do."

"Don't worry, you'll begin to understand everything. Is the wedding before Christmas or..."

"No, there's no reason to delay it. There's no trusting men, who knows when they may have a change of heart. The iron's hot at this time, but I wonder if... if..."

Abida didn't finish her sentence for her. But her heart was beating violently. Whatever Mona had to say she would have to say without her help.

"Saran ji doesn't like children at all."

Abida remained silent.

"I've fought with him several times... but he's ready to pay..."

"How much would this little thing need, and of course she's not a poor man's child."

"If I had given her to you then you would have taken her happily."

Abida said nothing.

"I didn't give her to you because I was stubborn. But I was never at peace. I always felt I had stolen someone else's baby."

Abida silently ran her little finger through Sabiha's hair.

"Have you noticed something? She looks more like you than me. There were times when I got really angry, used to think you were a magician, that you had begun stealing her from me from the time she was in my womb."

Abida said nothing, just sat quietly like someone who had committed a crime.

"But this was my foolishness. Actually, it was a family resemblance. Majid Sahib was your first cousin, wasn't he?"

Abida didn't answer her.

"Is it possible that one woman's child can grow in another woman's body?" Mona asked, half afraid.

Abida's lips still didn't move.

"Nothing is beyond God's grace." Mona made the sign of the cross on her and left without looking back.

After she had gone, Abida picked up her sleeping daughter, draped her silky soft, somnolent arms around her own neck like a necklace, then tiptoed to her bedroom.

She gently put the girl down where Majid had once slept. She was overcome by drowsiness again and yawning, she settled into her own spot and fell into a deep slumber the minute her head touched the pillow.

She hadn't known such beautiful, intense and carefree sleep in years.

In Majid's picture hanging on the wall, his open eyes were inert, unmoving.

How could there be any sign of sleep in them?

***